Rowdy

BY JAY CROWNOVER

Better When He's Bad

The Marked Men Series
Rowdy
Nash
Rome
Jet
Rule

Rowdy

A Marked Men Novel

JAY CROWNOVER

wm

WILLIAM MORROW

An Imprint of HarperCollins*Publishers*

ROWDY. Copyright © 2014 by Jennifer M. Voorhees. All rights reserved. Printed in the United States of America. No part of this book may be used or reproduced in any manner whatsoever without written permission except in the case of brief quotations embodied in critical articles and reviews. For information address HarperCollins Publishers, 195 Broadway, New York, NY 10007.

HarperCollins books may be purchased for educational, business, or sales promotional use. For information please e-mail the Special Markets Department at SPsales@harpercollins.com.

FIRST EDITION

Library of Congress Cataloging-in-Publication Data has been applied for.

ISBN 978-0-06-233305-6

14 15 16 17 18 OV/RRD 10 9 8 7 6 5 4 3 2

Dedicated to anyone who is trying to figure out where they are supposed to be. Don't worry, friends, the universe has a plan for you; you just need to listen to what it's trying to tell you and you'll eventually end up exactly where you were always meant to be.

FOR ANYONE WHO DOESN'T KNOW my backstory, the long and short of it is I thought I had my life figured out. I thought I was on the path I was supposed to be on. I thought I was doing what I was supposed to be doing and in return I was going to live the dream and have the typical happily-ever-after.

Not so much. The path I was meant to be on was vastly different. My happily-ever-after didn't involve love and marriage but instead a new career and a grand adventure I had only ever dreamed about when I was much younger. Really, what I thought I was supposed to be doing was just the status quo, the day-to-day rhythm I had fallen into because I didn't know any better, and frankly because I was scared of what lurked outside the comfort of what I had known for so long.

Well, screw that. What I was meant to be doing was so much better, so much more challenging, so much more enlightening and fulfilling than the status quo. I wake up every single day thankful that my path has changed so drastically. Sure, it sucked at the time. It was one of the lowest points in my life and one of the most terrifying journeys I have ever traveled, but coming out of it on the other side stronger, totally independent, and absolutely creatively fulfilled, all I can do is tell the universe thank you for shaking things up.

It's okay to be scared, I really think that's how you know that whatever it is you're meant to be doing matters, but it's not okay to *not* find that thing you're supposed to be doing because you're afraid of something new, because the path less traveled is daunting and dark. Embrace the change, find your passion, know what your true joy really is about, and pursue it until the end of time. Live the life you were always meant to live. Honestly, nothing on earth will make you happier or more grateful for every single moment you have.

Just get out there and do you. The universe loves that shit! ☺

Rowdy

Salem

I DON'T HAVE A LOT of great memories from my childhood. There were too many rules. Too many regulations. Too many disapproving looks from my father and not enough support or backbone from my mother.

We lived in Loveless, a tiny Texas town with an achingly accurate name. I was the minister's daughter, and if that didn't come with enough inherent expectations, the man who was beloved behind the pulpit but a tyrant in our home heaped them on ever higher. I was meant to be quiet, compliant, and conventional. Problem was . . . that was never me.

When I was nine, I convinced my mom to let me try out for a very exclusive dance team. I longed for something different, something that would make the day-to-day less agonizing. I was so proud, so excited when I made the team, only to have my father tell me dancing like that wasn't permitted and no daughter of his was going to make a spectacle of herself. He wouldn't stand for it. It was how everything in my life went, and my mom never seemed willing to take a stand and defy him, even if it meant giving her daughter something she so desperately wanted. Anything that went against my father's wishes or was deemed inappropriate and shameful got kicked to the curb along with any sense of uniqueness and enjoyment. My parents wanted to squeeze me into a too-small box, painted white and tied with a bow of tradition. Me being me would never be good enough.

It was a situation made even worse by the fact that my younger sister was the apple of my parents' eye. The perfect golden girl. I loved Poppy with all my heart, too. She was gentle and kind but she was also docile and obedient, ready to jump whenever my father barked an order.

I was never going to be perfect and compliant like my adorable little sister. I had no plans to end up a happy home-maker like my mother. And I sure as hell was never going to fit into the conventional mold of the traditional Mexican woman like my father so desperately wanted me to. So at nine years old, I decided that I would make my own way. I saw a light at the end of the tunnel, I just had to be patient.

When the time came, I broke free. I hit the road with exactly the kind of guy my father hated. I was barely eighteen, not really grown, but I had to get out. I had to run . . . I just didn't see any other way to survive. I fled Loveless, shaking the dust off my boots and never looking back.

I have very few regrets about the choices I made for myself back then. To this day I am a woman that stands by my decisions—good or bad. I'm independent. I'm strong-willed. I've made my own way in life, and have, up to this point, been extremely successful at it. There've been times when I stumbled. There've been times when I lay alone in the dark and wanted to cry. There were quiet moments that snuck up on me that reminded me my parents weren't the only people I ran from in that tiny Texas town. But overall I tried to accept full accountability for my happiness and well-being and that was the way I liked it.

I still kept in touch with my sister, Poppy. We were close even though she had married a man I wasn't too fond of a few years ago. She still lived in Loveless. So deep was my hatred for that place and the memories that lived there I couldn't even bring myself to attend my sister's nuptials, which had of course taken place under my father's watchful eyes in his church. I liked to move around, so Poppy would come visit and get a feel for whichever big city I was calling home for the moment. Her visits had become much sparser over the years, and now I could only get in touch with her every so often for a quick chat on the phone.

At first my gypsy ways had landed me in Phoenix and then Reno, all before L.A. had called to me, which had then been quickly followed by New York. I had tried New Orleans on for size and had a blast in Austin for a few years. Most recently I had landed in Vegas, and something about the lights, the noise, the constant flow of people, the way it really felt like a transient town, had stuck. I stayed in the neon jungle for far longer than any of the other places on the list and settled in to a really profitable career that hinged on all those decisions I had made that my parents were so sure were going to doom my future.

I had a great job, a killer apartment, and I was even seeing a guy that was hovering on the edge of something closer to serious than I normally liked, when I got a call out of the blue from Phil Donovan's son.

Phil Donovan was legendary in my world—a veritable god in the tattoo industry. He was the tattoo guy other tattoo guys wanted to be. He was the artist you wanted to say had worked on you. He was groundbreaking. He was famous. The list to apprentice under him was a hundred million miles long. Phil was a supremely talented man, and according to his son, Nash, he was sick and his odds on pulling through were slim to nonexistent. Nash had inherited Phil's shop in the heart of downtown Denver and had also been tasked with getting a new tattoo shop up and running in the more trendy Lower Downtown—"LoDo"—part of the city. Phil had thrown my name in the hat for Nash to consider as the shop's manager.

I had only met the older man once. It was during a convention in Vegas, and I had just wanted to meet the notoriously handsome artist. Well, Phil was indeed a gorgeous example of a rock-and-roller aging well, but he was also charming, polite, and something about his demeanor had spoken to my very wayward soul. We ended up talking for hours and hours. He offered to tattoo me, and there was no way I was going to say no. I spent the next day under his needle and ended up spilling my entire life history under his watchful purple gaze. It was like being absolved of every sin I had ever committed by a very tattooed and cool pope.

When he asked where I was from and I told him "all

over," he had just laughed. When I mentioned I grew up in a very conservative town in Texas called Loveless, I could feel something change in his demeanor. He became more intent, asked a truckload more questions, and by the time the elegant, beautiful, and very traditional Lady of Guadalupe tattoo was done on my calf, I felt like Phil knew me better than I tended to know myself.

We said good-bye and I never really thought much past that encounter other than I had a killer tattoo from Phil Donovan, which totally gave me bragging rights. Nash's call had taken me off guard, so I was prepared to blow him off. I was sad to hear about Phil and I didn't really want to leave Vegas. Colorado was cold and had mountains. I had zero use for either of those things. I was getting ready to hang up when Nash told me to look up the shop on the Internet. To check out the artists and their work. He told me that Phil was absolutely sure I would be interested in the job and the move once I did. I shrugged it and him off and hung up, but my curiosity was piqued, so I did indeed pull up the shop on my phone.

The Marked had a stellar reputation. The ratings were out of this world and the portfolios of the work its artists were producing were breathtaking. But it wasn't until I flipped over to the individual artists' pages that my entire world and my future went from Vegas to Denver in the span of a heartbeat.

There on the tiny screen of my phone was the one solid and always good memory I did have from my youth. The one thing that I had held in a warm fuzzy place no matter where I was or how I was feeling. There looking back at me was the grown-up version of the blue-eyed boy who was the one person in my entire life to ever make me feel accepted. The only person who had ever made me feel like it was okay just to be me and that being me was actually a pretty great thing.

Rowland St. James . . . Rowdy. The boy next door who was so sweet, so wide-eyed, so afraid of being sent back into the system, so afraid of being alone.

The first time Poppy dragged him over to the yard to play with us I remembered watching him struggle to figure out how to have fun, how to loosen up and have a good time. He was so little, with such big, sad eyes, my heart squeezed for him. Every little kid should know how to play, should want to roll around in the dirt and cause a ruckus, and it seemed like every little kid did, except for Rowdy.

I think I felt so bad for him because I knew exactly how he felt. I was barely a teenager, and even then I didn't want to think about how going inside with scraped knees or ripped clothes would go over with my tyrant of a father. I would get yelled at, I would be punished, I would have all my privileges—the few I had—revoked, and all the fun in the world wasn't worth the repercussions it caused, so I typically resigned myself to sitting on the sidelines and watching everyone else enjoy themselves. Only, once Rowdy was part of the picture, I no longer had to sit there alone.

That was how I first found out how artistically gifted he was. Drawing on paper was clean and tidy, it was normally boring, and there was no possible way I could get in trouble or end up grounded for playing tick-tack-toe or hangman. Little had I known that handing a few sheets of plain drawing paper and a few colored pencils to Rowdy was going to unlock artistic potential that would blow me away. Even at ten he had been able to craft images and landscapes that looked real enough they deserved to be framed and hung on a wall somewhere. The boy was skilled, and it was the first time I ever saw him really smile. He loved to draw, loved to sketch and mess around with paint, so whenever we ended up cast off to the side, that was what we did together. Draw and doodle. I sucked at it, but I loved that it made him so happy.

Even with our age gap and obvious differences, Rowdy just understood what it was like to want more and be more than we were currently stuck with. He was a kindred spirit, and he made my heart smile when my day-to-day was so dreary and desolate. We were two kids just trying to make do in households that didn't really want us or understand us. We might have been on the outside looking in at our own families and our own lives, but at least we could stand outside together. He was quite simply the best friend I ever had—he still was. Sometimes, though, I wondered if he was content to be on the fringe with me, okay with his nose pressed against the glass just because he was another person in my life who was blinded by Poppy's perceived perfection. We watched everything move around us, never feeling included or wanted, but he never took his eyes off of my little sister.

I had always known that Poppy was the Cruz sister

for him, but somehow I forgot that in my last moments in Loveless. Just as the Belvedere was about to peel out of my parents' driveway, I caught sight of his brilliant sky-blue eyes in the rearview mirror. I jumped out of the car, and in that split second something changed from kinship and our deeper bond of not belonging changed into something else. I saw him as older, saw him as so much more than a confused teenage boy. He was only fifteen, too young to have so much loss and despair in his heartbreaking gaze. Too young to suddenly look so grown-up and like something else. In that half of a heartbeat he became desirable and forbidden to my suddenly thundering heart. Neither one of us was ready for the other; at eighteen I didn't have a clue how drastic my actions were going to be or how long the effects would last, but I had to kiss him good-bye, had to let him know that he mattered in so many different ways even though I was leaving and never coming back.

Only now, thanks to serendipity and Phil Donovan, Rowdy was staring back at me, all grown-up and gorgeous. He was still blond, still smiling in a way that made my heart trip, but he was bigger, badder, and those blue eyes now had to compete for attention with a riot of ink covering most of his visible skin. It was like staring at everything that I suddenly wanted in the center of a crystal ball telling me that was what my future was supposed to look like.

Without even taking a second to think, I called Nash back and accepted the job. I think he said something about interviewing, but I could hardly hear him through the blood rushing between my ears. Sure I would have more details to figure out before I packed up and left, but I had a new destination and a clear goal in mind. I wanted to see if it was still there, the synchronicity we had, the undeniable connection and pull that had made us work together so well when we were too young and too lost to know what to do with it.

It took a minute to cut ties with the current shop I was working at, mostly because they had just signed a deal to do some kind of tattoo reality show and I think having me at the front desk was one of the big selling points. I also had to break it off with Mr. I Want More and head to New York for a photo shoot I had booked for a tattoo magazine. As each day passed I got more and more anxious. I wanted to be in Colorado, wanted to lay my eyes on the grown-up version of Rowdy. I was dying to see what the years had done to him besides make him undeniably sexy. He had always had the best personality. Affable and laid-back even though his life had been anything but a bed of roses. I always admired him. I envied the way he seemed to just roll with whatever landed in his lap. I was the exact opposite. I made everything into a battle, a fight for survival, and it was exhausting.

Fighting for everything made fighting for the things that actually mattered get lost in the noise and lose their significance.

I threw everything I owned into my car and once again hit the road. It was the first time I ever left one place headed toward another with a clear destination in mind. Not only the anticipation of facing the one happy thing I held on to from another life, but also the lure of helping to build a tattoo empire, of extending Phil's legacy out in the world with the next generation of tattoo gods, was exciting, and I loved a good challenge.

When I hit Denver in May I was stunned at how beautiful the place actually was. The city was so clean and the way the Rockies loomed out in the distance really was breathtaking. It had a life to it, a vibe that was different from any other place I had ever been and I instantly felt bad for dismissing it out of hand. When I sucked in a breath it was like I could feel the mountain air doing something to my insides. Or maybe I was just suffocating because of the lack of oxygen. Denver really was a mile above sea level, and for a city girl, trying to breathe at that elevation was proving to be a little tricky.

I found a tiny, furnished apartment. After all I was a master at uprooting my life and bouncing from one place to another. I gave myself a pep talk to convince myself that I wasn't crazy to move to an entirely new state on a whim and a picture of a pretty boy. I got myself gussied up, did my hair, slicked on some bloodred lipstick, and donned my most killer pair of heels, and went to charm my potential new employer.

My new boss was a babe. So was his business partner. Seriously they should be on a calendar featuring the hot tattooed and pierced men of Denver. They also considered me carefully. Checking out my ink, not in a leering, creeper way, but to see if I could tell the difference between good and bad work. I must have passed inspection because the tiny blonde with the baby and the attitude smiled at me and told them to hire me or else. Mr. Sexy with the flames tattooed on his head, Nash, like I wouldn't have known who he was from the eyes alone, offered me the job. Of course I accepted.

The guy with the black mohawk and all the swagger made a few sarcastic comments and flashed me a grin that would have made my blood heat if I hadn't noticed the very obvious wedding ring he was sporting. Those two were trouble. The very best kind, and I told them I knew it was going to be a good time and that I was excited about getting in on this opportunity with them on the ground floor. We were all set to go and I'd told them I was excited to start when I heard his voice.

It was deeper, smoother, but under the baritone was the soft Texas twang I remembered from all those years ago. When his head cleared the top of the stairs I saw his eyes widen, watched them fill with recognition and trepidation. I couldn't help but smile. Even though he looked less than thrilled to see me, everything about seeing him made me happy, and I knew, just knew I had made the right choice. I moved toward him like there was a force field pulling us together and listened to my heels tap on the wooden floor in time with my heartbeat.

I stopped right in front of him. Even with him hovering a step down below the landing and with me in heels, he was still taller than me. He was broad and strong. He was watching me like I was some kind of apparition.

I was. I was very much a ghost from his past just like he was for me.

I ran a finger over the bridge of his nose, fought the urge to lean forward and press my lips to his slack mouth.

I said his name, his real name, so he could tell it was really me—"Hello, Rowland"—and it made his entire body jerk in response. "You sure did grow up nice." We stared at each other in silence for a minute and I saw all the color bleed out of his face. He whispered my name back at me in a strangled tone.

He had a massive anchor tattooed on the side of his neck. It looked like it was alive with the way his pulse thundered rapidly under the ink.

I looked back over my shoulder and told the rest of our bewildered audience, "Strike that, it's going to be a great time. See you guys at work on Monday. E-mail me whatever forms you need me to fill out."

I made sure my hand brushed across Rowdy's chest when I walked past him as I made my way down the stairs. I could feel his heart racing, could feel the way he trembled. I'm sure it was more from shock than any kind of appreciation of my feminine charms, but I didn't care.

For the first time in my entire life I knew I was exactly where I was supposed to be.

CHAPTER 1

Rowdy

THE POOL BALLS CRACKED together with a loud *smack* and rolled aimlessly across the table. Not a single one, solid or stripe, found its way into a pocket. I leaned heavily on the pool cue I planted on the floor and glared at the table.

"Man, you are off your game."

In more ways than one. I snorted and looked across the pool table at my best friend, Jet Keller. He wasn't in town much anymore. He was usually off making up-and-coming bands into stars or busy playing rock star himself. It was a rare night when he was actually home and not attached to his very pretty wife. Normally I would be all over some bro time with Jet, but like he said, I was off.

I reached behind me and grabbed the bottle of Coors Light I had left on the high-top table. Beer normally was the answer to all of life's problems, but the things that were running around in my mind, the things keeping me up at night, no amount of beer could quiet. I shifted my weight on my feet and watched as Jet sank almost every single one of his shots. I had no idea how he managed to lean over the table and take the shots he did without his pants ripping in half. I kept telling him if he ever wanted to have kids he'd better buy some regular Levi's; it was a long-running joke between the two of us. I felt bad for the guy's balls.

I had known Jet for years and was used to his hard-rock style. It fit who he was. It fit his personality. He rocked it onstage and off. It didn't, however, fit in at the run-down dive bar well off the beaten path I'd dragged him to. I was avoiding the bar closest to the tattoo shop because I had no intention of running into my newest coworker.

It was hard enough seeing her day in and day out at the shop. It was a struggle hour by hour to keep the nine million questions I had from flying out of my mouth. I wanted to know everything, wanted all the answers, but knew even if she had them it wouldn't make up for the fact she had let me down all those years ago. So I just remained quiet. I kept my trap shut and went out of my way not to look at her, not to talk directly to her, and I sure as shit made sure not to be where I thought she might be outside of work. My avoidance tactics meant the watering hole by the shop was currently off-limits and so was the Bar, the run-down dive owned and operated by a close friend. Those were the only two places that I frequented with my friends and the rest of the gang from the tattoo shop, so it made sense that those would be the places Salem might pop up. Ergo, I dragged Jet's ass to a place that looked like it hadn't been cleaned since Colorado experienced the gold rush and where every pair of suspicious eyes were on us.

"It's been a strange few weeks."

Jet arched a black eyebrow at me and motioned for me to rerack the balls.

"That have anything to do with the babe from Vegas?"

I felt my shoulders tighten involuntarily. "Maybe."

I took my time getting the colored balls back in the triangle, and when I was done, I stood and leaned on the table with my hands braced on the edge. My tattooed knuckles almost turned white under the pressure. That was the thing with having a tight-knit group of friends that substituted as family. No one's business was off-limits and everyone wanted to stick their fingers in the mess and try and help.

I narrowed my eyes at him slightly as he ordered us another round of beers from the cocktail waitress that looked like she had been doing this since the womb. "Haggard" didn't even begin to cover her worn appearance, and it annoyed me. If I wasn't being such a nut case we could've been at the Bar, where Dixie was the cocktail waitress. She was a doll. A redhead with and easygoing attitude and a bright smile. She was also down for spending quality time with me naked and not expecting anything the next morning, so that made the fact I was getting snarled at by Betty, the Devil's very own cocktail waitress, even more aggravating.

I snapped at Jet, "What have you heard?"

He grinned at me in the way he had that let me know I was being a dumb-ass. I didn't get riled up easily. I never saw the point. Things always had a way of figuring themselves out and it was the harder people worked at trying to change the outcome that really made everything a clusterfuck. I firmly believed whatever was meant to happen would happen and there was no way to control the outcome.

He tipped the waitress and took the beers and handed me one.

"Just that she is something else. I heard she can give Cora as good as she gets, that she's awesome with the customers, that she knows her shit when it comes to managing a tattoo shop and that she's not just a ten, she's a ten times ten, and that you're avoiding her like she came from a leper colony not Sin City."

Cora Lewis was the business manager for the Marked, the tattoo shop I worked at. She was tiny, mouthy, and the real boss of all of us, and next to Jet she was my closest friend in the world. The fact that she had immediately taken to Salem, had brought her into the fold without even stopping to ask me how I felt about it, bugged me and also made me feel like the odd man out. Everyone seemed to love Salem, couldn't stop singing her praises and touting about what a lifesaver she had been with the shop expanding into a new location. If you asked anyone else I worked with, she was the saving grace of the Marked.

I wanted her to go back to where she came from and to take all the memories, the feelings that she had tied to her with her. I had worked long and hard to bury most of my pre-Colorado life and I didn't need a daily reminder that I had loved and lost both Cruz sisters.

"She's beautiful. She always was."

Salem Cruz had everything a modern-day pinup girl needed to have in order to be a showstopper. There were the curves she had for days. There were miles of amazing, dark hair that seemed endless and it had a brilliant shot of bright red in the front of it. She had eyes the color of obsidian winged in black liner and a mouth painted in a perfect bloodred pout. Every day she looked like something out of a hot rod magazine. Her style was perfectly designed to be both sassy and sexy in a way that made her almost impossible to ignore. Every day the little ruby Monroe piercing she wore above her lip winked at me and every day I tried not to notice that her tattooed arms were masterfully done and filled with artwork that I envied as a professional and as an artist. I also tried really hard not to remember when she wrapped them around me when I was young and scared all the time as she tried to make me feel better.

"You know her from way back when?"

Jet had no idea how loaded that question was.

"Yeah. I grew up next to her family in Texas. I spent a lot of time at her house when I was just a kid."

She had looked different then, far more conservative and traditional. Her hair was darker then, but her eyes were still midnight black and mysterious. Her smile was the same and so was the way I could feel my blood thicken when she walked past me or accidently brushed by me. Back then I thought it was wrong. I thought it was terrifying and dangerous to react to a girl that I knew wasn't for me, but now I knew Salem was irresistible and it was physically impossible not to react to her.

"So what's with the freeze-out?"

Normally I was charming, affable, and engaging with

the opposite sex. I just had a way of talking to them that let me get my way and left everybody happy at the end of the day. With Salem I couldn't do that. With her I couldn't find words that weren't accusation, blame, and downright hateful. I was mad at her for leaving and madder at her for suddenly showing back up.

"She left Loveless when I was fifteen. She packed a bag and took off in the middle of the night with the town's biggest weed dealer. Her parents were big in the church and her little sister worshiped her, so it was hard on everyone when she disappeared." I sucked down a heavy swallow of beer and sighed heavily. "It was really hard on me."

I had loved Salem's sister, Poppy, with every piece of my young soul. She was my one and only, she was the center of my entire world. At least she had been until I followed her to college and ultimately had her tell me we were never going to be a thing. Salem, however, had been my confidante, my confessor, and maybe most importantly she had offered a lonely and unwanted boy friendship and acceptance. She was my very best friend and I was lost without her. When she left without so much as a good-bye it had been the second time in my life that I felt like I was being abandoned. I was once again left behind by someone that was supposed to care about me forever. Salem left me gutted and hollowed out.

"So you were tight and then she bounced and this is the first time you have seen her in ten years and now you're all twisted up about it?"

If only it was that simple. The Cruz sisters had done a number on me coming and going. I would be perfectly happy to have never had to see or think about either one of them again.

If I didn't have my hair slicked up and styled like a character out of *Cry-Baby*, I would have shoved my hands through it in frustration.

"I'm not twisted up. I just don't have anything to say to her. A decade is a long time. She's a stranger." And anything I said wasn't going to come out right anyway. The words would be twisted with rage and memory.

Jet gave me a look and pointed the open end of his beer bottle at me. "Right. She's a stranger, a superhot stranger, and instead of talking to her or flirting her up like you normally do, you're acting like a mute weirdo. Nope, not twisted at all."

I contemplated cracking him over the head with my pool stick, but I had a soft spot for his wife, Ayden, and I wouldn't want her to get upset with me.

"Shut up. You're not around enough to make commentary on how I'm acting anyway."

I meant it as a joke, a way to change the topic of conversation, but I saw him flinch and his hands tightened involuntarily on his beer bottle.

Jet worked hard. He was hell-bent on making a name for bands he had faith in. He was killing it as the head of his own record label, but the trade-off was that he had to go where the music was. That meant he was forever off to L.A., Nashville, New York, Austin, or even Europe. It was hard for him considering he and Ayden had only been married for a couple of years and they were in love—really, really in love. I could see it wearing on both of them but neither one had said anything, and like I said, there was no stopping fate no matter what that nasty bitch had in store for you.

"Everything all right with you on the home front?" I didn't want to pry but it was way better than dredging up my past for him to dig through.

"Ayden and I are great. It's everything else that sucks." He shook his dark head and looked at me from under a frowning brow. "She's going to apply to transfer to the grad program in Austin."

I paused for a second so I didn't say something stupid.

"You want to move to Austin?"

He chugged back the rest of the beer in his hand and laid the pool stick across the table.

"Want to—no, but it makes the most sense. She can transfer to UT Austin and finish school and I can actually see my wife more than two or three times a month. It just sucks. Our friends are here. Her brother is here and Cora just had the baby." He shook his head again and his chest rose and fell in a heavy sigh. "It was her idea, but it still makes me feel like shit. I renovated the studio thinking it would be enough, but it just isn't."

It did suck but it was understandable.

"When will she find out if she gets in?"

"Not for a while. It takes some time to get into grad school, and even if they do want her she has to go and do an interview and jump through a million hoops before it's official. Try not to say anything to Rule or Nash. She hasn't told Shaw or Cora yet. She wants to wait until we know for sure what we're doing."

Rule and Nash ran the tattoo shop and Shaw was not only Ayden's best friend but also Rule's brand-new wife. All three of the girls in our little world were supertight, and if one of the dudes let this major development slip, there would be carnage to follow for sure. Those girls were a solid unit and the idea of one of them leaving was definitely going to be the cause of some serious emotional upheaval.

"That's some pretty big news. Keeping it quiet might not be the way to go. Has she told Asa she's thinking about leaving?"

Asa ran the Bar and was Ayden's older brother. He was a little bit of a wild card and the only reason he had settled in Denver was to be closer to his sister. The two had a strained relationship due to the fact that Asa had a history of being a major shithead and petty criminal, but they were just starting to mend some long-broken fences.

Jet nodded and propped a hip up on the table. I really did expect those jeans of his to split in half every single time he moved. It was endlessly fun to rip on him about it.

"They talked about it. He told her to do whatever makes her happy. I think it bummed her out he didn't ask her to stay."

I grunted and cocked my head to the side a little as I noticed a group of guys several years older than us giving us squinty-eyed looks from the far corner of the bar. I mean I knew we didn't fit in with the run-down ambience, the rough-and-tumble vibe of the place, but we were minding our own business and we always respected the locals' territory.

I told Jet absently while keeping an eye on the group,

"He spent her entire life asking her to do things for him. After he almost died it makes sense that maybe for once in his life Asa would want her to do something for herself. He knows you're what makes her happy. He isn't going to try and keep her from being happy anymore."

Asa was an enigma. He sort of just showed up out of the blue and had dragged Ayden into a mess full of her past and a group of angry bikers. The end result had landed Asa in a coma and Jet and Ayden in matching wedding rings. We all had welcomed the blond southerner into the fold, but everyone watched him with careful eyes. He was lucky Rule's brother, Rome, had come home from the war and ended up owning the Bar. For some reason the older Archer took a shine to Asa and had put him to work. I think we were all just kind of waiting to see how it played out.

The group that was watching us bent their heads together and the guy I figured was the leader met my gaze and flipped me off with a sneer.

I set my beer down and looked back at Jet.

"The natives are getting restless. We probably wanna go."

I didn't mind a good old-fashioned bar brawl. After all, I had played football up until I had dropped out of college at the end of my freshman year. I was still built like an athlete even if on the outside I looked more like James Dean. I was taller than most of them and definitely in better shape, but I liked to think I had grown and matured in the last few years. Avoiding bloodshed and broken knuckles that would mean I couldn't tattoo was obviously the better option.

Jet looked over my shoulder and dipped his chin down in

agreement, only our decision to depart came a split second too late. We were walking toward the door, eyes up and alert, when the men decided they couldn't just let us walk away. I stopped and Jet paused next to me when we were suddenly faced with three fairly drunk, middle-aged guys that looked like they worked long hours doing manual labor. The one that had flipped me off made it a point to scan me from the top of my head to the toes of my worn black cowboy boots. He made a face and elbowed one of his buddies in the ribs hard enough to make the other guy grunt.

"Who do you think this joker is supposed to be? Elvis?" His gaze flicked over to Jet. "And who are you supposed to be? Ozzy Osbourne? Marilyn Manson? Someone needs to remind you boys that Halloween is in October."

I felt Jet tense next to me but neither of us moved.

"How long did it take you make your hair all fancy like that? It would be a real shame if someone went and messed it all up."

I had awesome hair and it did in fact take longer than I liked to admit to get in the lifted, retro style. If this dude thought he was putting his hands anywhere near my head, he had another thing coming. I was going to tell him that we didn't want any kind of trouble, that we were happily on our way out the door, when I saw his arm start to lift up. I was going to grab his wrist and tell him to fuck off, when the guy he had tagged in the ribs beat me to the punch.

He reached out and smacked his mouthy buddy's hand out of the way and pointed at me.

"You look familiar."

I cut Jet a sideways look and he shrugged.

"I don't see how. It's our first—and last—time in here."

The guy considered me. I mean really looked at me for a long minute until it got kind of awkward. The guy with the mouth looked like he was ready to pipe up again when the gawker suddenly snapped his fingers and broke out into a huge grin.

"I know! You played college ball for Alabama."

I blinked and it was my turn to stare. No one recognized me from that part of my life. I mean no one. Those days were long past and I had only been on the field for one season.

"Uhh . . ." I heard Jet snicker a little next to me but I didn't want to waste this chance at making a clean escape. "I did play, a very long time ago."

"I graduated from the University of Alabama, so I follow the Crimson Tide like it's my religion. You were a running back. I remember everyone saying that you had a boatload of potential. I remember thinking the coaches had some serious balls putting you in first string. You were fast, fast enough to help them get to the Sugar Bowl that year. Rowland something . . . right?"

I reached up and rubbed the back of my neck. The rest of the superfan's cohorts had fallen quiet and were now looking at me in an entirely new way. Nothing like football to soothe the raging blue-collar beast.

"Rowdy St. James."

He nodded. "Right. Rowdy, because you were wild and unpredictable. No one could ever tell what kind of pattern you were going to run. Something happened, though.

I don't remember what but I remember you didn't play in the bowl game or the following season. I remember them taking about you on ESPN. You just vanished and everyone wondered why."

That was not something I wanted to discuss, especially not with a group of guys that had been all too eager to start shit a second ago.

I shrugged and forced a sheepish grin. "Well, you know, the pressure got to me. I wasn't ready for the big show. It just wasn't meant to be."

A professional football career really wasn't in the cards for me, but it had nothing to do with the pressure and everything to do with me not being invested in it. But I wasn't about to share that with these guys.

"You were a talented kid. It's a shame you didn't follow through."

I gritted my back teeth and offered a shrug. It had nothing to do with follow-through and everything to do with the fact I nearly beat the starting quarterback to death with my bare hands a few weeks before the bowl game. Man, what was it with the ugly past rearing its head and refusing to stay in the dark where I left it?

There was only one way we were getting out of here. I reached out and clapped the superfan on the shoulder and hollered as loud as I could, "ROLL TIDE!"

It was immediately followed by an answering holler from the guy that recognized me and that of course started an epic debate about college football and the Big Ten, which of course transitioned into talk of the Broncos and their tragic loss in the Super Bowl earlier in the year. Before the guys had noticed, Jet and I managed to slip out the front door, leaving the sounds of arguing male voices and clinking beer bottles echoing behind us.

In the parking lot Jet doubled over in laughter and I couldn't help but smack him on the back of his head as we made our way to the flashy Dodge Challenger he drove.

"Shut it."

"What the fuck does 'Roll Tide' even mean?"

He popped the locks on the car and we got in.

"How about, 'Thanks for saving us from having to fight our way out of there, Rowdy'?"

The car started with a sexy purr and I had to cringe when thundering guitars and screaming vocals assaulted my eardrums. I dug what Jet did for a living and there was no doubt that he was a very talented dude, but that metal music he liked and played was not my favorite. I reached out to turn it down without asking, which made him laugh again.

"It's a football thing. Something you musicians wouldn't understand."

"Hey, I watch football when it's on."

"I've watched games with you. You watch for five minutes then check out and either get falling-down drunk or go find something to write with and end up writing twenty new songs by half time. That is not watching the game, my friend."

He didn't argue with me. "Still, I had no idea you were seriously famous for throwing a ball around. I mean I knew you played when you were younger, but not that you were like on ESPN and shit."

I groaned and leaned back in the seat. "I didn't throw a ball. I caught a ball and ran with it, and the only reason anyone cared one way or the other was because I walked away from all of it without an explanation."

He looked at me out of the corner of his eye and I purposely looked away.

"I don't suppose you want to explain it now?"

"You suppose right."

"Well, hell. I thought my old lady was the master of keeping the past a secret. Turns out she don't got nothing on you."

I just grunted in response.

The truth was I never really thought about my past. I had put my heart on the line after I followed Poppy to college, watched it get shredded, and had decided then and there I was never going to invest myself in anything or anyone like that every again. I dropped out of school, not like I really had a choice after the incident with the quarterback anyway, and ended up doing the same thing Salem did, packed a bag and hit the road, leaving everything behind.

I left Texas—all the memories she held, football, college, and Poppy Cruz in the dust, where they had stayed until a few weeks ago when Salem sauntered back into my life like she had never left it.

Jet was right. I was twisted about Salem being in Denver. So twisted that I wasn't sure how I was ever going to get myself straight again as long as she was around. That girl had ruined me once when I was young. I would never forget the way I felt when she walked away. I didn't want Salem anywhere near me. I couldn't trust myself not to fall back into caring about her, trusting her, being captivated by her, only to have her move on once again, leaving me empty and alone.

CHAPTER 2

Salem

I LOOKED AT THE very pretty blond woman standing across the desk from me. She was obviously nervous. Noticeably out of her element . . . the tailored pantsuit and the Gucci purse on her arm were a dead giveaway that this was probably the first time in her life that she had stepped foot in a tattoo parlor. I gave her my most welcoming smile and cocked a brow at her as she put her manicured hands on the desk in front of me. It was my job to manage the traffic, to make sure clients knew what they were getting and that they were matched with the right artist. It was also my job to make sure I didn't let someone make a mistake that they would be stuck with on their skin forever.

The woman was probably the same age as me, around twenty-eight or twenty-nine, but she had that vibe about her that broadcast that she wasn't really sure what she was doing at the Saints of Denver. This was the new shop Nash had opened after his dad had passed. It was right in the heart of the trendy, more upscale part of LoDo and far more modern and slick than the shop that was on Capitol off of Colfax. The artists that worked here had been handpicked by Rule and Nash. They were skilled and pretty awesome, and since this was a brand-new shop, and Nash wanted to build a reputation for it as well as have it double as a retail space for clothes and other tattoo-themed merchandise, I was spending more of my time here than at the shop where the guys were based. They rotated days so that one of them was always at the new shop to help drive traffic in through the doors.

Today was Rowdy's day at the shop and normally that would thrill me—if he hadn't been determined to pretend like we didn't know each other and that I didn't exist. It was going on a month, and every time those sky-blue eyes landed on me he looked away a second later and his jaw ticked in aggravation. I tried to corner him, tried to get him alone more than once so we could talk it all out, but the boy was good at evading me and I had never had to chase a man before, so I wasn't really sure how to go about it and not seem desperate.

I saw the blonde gulp and she shifted nervously and I asked her, "How are you doing, doll?"

She snapped her gaze to me and her lips parted a little. She really was stunning in a very refined and country-club kind of way. Her eyes were the color of the ocean and looked terrified as she blinked at me.

"I . . ." She paused and I saw her gaze dart up to somewhere over the top of my head as I could literally feel Rowdy walk up behind me. I was so attuned to him, so aware of the space he took up and the way he smelled and affected the air around him, that I didn't have to look over my shoulder to know that he was there. The pretty professional gulped again and her eyes popped open even wider. Rowdy was hot, and when he smiled it was hard not to fall in love, but this woman looked like she was about ready to faint or throw up.

"Can I answer any questions for you, darlin'?"

Over the weeks I had learned fast that Rowdy was a big-time flirt. He always had a grin, always had a soft word and special little gleam in his eye for a pretty girl. His charm was effortless and so was the light humor he used to make his clients and friends feel at ease. If I hadn't known the little boy he used to be, I would've taken it at face value, but I knew there was more to that careless demeanor and laid-back persona he showed the world.

Watching the color flee from the woman's face as she gazed up at Rowdy over my shoulder, I asked her, "Do you want to sit down for a minute and look though portfolios or something? I can get you a glass of water and we can talk about what brought you to the Saints of Denver today." I smiled at her again, hoping it would help calm her down and maybe distract her from whatever had her paralyzed in terror.

Slowly her perfectly coiffed head shook side to side in the negative. She lifted her hands off the counter and I watched them as they curled into tight fists at her sides. She blinked at me again and then jerked her gaze back up to where Rowdy was looming behind me and she took a stumbling step back.

"I'm just not ready for this."

That was a pretty extreme response to chickening out on getting some ink, but I wasn't the type to judge. I'd rather have her get out now than waste everyone's time and back out on the day of the appointment or have a freak-out once she hit the chair. That was never good for business.

"You know where to find us if you change your mind."

Rowdy's voice oozed comfort and had a lull to it that seemed to calm her down. She clutched her purse and turned in a sort of frantic whirl and bolted for the door. It was odd, but definitely not the weirdest thing I had ever seen in a tattoo shop. I felt Rowdy shift behind me and knew he was going to walk away from me again without saying anything and I was done letting him ignore me.

Even though the shop was packed and the other artists all had clients they were working on, I still jumped up from the chair I was sitting in and grabbed the front of his shirt. It was black and had white piping on it with shiny pearl snaps up the front and I had been admiring all day the way the rolled-up sleeves showed off the colorful artwork that covered both of his forearms. I spent a good portion of my day checking him out and didn't feel bad about it at all. His sandy-blond brows dipped down at me and the anchor that covered the side of his neck started to jump when he reached up and wrapped his fingers around my wrist.

"Let go."

I instinctively tugged him closer so that he was forced to bend down a little, and those summer-sky eyes were all I could see.

"Stop avoiding me." My tone was curt, but I was done playing games with him. We had to work together, but more than that, I was here *for* him and at some point he was going to have to know that and understand the importance of it.

"I'm not avoiding you." All the welcome and honeyed sweetness that usually coated his words was missing when he talked to me. I saw the corner of his eye twitch when I pulled him even closer so that were almost sharing a breath.

"Yes, you are and I'm over it. You don't want to talk to me, don't want to catch up with me, then that's fine, but you haven't even asked about Pop—" I didn't get the rest of her name out of my mouth before his other hand slapped over my mouth and he used the hand he already had around my wrist to jerk me forward and pull me to his chest. He bent his head down so his lips were right next to my ear.

"Don't even think about going there with me, Salem."

I shivered, and not from fear. I was finally pressed all against him, only the time and place was totally wrong. A fact proven by Cora's sharp voice snapping Rowdy's name and telling him to let me go.

Immediately his hands were gone and so was the press of his hard body against mine. I turned back around to look at him and saw the way his nostrils flared and the way his bright eyes darkened. He was mad, really mad, and finally a bit of the boy I remembered was shining through.

"We're going to have to talk eventually." I kept my voice calm and even smiled at him. I felt like any move I made was just going to spook him further.

He backed up a few steps and narrowed his eyes at me. "Not if I can help it."

I cocked my head to the side and lifted an eyebrow at him. "Not talking about the past doesn't make it go away."

He made a noise low in his throat and shifted his gaze to the petite blond woman that had come from the upstairs area of the shop and stopped next to me. Cora had just had a baby with Rule's brother and I couldn't believe how amazing she looked. She was just as tiny and just as spunky as she had been before the baby, at least that's what everyone told me. Little baby Remy, or RJ as she was more commonly called, stayed at home with Cora's dad while Cora worked half days at the shop and her boyfriend went to work at the bar he owned. I had yet to meet Rule's older brother, but I was curious about the kind of man that could put up with her fiery personality full-time. She was a delightful handful even if she was about to butt her nose into something she had no clue about. Rowdy and I had ties that bound us together, it was just proving more difficult than I thought to unwind them and tie them back up into a pretty bow.

"What is going on? We have customers, you dumb-ass."

Rowdy shot a look over his shoulder and then looked back at me. I saw his eyes narrow and then his handsome face shifted and the cool cat that never got his fur ruffled resurfaced. The unflappable smile was back on his face and the midnight-blue shadows that had been dancing in his eyes vanished.

"Don't worry, we were just setting a couple of boundaries." He flashed the tiny blonde a wink and turned on the heel of his cowboy boot and made his way back to his station. He didn't have an appointment for another thirty minutes but I could guarantee that he would find a way to keep himself busy until then to avoid having to interact with me anymore.

Cora propped her hip on the counter and waited while I checked out two clients and checked another one in. Sure I was a little rattled by Rowdy's reaction to me trying to bring up my sister's name, but I was more unsettled by how angry he really seemed to be at me. I hadn't seen him in a decade and when I left Loveless he had been a teenage boy with his entire life stretched out in front of him. I couldn't imagine what had transpired in my absence to make him have such a burning resentment toward me.

Poppy and Rowdy had remained tight after I left. I knew that because before she had moved back home Poppy and I had stayed in constant contact; now our communication was far more limited. I knew that when they had graduated high school together Rowdy had picked the University of Alabama to attend because that's where my sister decided to go, even though Notre Dame had offered him a better recruitment package. What I didn't know, what I wondered at now, was how things had happened between them that had set Rowdy running away not just from my little sister but also from his entire future and education. I needed him to talk to me if I was ever going to put everything I had missed in the last ten years together to get a clear picture of who Rowdy was as a grown man.

Cora waited until I got off the phone and asked me to go upstairs with her. I didn't really want to but I figured I couldn't say no. Nash and Rule ultimately signed my paycheck, but I realized fast that Cora was sort of the rudder of the group. She steered the ship and I didn't want to be the one causing waves so early on in my employment here.

I liked Denver. I liked the welcoming and fresh vibe it had. I liked my coworkers and the men and women in their inner circle. Rule's wife was a sweetheart and there was no doubt the tattooed heartthrob had met his match in the classy blonde. Nash's girlfriend was just a peach. She didn't really talk much but when she did she was always kind and insightful and she looked at Nash like he hung the moon. I had only met Jet once but his wife, Ayden, popped in and out of the shop to talk to Cora at least twice a week, and I always thought she was a riot. And of course I adored Cora. She was smart, sassy, and full of attitude. She was just my kind of gal, only right now I was dreading getting dragged over the coals by her, but that didn't change the fact that they were all really good people and I couldn't have asked for a better place to land when I finally realized where I was supposed to be.

The upstairs was mostly empty. There was an office Cora shared with the boys and a whole bunch of empty space that was just waiting to be filled up and turned into a trendy, retro tattoo boutique. It would make money. The boys just needed to stop waffling about what they wanted to put up here and just do it. I think the idea of shopping and building an online store was kind of daunting to them and really Phil's passing was still pretty fresh, so everyone was just trying to find their footing as business owners still. It was a good thing I was here. This was right up my alley.

I loved clothes. I loved tattoo and pinup culture. I couldn't wait to make the Marked and the men behind it a household name.

I walked into Cora's messy office and sat in the chair across from her desk. She didn't walk around the other side but instead just jumped up on the edge in front of me and swung her legs back and forth. She had eyes that were two different colors, so it was easy just to stare at her in awe. I had to respect that she didn't beat around the bush when she immediately laid into me.

"Look, Salem, I like you. I like you quite a bit actually and I think you are just what we all need for the next phase of this business once the boys get their shit together. But Rowdy is my family and he's been off of his game since that first day we hired you and I don't just mean professionally. I don't know everything, but I do know that ever since you showed up he hasn't been himself and *that* I don't like at all."

I pulled my hair over my shoulder and ran my fingers through the dark strands.

"What exactly *do* you know?" I kept my tone light and curious, wondering if maybe he had shared with her his underlying reasons for seeming so fired up about me popping back up in his life.

She lifted a shoulder and let it fall. She really was just the cutest thing ever.

"I know that he burns through girls at an alarming rate and that they all thank him afterward. I know none of them stick and yet he can't seem to keep his eyes off of you."

Well, that wasn't exactly what I had been after and I

think she knew it. When I arched a dark eyebrow at her she gave me a coy grin.

"He never sticks with the same girl for more than a minute, which isn't exactly unusual with this crew. The rest of them put plenty of miles on the sheets until they found the right girl. Only Rowdy has mentioned more than once that he already met the right girl and she didn't want him, so now there is no reason to look for *the one*. He told me that *the one* just happened to be your sister. She broke him, so now he's all about a good time and not taking anything or anyone too seriously. At least he was until you walked in the door. He seems pretty fucking serious about you."

I crossed my legs and looked down at the peep-toe cut out of my pumps. They were black and had red bows on the heels. They were supercute and went awesome with my fitted, red pencil skirt. I dressed the way I did to feel sexy and in control. I rocked a look that attracted attention, and I did it mostly because I had been so disparaged when I was younger and I liked the positive response it always got. No amount of style and panache could dull the sharp edge of the blade that cut through me at the reminder that Rowdy had loved my little sister.

I looked back up at Cora and nodded a little. "He did love Poppy. The family that lived next to mine in Loveless took Rowdy in as a foster kid when he was ten. They were supernice but had a bucket load of kids, their own and ones from the state. Rowdy was shy, quiet, and really sad. Poppy and I were playing tag out front one day and she just happened to see him sitting on the front porch. I remember him watching us but not saying anything and she ran over and asked him to play with us."

I felt a soft smile pull at my lips at the memory. Even then he had been tall for his age and lanky. There was also no way to miss that glittery gold hair and those bright blue eyes in a town that was predominantly inhabited by Mexican-American families. He was something else. Something new and uncertain, something exciting and unexpected in a life that had forever seemed monotonous and bleak. Even though sadness and discontentment bled off of him back then, I could still see the strength and defiance in him that I so longed to have in myself. I wanted to soothe him but I also wanted to watch what happened when someone with that much untapped potential was set free. I wanted to live through him and stand beside him so I could feel what finally being untethered from the chains of conformity felt like. I also wanted to hug him and tell him it was okay to be sad, to be angry, to be lost and frustrated. I wanted to tell him he was all right just the way he was, like I so desperately longed to hear. Now I still wanted to tell him everything would be all right, but he wouldn't stand still long enough for me to explain that I was here for him and now that we were both free we could flourish and grow into something amazing and unbreakable together. He just had to give me a chance.

"I think he loved her from that moment on." I sighed and looked down at my hands where they had unconsciously laced together. "My dad is a very traditional man. His family immigrated from Mexico City when he was just a baby and he really believes in the old way of doing things. He is hyper-religious and didn't mind Poppy being friends with Rowdy because he was an orphan and his foster family were active members in our church, where my dad presided over the congregation. But he never would've condoned a romantic relationship between the two of them and Rowdy always knew that. It never stopped him from wearing his heart on his sleeve, though. I think he was just waiting for the two of them to get older, for them to go off to college, and then when Poppy was out from under my dad's thumb, she would see they were meant to be together."

Cora's legs stopped swinging and she looked me dead in the eye.

"So what happened?"

I barked out a dry laugh and pushed my long hair back over my shoulder. "Good question."

Now it was her turn to lift an incredulous eyebrow, only hers was dotted with a sparkly pink piercing.

"You don't know?"

"Nope. All I know is he left school, left her, and just dropped off the map. I asked her about it a few times here and there over the years but she never gave me any details."

"Are you here for the job, Salem, or are you here for Rowdy?" It was very Cora to ask the question so bluntly.

I could play it coquettish, smile and brush it off, but I liked her honesty and forthrightness, so I figured I should offer her the same. Plus I wasn't afraid of any of this crew knowing I was here for one of their own. They should know that eventually they were going to have to share Rowdy with me.

ROWDY   41

"Both. I came for both."

She made a noise that was a mix between a snort and a laugh and hopped off the desk.

"I don't think he has any idea what to do with you. I think he's afraid of you."

I got to my feet and smoothed my hands down the fabric of my skirt. I watched as she made a noise of distress and pressed an arm across her chest. Her dual-colored eyes got big in her face.

"Are you okay?"

She made a face and turned a little pink. "I have to go. Apparently it's time to feed my kid."

Aww . . . how sweet was that? "No worries. I got the shop for the rest of the day. I can manage whatever is left for the afternoon crowd."

She nodded and reached for her purse. I wasn't surprised that it was zebra striped bright yellow and black. Cora was definitely colorful in appearance and personality.

"Try and play nice with Rowdy for the rest of the day. Obviously the two of you need to have a come-to-Jesus talk, and if I have to put my foot up his ass in order to make him see that, then I will be happy to do it."

I followed her to the top of the stairs and put a hand on her shoulder before she could head down.

"No. He needs to get there on his own. I've been letting him tiptoe around me for weeks and I've given him plenty of time to adjust to the idea that I'm back in his life and that I'm not going to go away. He's obviously not ready for me yet."

She laughed a little and we made our way back into the

shop. The waiting room had gotten busy in the fifteen minutes I was upstairs, so it was going to take a second to get
everyone situated and straightened out. She leaned over and
whispered so only I could hear, "Just so you know, I would
pay a small fortune to see him in those tight football pants
he used to wear when he was younger. I Googled him once
and saw a picture from when he played for Alabama."

She waved her hand dramatically in front of her face and
gave me a little wave on her way out the front door. I had to
laugh and just happened to look over my shoulder to catch
Rowdy staring at me.

For once, the angry gloss was gone from his eyes as he
watched me unblinkingly. I saw it clear as day in that split
second. The reason there was so much division and disso-
nance between us. The reason he couldn't handle me being
back in his life suddenly was mapped out in that sea of blue
on blue. When Rowdy looked at me all he could see was the
past and what he had suffered through then, the loss he had
felt at my hands and the heartache he had been gifted by
my sister. But for me, when I looked at him all I could see
was the future and every promise and possibility that was
wrapped up in the sexy, blond, and tattooed package that
was grown-up Rowdy St. James. Some way, somehow, we
had to start looking at the same thing if I was ever going to
have a shot at showing him there was life after *the one* and
life after loss, especially if *the one* was the wrong person for
him all along and the loss was right in front of him wanting
to make amends.

CHAPTER 3

Rowdy

I WAS NEVER THE KIND of guy to turn my back on a good time. It was rare anymore that the entire group of friends I had immersed myself in and now called my family were all able to get together at the same time on the same day. So when Jet called me on his last night in town before he flew out to listen to some band play in Portland and demanded that I show up at the Bar because everyone was going to be there, I couldn't think of reasonable or noncowardly excuse not to go.

It was getting harder and harder to avoid Salem without making it absolutely noticeable and now that Cora had witnessed my epic overreaction when Salem had been on the verge of mentioning her sister . . . well, there was just no escaping the endless questions and speculative looks coming from those two-tone eyes. I loved Cora something fierce, but I didn't have any desire for her to start sticking her fingers into old wounds. Those suckers had long since scabbed over, and even if the scar tissue they left behind was ugly and gnarled, it was way better than the festering hurt and leaking heartache the actual memories had tied to them.

In an effort to prove not only to the girls but also to myself that I could play nice and that just seeing Salem in all her pretty, bronze beauty wasn't going to drag me back to places I never wanted to go, I put my best FTW attitude on and went to the Bar. I figured I could do this for one night. I could fake my way through pretending like the very sight of her didn't undo me from the inside. I just had to remind myself she was simply a stranger that I no longer knew. She was just a random and lovely Latin goddess covered in some of the prettiest, most detailed ink I had ever seen. I was a pro with the ladies and Salem was most assuredly all *lady*. I could be charming and slick. I could be engaging and friendly, and hopefully that would put her at ease and I would feel a little less like she was here in Denver to bring every terrible memory that haunted me to my front door.

I thought it was a rock-solid plan. I thought I was going to pull it all off with no trouble, but then I hit the entrance. The first thing my eyes landed on wasn't Ayden trying to get Jet to two-step with her to "Family Tradition," or Rule and Shaw whispering with heads bent close together, or Rome tugging his little pixie around the side of the bar to where I knew his office was back behind all the liquor storage, or Nash and his pretty Saint pretending to play a game of pool while they really just made out next to the felt-covered table. No, the first thing my traitorous gaze clapped on to was Salem's unmistakable curves where they were propped up so enticingly when she leaned over the bar as Asa beckoned her closer.

Of course the first thing that slammed into my brain was the way her black-and-white skirt hugged her backside and hips as she leaned over on those crazy tall heels she liked to wear. Right on the tail end of that thought was the notion that Asa was probably getting one hell of a show if she had a low-cut top on, and for some reason that made my head feel like it was going to fucking implode. My back teeth clenched together and I literally saw a hot red haze when she tossed back her head and laughed at something the blond southerner said. Her dark hair swished across the curve of her ass and her husky laugh made something in my gut and below my belt get tight. Before I could think about what I was doing, I found myself walking toward the bar with hasty steps.

I saw Asa notice my approach and he grinned at me knowingly as he purposely moved away to help another customer. I had to give it to the guy, he had killer taste in women. More often than not, now that he and I were the only unattached members of our little unit, we found ourselves good-naturedly fighting over the same girl at the end of the night. It was never anything serious and more than once it had turned into a sort of game to see which one of us could get the girl first. Considering both of us were blond and had our fair share of charisma, it was always a crapshoot to see who would win. He had the southern drawl working in his favor, but I had the fact that I was rocking plenty of ink and a retro-cool vibe a lot of ladies couldn't seem to resist. I posted up next to Salem and took the Coors Light Asa set in front of me without having to ask for it. I narrowed my eyes at him a little and saw his grin go from friendly to speculative.

"What's up, Rowdy?"

He always sounded like he had just stepped off of a farm in Kentucky. Ayden's accent was hardly noticeable unless she was mad or excited, but Asa used his twang like a weapon against all unsuspecting women. I felt Salem turn from where she was leaning to look at me, but I ignored her and focused on Asa.

"Not much."

"You haven't been around much lately." Now that all my friends were either married, practically married, or involved with their one true love, I tended to spend my free time hanging out here and shooting the shit with him. He would definitely have noticed that I had been cowering under a rock covered in my own fear and uncertainty for the last month or so. I went to make a smartass remark about him enjoying not having the competition around, when I heard Salem snort.

I'd avoided being too close to her because she made me uneasy and I was just so physically aware of her. When I grabbed her the other day I had been driven by panic and fear, not out of a sudden need to touch her. However, being this close, seeing the midnight-sky color of those eyes and the way her mouth was always painted in a perfect, sexy pout, had blood rushing to parts of my body I didn't want to be happy to see her. The way that ruby sitting at the corner of her mouth winked at me like it wanted me to bend down and lick it had me so that I suddenly couldn't remember why I didn't want to be close to her. The way her raven-dark brows danced up as I stared at her suddenly made me want to get as close as I could.

"I've been busy." I answered Asa's question offhandedly while I continued to stare at this stranger that I had once known better than I knew myself.

"Busy with what?"

I jerked my head around and noticed he had a shit-eating grin on his face. The fact that I was dumbstruck by this woman was obviously apparent and he had no qualms about torturing me with that knowledge.

I picked up the beer to have something to do with my hands and tilted my head to one side as Salem and I continued to watch each other. I was looking at her like she was going to attack at any second. I watched her like she was going to pounce and pull away all the good stuff I surrounded myself with now and all I would be left with was a blanket of threadbare awfulness that covered a life I didn't want to remember.

She was looking at me like I was the toy inside a Cracker Jack box. Her eyes shone like she had just found something she had been looking for and it was so much better than she imagined it being.

I took a big swallow of beer and told her flatly, "I want to know why you're in Denver, Salem."

She picked up her drink, something pink that smelled tangy and sweet, and took a sip. She pushed her heavy fall of hair over her shoulder and I looked down. Yep, Asa had gotten an eyeful. She had on a red lacy top that was cut low over the swells of her breasts and it looked like if she leaned in just the right way, the entire thing would fall down and expose her entire chest. She dressed provocative and alluring, but it was always sophisticated and very pulled together. She really did embody a modern-day Bettie Page.

"I'm here because Phil wanted me here. He knew this was where I was supposed to be if I wanted to be happy."

I wasn't expecting that answer, in fact I felt kind of like a dope for thinking she was going to say it had something to do with me being here. The little ding to my ego surprised me and I frowned.

"What does that mean?"

She just shrugged. "It means I've moved around a lot since I left Loveless. I never stay in any one place for very long and I've never managed to settle. I always thought that meant I was adventurous, that I had the soul of a gypsy, but Phil made me realize that I was always just looking for a safe place to land, a place to call home. I have never had that before."

"Denver is your safe place? You want this to be home now?"

I got it. I mean, Phil had found me slumming in a disgusting tattoo parlor in Oklahoma apprenticing under a guy that was more interested in running meth out of his shop than tattooing or teaching me how to tattoo. Phil had a friend of a friend that mentioned me to him, and the fact I was young, really eager to learn, and legitimately loved art. He made a special trip to come see me, and without my knowing how it would play out, Phil Donovan had rescued me, brought me to Denver on his dime, taught me what I needed to know to have a successful career and how to make money off of art.

Most importantly Phil had brought me into the fold of his family. Lonely wasn't easy but I had done it for so long that at first I didn't recognize what any of it was. Phil made Denver my safe place and my home as well.

She smiled and that sexy-as-hell piercing above her lip winked at me again. Now there was no question things below my belt were getting hard and taking all kind of notice of her against my will.

She told me coyly, "Sort of. My home is a little more complicated than coordinates on a map."

I was going to ask her what in the hell that meant when the door to the bar opened and a young woman sauntered in. I heard Asa suck in a breath from across the bar and heard Saint call out "Royal" as she waved to the new arrival from where she was still wrapped around Nash by the pool table. The auburn-haired beauty gave a general wave and then glided across the floor like it was her own personal catwalk as she went to join her friend. Just like that, Nash was in the center of a sexy redhead sandwich as the two girls hugged and giggled all around him. Lucky bastard.

"Who? Is? That?"

Asa's drawl was suddenly tight and thick in a way I had never heard before. His eyes, which were normally all shiny and bright like a gold coins, darkened to something intense and intent like I had never see in him before.

"Royal. She lives across the hall from Nash, and since Saint practically lives with him now, the two of them are inseparable."

The two redheads were an odd mix and as opposite as

two girls could be. Saint was low-key, soft-spoken, and about as humble and sweet as one person could get. She had coppery hair and freckles, so I liked to tease her that she looked like Pippy Longstocking. Royal Hastings had been genetically gifted in every way a young woman could be. She was tall, had perfect skin, cocoa-colored eyes, and auburn hair that went on for days. Her body was the kind of thing I used to think never really existed outside of a *Sports Illustrated* Swimsuit issue, and if all of that wasn't enough in a supersexy package, she was also really nice, superfunny, and just quirky enough to make her approachable and engaging.

"I want." Asa's voice dropped an octave and I saw Salem look back and forth between the two of us. I hated to even think it but it sure ran through my mind that if he set his sights on Royal, that meant I didn't have to get all queasy and weird about him flirting with Salem so I told him, "Go for it. She's single."

His eyes shot back to mine and he scowled. "Why is a chick that smoking hot single?"

In guy speak that totally meant "what is wrong with her?"

I lifted a shoulder and let it fall innocently. "She works a lot and has weird hours, I guess."

He put his hands on the bar across from me and leaned forward a little. "What does she do?"

That was the tricky part. When I told him what the stunning young woman did for a living, I knew his interest would immediately be dampened. I tossed it around in my head for a second, toying with how to tell him, when Salem suddenly interrupted our back-and-forth banter by stating, "She's a cop."

Asa's eyes bugged out huge in his face and he took a step back from us like the news held an electrical shock.

"How do you know that?" His tone was harsh when he asked her the question.

Salem lifted a bare shoulder and let it fall. I decided I wanted to lick along her entire collarbone and suck on the curve of her shoulder where it met her elegant neck. What was wrong with me? I was supposed to be running away from her and the hurt I knew she could inflict.

"She comes into the shop with Nash's old lady all the time. One time she was in her patrol uniform. I asked her to show me her gun."

All the color fled out of Asa's face and he shook his head back and forth like the action would dispel the truth in Salem's words. Just to drive the point home I nodded and added, "She really is. I didn't believe it when Nash first told me but it's true. She even got jumped by a junkie while she was on patrol a little while ago and ended up walking around with a black eye and a busted lip. She carries a badge and enforces the law, my friend."

He swore under his breath and gave me a lopsided grin. "*That* should be illegal. No girl that hot should be allowed to protect and serve."

He wandered away to fix some drinks for Dixie, who was watching the exchange from the end of the bar. When I caught the pretty cocktail server's eye, she smiled at me and I had to swallow back some beer to avoid the automatic grin back. Flirting with a pretty girl came as naturally as breathing to me, but Salem was watching me carefully with those ebony eyes of hers, and for some reason giving Dixie my *I'll show you a good time* grin didn't really sit right under the scrutiny. She pushed some of her long hair over her shoulder and I watched it slither across her bare skin. Flirting might be second nature to me, but this woman was effortlessly sexy and oozed sensuality like it was an expensive perfume. She was way better at playing this back-and-forth game than I was ever going to be and that was just more reason to keep my distance from her.

"Pretty girls shouldn't be police officers?" Her tone was a little snide, so I pushed off the bar and inclined my head to where Asa was still talking to Dixie.

"Asa has a long history of being on the wrong side of anyone with a badge. It isn't her so much as what she does. He isn't the kind of guy that likes it when a hot girl is off-limits and to him what she does for a living makes her most definitely off-limits."

She lifted a raven-tinted eyebrow and cast a speculative look between Asa and the striking redhead that had tossed her head back and was laughing loudly as something Saint had said.

"It's a shame he feels that way. They would make a really beautiful couple."

Well, that made me feel less like strangling Asa for not only getting an eyeful when Salem had been bent over the bar, but for smiling at her and being so easy around her when she made me feel like I was back to being an unwanted and out-of-place little kid.

"So you just dropped everything—left your entire

life—to come help Nash and Rule with the new shop because Phil wanted you here? You didn't leave anyone or anything behind?"

There was resentment there. I could hear it in my own voice, and I couldn't seem to help it. My mom had died in a random act of violence when I was a really little kid. I didn't have too many memories of her. But I could recall that she was nice, pretty, and was always smiling or laughing. I remembered her being happy.

I had gone into the system when I was only six years old. I had no other family or at least no one with my blood willing to claim me, so I bounced from foster home to foster home until I landed with the Ortegas when I was ten. I knew logically my mom hadn't left me alone in the world on purpose, that fate was a tricky thing and could be really fucking nasty when she wanted to be, but there was no denying that whenever someone I cared deeply about walked away from me it brought back all those feelings I had long since held on to of being abandoned.

Instead of answering my sarcastically asked question, she propped her hip on a bar stool and leaned a little to the side while she considered me solemnly. I always thought she had great eyes. When I was younger I thought they looked like velvet and something soft. Now, while she watched me unflinchingly, I thought they looked dark and enigmatic. I didn't like that she came across like she knew every secret the universe had and that she was just waiting for me to catch up to her so she could whisper them in my ear.

"Why haven't you asked me anything at all about

Poppy? Not how she is? Not where she's at? Not what she's doing? You wouldn't even let me say her name yesterday and I'm wondering why. I know the two of you had a pretty bad falling-out, but there is something more there. You two were attached like Siamese twins when I left Loveless. So enlighten me, Rowdy. What really happened between you and my sister?"

I couldn't stop the way her sister's name made me take an involuntary step back. I didn't ask because I really didn't want to fucking know any of that information. This was exactly why I had been avoiding Salem like a coward for the last month. I just wanted to go back to a point where I was happy pretending like the Cruz sisters were nothing but a distant memory I only dusted off when I had too much to drink or sentimentality snuck up on me and gave me a sucker punch.

I was saved from having to choke out a lame response when Ayden popped up at my side and grabbed my elbow. Her eyes were the identical shade of rich whiskey as Asa's and they were shiny and bright with both tequila and mischief.

"Come dance with me. Jet is being difficult."

I looked over my shoulder and saw that my friend was glaring at me in warning. Since ruffling Jet's feathers was at the top of my favorite-things-to-do list, there was no way I was going to tell her no. I wasn't really a country-and-western kind of guy, but I did have on cowboy boots and I was never going to complain about getting my hands on a girl that was as pretty as Ayden.

I looked back at Salem and could practically see the wheels in her head turning behind her dark gaze, but before

I could say anything to her she reached for her drink and pushed off the bar.

"We're gonna have a reckoning eventually, Rowland. You were always really quick on the field, but off of it you kind of stumble."

She swished her way around me, her hair slinking across my bare forearm and making my guts clench. I watched her as she wound her way to where Nash and Saint were still talking to Royal and saw her embrace the auburn-haired stunner in a one-armed hug like they were long-lost friends.

I looked back at Ayden and told her before she could even start, "Don't. Just don't."

I let her tug me toward the tiny dance floor and easily fell into a quick two-step with her as David Allan Coe crooned "Mama Tried" on the digital jukebox.

"Rowland?" She giggled a little and I scowled down at her.

"I haven't been that guy in a long time."

"Where did 'Rowdy' come from, then?"

I grunted but flashed a very toothy grin at Jet over the top of Ayden's head as he raised both middle fingers up at me and mouthed every dirty word he knew. I pulled his lady closer and smiled cheekily down at her just to rile him up even more.

"I was an unruly child. I had a lot of energy that no one seemed to know what to do with. I was always in time-out, always in trouble at school, and no one really seemed to want to get a handle on it. I was put with a family when I was ten that already had a bunch of other kids, their own and other fosters. The mom—Maria—didn't speak the greatest

English and used to mutter at me in Spanish. She was trying to tell me to settle down, to act right, but I was just rowdy. My teachers, the other parents at church, some of the other kids started calling me that and it was easier for her to say, so it stuck and it fit."

Her eyes had widened huge in her face and her mouth had sort of dropped open in a little gasp. I gave her a squeeze to let her know it was a long time ago and that it was all right now, but inadvertently my gaze once again sought out that dark head of hair and those ridiculous curves encased in a skintight skirt. At least it had been all right until she showed up.

Ayden wrinkled her nose at me and gave me a squeeze back. "Did Jet tell you about Austin?"

Her voice was quiet. I almost didn't hear it over the clatter of the heels of our boots on the wooden floor.

"He mentioned something about it."

"What do you think?" She sounded hesitant and I saw her gulp a little after she asked it.

"I think we're all adults and know how planes work. Austin isn't Antarctica, and just because you'll be in a new zip code physically doesn't mean you won't be here in heart and spirit still. You guys are family no matter how many miles might be between you and us."

I saw her nod a little and her eyes got glassy and hot.

"I'm scared."

I sighed a little and pulled her into a hug that had her squealing in surprise and her long legs kicking up behind her. I kissed her soundly on the temple and told her matter-of-factly, "That's how you know you're doing it right, honey."

I put her back down and she lightly smacked me on the center of my chest with a laugh.

"Yeah, but I'm still freaked out. I'm worried about Asa. Who's going to keep him in line and keep an eye on him when I'm gone? He's a trouble magnet."

"I would think it's past time your big brother keeps himself in line and there is an army of us here to remind him what he has to lose if he slips up. Worry about you. Worry about your man. Just go and be happy and enjoy being in love and being married. It'll be fine, Ayd, and if it's not there isn't anything you can do about it anyway."

She made a noise in her throat and lifted her eyebrow at me. "So what's the story with you and Salem? There seems to be more going on there than you originally let anyone in on."

Over the top of her head I saw that Jet had climbed to his feet and was stalking toward us. I winked at him and was treated to another nasty look.

"It ain't a fairy tale, if that's what you're hoping for."

"She's fun and kind of eccentric. I like her."

"Salem's easy to like." She was warm. She was smart. She was caring and compassionate. She was the only person in my young life that had made me feel at peace, and when she took that away, when she had abandoned me to my own devices, that was when I really had latched on to Poppy with a ferocity that bordered on obsession. I wasn't going to make the mistake of being taken in by Salem's welcoming personality again. It left too big of a void when it was gone.

"So why are you acting like she kicked your puppy? It

isn't like you, and frankly I'm not a fan. She's a great addition to the shop and you guys are lucky to have her."

Jet had finally reached us and put his arm around Ayden's middle. He pulled her backward to his chest and I let her go without a fight.

"You suck." His tone was surly as he looked at me hard.

I laughed and shrugged. "Then get off your ass and dance with your wife. She comes and listens to that ear murder you call music, the least you can do is twirl her around a dance floor once in a while."

He grunted and begrudgingly let Ayden pull him into a slow dance as I stepped away from the darkly beautiful couple. I headed to the bar for another beer and thought about what Ayden had said.

The truth of the matter was that the shop and even Rule and Nash were indeed lucky to have Salem here . . . but me— well, I kind of always had the idea that if it wasn't for bad luck, then I would have no luck in my life at all. I lost my mom. I lost Salem. I lost my first love and that was all before I was old enough to drink legally. Bad luck was something I was intimately acquainted with.

I figured all the good fortune I had since meeting Phil and coming to Denver was fate's way of repaying me for a childhood of being lost and loveless.

CHAPTER 4

Salem

H<small>EY, WILL YOU PLEASE</small> call me back? This is the fourth message I've left you in two weeks, Poppy. I'm starting to get a little bit worried."

I scowled at the phone and shoved it back in my purse as I jumped around a puddle the afternoon rain was leaving on the sidewalk. Denver got hot in the summer, not desert hot or Texas hot, but it was still nice and warm, so I was surprised that when the sky opened up like it seemed prone to do midafternoons, the raindrops that fell were freezing cold and the size of quarters. The weather in this state had a serious identity crisis but I guess that was okay because if you hated what was happening weatherwise it would change five minutes later.

I shivered since I was wearing cute black shorts with big silver sailor buttons and a flouncy off-the-shoulder shirt this morning, and now I was freezing as I walked to the coffee shop at the end of the block to grab something to warm me up before I headed back to the shop from my lunch break. I didn't even want to think about what the rain had done to my hair and the heavy eye makeup I usually wore, so instead I focused on how irritated I was at my baby sister.

Poppy and I had always been very different. Where I was resigned to the fact that Loveless and my parents' home were not places I was ever going to thrive in and find happiness, she was still there and still the apple of my stern father's eye. I had prayed that after she went away to college and saw more to the world, she would branch out, live a little, and realize there was more to life than being a perfect daughter. Much to my annoyance she had returned home right after graduation and had fallen quickly into all her old patterns even when I pleaded with her to come and stay with me. A marriage to a man that was far too similar to my father for my liking had quickly followed and so had Poppy's distancing herself from me. A choice I was sure wasn't entirely her own.

Even though my parents and her husband didn't love that Poppy still stayed in touch with me, it was her one act of defiance and we talked whenever she could get away with it. I had questions—a lot of them. I wanted answers and it was impossible to get them from Rowdy, considering he was about as welcoming as a concrete wall. There was more to their falling-out than the simple "he wanted different things than I did and it meant we couldn't even be friends anymore" that Poppy had initially given to me when everything broke loose all those years ago. Something major must have occurred for Rowdy to be so adamant that he didn't even want the slightest info on my sister. She was supposedly his first love and Poppy normally told me everything there was to tell, so all the subterfuge between the two of them had me extra curious.

My sister was not what one would call lucky in love. She was too eager to please, both the men in her life and my father. That led to her dating and ending up in relationships with some real gems. I don't think she would know the real deal in love if it bit her on the nose, and that was one of the reasons I tried to keep tabs on her and was worried she hadn't called me back. Her husband was a real piece of work. Oliver Martinez was a bossy and menacing carbon copy of my dad and that made me really nervous. Poppy wasn't strong enough to walk away or willful enough to stand up for herself if a man in her life was trying to control her.

I ordered a floofy coffee drink and a brownie because they looked good, and tried to wring some water out of my long hair. I was shuffling back to the door, my eyes down as I put the brownie in my purse, and I didn't see the woman I almost plowed down until it was too late. I barely caught her around her wrist as she bounced off of me and the collision sent her phone flying to the floor.

We both gasped and I stammered out an apology because even though my coffee hadn't spilled everywhere it still sloshed a little from the violence of the impact and got on the back of both of our hands.

The woman waved me off and bent to retrieve her phone as I rushed to apologize again and again. I was even more apologetic when I noticed it was the same elegant, blond woman from the other day in the shop.

She was wearing another sharp suit and her hair was pulled up in a tight bun on the top of her head. Her eyes were wide as she recognized me.

"Sorry. I was reading e-mail on my phone and not paying any attention."

I snorted a little and flicked my hand to shake the cooling liquid off the back of it.

"I was juggling a hundred things and my mind was a million miles away. I have a few minutes before I have to head back to the shop; let me buy you your coffee to apologize."

She shook her head. "Oh no, you don't have to do that, really. I should have been paying attention."

I just ignored her and turned and walked to the line hoping she would follow me. She did, still telling me the gesture was unnecessary, but by the time it was our turn to order she had quieted down and I wasn't surprised that she got a simple black coffee and didn't add anything to it. This woman really seemed to be absolutely no frills and no nonsense, which again had me wondering why she had ventured into the tattoo shop in the first place.

"I'm Salem Cruz, by the way." I stuck my hand out and she shook it briskly.

"Sayer Cole. I actually work at the family law building that's a couple of blocks over."

I nodded and grinned a little. "You would be surprised how many lawyers are running around with tattoos nowadays. I sure hope it wasn't your job that convinced you to forgo getting some ink."

She balked a little and turned a hot shade of pink. "No.

I'm actually pretty new to Denver and was just out exploring." She cleared her throat as we made our way back to the door. I was relieved to see the rain had let up some. "I stuck my head in on a whim. I'm not really sure what I was thinking."

She looked away from me as soon as she said it and I had the distinct feeling she wasn't exactly being honest with me.

"I'm new to the city, too. So far I love it here. Where did you move from?"

"Seattle. I spent my whole life there. I needed a change."

I could relate. She asked me where I was from and I just laughed and told her all over. When she asked what had brought me to the Mile High City I looked at her out of the corner of my eye and asked, "Are you going to think I'm ridiculous if I tell you it has to do with a guy?"

She shrugged a little and we stopped at the corner of the block. Her gaze darted away and again I got the really strong impression that she was only telling me half of what she meant. "No. I'm sort of here for a guy, too. Not in the romantic sense but a certain guy was definitely a motivating factor in why I accepted this transfer when my company decided they wanted to open an office in Denver." She inclined her head in the opposite direction of the way I had to take to return to work and told me with genuine kindness lacing her tone, "I hope it works out for you."

I laughed. "I'm pretty persistent. If you change your mind about adding a little rock to your roll, come back by the shop. Those boys are doing some really spectacular work."

Her gaze drifted over the expanse of my tattooed arms.

"I never realized how beautiful it could be, or how much art was really involved in tattooing."

"If it's done right it is as beautiful as anything painted on a canvas and it's the one kind of art you really can share with the world wherever you go."

The lights changed, and as we headed off in opposite directions I wondered about the polished young woman who seemed to have a lot of secrets. I silently hoped whatever had brought her to Denver worked itself out as well. Secrets or not, she seemed really nice.

I pushed open the doors of the shop and had to wind my way through the people cluttering up the waiting area to get behind the desk. Cora was talking to two girls that were showing her pictures and the buzz of tattoo machines was steady in the background. Nash caught my eye and inclined his head at me. I stashed my purse after rescuing the brownie so I had it on hand for later and asked him what was up.

He rubbed his hands over his shaved head and I wondered how often Saint did the same thing to him. Those flames he had tattooed along each side of his scalp were bright and fun. If he was my guy I would have my hands all over them every chance I got. His purplish eyes flashed at me with a mixture of good-natured humor and aggravation.

"What do you need me to do in order for you to get that store upstairs up and running? I thought I had an idea, but every time I think I'm moving forward something happens and I get pulled in the opposite direction."

"I need you guys to give me some images, some kind of logo, so I can contact a screen printer and get the designs put on T-shirts and other apparel." It had to be cute stuff and trendy stuff that fit with the vibe the guys had going on. "I think you should all base your design ideas off of tattoos each of you already has. The fangirls would go bonkers for it. You have that dragon, Rule has that snake on his arm." I nodded when his eyes got squinty in thought. "Cora has all those flowers, and Rowdy has that anchor on his neck that is impossible to miss. All different, all distinct, and I think it would make a statement. That way we aren't just branding the tattoo shops—we're branding the people behind them." I reached out and squeezed his impressive bicep. "I also think you should do a special limited-edition design for Phil. Something old-school, something badass that pays tribute to him and his hand in leaving this behind for you guys."

I saw his Adam's apple slide up and down and his eyes blinked fast for a second until he cleared his throat and dipped his head down in a nod.

"You are exactly the person we needed to make this happen. My dad really did know his shit."

I grinned. "He was a very smart and tricky man."

"He wanted you here for more than the shop, didn't he?"

I lifted a bare shoulder and let it fall. "Sometimes it takes someone from the outside to notice what is missing. Phil was really good at that."

Nash grunted his agreement and lifted a hand to wave his client over as he entered the shop.

"He was." He took a step around me and then paused and looked down at me. "The store was all Rowdy's idea. The concept, the idea to branch out, was all him. I think I'll give him a call and tell him he can be your point person on getting up and going. Rule and I have too much other stuff to deal with right now."

It was there in those fabulous eyes, the same kind of compassion and need for the people around him to be happy that glowed out of his father's eyes. He was Phil's son—no doubt about it. I laughed and turned back to the desk so I could help Cora manage the still-growing crowd of potential clients.

"Whatever you say, boss."

IT WASN'T UNTIL HOURS and hours later that I finally got to my brownie. It had been a packed day for appointments, and there were two late walk-ins that a couple of the new artists agreed to stick around and do, so it was almost nine at night by the time I got around to doing the cash-out for the day and locking everything up. Even on a busy day here it didn't come close to the chaos I was used to at the shop in the casino. That place had almost fifteen artists on staff and was open until two in the morning. The shops in Denver were successful and busy but they felt way less like a spectacle than my previous job had. I was surprised how much I liked the closer-knit, more mellow feel of my new gig and I appreciated that they were really cranking out amazing works of art versus cookie-cutter, flash tattoos that tourists picked off a wall.

I was the type of person that got bored and hated routine. I think that was one of the reasons I was always on the move so much. I never wanted to be predictable. I never wanted to know what was in store for me from one day to the next. I'm sure it had to do with growing up in a house where routine was everything, where not one second passed that wasn't accounted for and planned down to the minute detail. My dad lived and died by rules and regulations, so it made sense that as soon as I was able I decided to never have a plan. I was always content to just land wherever the wind took me—only now that had changed. I felt grounded here. Felt like I could wake up to the mountains, fresh air, and crazy weather for an endless number of days and never get tired of it.

I also knew without question that I could stare into Rowdy St. James's cerulean eyes for an eternity and never see anything prettier—even when he was looking at me like I was something toxic and dangerous.

I was munching on the brownie and called Poppy again, this time leaving a message where I chewed her out and threatened to get on the next plane out of Denver if she didn't call me back tomorrow. I was putting the cash from the day's deposit in the safe that was in Cora's office and making sure all the doors were locked upstairs when I caught sight of myself in one of the crazy fun-house mirrors the contractor had put up here to tie the boardwalk theme of the shop together.

It was the mirror that stretched me out and made me look like a giraffe. It also reflected that I had thick black smudges of eyeliner under each eye and that my normally sleek and styled hair was a frizzy mess from the rain. I couldn't believe I had worked the entire last part of the day looking so rumpled and messy. I shook my head at the silly reflection and went to turn the lights off when I heard footsteps on the floor below me.

The only people with keys to either shop were the guys and Cora, so I just assumed it was one of them and waited to see if the footsteps were going to hit the stairs. They did, and when I heard the distinctive click that could only belong to a pair of well-worn cowboy boots, I felt my heart start to pick up speed.

Rowdy's slicked-up hair cleared the top landing and his bright gaze landed on me. He didn't smile or grin. He didn't quip one of his fast responses at me; he just stared at me steadily as he closed the space between us until he was standing in front of me. He towered over me and I had to tilt my head back to look up at him. Flirty-fun Rowdy seemed reserved for any female that wasn't me and I didn't know if I liked that or if it annoyed me just yet.

"Hey."

His eyes flared hot at the center and I saw the corners of his mouth tense in a frown as he continued to just stare at me without speaking.

It took a solid five minutes before he decided to open his mouth. "Nash called me and told me to swing by and see if you were still here. He wants me to talk to you about the store."

I lifted an eyebrow at him and took a step back. When I did so he took a minute to breathe the space in and run his thumb along the edge of one of his ruthlessly trimmed sideburns. His eyes also swept over me and landed back on my face with his frown still in place.

"Why are you such a mess?"

I snorted and flipped my tangled hair over my shoulder. "I got caught in the rain on my lunch break and almost ran some poor woman over in my haste to get back to work. I can't believe no one told me I looked like a drowned rat all day." I rolled my eyes and went to move another step or two back from him but he caught my wrist in his hand and tugged me closer.

My lungs stopped working and my heart fell out of my chest and landed at his feet when he took his free hand and ran his thumb along the delicate curve below one of my eyes where all my eyeliner had retreated to.

"This actually looks familiar. I remember the first time you snuck makeup from one of your girlfriends at school and couldn't get it off." He repeated the process on the other eye and I had to suck in a breath out of desperation because his face was starting to get blurry from lack of oxygen to my brain. "You didn't know the stuff was waterproof and spent an hour trying to scrub it off with the hose in the backyard because you knew your dad would lose his shit if he caught you with it on. You just ended up looking like a soggy raccoon."

I remembered the incident just as clearly as he seemed to, only I was having a hard time thinking straight because his thumb was now dancing across the high arch of my cheekbone and skipped even lower to glance across the ruby I wore right above my lip.

"You ran home and asked Maria what to do. She sent you back with olive oil and saved the day." I gave him a lopsided grin. "It wasn't too long after that that I started wearing as much makeup as I could cake on my face just to get under his skin. Some habits stuck with me, I guess."

I saw his chest shudder as he took a deep breath and something dark moved across his sky-blue eyes. He opened his mouth like he was going to say something else then changed his mind and snapped it closed. He dropped my wrist like it was on fire and took a step back from me. I didn't bother to try and hide the disappointment that his retreat caused.

"So talk to me about the store."

I sighed a little, but if he wanted to talk business I wasn't going to look a gift horse in the mouth. At least he was carrying on a conversation with me.

I ran over the basic ideas I had given Nash earlier. I told him that I really thought their clients would love the opportunity to represent not only the shop but their favorite artists and I was happy that he seemed to agree. He told me his idea about offering prints and graphic pieces of art to sell as well as apparel and I had to admit I was impressed with his entrepreneurial mind. He had always been a lot more than a pretty face and a jock. I was happy to see he hadn't lost that as he had grown into adulthood.

We tossed ideas back and forth for twenty minutes or so and I told him he was in charge of wrangling Rule and Nash because he knew them better than I did in order to get them to give me designs I could use. He readily agreed and then we fell into an awkward silence as it was obviously time to go. He told me he would have something for me by the end of the following week and I nodded in agreement. We turned in different directions, him toward the stairs and me back toward the light switch on the wall, when he suddenly said my name in a very strangled tone.

"Salem . . ."

I looked at him over my shoulder and lifted a brow at the intent look on his handsome face.

"Yeah?"

His boots clattered on the wooden floor as he stalked toward me. His mouth was in a tight line and his eyes were bleeding blue fire at me.

"What is that?"

He walked right up to me. He didn't stop until his chest was almost pressed into my back. For someone who had actively avoided me for weeks and weeks and didn't seem thrilled to have to share the same space as me, he sure didn't have any kind of problem at all putting his hands on me.

He collected my heavy fall of two-tone hair in his hands and pulled it all up and off the bare expanse of my shoulders and neck.

From one shoulder to the other I had a field of Texas bluebonnets and in between all the flowers were tiny little sparrows. It was a big tattoo, bright and pretty, that took up a lot of real estate on my skin and in my heart. The flowers and birds were so lifelike it looked like a photograph not a painting made of flesh and ink. It was the first tattoo I had ever had done and it had withstood the test of time pretty well over the years. Normally it was hidden by my hair or whatever I was wearing for the day, but with this shirt, the entire thing was on display and it was no wonder he was looking at the ink like it was going to jump off my skin and wrap him in memories.

"I got it done as soon as I left Loveless." My voice was a little shaky even though I meant to sound defiant. The flowers were the exact same color as the heartbreak in his blue eyes that day I left.

"I drew that for you." He sounded mad. He sounded hurt. I couldn't blame him for either.

"I know you did, Rowdy. I might have had to leave Texas, but it was never my intention to make you think I was leaving you and Poppy as well."

His finger traced along the field of flowers and he said more to himself than to me, "You never thought it was weird I liked to draw. Everyone else always told me to focus on football. Everyone said I was going to go pro, so I shouldn't waste my time with studying or messing around with art. You always told me to do what I wanted. You were the only one that ever said it was okay that I was really good at more than one thing. I drew this picture for you for your birthday when you turned sixteen."

I was going to jump out of my skin and then I was going to jump him if he didn't stop stroking me like that. I let out a shuddering breath.

"It was beautiful. The gesture and the picture. You always were extremely talented and I thought your art should be on display. I never forgot you, Rowdy. I always took you with me wherever I ended up."

He said my name again, only this time he sounded confused and lost. I gasped a little as his hands suddenly gripped my shoulders and he spun me around. Before my mind could catch up to what was going on, he was backing me up toward that fun-house mirror. When my bare shoulders hit the chilly glass I gasped, which worked out perfectly for him because he suddenly dropped his head and clamped his mouth over mine.

My brain might not have known what to do with his sudden switch in demeanor toward me but my body had no trouble responding. My back arched. My arms reached up to twine around his neck. My nipples got hard and my mouth did its very best to seal itself to his forever. My tongue twisted around his and I whimpered as his hands slipped around my waist to pull me up higher on the toes of my heels in order to match his impressive height. Thank God I typically wore ridiculous shoes, or getting all the good stuff lined up would have been impossible.

It wasn't a sweet kiss. It wasn't a delicate kiss. I could taste the past and his resentment in it. I could feel that he was chasing down ghosts as his teeth nipped a little harder than they should have along the plush curve of my bottom lip. None of that mattered, though, because this was Rowdy and to me he felt like everything that had ever been good or made me happy in this whole entire world.

His hands were a little too hard, his breathing a little too fast, and when I leaned even more fully into him I could feel that his heartbeat was erratic and unsteady. I was trying to climb up him, trying to get inside of him, and just when I got my hands up to the back of his head so I could pull him even more fully to me, my phone decided to ring from where it was stashed in the back pocket of my shorts.

Carl Perkins was singing "Honey Don't," and while I would have been glad to ignore it and continue kissing the boy I had always wanted to kiss in another way than good-bye, I couldn't because it was finally my sister calling me back.

I dropped back to my feet and let my arms drop from around Rowdy's neck. I dug the phone out and hit the touch screen to answer the call.

"Poppy?"

As soon as my sister's name fell off of my lips Rowdy's entire behavior changed. Dark shutters fell across his pretty eyes and he stepped deliberately away from me. Without another word he turned on his boot heel and headed for the stairs. He didn't say good-bye, didn't look back. There was no acknowledgment that we had been involved in a very serious lip lock just seconds before. He just vanished, leaving me all keyed up and with more questions than I had had before. Damn him and damn the past that seemed to be standing in the way of where I wanted to be.

CHAPTER 5

Rowdy

IT WAS SO HARD to keep the memories at bay once the door they had all been closed behind was flung open. One after another they chased me across all of my waking hours and danced behind my eyelids at night.

I remembered the first time Poppy ran across the yard between our houses and asked me if I wanted to play. I was so used to being overlooked, so used to being forgotten and alone, that I almost ran in the other direction. She was so cute—all knobby knees and long pigtails. She smiled at me and told me we could be friends forever and I remembered even at ten years old thinking I never wanted to be without her smile and her kindness.

I remembered Salem being patient and funny as two kids trailed after her like she was the queen of the world. She never tired of the questions, of the attention, of fixing up my hurt feelings when I had a bad day at school—which there were a lot of—and she never looked at me like she found me lacking even when everyone else in my little world was trying to guide me in a direction I wasn't sure I wanted to go. She was always my biggest cheerleader and it never mattered if it was because I scored a touchdown or drew her a picture.

Along with all those memories came the other ones, the ones that made it hard to breathe and made my head throb and my heart hurt.

I remembered Poppy and her big, sad eyes telling me she would never love me the way I loved her, that we would always be from two different worlds, and therefore it would never work out. I literally put my young and soft heart in her hands and she had chucked it back at me like it was nothing. I had had a crush on her—was so sure that I'd loved her—for what felt like forever. I just knew she was my *one*. She was steady. She was unfailingly kind and generous. She was lovely inside and out, but to her I wasn't enough. I didn't have the right background, the right upbringing, and in all honesty the right skin color for her to ever be able to bring me home and tell her dad she was spending the rest of her life with me. I would have given her the world—only she didn't want it—or me.

I also remembered standing in the driveway watching Salem and her dad scream at each other while she threw all her things into the back of a rusted-out Belvedere and her telling him point-blank she was never going to step foot in his house or in Loveless again. She was my best friend. She was the one that always made everything better, and even at fifteen I remembered thinking I would never make it the rest of the way through high school without her. How was I supposed to pick which college I was going to go to?

I was going to tell my foster parents, Poppy, everyone, that I didn't want to play football, I wanted to paint and draw. I wanted an art scholarship not an athletic one and Salem was the only one that would support me in that. I needed her to give me the strength to fight for it, but in the blink of an eye she was gone.

She saw me where I was lurking and got back out of that car so that she could give me a kiss—a real kiss—on the lips and I remembered she tasted salty and sweet because she was crying as she told me good-bye. It was my first kiss and the memory of it was tied to watching yet another person I cared about leaving me on my own. She tried to tell me she would write, call, send a carrier pigeon, but I just walked away from her because I couldn't listen to it and I knew she was lying. Once she was gone, I wouldn't matter anymore, which had proven to be true.

Now all those memories were tangling and colliding with the new ones I had of the way grown-up Salem felt pressed against me. The memory of the way my dick twitched when I saw her standing at the top of the stairs that first day she got hired to work at the shop. There was the irritating remembrance of the way she burned as hot as the sun when I touched her and that she still tasted salty and sweet, but now I was old enough to want to know if she tasted that way everywhere on her body, not just on her pouty lips. I couldn't stop seeing the way her dark eyes gleamed like polished onyx, or stop thinking about the way her full mouth felt better than anything I could ever remember feeling, and the fact she tasted like chocolate and history in the best and worst way was haunting me every minute of every day. I knew that if her phone hadn't gone off I was a split second away from trying to get my hands in the waistband of those short-shorts she had been wearing, and even closer to tugging the shoulder of her sexy top the rest of the way off. I wanted to touch all that caramel-colored skin and put my mouth on the pointy tips of her breasts that I could feel poking into my chest.

It was all crashing and colliding so loud and hard that I felt like I couldn't see or hear anything else. I actively avoided going to the new shop and even harassed Rule into taking my shift that week so I didn't have to see her. I couldn't get on top of it and as a result I was drowning in the past and running away from the future. I was exhausted.

Even though I told her I would get her some drawings by the end of the week, I totally blew it off and now it was Thursday night and I was well on my way to getting absolutely shit-faced with my friend Zeb Fuller at the Bar. I also fully intended to take Dixie home because the quickest way to get over the idea of someone was to get into the idea of someone else. And even if Dixie wasn't game to play surrogate lover, then maybe I would take the blonde that was eye-fucking me from the end of the bar home with me and her hot, brunette friend was totally welcome to join us. I smiled at her for good measure and saw her flush and turn to whisper to her friend.

I caught Asa's eye; he was watching the show with a smirk and shrugged. I turned back to Zeb, who didn't look half as impressed as the southern bartender did.

"What?" My tone was a little surly and a whole lot sloppy.

I was chugging Jäger shots like they were water and I think they had finally caught up to me.

Zeb was a good dude. He had been a client first and then morphed into a friend after we spent several hours covering up the nasty jailhouse tattoos he had gotten over the couple of years he had spent locked up. The guy was an amazing craftsman. I was pretty sure he could build a house with nothing more than some Elmer's Glue and some toothpicks, but life hadn't always been a picnic for him and that being the case, I had wanted to help him out. I was the one that suggested Nash and Rule look into hiring Zeb as the contractor on the new shop, and much to my relief it had worked like a dream for everyone involved.

With all my friends being married, or having babies, or settling down with sexy nurses, I was on my own way more than I was used to be, so I had taken to calling Zeb when I needed a drinking buddy for the night.

Zeb lifted his Jack and Coke and just looked at me over the rim of it and told me "nothing" in a tone that clearly meant something.

I squinted my eyes a little and tossed back the newly filled shot Asa had placed in front of me with a lifted brow.

"What's with the look, then?"

Zeb was a massive guy. I think he was even bigger than Rome, which was almost unheard of as far as I was concerned. He was as covered in ink as I was, and with his shaggy dark hair and scruffy face he was one intimidating bastard. I think I was lucky we were friends or else I might have regretted being a dick to him.

"I don't know what's more pathetic, the fact you are wasting your game on some random bar chick . . ." He grunted at me when I scowled at him. "Or the fact that you're a grown-ass man trying to drink your girl problems away."

I was twenty-five but felt like I had lived a hundred lifetimes from the moment the cops had showed up at the apartment door in the middle of the night to tell me my mom was dead. They had explained that she had taken a bullet when some punk kid tried to carjack her when she hadn't moved fast enough to suit him. They put me in the system that night and I had never escaped. I had been a grown-ass man since that moment on, and Zeb was right, I should be man enough to face Salem and the way she had me tied up in knots.

"What do you know about it?" I sounded petulant and irritable.

Zeb rolled his dark green eyes and his normally unsmiling mouth twitched at me in unsympathetic humor.

"I know she's about this tall." He held his hand out to about shoulder height. "She has a figure that makes it hard to think and eyes and hair that were made to get lost in when the lights go out."

I felt a muscle tic in my jaw as I leaned on the bar and asked Asa as he walked by, "You telling stories?"

He laughed at me and I wanted to lunge over the bar and choke him.

"Hey, she's a fox and radiates hot sex and good times like it's effortless. I was just sharing my appreciation of a pretty girl. It's not my issue that you can't seem to see her looking at you like you're her favorite drink and we're in a drought."

Oh, I could see it all right. I just didn't have the first clue as to what to do with it. Well, that wasn't entirely true. After that kiss I had a pretty fucking clear idea where everything I was feeling toward Salem was headed, right into my bed, but I wasn't sure I could handle that. Just her saying Poppy's name had been enough to tame the raging hard-on kissing her had awoken and had done more to get my head out of my pants than any shock of cold water ever could.

Could I ever really have loved Poppy the way I thought I had if just the sight of Salem, the idea of putting my mouth on her, did more to wind me up than Poppy ever had? I don't think there was really any way I would've been able to kiss Salem if all those feelings I had for Poppy in the past were really as important as I had always made them out to be.

I mumbled something that made no sense and picked up my beer.

"It not just some random chick that I'm trying to navigate around. I know this girl and she knows me."

Zeb chomped on a piece of ice from his drink and I thought he looked like he could be out in the woods somewhere living off the land. He was the epitome of what a Coloradoan should look like. I thought we should maybe put him on the state flag to represent us all proudly. Yep, I was drunk.

"That's your problem, Rowdy. You never want a chick to know you. You just want to hit it and quit it so you don't have to put any effort into it."

I growled a little and motioned for another shot. "I put effort into it once. More effort than any young man should, and it blew up in my face. I learned that lesson the hard way. No more effort . . . just a good time for me and a great time for her. Everybody wins."

Zeb made a noise and nodded when Asa asked him if he wanted another round.

"One girl burned you a long time ago, so that means all girls are made of the same flammable material? Gotta say, I always thought you were smarter than that."

I was getting annoyed. We were supposed to be brothers-in-arms—bros before ho's—and all that noise. I didn't ask him to hang out so he could shove logic and brutal clarity at me.

"You don't understand."

He rolled his eyes at me.

"No? I was engaged when I got arrested. I loved the holy shit out of that girl. She told me she would wait, that I was her one true love and even bars and time wouldn't be able to keep us apart. It took a little less than two months for her to stop visiting, a little over six and she was engaged to a ski pro. She has two kids now and drives a minivan. You think that means all women are like that? That there isn't one out there that would really wait if she loved me?"

We just stared at each other until he shook his head.

"I don't. I think there are good women out there that will stand by their man no matter what. I think there is a woman out there that won't give a shit I did time and she will love me anyway and be willing to see what I have to offer now. Sure, until I find her I have no qualms about doing easy—easy has its place and can be a good time. But when it gets hard, when the girl is worth it, I'm not scared to do the work." He laughed. "I like doing the work, especially when it's hands-on."

The liquorish taste of the Jäger danced on my tongue as I tossed the shot back. I needed to stop. Things were starting to get wavy and I felt like if I let go of the grip I had on the edge of the bar I was going to slide off the bar stool and land on my face.

"There is only one first girl to hold your heart. That first sets the tone for everything and everyone that comes after." I didn't sound so sure about that anymore and it wasn't just because of the booze.

Asa paused and leaned across from me on the other side of the bar and reached out across the expanse to flick me between my eyes. I swore at him and jerked my head back.

"You're a dumb shit. There a million first girls for a million different first things. There's the first girl you slow-dance with, and the first girl you go to bed with. There's the first girl to give you a kiss, and then the first one you take home to your mama." His amber eyes lit up with humor. "There's the first girl you fight with and the first girl you fight for. There's also the first girl you have to let go of. There's the first girl you love, obviously, and the first girl to break your heart. There's always a first girl, Rowdy, but there is also the girl that is going to come after her until you get to the last girl. The last girl is the one that really matters."

I always told myself that Poppy had been my one and only but I wasn't going to lie she wasn't my first girl for most of what Asa said. Sure she had most definitely been the first girl to break my heart and she had done so spectacularly. The first girl I had sex with was Joanne Morse when I was fifteen. The first girl I had slow-danced with had been Megan Drake during homecoming the year I scored three touchdowns in one quarter. She was also the girl that had gone down on me for the first time. Once I figured out I could pine for Poppy but still get laid as long as I smiled at a girl and told her she was pretty, I had pretty much run through the entire available and age-appropriate female population of Loveless by the time I graduated high school. The first girl to take home to mama was never going to happen since my mama was in the ground and the girl that had given me my first kiss was the reason I was acting like a drunken idiot tonight. He was right: there had always been another girl after the first and I had never had a last girl yet.

"You guys suck. I just wanted to get drunk and get laid." They both chuckled at me and I let my glassy eyes land on Dixie as she sauntered up to my side and put a hand on my shoulder.

"I am totally willing to help you out with the last part, Rowdy."

I liked Dixie. I liked her as a person and liked everything she was working with that made her a pretty girl. She never asked for more than I wanted to give and we always had a good time when we got naked together. She was a sweetheart, but right now, looking at her and the sexy anticipation in her eyes, I knew there wasn't any way I was going to be able to go through with taking her home. My mind was on someone else and I didn't want Dixie to be reduced to a drunken hookup because I was acting like the world's biggest coward by avoiding the woman I really wanted to be with.

I covered her tiny hand with my own and pushed away from the bar with a lurch. "Not tonight, sugar. These two sorta ruined my mojo."

There was no way I could drive, so that meant my SUV was staying in the parking lot and I was taking a cab to my apartment.

"Sorry."

She just shook her head at me and smiled. "I always knew someday someone was going to catch your eye and you were never going to look at any other girl again. It's the way all of you guys seem to be. As much as it sucks, I have to say it also gives me hope that a guy will look at me that way one day."

She was turning my rejection into an act of chivalry. Man, she really was a doll.

Asa called me a cab. Zeb helped pour me into the backseat and the poor driver watched me in the rearview mirror all the way to my complex like he was afraid I was going to hurl all over everything I gave him a fat tip to make up for causing him to worry and stumbled into my lonely apartment.

I was really drunk. My head was spinning from booze and memories, so I did what I always did when I was that keyed up. I got out a sketch pad and some charcoal and I drew. I was pretty sure none of it would look like anything legible in the morning when I sobered up, but for the moment it made me settle, focus, and some of the things that were chasing me finally quieted down enough that I could shut my eyes and slump over in a blacked-out heap.

I JERKED AWAKE WITH a start the next day and sent the sketch pad falling to the floor as I scrambled to find my phone from wherever it had landed last night in my train wreck. It was on the kitchen counter next to a bowl of cereal I had poured but obviously never ate, and the Marked number was glaring at me as the Cramps' heavy and psychedelic guitars rattled my fuzzy head.

"Yeah?" My voiced sounded like I had smoked ten cartons of cigarettes all by myself last night.

"Rowdy?" Salem's voice was concerned and I flinched involuntarily.

"Yeah. What's up?"

I added milk to the waiting cereal and took a bite.

"Do you know that it's after noon? Your first appointment has been waiting for thirty minutes."

"Fuck me." I tossed the cereal bowl into the sink and rubbed a hand all over my face. "No, I had no idea. Can you reschedule it and give them a discount for the inconvenience. I'll be there in a few minutes." I needed to wash the Jäger out of my system and go back to the bar to get my car. It was going to take more than a few minutes but she didn't need to know that.

"Are you okay?" Again with her concern and my dick twitching in my pants at the sound of her voice.

"I got tanked last night and blacked out on the couch. I'm fine, just a little annoyed at myself."

"Okay. I'll handle the client."

Her tone had switched from worried to slightly disappointed and I felt it deep in my gut. Whatever was going on between the two of us, whatever she was doing to my head, I still needed to keep things professional between us at work. I owed that to the guys, to my clients, and even to Salem.

"Thank you. I'll contact him as well and apologize, and I'll have some designs for you to look at Sunday if you want to meet up."

She made a weird noise and I heard her move the phone to the side to talk to someone in the shop.

"Fine. You can bring them by my place or just e-mail them to me when you have them ready. I need to spend Sunday and Monday at home this week."

I wanted to ask her why, and immediately thought she wouldn't be spending those days alone, and then wanted to kick myself because it wasn't any of my concern. I agreed and she told me she would text me the address.

I hung up and let my head fall forward on my neck. I was a goddamn mess and I needed to get my act together. It didn't help my state of mind when my gaze landed on the abandoned sketch pad from the night before that the image staring up me was the one I had spent all night trying to run from and trying to drink away.

It was all there . . . her dark eyes, her endless waves of ebony hair, her perfectly sculpted mouth complete with the winking jewel above her lip, her knowing grin. Plus, the knowledge of every secret I had was there in that hastily drawn image. Even in a drunken haze so bad I could barely remember getting home, she was at the forefront of my mind and I couldn't get around having to deal with her and the hurt she had left behind.

I picked the pad up and tossed it on the couch in disgust. This was getting out of control and I really had to do something about it.

I took a shower hot enough to scald and rushed to get out the front door in under twenty minutes. My next appointment was at one thirty and I didn't want to disappoint anyone else today. I hated that feeling.

Work was a nightmare. I was usually the one giving everyone else a hard time, usually the guy ready with a quick retort. But there was no denying that I looked like hammered dog shit and was acting like a bear with a thorn in its paw, so Rule and Nash were ruthless about it all day long. I took the ribbing good-naturedly and made it through the rest of my clients with no incident. I was hoping Salem would still be there when I arrived, but she had left to go to the LoDo shop not long after calling me, which left me feeling unfulfilled and unsatisfied on top of being more hung over than I could ever remember being.

Nash wanted me to go with him to grab something to eat for dinner since Saint was working a late shift in the ER and Rule had taken off to go home already. Rule was always bolting home right after work anymore and I think it bummed Nash out. The two of them were really tight and now, with all the business stuff going on and each of them settling into domesticated bliss, their bro-times were few and far between.

I had to decline because I needed to work on the drawings for the store. I wanted to show Salem I wasn't really as much of a screw-up as I had appeared to be in the last few days. Nash told me he understood and promised he would have some sketches to me within the next few weeks as well, and left me alone to draw.

I sketched out a pirate ship. I sketched out a mermaid like the one I had put on Rule a few years ago. I sketched out a gypsy and then had to argue with myself not to throw it in the trash when I realized how much the design looked like my drunken doodle from the night before. All the images were bold and graphic. They were old-school tattoos with enough flare to make them appealing to a consumer not in the business. I liked them so much I decided on the spot I couldn't wait until tomorrow to show Salem. I didn't care that it was almost eleven o'clock at night or that I might come across as crazy, I texted her and asked her if it was all right if I brought them by tonight. I really could've just snapped photos with my phone and sent them to her but I didn't want to do that. I wanted to show them to her in person.

I hadn't felt like this, the rush, the chill of anticipation rushing up and down my spine, since the last time I had created something on paper to show her. I was fourteen and Salem was seventeen. Her dad had refused to let her go to her prom because as usual she had broken one of his endless rules. She was so sad about it, too, because the captain of the football team had asked her. It was going to be her dream date. Instead she had spent the night in her room alternately crying and cussing about her dad. Because I was always hanging around, always at her house instead of my own, I had ended up on her bedroom floor while she cried in bed, trying to make her feel better. Granted I was just a clumsy teenage boy, so there wasn't much I could do, but when she told me how sad she was that she would never have a picture to keep—a good memory from prom and her high school days—because her father had thwarted her once again, I knew there was one thing I could do.

I knew Salem's face as well as my own and it took less than five minutes to draw her out and put her in a fancy princess dress that she would never wear in the real world. The captain of the football team was a little trickier. By then I was only on junior varsity, so I knew basically what he looked like, but the only way I could really figure out how to draw him was in a football uniform. So I drew her a prom picture with her looking beautiful and perfect on the arm of a jock with a jersey on and a football helmet under his arm.

When I gave it to her she stopped crying instantly. She laughed and laughed. At first I thought she was laughing at me and then she had launched herself off the bed and tackle-hugged me to the floor. She told me it was way better than any prom picture could ever be and I still remembered feeling so proud of myself for cheering her up.

I also remembered Poppy sticking her head in the room to see what the ruckus was all about and giving both of us a disapproving look when she saw Salem sprawled all across the top of me. I hadn't cared even though Poppy was the one I was supposed to be in love with. I wanted to make Salem happy. She was always going out of her way to make me feel like I belonged, like I mattered; I wouldn't be judged for returning the favor.

The place Salem rented was right in the heart of Capitol Hill and not too far from the Marked or where Nash lived. She was just a few streets up and over. I found her name on the call box and buzzed her to let me in. She didn't answer the first time and I wondered again if she was alone. When I buzzed the second time I laid on the button until the noise annoyed me and I had to jump back when she suddenly appeared at the security door. She pushed the heavy door open and I had to step to the side as an energetic black bundle of fur and fluff darted past me. Salem went racing after the puppy and I was left there staring after both of them like an idiot.

She was hollering "Jimbo! Get over here, Jimbo!" and the black Lab puppy was happily ignoring her as it pranced around from yard to yard.

Salem had her long hair tied up on top of her head, a pair of black glasses covering her dark eyes, and she was wearing the same shorts she had on from the other night when we had gotten up close and personal at the shop. Only tonight she had on a white tank top that clung to every curve she had and it was pretty obvious she wasn't wearing a bra.

I had to admit the more she stripped out of her fancy outfits and perfectly made up face, the more I was drawn to her. This Salem reminded me of the girl that had given me hope, the other Salem made my dick hard and had my head spinning, and I was irrevocably drawn to both of them.

The dog made a beeline for me and I bent down to scoop his fuzzy little body up. His tongue darted out to slime all over my face and his tiny tail whipped back and forth. Salem dashed up to the front of the apartment complex and took a minute to bend over at the waist to catch her breath.

"Stupid dog." The dark fur ball turned at the sound of her voice and tried to escape my hold to get at his pretty owner.

"You got a puppy?" I handed him over to her and she tucked him into her chest as the dog attacked her face with his love.

"Yeah. I've never really stayed anywhere long enough to get attached to a pet. My neighbor mentioned that her boyfriend was trying to get rid of a surprise litter of puppies, and once I saw his dopey face I couldn't resist."

She headed for the door and looked at me over her shoulder. "He's why I have to be home over the weekend. He isn't awesome at being alone for too long yet."

I lifted an eyebrow and followed her into the building. I couldn't take my eyes off the sway of her rounded backside or the long length of her bare legs.

"Jimbo?"

The name was funny and fit the big, goofy pup.

"Yeah, Jimbo. Why not?"

Why not indeed? She walked into the apartment, set the dog down, and turned to look at me. I saw myself reflected in the lenses of her glasses as she watched me carefully.

"This really couldn't have waited until the weekend, Rowdy?"

Her feet were bare and I noticed her toenails were painted a deep, rich red. Even dressed down and covered in dog slobber, she just had something about her that called to deep parts of me. She sighed and walked into her kitchen when I didn't answer right away. She offered me a damp paper towel and I used it wipe the dog drool off as she did the same.

The only way we were going to be able to work together, to get past the roadblock of the past, was if I was completely honest with her. I finally had to tell her how entwined in the memories I had of her—both good and bad—I still was.

I told her in a husky tone shaded by the past, "I was excited to show them to you. They made me feel like I used to back in the day. I loved drawing stuff for you to look at. No one else ever gave a shit about it, but you always loved it— told me to stick with it if I enjoyed it. I don't think I would be any kind of artist today if it wasn't for you, Salem." I lifted an eyebrow at her as she crossed her arms over her ample chest. "Thank you."

"Oh, Rowdy." She shook her head. "It was all you. You were always great. It's so sad you didn't have an army of people to tell you that every single day when you were little."

"No. I just had you." I walked over so that I was directly across from her with only the counter of the kitchen between us. "I feel like you and the past have been chasing me down ever since you walked into that shop, Salem." She didn't answer me but I noticed a little pink work its way into her dusky cheeks. "What are you going to do if I decide to let you catch me?"

I was fast, but she was right, off the field I did tend to stumble here and there, but for the first time in a long time I felt like I just might have found my footing, and with it, I suddenly wanted to walk right up to her.

CHAPTER 6

Salem

WHAT WAS I GOING TO DO when I caught him? That was easy. Strip him bare—both physically and emotionally, and then I was never going to let him go. I didn't think he was ready for me to be that honest, though, so I told him, "I'm going to find out why you're running from me." I tilted my head to side and asked him point-blank, "Are you still in love with my sister, Rowdy? I need to know that story."

After his reaction when she called me the other day, it was something that had been on my mind and poking me under the skin endlessly. I knew he had cared deeply for Poppy, and that in her usual way my sister had let my dad's decisions function as her own. What I didn't know was if he was still hung up on her, and still pining away for something that had never even had a chance. His youthful infatuation following him into adulthood seemed unlikely after so much time. But if that was the case, then no matter how much I wanted him, or how badly I wanted the wonderful thing I just knew we'd have together, there was no way I was fighting memories or the ghost of my sister to have it. I had too much pride and valued myself far too much to do that. I wasn't going to compete with his idea of first love, not when the person was very much alive and an integral part of my life.

I'd tried to pull the answers out of Poppy the other day, but she was skittish and had blown past the topic like it didn't matter. Something was going on with her. She told me she was busy and that she couldn't talk and hung up on me after only a few minutes of conversation. That wasn't like her and it amped my concern for her up ten notches.

I watched Rowdy carefully as he set the papers he had in his hand on the counter and walked around to the side I was on. He didn't stop walking until he was right in front of me and I stiffened in an automatic response when he caged me in with an arm on either side of my hips. His head dipped down a little so that we were eye to eye, and I swore I could drown in that blue ocean of his gaze forever. His blond hair was lighter than normal without all the junk he usually put in it to style it up in that pompadour he wore, and the way it fell across his forehead made him look like that little boy who'd always made me so happy in those lost years. My fingers itched to reach up and push it away. They itched to touch him in any way he would allow.

He leaned a little closer to me and I felt his breath move the bloodred hair at my temple.

"I asked Poppy to marry me. I was eighteen, had the world at me feet, and was pretty much guaranteed a shot at playing pro football. I offered her everything and she told me she considered me her brother. She looked me dead in the eye and told me no matter what I did it would *never* be enough because your parents wouldn't approve because they knew where I came from. That I wasn't the right guy for her."

I felt his chest expand and his breath hitch as dark blue clouds shadowed his hot stare. His lips touched my skin right next to my eyebrow and I was stunned my glasses didn't fog up from the all heat he was generating. But while I was admittedly getting turned on, I also felt like everything inside of me where my heart and hope lived had turned into stone.

Rowdy asked Poppy to marry him? That was the first I had ever heard of that and I felt like it was life changing. They were both so young. I always assumed it was just puppy love but apparently his feelings for my little sister had been much more complex than I remembered or believed them to be.

"You asked her to marry you?" I wanted to shove him away from me. I really wanted to grab my sweet little puppy and run all the way to someplace where Rowdy St. James was lost back in my memories and I didn't have this new information hammering away inside of me.

"I did. Poppy didn't just say no, she took everything I thought I knew about love and ripped it apart from the inside out. The pieces of my heart were so tiny when she was done with me I didn't bother to look for them. So no, Salem. I am not still in love with Poppy. She broke me and I haven't bothered to try and love anyone since."

I couldn't take it anymore. I put both of my hands on the center of his chest and shoved him away from me. I felt like I needed to escape, like his words were building a cage around all the grandiose ideas I had been following when I left Vegas.

"She never told me. We talked all the time back then, and not once did she tell me that you fucking asked her to marry her."

I was watching the fantasy I had of showing him that there was so much more to us now that we were older disappear into smoke. I felt like he had just pulled a quarterback sneak and I was on the defense looking like an idiot while he ran the ball into the end zone. I never would have come here, never would have made myself at home if I had known just how barbed the ties were that held him anchored to the past.

I spun around to glare at him and to tell him to leave, but it got lost as I gasped in surprise because he had followed me and was once again all up in my personal space. He gripped my upper arms and hauled me up onto my toes.

"You started all of this, Salem. You don't get to back away just because you don't like what's hiding in the dark once the light you're shining hits it."

"Why didn't she tell me?" The words were whispered and I couldn't look away from the burning blue of his aqua-colored gaze. Again my fingers twitched to get that blond lock of hair off of his forehead or maybe smack him across his handsome face.

"That part of the story is hers to tell."

"That's why you quit school, why you stopped playing ball? She turned you down and you ran away from it all?"

Slowly his head rocked back and forth in the negative

and he pulled me up even closer so that our chests were pressed tightly together. Instantly I regretted not putting on a bra as the tips of each breast got excited being so close to all the hard heat of him. I let my hands curl tightly around the hard flex of his biceps.

"I never wanted to play ball at that level. I wanted to draw. I wanted to paint. I wanted to be creative and make art. I wanted to learn how to be a better artist, but I didn't know how to do that and chase after Poppy at the same time. I thought once she got away from your dad she would finally be able to see me. That she would see who I really was and realize that regardless of the circumstances that put us in each other's path, I was worth something." His mouth turned down and he dropped his head so that our foreheads touched where I dangled in his hard hands. "There was never any chance of that happening. She met a guy the first day of school. An appropriate guy with the right kind of family and the right kind of heritage to take home to your dad. I hated him on sight."

He let go of one of my arms and reached up to snatch my glasses off, which made me blink up at him as he went a little fuzzy around the edges of my vision. He used the pad of his thumb to rub the high arch of my eyebrow and I thought I was going to melt into a puddle at his feet.

"I beat the shit out of him. Cracked a couple of his ribs, fucked up his nose, and left him in miserable pile of broken and bloody despair. The thing is, he also happened to be the starting quarterback and all of that went down a few weeks before a major bowl game."

I gasped and his frown switched to a grin. I didn't notice he had been walking us backward the entire time he was talking and now I was backed up against the kitchen counter. He grabbed me around the waist and hefted me up so that I was perched on the edge and made himself at home between my legs.

"The school kept it quiet because he was getting ready to be drafted and they didn't want him to lose his authority over the rest of the team by having to admit he got his ass kicked by a freshman. I lost the scholarship I got recruited with and was pretty much banned from playing football at any college level for the next couple of years. To me it was like getting a Get Out of Jail Free card. I didn't want to be in Alabama. I didn't want to see your sister ever again. And football was never really where my heart was at anyway. All of it felt like it was being forced and I was sick of all of it."

I was still trying to get my head around the fact that he had proposed to my sister and now he was telling me he had tried to kill her college boyfriend with his bare hands. None of that should be a turn-on. None of it should make it okay that his hands were running up the outside of my thighs and into the hem of my shorts where my legs were bracketing his lean hips, but even with all these new revelations I wasn't inclined to make him stop.

"You beat up some guy just because he was seeing Poppy? You were that jealous?" That didn't ring as one hundred percent true considering Poppy had dated a lot in high school and it never seemed to bother him. It was hard to think because his hands had found their way around the back of my legs and were now cupping my ass as he pulled me closer to the edge of the counter. There was no missing that our proximity was having an effect on him as well. The hard ridge in the front of his pants was unmistakable and I wanted to rub against him. It felt wanton and kind of wrong now that I knew what had happened with him and my sister in my absence.

"That's also not my story to tell. I beat him up because he was a grade-A asshole and I never liked him. He was the kind of guy that made me know for sure football was never going to be what I wanted to do. I was jealous that she cared about him and not about me, but that didn't have anything to do with why I kicked his ass. So there you have it, Salem. I'm running all the time because those memories hurt when they catch up to me and I've had enough hurt in my life."

I sucked in another breath and put my hands on his shoulders as one of his hands left my ass and danced along the inner curve of my thigh, where all the best parts of me and him were pressed intimately together. I felt him run his knuckle along the edge of my panties and couldn't help but gulp a little bit. I needed to tell him to stop but I just couldn't seem to find the words. "That's why you're running from the past. Why are you running from me?" I sounded husky and turned on. I really should develop some shame but he felt so good and those eyes were so clear and vivid I couldn't look away.

He chuckled a little and I could feel it everywhere we touched. His fingers were getting bolder and my desire to keep some kind of control of him—of the situation—was fading into nothing.

"You always saw me, Salem. You understood me when I didn't even get myself. You were my best friend and then you left. I can't care about someone, attach myself to someone, when they're just going to leave me in the end." He breathed in and out in a heavy way and I couldn't stop myself from finally putting my fingers on that unruly piece of hair hanging in his eyes. His next words twisted my heart so much that it ached. "Not after what happened to my mom."

I was going to tell him I was sorry. I never meant to just drop out of his life altogether, but I was young and finally free from my father's reins, so I had gone a little crazy and lost some of myself. I needed him to know he had been my best friend as well. I wanted to tell him how he was the only good I could remember from growing up but his mouth moved from my temple to my lips and just rested there.

He didn't kiss me, didn't breathe me in, didn't tease me with his tongue. He just rested his lips against my own as we stayed pressed together in silence, tension thick and throbbing between us. I felt like I was stuck. Caught in some kind of slow-motion movie reel where every touch, every move he made was agonizingly deliberate and torturously drawn out. Those talented fingers of his were skating very close to the edge of where fabric and skin met underneath my clothes and he was no longer anywhere near my inner thigh but so much closer to places that were hot and damp. Places that were beginning to coil tight with want and need.

"What about you, Salem? Did you think of me as a brother?"

When he spoke I felt his words as they brushed across my mouth more than heard what he said. I gave my head a tight little shake and let my fingers curl into the strong cords at the base of his neck.

"No. I thought you were a beautiful and sad little boy and then I thought you were a clever and talented teenager." I gasped and let out a tiny shriek of surprise because there was no longer fabric between his questing fingers and my wet and eager flesh. "Now I think you're a gorgeous and complicated man, but none of my feelings for you have ever been familial. I never considered you like a brother, Rowdy."

It was hard to get the words out, hard to breathe because he was touching me, stroking me from the inside out, and finally his mouth was rubbing achingly across my own. How was a girl supposed to have a single coherent thought when all of that was happening to her and the guy doing it looked and felt like Rowdy did? When he was the only bright spot in an otherwise cloudy childhood.

"Tell me you're here for me." His voice was low and I could practically feel the intensity of his gaze and he shifted me a little so his fingers could move deeper, play harder with all the most sensitive female parts of my body.

I didn't want to tell him that. Even if it was the truth.

He kissed me. Really kissed me. His lips and tongue taking no prisoners as his thumb landed on my clit and pressed down with enough force to make me jerk in his hold. I kissed him back helplessly, sat there and let him play with me and my body like I was powerless to stop it . . . because I was. His fingers circled inside of me, his touch just right as he continued to ravish my mouth.

He pulled back and dropped a hard, biting kiss on my mouth. He leaned a little closer, his hand pressing in with him as he used the very tip of his tongue to touch the very center of my top lip and then he brushed a kiss across the ruby that sat right above my mouth. It made me shiver and had my nails digging hard into where I was holding on to him. I cried out and arched my back when he found that perfect spot, that magical place inside of me that not every man had found before. I saw a flash of white as he grinned at me and then it disappeared as he buried his face in the curve of my neck and started kissing and sucking along the taut flesh that was there.

"Tell me, Salem. Tell me you came here for me."

I was so close, could feel pleasure and something more burning along all my nerve endings. I was squirming in his hands, my body was bowing and quaking against his, and I knew I was going to break apart at his touch any second now. My nipples were tight and aching. My skin was overly sensitized and everywhere he touched I felt it electric and sparking right where his hands were, not to mention he had honed in right on the coiled core of my desire.

"Rowdy . . ." His name escaped on a strangled groan, as his teeth sank into the side of my neck where my pulse was thundering. The noises I was making told him exactly how his touch was affecting me, it was over and he knew it. I felt him growl against my pulse, I felt his muscles go tense as my body broke and spasmed around his fingers. It didn't just feel good and sexy-sweet, it shook me to my very core.

I liked sex, and had never been scared to admit it, but I

had never been touched, never had a man put his hands on me and have it feel like I was better for it at the end like he had just done. I felt like he was showing me something new, teaching me something I didn't know about myself, and it left me stunned.

Rowdy pushed back just enough so that we were staring at each other. He pulled his hand out of my shorts and rested it on the top of my bare thigh. We were both breathing hard and just watching each other. His eyes glowed and there was a grin and something else dancing across his face.

"I came for you." My voice squeaked out high and thready.

He laughed, deep and rumbling. "I know. I was right there with you, but I still want you to tell me you're here for me."

I pushed him back from me with a scowl and jumped off the counter. The way my chest pressed against his much harder one made my already excited nipples hurt with the need for attention.

"Fine. I'm here in Denver for you. I met Phil a few years back and he had me spilling my guts to him while he tattooed me. He asked where I grew up and I told him Loveless, Texas. He had to have known you and I had a lot of history. He put the wheels in motion before he passed away but the truth is I came here for you."

He opened his mouth to say something else but the puppy, who had remained surprisingly quiet during all our commotion, came hurtling out of my bedroom with the remains of a tattered and slobbered-on high heel in his mouth.

I sighed as he brought his prize over and dropped it at Rowdy's booted feet with a proud "woof."

I grumbled, "Looks like he wants to play."

Rowdy chuckled and bent down to scratch the dog behind the ears. "So do I."

I couldn't stop my gaze from rolling over the way his pants were straining in the front. I bit my lower lip and saw his gaze narrow in on the motion.

Now that there was some space between us, I got my wits back and told him, "Look, I had no idea you asked Poppy to marry you. I have all these memories of how sweet you always were, how in sync we always were, and how you always made me happy. I decided to chase those old feelings down. I was always missing something no matter where I was at and I kind of felt like that something was you. I didn't think it all the way through . . . I never do."

I shifted uneasily on my bare feet as he continued to watch me in silence. "I want you, Rowdy. You're gorgeous and extremely talented, but I'm not going to share a guy with my sister. Not any guy, not ever." I wondered if he even knew she had married someone else just a few short years after rejecting him.

He lifted one of his golden eyebrows at me and rose back up to his full and impressive height.

"Poppy isn't here."

"It doesn't feel that way. I don't know that I'm going to be able to get my head around the fact you asked her to marry you, Rowdy." I looked at the little dog that had wiggled between us and plopped his fuzzy bottom on my feet. "I always thought it was just puppy love, not something real."

He rubbed one of his sideburns with his index finger and a boyish grin flirted with his mouth. He was a dangerous mix of the boy I remembered and the complicated man I was starting to get to know on a much different level.

He put his finger under my chin and lifted my face back up so that we were looking at each other.

"I haven't done something real, Salem. I loved Poppy for a lot of reasons and I don't know looking back on it now that any of them would have lasted or would make any kind of sense now. What I do know is that when I saw you that day you got hired at the shop, it was like walking face-first into a wall, and not only did my dick get hard just by looking at you but something in my chest felt like it broke loose. I don't know if any of that is good or bad yet, but what I do know is that it feels pretty damn real. More real than anything I ever felt for your sister. I know it all feels less like something that's going to be easy and a good time and more like something I have to work my way through. I also know feeling all of that scares the living shit out of me."

Well, it wasn't exactly a sweeping declaration of love and they weren't words that put all my apprehensions to rest, but there was no denying the magnetic, physical response that we most definitely brought out in each other. I just needed a minute to get my head and my heart on the same page and I told him as much.

"I need to figure out how I feel about the fact you were

willing to spend the rest of your life with my sister, Rowdy. Nothing has ever mattered enough for me to want to put it all together before. Normally I get bored and move on when things get difficult or complicated. Including my feelings. It's easy to run away and much harder to stay."

His eyes darkened to a fathomless turquoise and he took a step back from me. "Already been in your rearview once, Salem. I have no intention of ending up there again."

I sighed and bent to pick up the dog when he whined up at me. I rubbed my face in his soft fur and looked at Rowdy over the top of Jimbo's head.

"I'm not going anywhere."

He snorted and turned so that he was walking toward the door.

"I'll believe it when I see it." He nodded to where he had left the drawings on my counter. "Take a look at those and let me know what you think."

He had the door open when I called his name: "Rowdy." He looked at me over his shoulder and I saw everything I wanted from him in that electric-hot gaze. "We started out as friends, maybe we should try that first and it'll give you time to see I'm here to stay and give me some time to figure out if I can work through your history with Poppy in my head."

He considered me for a long, silent moment and all I could hear was Jimbo panting and my heart thundering. If he said no, if he told me he wasn't interested in rekindling that easy camaraderie we had always had, I wasn't sure what I was going to do. I needed to have him in my life but I needed a minute for clarity as well.

"I have plenty of friends, Salem. I don't want get any of them naked or take any of them to bed. We don't need to try and be friends again—we always were. That never went away—you did. You started this game of chase, so when you figure your shit out let me know because I'm already caught."

The door closed behind him on that definitive note and I was left staring after it not sure what to say or how to feel.

I was fine on my own. In fact I thrived and had made a pretty wonderful life for myself all on my own. I wasn't the type of woman that ever felt like I needed a man to be complete or fulfilled, but staring at the closed door and having my body still burning and sensitive from his attention, I suddenly wanted to call him back and ask him to stay. He was messing not only with my feelings, but also with what I thought I had always known.

I kissed Jimbo and set him down after collecting my destroyed shoe and walked over to the counter where Rowdy had left the images for me to look at. I spread them out and just stared at them in awe. He really was amazingly skilled. The sketches looked 3-D and so lifelike that I had to touch one to make sure it was just plain pencil on paper. People were going to lose their minds when I got the graphics put on cute little tank tops and fun T-shirts. The gypsy would look awesome on the back of an old-style mechanic's jacket.

I was designing stuff in my head, so it took a second to register as I stared at the girl's lovely face that she looked familiar. I picked up the picture and held it closer to my face since Rowdy had snatched my glasses and I could hardly see.

She had long, dark hair. She had endless midnight eyes. She had a heart-shaped mouth with just the hint of a smile on her face. She was lovely, soft and romantic-looking. She was the spitting image of me. The face, all the features, everything was me if I was a 1940s fortune-teller.

I made a strangled noise low in my throat and let the picture fall from numb fingers. He was still mad at me, holding on to a lot of anger and feeling abandoned from when I left all those years ago. With his history of love and loss I couldn't blame him. He didn't trust that I was here for the duration, that he was enough to keep me rooted in Denver. He was leery and kind of harsh, but even in all of that he still saw me as something so beautiful it almost hurt me to look at it.

It made me want to cry, mostly because as much as I loved the picture, loved the way he viewed me, I couldn't stop my very next thought from being, was that how he still saw Poppy as well?

Crap. This game of catch was turning out to be way trickier than I had anticipated.

CHAPTER 7

Rowdy

NOW THAT THE TABLES had turned and Salem was the one avoiding me, giving me sidelong looks and running the other way when I crowded her, I saw just how annoying and frustrating it must have been when I was the one doing it to her. I took every opportunity that presented itself to touch her, to be near her, to crowd her and press in on her. I was the one treating her like prey and she was looking back at me like a deer caught in the headlights with those deep, dark eyes.

I knew something was going to have to happen one way or another between the two of us. Either she was going to get over all that nonsense in her head about Poppy and let me take her to bed, or she was going to decide it was all too much and not meant to be and cut and run like she apparently had been doing all her life. I wasn't sure which outcome I was gunning for since both had pros and cons.

On one hand I wanted to get naked with her, tangle myself all up with her in all the raunchiest and dirtiest ways I could think of, but I didn't want to have sex with her and then have her pull up stakes and leave me hanging. I had a feeling if I ever ended up in bed with Salem, it would mean an end to my hit-it-and-quit bedroom habits. There was no quitting with her, not considering how strongly I still reacted to her after a decade of no contact between the two of us. As a result I think subconsciously I was pushing her, trying to make her run because I knew all along that's what she was more than likely going to do. It was her pattern. I was just trying to speed the process up before I could get any more invested in her and the fact I wanted her so bad I could taste it. The thing was, no matter how hard I pushed her, how close I got to her physically, she never told me to back off. She just gave me a knowing look, like she knew all the plays before they were called out and already had a defensive strategy in mind to counteract them.

It was Friday afternoon and I had been at the Marked, but my last appointment canceled due to an emergency, so I had a couple hours free. It was Rule's day to be down at the Saints of Denver, so I knew he was going to give me a load of shit for lurking around the new shop when I should be working, but I didn't care. When I pushed open the door I was surprised to see his spiky head behind the counter and not Salem's. He was on the phone and just rolled his eyes at me when I propped myself up on the opposite side.

"Let me call you back, Rome. Rowdy just got here." He paused and then grinned. "Yeah, thanks . . . I'm scared shitless but I'll figure it out."

I lifted an eyebrow at him and he did the same back at me, only his had metal in it.

"What's up?"

"Nothing. Just thought I would stop by. What's up with you? Why are you scared shitless?"

Rule shrugged. "Things just keep changing. It's hard to keep up sometimes. Rome was just telling me it's all payback for being such an asshole for so long."

"What's he talking about? You're still an *asshole* most of the time."

He laughed and leaned back in the chair with his arms up behind his head. "True. You wanna be straight with me and tell me the real reason you're here instead of being where you're supposed to be? Because I'm pretty fucking sure it has something to do with our pretty new shop manager."

"I don't want to tell you shit."

He snorted and told me, "She had a meeting with the screen printer. She should be back in an hour or so. Those designs you mocked up were killer, dude."

I shrugged nonchalantly. "Still waiting on you and Nash to give me something I can give to her."

He let his arms fall and rose to his feet as the front door opened. "My mind has been on other things lately. I'll get to it soon. Promise."

He greeted a client and I turned to go up the stairs. He stopped me by calling out my name.

"The girls are all up there. You might want to steer clear for a minute or two."

I just waved him off. I was used to Cora's attitude and Ayden's sass. Shaw was the sweetest thing in the world, and whatever they were up there discussing couldn't be anything that would send me running for the hills. Besides, maybe I could pick their collective lady minds and figure out what Salem's deal really was. There were just too many secrets and unknowns lurking behind those dark eyes.

When I hit the top of the steps I immediately knew I should have heeded Rule's warning. The girls were huddled in a tight circle and they were all making whimpering sounds like they were crying. All three of them had their heads bent close together like they were in a huddle before a major play and I felt all my protective instincts fire up. I wanted to hurt whoever it was that was responsible for making these fantastic, important women cry and then I realized they were probably all just overreacting about Ayden's news that she was moving.

The all broke apart when my boots clattered on the top step and three pairs of watery eyes shifted in my direction. I smiled at them, my instinct to try and make the situation better.

"Don't worry, girls, Austin isn't that far away. Jet will bring our girl back on the regular. I'll make sure of it."

I saw Ayden's eyes get huge in her face as Shaw and Cora both turned on her with furious scowls.

"What?" Shaw snapped the question and Cora followed quickly behind.

"Yeah, what?"

Ayden held her hands up in front of her and glared at me.

"You suck, Rowdy."

I frowned and looked between all of them, totally lost.

"What in the hell are you all crying about if it isn't because you're moving?"

"MOVING!" Shaw's shriek was enough to have the mirrors and windows rattling in their frames as her cheeks turned a hot red.

Cora shoved Ayden in the shoulder and my buddy's girl just shook her dark head. "I was going to tell you guys once I officially got accepted into the grad program at UT Austin. Jet and I just can't keep spending so much time apart. I hate it. He hates it and we had to figure something out."

Shaw just gaped at her as Cora crossed her arms over her chest. They both watched Ayden while she glowered at me. I shifted uncomfortably and made my way farther into the room.

"If you weren't crying because of Ayd leaving, then what on earth has all of you in tears? I don't like it one bit and I'm ready to beat someone up for all of you."

Shaw jerked her gaze away from her friend and stared at me for a solid minute before blinking her big, green eyes at me. She let out a high-pitched laugh and pushed some of her almost white hair out of her face.

"I'm pregnant. I'm not supposed to be, but somehow, as usual, Rule doesn't do things the way he's supposed to and now we're having a baby."

Holy shit! The ultimate wild child having a child of his own. Oh, how the times had changed on all of us.

I walked over to her and wrapped her up in a rib-cracking hug. "Congratulations. You two are gonna make a beautiful baby, but why are you all crying over it?"

Cora lifted her eyebrow at me. "Happy tears. It's exciting." She pointed at Shaw and her mouth kicked up in a half grin. "I knew it wasn't a stomach bug."

Shaw shoved her hands through her long hair and sighed. "I just didn't believe it for a long time. I mean we just got married. I still have to get through school and I'm not even close to doing a residency yet, but I'm already trying to imagine how any and all of that works with a baby. Rule was the one that kept saying I was probably pregnant but I thought he was out of his mind." She shook her head and laughed again. "We're always careful, but it's just like him to make his own rules and have that not matter."

Cora reached out to squeeze her shoulder. "Don't worry. You've got all of us around to rely on. You'll be fine and I'd pay a million trillion dollars to see Rule as Mr. Mom. It's going to be fantastic. If his brother can take to fatherhood like a duck to water, the younger Archer will be fine. Those boys have more love in them than they know what do with. They were made to be daddies."

Ayden looked like she was going to cry again and I was suddenly very aware of the fact I was the only person in the room with a penis.

"I can stay. If you need me here, I'll stay." Ayden whispered the words to her best friend and her voice broke. Ayden and Shaw were in tears again and then they were hugging and sort of rocking together.

"Don't be ridiculous. I hate that you aren't with Jet, too. It's where you're supposed to be." Shaw would always have a heart the size of my home state.

I looked at Cora like she might be able to help, but for a pretty tough chick she looked like she was going to break apart again as well.

"Well, damn. I didn't mean for any of that to happen. You all know I'm usually better around the ladies than this."

Cora walked over and hooked her arm through mine and rested her head on my shoulder.

"It's okay. She would've had to break the news eventually. It's just a lot to take in. Those two are tight. It's gonna be hard for them to adjust to not having the other right around the corner for every little thing. Honestly, we all saw this coming. Ayd needs to be where Jet is and Jet needs to be where the music is. It'll be fine. It always is."

"I can't believe Rule's gonna be a daddy."

We both sort of laughed and she turned her head to look up at me with her multitoned eyes.

"Would serve him right if she ends up having twins."

I barked out a laugh that had the other two girls pulling apart and scowling at us. Cora moved out of striking distance as Ayden stalked over and punched me solidly in the gut. I grunted a little and caught her up in a tight hug as well.

"Sorry. I didn't mean to spill the beans."

She just shook her head and wrapped her arms around my waist. "Probably better it came from your pretty face than from me anyway. I would have screwed it up."

"You'll be here when she needs you."

She nodded her silky hair under my chin. "Always."

"What are you doing here anyway? Why aren't you at the Marked?" Ever the busybody, Cora would have to be the one to point out I wasn't where I was supposed to be.

"My last appointment canceled, so I thought I would swing by and see what was going on."

She snorted. "You thought you would swing by and get Salem all riled up. I don't know what the two of you have going on, but it's like watching two boxers circle each other in the ring. One of you is going to get knocked out by a sucker punch sooner or later."

Ayden made a noise and pulled away from me. "A sucker punch called love. Rowdy likes her. Jet told me he hasn't been with anyone else since Salem showed up, so we know it's serious. You never keep it in your pants for very long."

I fake-growled at her and stepped away from the girls. "Salem and I have history, is all. She used to matter a lot to me and now that she's back we're just trying to figure it out. The then and the now can be a little bit tricky."

"Does she know you swore off ever getting serious about another girl because of her sister?"

"Yeah. I told her all about it this weekend; that's why she's been dodging me. She says she doesn't really know what to think of it. Salem thought it was simple puppy love."

"Even puppy love can have some nasty teeth." Cora's tone was matter-of-fact. It was something we shared, a tie that bound us together the others didn't have. Cora's first love had cheated on her, left her broken and soured on the idea of what love should look like as well, so I just nodded at her assessment.

"It sure can, but now I think I want to see what's past *the one*. What the one after might look like. Salem was my best friend when I really needed someone and now she's here and I want her to be an entirely different kind of friend." I wiggled my eyebrows up and down, which made all the girls laugh. "The kind with benefits and missing clothes."

"They do say friends make the best lovers." Shaw sighed in a dreamy way. "You deserve someone that can make you happy, Rowdy."

I never really thought I wasn't happy, but now standing here in a room full of good women that loved difficult and complicated men I wasn't so sure. Then I found myself in the middle of a hug between the three of them that just made my heart swell. These were good women that loved hard and loved completely and I was a very lucky guy to have them in my life.

"Well, this is quite the love fest."

Salem's voice held a mixture of humor and irritation. I met her midnight gaze over the top of the girls' heads. She stood watching me and I could tell she was trying to decide if the sight of me being smothered in love by three beautiful women was hilarious or annoying. The other girls broke away and I took a step toward her. I saw awareness flare in her dark gaze and she took an automatic step back. I reached out a hand to grab her wrist because one more step back in her haste to get away from me and she was going to topple backward down the steps. I felt her pulse thunder out of control under her delicate skin.

"I was looking for you." I let my voice drop a little lower and made sure she could tell I was checking her out as my gaze scanned her from head to toe.

She was back in her formfitting, supersexy garb that put every curve she had on display. Her hair had a bunch of big, loopy curls in it and her face was painted in that pretty retro way that made her look like a rock-and-roll dream. I still preferred her with no makeup and less camera-ready.

"You were?" She sounded sarcastic and smirked at me as she looked at the other three girls in the room.

I rolled my eyes at her purposely obtuse attitude and pulled her a little closer so that she was the only one that could hear me when I told her, "I want to take you to do something on Sunday when we're both off."

She blinked at me and her glossy mouth dropped open in silent denial. I could see the indecision flash in her eyes but I just smiled at her and told her, "Don't worry. What I have in mind doesn't have anything to do with a bed or you being naked in it."

She wrinkled her nose at me and shook her arm free. "Fine." She always had been defiant. There was no way she was going to turn me down and look scared in front of the other girls.

I nodded in satisfaction. "Don't dress like that, though."

Her ebony eyebrows furrowed together and her cheek twitched at me. "Why?"

"You need to be able to get a little dirty. I'll pick you up around noon. Grab the dog; he can come, too."

I could see I had her curiosity piqued but I didn't give her a chance to ask any more questions. I wanted to do something that took us both back in time, put us in a place where we remembered how to be around one another without all the baggage and weight of the past holding us down. I thought I had a perfect idea.

I smiled at Shaw again and slid past Salem to head down

the stairs. I made sure to press into her space, to brush across her chest just so I could feel her quick intake of breath.

"Congratulations again, Shaw. This is going to be an awesome adventure for you and Rule. Remy needs a little playmate."

Salem broke into a blindly pretty smile. "You're pregnant?"

Shaw nodded. "We waited until we saw a doctor to know for sure and Rule wanted to tell Rome and his parents first."

Salem tossed her head back and laughed. The sound was husky and rich. "I haven't been in this city for very long but even I know adding more Archers to the population is bound to be a good time down the road. How exciting for the two of you."

And just like that I was outnumbered by waves of estrogen once again and I couldn't get away fast enough.

Rule was working on a client and bent intently over an intricate design of a Hindu god that spanned a burly man's bicep. I lurked over his shoulder until he looked up at me, his pale blue eyes sharp and knowing.

"Other things on your mind, my ass."

He chuckled at me and looked back down at what he was doing. "We had to be sure. It's not like it was something we were planning on. Now that I know for sure, I'll be able to focus more on the shop and the store."

"Everything happens for a reason."

Rule paused and lifted the machine up off the client's ink-smeared flesh. He looked back at me again and this time his eyes were winter cool and his expression pointed.

"Or sometimes accidents happen and we just work with

them, consider them a blessing. Not everything is preordained, Rowdy. You should know this by now. Shit really does just happen. Look at Rome and Cora. None of what happened with them was on the agenda, but it happened and it all worked out."

I disagreed, but I wasn't going to argue the point and take away from the excitement of the fact he was starting a family with the perfect girl for him. And it was my firm belief that Rome and Cora had been thrown together by something far bigger than either of them so they could save each other. Little baby Remy was just a happy result of the fact the two of them were meant to be.

"Either way, congratulations, dude." He nodded his thanks. I left him to finish his tattoo.

I always figured the things that happened, good or bad, had to be happening for a reason. There had to be a reason my mom was taken from me when I was too young to take care of myself. For a long time I reasoned that she had to go so that I could be taken in by the Ortegas and placed next to Poppy. I would have never met her otherwise. When Poppy had dashed all the dreams and hopes I had built on her young shoulders, I thought her turning away from me had been orchestrated to get me out of football, to get me on the path to my true calling and to Phil. Now all those little things, all those little pieces, were building a road to the other Cruz sister. I never considered a reason for all those things happening, but now I wasn't so sure that Salem wasn't the final destination my mother's tragic end had been pointing me to from the very beginning.

SALEM WAS LOOKING AT ME like I was off my rocker.

The puppy was bounding around like a lunatic on the end of the leash. I think out of the three of us making the trek to City Park, he was the only one who was overjoyed to be headed out for day outside in the sun. His antic were making me have to hold onto the handle of his leash in a tight grip. The park was right off of Colfax. It was huge, green, and crowded with locals and tourists alike out to enjoy a beautiful Colorado summer day. I picked it because it was within walking distance of Salem's apartment and that gave her an easy out if things got weird or if she decided she wasn't going to get past the fact that she thought Poppy was very much standing between us even though I had no clue where the other Cruz sister was even at and frankly didn't really care.

"The park? Are we twelve years old?"

She had heeded my warning and dressed down for our Sunday outing. Her dark hair was tied in long braids down either side of her head, the red stripe making her look like she had a flashy hot-rod racing stripe in her hair. She was wearing cutoff jean shorts that showed off her caramel-colored legs that had beautiful ink sprinkled across the surface and she was rocking black Chucks that were identical to my own. And just because she couldn't help but emanate sensuality and dark beauty, she had on a tight plaid shirt that was tied up over her navel, flashing her taut tummy and a secret tattoo that dipped below the waistband of her shorts that I was dying to check out. She looked perfect and she didn't have a drop of makeup on her face. The only thing I wished was different was that I could see her eyes, but they were hidden behind a massive pair of sunglasses that just showed my reflection back at me as I stared at her.

"It's Colorado. We do things outside here when it's nice. It'll be fun, I promise."

The puppy looked at us, his tongue lolling out the side of his mouth, and I laughed at the goofy picture he made.

"You really want to do this?" She tossed the football I had handed her when we started our walk from one of her hands to the other and I grinned at her.

"Yep. You used to have a pretty good spiral."

I was sure if I could see her eyes she would be rolling them at me. "I still do."

That made me laugh, and once we got to the park and found a place that wasn't overly crowded where we could throw the ball back and forth and let Jimbo run off the leash without bothering anyone else, I put my own sunglasses on and told her, "We used to toss the ball back and forth all the time. It was fun. We deserve to have things that are still fun from then. I just thought maybe it would take us back to a time that was easier for us to be around each other."

She didn't say anything for a minute but she did sink her teeth into her bottom lip and I wanted to tackle her to the ground and replace her teeth with my own. She tilted her head to the side and asked, "How long has it been since you've done this?"

I shrugged. "Sometimes when we have a barbecue the guys will toss the ball around with me, but Rule had a twin brother that passed away and he was a jock, a quarterback, so I don't think tossing the ball around has the same kind of good memories for them as it does for me. You're the only girl that I ever played with." And I wasn't talking about sex. She was the first girl to ever show me what a good time outside of the bedroom could be like and while I was greatful for that I was ready to add something far more adult and naked to the mix now.

She bent down to take Jimbo off his lead and I groaned out loud as the denim tightened enticingly across her backside. She was going to be the death of any kind of restraint I might've had.

The dog yipped and pranced around as she turned and jogged several yards away. Jimbo jumped around her knees and had her laughing as she chucked the ball in my direction like a pro. The dog chased it through the air as I caught it with one hand. There was a little sting behind it as it connected with my palm. She did have a pretty good arm still.

I tossed the ball back at her far more gently than I would have if I was playing for real and laughed at the silly puppy as he zoomed back between us, barking his little head off and trying to jump in the air to catch the ball with each pass. It was like a giant game of keep away.

"I remember when you told me you were going to try out for the team." She huffed a little because I purposely tossed the ball a little over her head so I could watch all her best parts bounce and her shirt ride up on her toned tummy. "You sounded so sad about it."

I had to run to the side as she retaliated and I almost tripped over the dog as he got right under my feet. I scowled at her as she laughed and put a little more heat behind the next toss.

"I didn't want to. I was just tall and big for my age. Everyone kept telling me I needed to. Your dad asked Poppy to mention it to me and the next thing I know I'm signing up for the junior varsity team and then starting on varsity a couple of months later. I never even thought about being an athlete before then. No one was as surprised as I was that I was good at it."

She chucked the ball back at me and it hit me right in the gut. I grunted a little and bent down to pet the dog as he lay at my feet.

"You were the best. Everyone said so." She sounded wistful about it.

I lobbed the ball back to her halfheartedly. "Maybe, but being the best at something you don't love makes it a chore and no fun. Plus it still wasn't enough to get me what I thought I wanted."

"My sister."

I wasn't going to lie to her, so I nodded. "I don't think I had a clue what I was fucking doing back then."

She sighed. "Me either. I knew I had to leave, had to get away from my dad, but I didn't really plan past that. The guy I left Loveless with left me in Phoenix after taking all my money and my cell phone. I ended up almost homeless and totally broke."

I swore at her revelation and fell back a step as she really heaved the ball at me in her resurrected anger.

"I got a job waitressing, slept on the couch of this girl I

met at the restaurant until her creep of a boyfriend tried to come on to me and she caught him in the act. Of course she blamed me and put me out on my ass, so I had to scramble again. I took a job at a strip club because it was the only work I could find on such short notice."

I dropped the ball and gaped at her in surprise as she smiled sadly at me.

"A girl had to do what she had to do in order to survive, Rowdy. I'm not proud of it but I did dance for about six months. While I was there I met this guy that ran a burlesque club in Reno. He offered me a job with more clothes and better pay, so I took him up on it. He told me my looks were going to make me a hit and he was right." She shook her head a little ruefully.

I didn't know what to say, so I tossed her back the ball and she hopped around to make the catch because I was way off the mark after listening to her recount her days after she left me.

"I was in Reno for less than a month when I got asked to be in a hot-rod magazine photo shoot. I said yes and then next thing I knew I was getting all kinds of offers to model—tattoo magazines, trade shows, conventions, and retro-clothing websites. I just had to look pretty and I got paid pretty well for it, and I got to keep my clothes on for the most part. It was fun. I traveled, met cool people, but it wasn't enough. Being a pretty face can't last forever and I wanted something to be proud of, something I could put my name on."

She didn't throw the ball back at me, instead she cradled it to her chest and pushed her sunglasses up on the top of her head. "That's why I got into the clothing line, why I wanted to be hands-on in the tattoo shop in Vegas. I wanted to leave a mark."

"You can do that here, probably more so." My voice was soft and I wasn't sure if she even heard me.

She suddenly snapped the ball hard at me and I caught it with an "oof." It was quickly followed by a grunt as her smaller body barreled into my surprised frame as she took me to the ground in a really effective tackle. She straddled my waist and put her hands on my chest so that she was hovering over the top of me and looking down directly into my stunned eyes as she reached up to pull my sunglasses off of my nose.

"I want to. Leave a mark, I mean. I want to leave one on the shop for Phil and because I think you guys are doing his legacy proud." She leaned down a little and I knew there was no way she could miss the hard ridge that she was currently sitting astride. If the football wasn't trapped between us we would practically be lying on top of one another. "I want to leave a mark on you as well, Rowdy."

I grunted and shifted the ball out of the way so I could wrap one of her braids around my hand and tow her toward me. "You did that a long time ago, Salem."

She shook her head side to side and bit her lip again. She was going to kill me with that. It took her from sinfully sexy to sweet and soft.

"Not a scar, not a wound . . . a *mark*. Something good. I want you to have good memories of me like I have of you."

I got her close enough that I could get my teeth in the

plump curve of her lip where she had just been biting it. She groaned into my mouth and I felt her fingers curl in the fabric of my T-shirt.

"Spend the weekend with me, Salem."

Her obsidian eyes went a shade darker if that was possible. This time there was no indecision. Poppy was nowhere to be seen because all Salem could see was me and the desire I had for her flooding my gaze as I pleaded with her through my eyes.

"Okay." Her voice was just a husky whisper but it was the sweetest thing I has ever heard.

I had to tell her, "Nice tackle, by the way."

She pressed a laughing kiss to my mouth and climbed to her feet.

"I've been waiting to tackle you for years."

Good . . . because I couldn't wait to return the favor and I was refusing to think about what it was going to do to me when this stopped being fun, when this stopped being her new adventure, and she decided it was time to move on. She was here for a reason, she was here for me, and I fully planned on enjoying her while it lasted. I already had marks from her, I would surely survive the next set she left . . . especially if they included claw marks on my back from all the things I was planning on doing to her in bed.

I was lucky she had come here for me but knew that my good fortune rarely held out when it came to matters of my heart.

CHAPTER 8

Salem

ITHOUGHT ONCE ROWDY secured my agreement to spend the weekend with him he would wrap up our time at the park and hustle me off to the closest horizontal surface he could find. Like always he was determined to throw me a curveball, and after a very steamy and not-at-all-appropriate-for-puppies-or park-patrons make-out session that had me all flushed and turned on, he got to his feet and grinned down at me.

"Not the right time or place for that, Salem."

I just gazed up at him, a little drunk on lust, as he scrounged up a tennis ball for Jimbo and decided the dog made a better fetch partner than I did. I just watched the two of them in silence for a while, mostly because at some point it got really hot and Rowdy took his T-shirt off, which meant I couldn't look away even I wanted to. I pulled my knees up to my chest and rested my chin on top of one to enjoy the view.

There was nothing little boy about him anymore. He

was all hard lines on a lean frame covered in strong muscles and bright ink. I had Internet-stalked him enough to know that when he played football he had been a lot bigger, wider, and more bulked up with muscle, but now he was more streamlined he looked more like an underwear model than a professional athlete. All those corded muscles that ripped across his chest and abs were covered with a layer of scrolling tattoo work that put most of anything else I had ever seen and worn myself to shame.

To go along with the unforgettable anchor that glimmered with a sexy sheen of sweat on the side of his neck, he also had a massive pirate ship tattooed on the center of his chest. It was immersed in a raging storm and fighting blue waves that were the same color as his brilliant eyes. Across the top of the ship, in the masts, was a waving banner with the words GUIDE ME HOME in tattered script and it broke my heart for him. Below the ship was an impressive sea monster with tentacles and mean eyes looking to pull the boat deep into the sea. It was a massive story told across his flesh in a truly beautiful way.

He also had the name "Gloria" in huge letters all along his ribs on one side and it would have really rubbed me the wrong way if I hadn't known Gloria was his mother's name. Each giant letter had cute little cherub angels holding it up. On his back on the opposite side of the memorial tattoo was a pinup girl that ran from his shoulder all the way to the top of his low-riding jeans. She was dressed like a pirate and I swear she was smirking at me while I drooled over him every time those muscles tensed and flexed as he threw the ball.

He had sleeves tattooed on either arm. One actually similar to my own and covered with really traditional, old-school, sailor-style work. The other, though . . . it was probably the most beautiful thing I have ever seen put on someone's skin in ink. Around his bicep and down to his elbow was a mélange of Monet's water lilies. The tattoo looked like someone had plucked the oil painting off the wall and wrapped it around his arm. From his elbow down to his wrist was a re-creation of Van Gogh's *Starry Night*. They were just beautiful and seemed like they should be out of place on such a rock-and-roll guy that used to be a jock. But no, on Rowdy the classic works of art not only fit, they served to make him even more stunning and interesting.

When he made his way back to me he was carrying my worn-out but obviously very happy puppy. He also wasn't alone. Three teenage boys trailed behind him staring at him in obvious admiration. He handed Jimbo to me and pushed his Ray-Bans to the top of his golden head.

"They're one short for a game. Do you care if I play with them real quick?"

I shook my head. Really I think they wanted to use Rowdy to impress the gaggle of teenage girls that had collected close by.

"Nope. How about you go be a boy and I'll head back to my apartment and make some lunch real quick? I'm hungry and Jimbo looks like he needs a nap."

One of Rowdy's blond brows shot up and the corner of his mouth hitched up in a grin. "Go be a boy?"

I flicked my hands toward the waiting teenagers and

pulled my sunglasses down so that I could look at him over the rim.

"You know, go roll in the dirt and get all sweaty and stuff. Go relive your glory days."

I got to my feet and put my squirming dog down so that I could reattach him to his leash. Rowdy reached out and tugged on the end of one of my long braids.

"Something tells me my glory days are just starting." Well, shit. Wasn't that just enough to have my heart doing a slip and slide all the way to my toes and back to the center of my chest?

"I'll see you in a little bit."

He turned away and I heard the boys' excited chatter and the teenage girls' collective sigh. I couldn't blame them. Watching him move while he was only half dressed was definitely a show not to be missed.

I got back to the apartment and gave the puppy some water. I decided I needed to take a shower since I was covered in sunscreen and had bits of grass stuck to me from sitting on the ground all afternoon. When I got out of the shower I put on a sundress that was fitted on top but flared out at the waist—very June Cleaver style—and left my hair wet and unstyled and my feet bare. I was so used to being polished, all shiny and perfect, that being casual at home was just starting to feel comfortable. My quirky and polished style was the armor I wore to show the world and in some way, my dad, that I could look how I wanted, act how I wanted, and still be a successful, beautiful person entirely of my own making. It was strange that Rowdy seemed to prefer the scrubbed-down, bare version of me but I wasn't going to complain. Looking flawless and put together all the time took a lot of work and sometimes I just didn't want to put forth the effort.

I never really shared what had happened after I left Loveless with anyone. I had learned some hard lessons and made choices I wasn't exactly proud of, but I had made it on my own and that was something I would never let anyone take away from me. I never had to go back or ask my parents for anything and that alone was enough to shadow the shame and regret that was attached to some of my more impulsive decisions. I carved my own path when it would have been so much easier to relent, and I had done it with my own style and my own flair, which was why I had decided it was okay for me to live my life on my own terms even if that meant not staying in any one place for very long.

That was part of what was confusing me about this situation with Rowdy. I never hesitated to go after what I wanted, to make my intentions known. But he was tangled up in the past and he had cared deeply for someone I loved irrevocably and that just made the whole mess so complicated that it made my head hurt. Even if Poppy hadn't returned his feelings, I didn't like the idea that I was just a substitute for the sister that had gotten away from him. I had way too much to offer to settle for being anyone's fill-in. This time just doing whatever I felt like didn't seem like it was going to come consequence free.

I was scrounging around in the fridge looking for something to make for lunch and the pickings were slim. I wasn't exactly a gourmet cook and I lived right off one of the main roads that ran through Denver, so spending time in the kitchen wasn't something I did very often. I decided that peanut butter and jelly sandwiches and some potato chips were going to have to do and figured Rowdy would be all right with it considering our entire day had been spent reliving moments from our youth. I was putting the sandwiches on a plate when there was a sharp knock at the door that had Jimbo rousing from his nap and barking.

I pulled to door open while I was licking the last of the peanut butter off the knife. Rowdy was propped up on the other side, still missing his shirt and even more rumpled and sweaty than he had been an hour ago when I left him in the park. His shirt was hanging like a tail out of the back of his jeans and all the ink that covered him was glistening like wet paint across his smooth skin. His blond hair was messy and falling across his forehead and his aqua-colored eyes were blazing like a beacon out of his face.

I let the hand with the knife fall to my side as we stared silently at each other. His gaze drifted over my damp hair, across my startled face, and down to my bare feet. He took one step inside the door, which forced me to take one back.

"Did you win?" I sounded shaky and nervous even though I didn't really feel uncertain. I was way more along the lines of breathless and needy.

"Oh, I think I'm about to win for sure." A sexy smirk pulled at the edges of his mouth. "Do you have anything on under that dress?"

It was a bold question followed by him taking the knife

from me and tossing it dangerously in the direction of the kitchen. It clattered loudly as it landed in the sink, and even that wasn't enough to drown out the sound of my heart pounding loudly in my ears. He was totally in my face and I knew that sandwiches were no longer on the menu for lunch.

I was.

"Why don't you find out for yourself?" I could play this game with him. After all, there had to be an offense and a defense in order for there to be a game in the first place.

He growled at me low in his throat and kicked the door shut behind him with the sole of his sneaker as he prowled toward me. He didn't stop coming at me until we were pressed right up against each other. He smelled like the outside and the grass from the park. He felt hard and strong and any idea that this was still the boy next door melted away as the erection bulging at the front of his jeans came into contact with my stomach. His eyes burned hotter than the summer sky, and when he slid his hands around, underneath the thick fall of my still-wet hair, I felt like it was all too much and I was just going to melt in a puddle of anticipation and longing at his feet.

He didn't say anything else, just started walking in the direction of the bedroom, forcing me to match him step for step as he waltzed me backward. The bluesy and folksy sound of Old Crow Medicine Show wafted out of the bedroom, guiding his way in the right direction.

"I stink." His voice was gruff and sent chills racing up and down my spine as we backed into the darkened bedroom. My bed wasn't even made and half of my wardrobe was lying across the floor. None of it slowed him down as he kept his pace going until the back of my legs hit the edge of my bed.

I wrapped my fingers around each of his tattooed wrists and gazed up at him. I licked my bottom lip and he groaned.

"I kind of like it."

"Shit." It wasn't really a word, more just an exhalation of sound, and then his mouth was on mine and nothing else mattered anymore. There was nothing more than the way he made me feel and the way that all the wildness and restlessness that always hounded me seemed to fade away under his lips and at his touch.

He kissed me hard. He kissed me long. He kissed me breathless and then he pulled back and did it again from another angle. The boy was good with his mouth, so good that I didn't notice the fact that his hands had found their way to the hem of my dress and the fabric was slowly being inched up the outside of my legs. His tongue twisted around mine, his teeth nipped at the tip of it, and I gasped loudly in the quiet when his big hands closed over either side of my naked backside. Maybe I had been planning for it all along, but putting anything on under my dress after my shower had seemed like a useless step when I knew I would be taking it off for him at some point.

"Nice." There was nothing but appreciation in his tone and his breathing kicked up a notch as his bare chest moved against mine.

He released one side of my ass and ran his hand up my spine so that he could undo the long zipper that held the cute frock closed. I moved my hair out of the way for him, and between one sigh and the next I was naked in front of him and he was obviously enjoying my curved form. He swore again and reached out a fingertip to touch one of the small silver hoops that decorated both of my nipples. They capped the dusky peaks and glittered with a ruby jewel that matched the one above my lip.

He let go of my rear end completely and used his thumbs to trace across the big lotus flower that marked one side of my hipbone and the arching, sprawling cherry blossom that decorated the other. They were both delicately done and popped brightly against my dark skin.

"Beauty against all odds and the fragility of life." His voice was hushed as he bent down and dropped a kiss on my clavicle.

"I guess that's one advantage of getting naked with a tattoo artist—it cuts down on the show-and-tell."

He laughed a little and I felt it all the way to my core because he was bending me over one of his arms that he had snaked behind my back and using my new arched position to circle each pierced nipple with his tongue. I was pretty sure nothing in my entire life had ever felt that awesome. Each peak puckered and pulled at the attention, and when he used his teeth and sucked the little metal ring into his mouth, it made them hot and wet when they landed back against my skin. I really thought I was going to die from sensation overload.

I was clutching at his shoulders to try and stay somewhat grounded and not totally get lost in the pleasure when he moved a single step closer and I lost my balance and toppled over onto my back, hitting the mattress with a little bounce. He was looming over me and the smile on his face couldn't be called anything but wicked.

He kissed my breastbone right between the full swell of each breast and drew a moist line all the way down the center of my body with his tongue, stopping to dip it in my navel and to put biting little kisses on each of my tattoos that framed the very exposed, very sensitive part of my body he was obviously heading toward.

"Rowdy . . ." It was part question, part demand because I was ready for him. I felt like I had been waiting for this, for him to put his hands on me, for him to put his mouth on me forever, even though it had only been a handful of weeks.

He blew out a breath that made my already damp folds quiver in need and I felt him chuckle against the soft skin of my stomach.

"I've heard you say my name in a lot of ways, Salem. Gotta say hearing you say it in bed when I'm about to eat you up is probably my favorite to date."

I was going to tell him to go to hell but lost the ability to think, to speak, when without any warning he dropped to his knees at the edge of the bed and pulled me to his face. It was too much. Too intimate. Too invasive and intense. It was the best thing ever. The boy really was beyond good with his mouth.

He ran his tongue the entire length of my opening. He put my legs over his shoulders and gripped my ass in hard hands as he explored every inch of my quaking and spas-

ming inside with his mouth. I squirmed on the bed, the pleasure almost too much to handle as he used the edge of his
teeth on my clit. Sensation raced along every nerve ending I
had and I couldn't breathe past everything I was feeling.

I got a handful of his hair to keep me tethered in the
moment and must have given it a harder yank than I intended
because he hissed out a breath that I felt on every damp surface of skin I had between my legs. He muttered something
dark and sexy that I couldn't make out and snaked one of
his hands from my rear to the front, and just as he trapped
that little tiny bud of desire between his teeth and sucked—
hard—he maneuvered his very talented digits in to replace
his stroking and seeking tongue and I lost my mind.

The double stimulation, the twist and twirl of his
strong fingers combined with the relentless suction of his
hot mouth, was too much to take. There was no buildup,
no steady climb to a blissful orgasm. No, instead it all barreled at me in a blinding rush that swept me away on a wave
of overwhelming pleasure and release. It made him chuckle
again, which had ripples of undiluted gratification chasing
the sound along all the sensitive flesh he was still manipulat-
ing and playing with.

I had never had an orgasm that actually made me hurt
before. It hurt so good that I felt it in every cell, in every
breath, in every blink as I peeled my eyes open and tried to
remember where I was, who I was, and who I was with.

I still had ahold of his hair, so I gave it a tug to get him to
let up on all my quaking folds. He let my legs slide limply off
his shoulders and crawled up the bed so that he was hover-

ing over me. He braced himself over me with his hands on either side of my head as he smirked down at me. He looked entirely too pleased with himself.

"Oh, Salem . . ." He let out a long sigh and bent to kiss me on the temple. "You're without a doubt going to me make so glad we're both all grown up."

That was the sweet, flirty side of him he usually reserved for everyone else but me. I knew it for exactly what it was. A way to keep this on a light and playful level. A way to keep it in perspective, because even though I had been the one on the receiving end of his attentions while he teased and played with me, I knew he had felt the deeper connection we had, too. There was doubt that something was happening between us that had shades of the past and flavors of the future all mixed together in one giant ball of emotion and experience.

I rubbed my hands on his cheeks, let my fingers tickle the soft brush of his sideburns, and used my thumb to brush along the damp curve of his lower lip. I trailed my hands across his broad shoulders and over the defined planes of his tattooed pecs. I traced the words scrolled there and met his gaze solemnly. "Grown-up Rowdy has definite parts I like, but so did boy-next-door Rowdy."

I saw him turn that over in his head for a minute, but I was well on my way to getting his belt unbuckled and his jeans out of my way, so if he had a response it was lost as I tried to get him as naked as I was. He had on black boxer briefs and I took a second to appreciate how good he looked half stripped with the straining head of his cock poking out of the waistband of his underwear. I wasn't the only one with some hidden surprises under my clothes. I pushed his garments down to his knees and urged him to roll over on his back. He did and stacked his hands behind his head with his erection pointed up at the ceiling while I checked out everything he was working with down there.

I felt both of my eyebrows shoot up in surprise. "A magic cross?" I had been in the body modification business for a while, and had seen my share of dicks wearing adornment. I had to say this was a first, however. I was intrigued by his hardware and turned on by it at the same time.

Across the plump and ready head was a vertical apadravya piercing that left the top of the barbell visible both above and below the head. Running horizontally and just a little bit behind the apa was an ampallang piercing that, combined with the first, gave the appearance of a cross through the head of Rowdy's cock. That meant there were four little shiny balls of delight resting on the surface of his already impressive erection, making any experience with him magical indeed.

"One of my closest friends is a body piercer. Not often do you find someone you trust enough to let them get close to your junk with a sharp and pointy object."

I used my thumb to circle between the points and watched as the action made his eyes glaze over. His stomach muscles went taut and the thighs I was sitting on tensed and released as I brushed across each ball with my finger. He looked good naked. We looked good together naked. I liked the way our ink blended together into one giant mural.

I pressed into him and moved my hand to grab the rest of his shaft in a firm grip. I also liked the way the nontattooed parts of us contrasted together. I was burnished and dark, he was golden and fair. I squeezed him around the base of his erection and used my other hand to pet the tight lines of his stomach. I'd never been with someone as pretty as Rowdy St. James and I wanted to enjoy every tactile sensation I could.

I let him go and snaked my hand between his legs just a little bit to rub his tightly drawn sac.

He barked out my name and jackknifed up at the caress. I guess playtime was over.

He shucked off his shoes and shimmied out of the rest of his clothes, a sight I wish I could just watch forever, and prowled toward me, his eyes glowing like a lighthouse signal trying to tell me he was where home was all along.

"Condom?"

I scooted over on the bed and fished around in the bedside table until I found one. I tore it open and motioned him closer. He took a step between my spread legs and dropped a kiss on the top of my head as I worked the latex over him and over all that metal. I gave him one last squeeze for good measure and he whispered into my hair, "One isn't going to cut it."

"I did promise you the weekend." I was suddenly thankful neither one of us had anything else to do until we went back to work on Tuesday.

"Thank God." He pulled me up and over him, let me adjust myself into position as he rubbed his palms up and down my ribs. I sank down so that just the pierced tip of him dragged across my swollen folds, and we both groaned at the contact. Those little metal balls made every move I made, every way he shifted and flexed against me, even more intense. I felt him in every part of me as I set myself all the way down and fell forward on my hands so I could get at his mouth with my own.

I kissed him the same way he kissed me—hard, consuming—with tongues dancing and breaths mingling as his fingers dug into the rounded curve of my hips and forced me to start moving up and down.

At first it was a sexy glide that had us both panting and our fingers clenching into one another. He felt so good, and the way he looked at me, it was turning me inside out and I was having a hard time trying to keep a steady rhythm. I rose up on my knees a little higher as we ground into each other and then let my head fall back on a breathless gasp when one of his hands suddenly disappeared between my legs where we were joined and zeroed in on that hot spot he seemed to be able to find every single time.

My hair pooled in a black puddle across the top of his legs as I started to frantically move on him. Between the stroke of his fingers, the friction of the barbells, and just the general drag and pull from his cock, it didn't take too long for me to feel the end racing up on me.

He said my name and his free hand left my waist to cup one of my breasts. He brushed his thumb back and forth across the tight and achy point until I was seeing stars and having a really hard time holding on to any kind of regular motion. Pleasure was riding hard at the base of my spine, my skin was glowing and slick with exertion and the need to let go. If he didn't catch up I was going to go over the edge without him and I wasn't going to feel bad about it.

I squealed in surprise when he moved rapidly and flipped us over. He used a knee to shove my legs farther apart to make room for him to move as he swiveled his hips in a way that made my eyes cross as he picked up his pace as soon as he was situated in the new position. He caught my hands in one of his and stretched them up and over my head. The other he used to brace his weight as he thrust and pounded into me like he was chasing all the desire he had built up between us to claim as his own. The pressure of his thick cock in my swollen channel was already enough to have me ready to come, but the added sensation of those metal balls dragging and massaging along every wall, every nerve ending, and I was sure he was going to have my head exploding on top of having a body breaking apart in a blinding orgasm. Rowdy let his head fall so that it was resting in the crook of my neck and I felt the sharp sting of his teeth in the delicate skin there, and that was all it took for it to be over for me.

I felt my inner walls grab him, felt the bottom drop out of his control, and suddenly he was moving just as desperately and frantically as I had been. I loved the way his heart thundered in tune with my own. I loved the way his strong body bowed and felt like stone all along my much softer curves. I loved the way he panted his completion in my ear and the way he collapsed on top of me when he was all wrung out and empty. I loved that sex with him was everything that sex should be and then some. He was really good with a lot more than just his mouth and had just shown me everything I had been searching for when I set off blindly for Colorado.

It might be wild, uninhibited, and a little dirty, but sex with him still felt like a safer place than I had ever been before.

He hefted himself up in a push-up and I shamelessly watched the way it made his biceps bulge.

"Probably the best touchdown I can ever remember." He was trying to make a joke but his eyes were dead serious, so I didn't answer. I just lifted a hand and cupped his cheek while we watched each other.

It was a nice moment, another sweet memory that I could tuck away and add to the ones I already had because of him, but it was broken by the keening whine of a puppy.

I sucked in a breath as Rowdy moved off of me and rolled to look over the edge of the bed.

"I think we might have scandalized him." He scooped up the dog and put him on the bed as he swung his long legs over and rose to his feet. "I forgot all about him when I saw you licking that damn knife."

I had forgotten about him, too. I was a terrible puppy mom. Jimbo licked my chin and he did indeed look like he was giving Rowdy a jealous-puppy-dog glare.

"I made some sandwiches. I'll let him out and we can eat."

He nodded and looked back over his shoulder at me with a flash of white teeth.

"Now ask me if I won, Salem."

I groaned and threw a pillow at his smug face. "I think we both won, smartass."

He went toward the bathroom laughing the entire way.

CHAPTER 9

Rowdy

I DIDN'T LEAVE SALEM'S place until it was time for me to go back to work on Tuesday. By then we were both worn out, and the idea that it was just some down and dirty sex to get the urge gone was a joke.

All the reasons I had adored her, needed her, admired her when I was younger came back in a knee-weakening flash right on top of the fact that no girl ever in my extensive history of fooling around had ever blown my mind in bed the way Salem did. She was funny. She was quick and sharp tongued. She was wicked street-smart and called things plainly as she saw them but that never made her seem harsh. She was also sweet, sexy as all hell, and absolutely the most beautiful thing I had ever seen stripped naked and writhing under me. If ever there was a friend I wanted to have benefits with, it was her.

I was also grateful she had let our weekend together pass without a single mention of the elephant in the room—her sister. We joked around about Texas, talked about some of the good things we both remembered, and basically tried to cram a decade of catching up into two days between bouts of sex that made me hot and bothered thinking about them. We reminisced about Phil and compared the tattoos he had left on us to remember him by. For her it was an intricately done Lady of Guadalupe—the patron saint of Mexico—a shout-out to her heritage and traditional tattooing. Mine was the memorial tattoo for my mom. Considering Phil was the only other parental figure I had ever had in my life, it seemed fitting he was the one to pay homage to my late mother with his craft.

Salem just got me. She got my art and why it was so much more important to me than football had ever been. It was nice to spend time with someone that I didn't have to try and justify all my life choices to. It also kind of nice to spend more than one day with the same girl even if I was scared of getting too close, of ending up too wrapped up in her because she had a history of leaving. I didn't tell her any of that, though, because I didn't want to put a damper on the time we had together.

When I worked at the new shop for my shift on Wednesday it was a little awkward. Mostly because I wanted to bend her over the front desk and plow into her over and over again. She kept things professional but far more pleasant than they had been when we worked together up to this point. She asked me if I wanted to go to lunch with her, and while my idea of lunch would've been a quickie in the backseat of my SUV, I agreed to go with her anyway, and having burgers and fries turned out to be almost as enjoyable as the quickie would've been. I really did like hanging out with her. I always had.

The rest of the week was busy. I had a full schedule plus Rule and Nash had finally gotten me a set of sketches to work with for the apparel and I had handed them off to Salem to get to work. That meant any night I thought about calling her up she was working late and I didn't want to pull her away from her project. It was a weird thing to be running around after a girl. I was used to them coming to me, and when one didn't have the time I usually just found another one that did. I couldn't do that with her. No one would be a substitute for all her bronze beauty and endless-night eyes. I wasn't going to sell myself short on getting what I really wanted even if it meant my pants got a little too tight every time I looked at her.

I was back at the new shop on Friday and I would have been lying if I didn't admit I was more than looking forward to spending a day ogling Salem's backside while working. I had every intention of asking her if she wanted to do something with me when we got off of work as well. Of course by "do something," I meant go to bed and not leave until the next morning but I would let her fill in the blanks.

I was on the corner at a stoplight, getting ready to cross the street to the shop in LoDo, when the classy blonde that had bailed on getting a tattoo a few weeks ago was suddenly hovering at my elbow. I nodded at her and gave her a friendly grin. She looked like she cost a million bucks and could give Shaw a run for her money in terms of having the bluest blood.

I figured I would say hello since she looked like she was trying to figure out something to say to me in order to break the awkward silence hovering between the two of us.

"Hello again."

She blinked at me and I saw her gulp like she was extremely nervous. She looked like she was afraid I was going to mug her or something.

It happened. I wasn't exactly petite and I did have a giant tattoo on the side of my neck and a couple scattered across my knuckles, so I knew that I could come across as intimidating. Especially to a single woman alone on the street with me. However, I had a weird feeling she was standing on this corner specifically for me.

"Hello." Her voice actually had a quiver in it and her blue eyes were darting around as she looked everywhere but directly at me. She was really attractive in a high-class way and she looked familiar beyond the fact I remembered her from the shop. She shifted on shoes that looked like they probably cost more than I made in a month and fiddled with an earring that was undoubtedly a real diamond.

"Are these your stomping grounds or are you working your nerve back up to get some ink?" I was always fairly slick around a pretty lady and I wanted to set her at ease.

"I work around the corner. I'm a lawyer. I practice family law."

She looked like a lawyer. "That sounds boring." The idea of being trapped in an office or in court all day sounded like my own personal vision of hell.

She laughed a little and stopped fidgeting with her earring. "I do a lot of work with kids and children's rights, so it's okay. I'm Sayer by the way."

She stuck out her hand and I shook it to be polite. She even had a highbrow name. "Rowdy."

Something crossed her gaze and she gave me a smile that was shaded with a sadness that I didn't understand. She was kind of an odd bird.

"That's unusual."

I shrugged. "I grew up in Texas. Everyone gets a nickname."

She made another strange face and sort of sounded like she was choking. She lifted her hand to her throat and I thought for a second her eyes filled with tears, but she blinked them away.

I frowned at her and asked her if she was okay. She nodded at me and took a deep breath.

"I'm sorry. I just . . ." She shook her head a little and clutched the strap of her purse. "Have you ever thought you knew someone—like knew everything about them—and then—*poof*—it turns out they were a total stranger all along?"

I had no idea why she was asking me that, or who she was, or what she was all about, but I felt kind of bad for her because she seemed a little lost and that was something I could entirely relate to. Not everyone got a pristine backstory.

"More than once."

I had thought Poppy was *the one* and I had been wrong about her and who I thought she was. I had needed Salem, relied on her to be my calm in the storm, but she had left me adrift in the treacherous ocean of uncertainty, and now I didn't know what to do with her and the way I wanted to cling to her in a dangerous way all over again. She wasn't who I had thought she was either—then or now. Probably the most important person I had thought I knew inside and out was myself. It wasn't until Poppy broke my heart, left me empty, that I had to really look at myself and figure out who I was going to be without her and without the love I had nurtured for years and years. It took striking out on my own, giving myself over to art and a new life in a new place, for me to figure out who Rowdy really was.

"Did it make you feel like you should have known better all along?"

"It made me feel like I should have paid closer attention to the signs that were already there."

This was an odd conversation to be having with a stranger on the corner of a busy intersection.

"Maybe that's what I should've done."

I smiled at her, after all she was good-looking, and a few weeks ago I probably would have asked her out even though she was miles out of my league and not even slightly my type.

"If it was a guy that pulled one over on you, don't sweat it. You're a pretty girl and we're generally not worth it."

She shifted a little and gave me that smile laced with soul-deep sadness again. "Oh, he definitely isn't worth it."

My phone beeped in my pocket and I pulled it out to see a text from Salem saying my first appointment was waiting on me. I swore under my breath a little and gave the blonde one last grin.

"I always say things happen for a reason. If he fooled you for a while there was a reason behind it. You weren't meant to know the truth until it was the right time. I gotta run, but take care, okay?"

She looked like she wanted to say something else and I could have sworn she was going to reach out and grab my arm but I didn't have time to chitchat with her anymore. When the light changed I bolted across the street and hustled to the shop.

It took Poppy telling me no to get me to the point where I could leave. It took what I had always thought was a shattered heart to make me finally admit that what I wanted for myself was something different from the path I had been on all along. I needed Poppy to get me to Phil and I needed Phil to get me to Denver and the family I had always wanted but had never had. All the bad things had led to all the great things including the raven-haired goddess that was glaring at me with baleful eyes as I scooted into work almost fifteen minutes late. If she had never left there was a good chance I never would have latched on to her sister in the first place. All of it was a chain reaction getting me to the here and now and to the fact that all that first love I was so convinced was everything was really turning out to be nothing.

"Don't look at me like that. I got waylaid by a pretty lawyer on the corner. I would've been on time if she hadn't stopped to talk to me."

Salem's eyebrows shot up and her bloodred lips quirked up at the edges. "The same one that came in here? Sayer? She's the one I spilled coffee on the other day. She's very nice."

I nodded and leaned on the counter, way more interested in talking about us than the lawyer. "Wanna hang out tonight?" I wiggled my eyebrows at her, which made her laugh.

"Sure. I have something I want to show you anyway. I can come over to your place later."

My mind immediately detoured into the gutter while I thought of all the dirtiest, sexiest things she could possibly have to show me.

"Cool." I rapped my knuckles on the counter and told her suggestively, "Bring the puppy. I don't think I'll be sending you back to your own place."

She rolled her dark eyes and flipped her long hair over her shoulder. "Pretty sure of yourself, Rowdy."

My client was watching me from my station, and I had kept the poor girl waiting long enough. I pushed off the counter and didn't bother to answer Salem. She knew as well as I did that the two of us alone in a private place was going to end up in nakedness and sexiness, so there was no use in trying to deny it.

My client wanted a massive Claddagh heart and entwined hands on her back with a bunch of intricate roses all along the bottom. It was a huge piece that was going to take multiple sessions. It was a neat design that I was pretty proud of. I just hoped the girl was tough enough to sit through the entire outline, which was bound to take at least four hours.

Since the design covered most of her back, she had to get topless. A situation that could be awkward and a little weird if the client was an exhibitionist or angling for more than just ink from an artist. Luckily this girl was a pro and put her hoodie on backward and settled into the chair like a champ. I told her I appreciated her attitude and the fact she wasn't trying to flash me.

The girl laughed and told me if she was going to be flashing anyone in the hopes of getting a number, it would be Salem, which had me laughing so hard I had to take a second to collect myself before putting any ink to her waiting skin. Salem turned around from the desk to give us a questioning look, which had me rolling all over again. I winked at her and she scowled at me before she turned back to the client she was talking appointments and designs with.

"She's really something." The girl sounded wistful and it made me smile.

"She is."

"I liked the other one, too. The mouthy blonde, but the new girl seems a little easier to handle."

I grunted and held my breath as I traced a particularly long line along her ribs. I knew it had to hurt but the girl didn't even flinch.

"Easier is relative. I think they were kind of hatched from the same egg."

"She doesn't happen to like girls, does she?"

God, I hoped not. "Not that I'm aware of."

The girl hissed out a sharp sound as I put the ink on her spine right at the base of her neck.

"That's a bummer. She probably likes you. Am I right?"

I paused in what I was doing for a second and looked up to see that Salem was watching me. I grinned at her and saw a hot red flush rush into her cheeks. Busted. At least I wasn't the only one daydreaming about what it was like when we got naked and tangled up together.

"We go way back."

"You look like you belong together."

We did? I didn't know anything about that, but I didn't hate the idea and we had always sort of been a matched set, so I just murmured my nonreply and settled in to do some serious tattoo work.

I WAS IN THE MIDDLE of trying to pick my place up and make it look less like a bachelor crash pad when I heard a knock on the door and Jimbo yip from the other side. Not having empty beer cans and fast-food containers littering every surface was going to have to pass as clean.

My place was pretty basic guy fare. Big leather couch, bigger flat-screen TV, and a fridge that was stocked with Coors Light and that was about it. It would never be considered homey, but most of my overnight guests I didn't want to stick around for too long anyways, so it worked for me.

I pulled the door open and the little dog lunged at me. I wasn't ready for him, so his fuzzy body hit the floor with a thud that made Salem gasp. I was going to pick him up and check him over to make sure he was all right when he scrambled to all fours and took off to explore the new place with his nose to the ground.

Salem shook her head at him and handed me the dog bowls and bag of dog food she had carted over. A little thrill raced across my skin that she had heeded my warning about not letting her go back to her place. She had brought enough stuff to keep Jimbo comfortable for the night.

"You can't get mad if he pees on any of your stuff. He isn't housebroken all the way yet."

She waltzed past me with a flip of her hair and my eyes zeroed in on the fact she had a very short denim skirt on. It wasn't what she had worn to work. Thank God. I could barely concentrate on my job as it was with her dressed in the formfitting outfits that she typically wore.

"I'm sure he'll be fine. I don't really have much for him to get into."

As I said it, her gaze wandered around the sparsely furnished space. She looked back at me with a frown.

"How long have you lived here?"

"Five years." I'd moved in shortly after settling into Denver permanently, right after my apprenticeship with Phil was over and I was working full-time at the shop.

"Everything looks brand-new."

I set Jimbo's stuff down and filled the bowls with food and water. The black ball of fur came barreling down the hallway to inspect the goods when he heard the food hit the dish. He jumped on my legs until I gave his ears a scratch and I figured we were friends again and I was forgiven for doing such awesome and unspeakable things to his master.

"I don't spend much time here. Really I'm only home to shower and sleep."

She made a face of disbelief at me and continued to prowl around. "That's all?"

I shrugged and crossed my arms over my chest. "I never took a vow of celibacy and I never said I slept alone."

"So after I leave tomorrow someone else takes my place?"

That was the way it had always been. Now I didn't think there was a woman alive that could take her place.

"No. When you leave tomorrow I'll just lie in bed and think about the ways I can get you back there as soon as possible. I haven't been a repeat offender for a really long time, Salem." I made sure she was looking at me as I motioned between us. "You are a first for me."

I could tell she wasn't sure if she believed me or not, but whatever hesitation she had about getting into bed with me, both literally and figuratively, always lost out to the fact that she wanted me. That was always there, hot in her black eyes and clear on her expressive face. I decided the subject needed to be changed before we got into stuff that was too heavy to get out from underneath of.

"You said you wanted to show me something. I'm hoping it involves you taking of several layers of clothes in order for me to see it."

She snorted and rolled her eyes at me.

"No. Just one layer."

She shrugged out of the red cardigan she had on and held up her hands in a ta-da gesture. "What do you think? It's the first mock-up of one of the shirts I had the screen printer make."

She was wearing a black tank top that was molded to her curvy frame. There was a fine ribbon of lace around the neck and the bottom, making it look very feminine and pretty. The old-style gypsy was on the front, looking even more like the woman that had inspired her when I saw the two faces together.

She turned around and I saw the Marked logo on the back along with the shop's Web address. It was a lot more fashion forward than anything I would have pictured when we started talking about doing a retail venue along with tattoos. The girls that frequented the tattoo parlors were going to eat it up, and if they filled the tops out the way Salem did, their husbands and boyfriends were going to be throwing money at us to make it happen. She was really good at this and I had to admit seeing my design stretched across her chest gave me a certain kind of pride that made me want to pound on my chest like King Kong.

"It's amazing."

"Right? Once I get the ones Rule and Nash finally finished done, I'm gonna have just a few made for the girls to wear so we can build up some buzz. You guys did a great job with the designs. They're all a little rough but still girlie enough that they won't alienate the female buyer. I think this is going to be a huge success."

I couldn't stop looking at the face that looked so much like hers.

"You picked the gypsy."

She looked down at herself then back up at me. "She's my favorite."

I chuckled a little and rubbed the back of my neck. "She's you."

Her mouth quirked up in a grin and she took a few steps

toward me. When she was within touching distance she put her hand in the center of my chest where my heart was beating out a tattoo that was totally foreign to me.

"I know." She had to lift herself up on her toes so that she could kiss me on the underside of my jaw. "That's why she's my favorite. It makes me all gooey and squishy on the inside that that's how you see me."

I put my hands on her waist as she trailed kisses along the edge of my jaw and worked her way to my earlobe. I bit back a groan when her teeth closed over it.

"You're beautiful. You have a darkness and a wildness in you. You look like a modern-day gypsy."

"You make the darkness and the wildness calm down." She had her hands under the hem of my T-shirt at my lower back and was tugging it upward. I caught the back of my collar in one hand and ripped it off over my head and tossed it in the general direction of the couch.

"Yeah?"

She ran her hands along the ridges of my ribs and then up and down my side where my mom's name was. The reminder of what happened when I loved someone wholly and how hard the lonely was when that love went away was almost enough to have me pulling back, but her lips landed right in the center of my chest just as her hands found their way to the front of my pants. She made short work of my belt buckle, and between her determined fingers and the wet tip of her tongue tracing random designs on my skin, desire and want kicked fear's ass to the curb.

"Yeah. You sort of feel like where I always wanted to be."

Well, fuck me. Didn't that put trying to keep a safe distance and not letting my heart get involved seem damn near
impossible?

I threaded my fingers through her soft hair and held her
head in my hands as she took a few steps forward and backed
me up so that I was leaning my ass on the back of the couch.
Her eyes gleamed up at me as she reached around my waist
and started to tug my pants off. I kissed her because I had to.
I kissed her because I wanted to. I kissed her because kissing
her was starting to make me feel like I had found something
I wasn't really aware I had been looking for. Mostly I kissed
her because every time she kissed me back I felt her settling
a piece of herself even more deeply inside of me. I leaned
forward a little to give her some clearance when she put her
fingernails in my ass cheeks to get me to move, and grinned
when she sucked in a surprised breath when she encoun-
tered nothing but naked skin underneath the denim. She
wasn't the only one that knew how to dress, or underdress,
for an occasion.

She used her index finger to trace a sensitive pattern between the piercings that decorated the head of my exposed
cock and told me in a quiet voice, "You always made me
really happy, Rowdy. I'm sort of infatuated with all the different ways you make me happy now that we're all grown up."

Between the words and her touch there was no stopping
my dick from twitching in her hand or the tiny bead of excitement that leaked out of the tip. She caught it with the pad
of her thumb and looked up at me with a grin. I was going
to ask her what she was smiling about when she suddenly

dropped down on her knees in front of me and had the slick head between her red lips. If there was ever a sight that was going to push me into an orgasm with very little effort on her part, it was that. Her pretty mouth, with that glittery ruby above it, open wide, was sucking me in as I gritted my teeth and exhaled hard through my nose as pleasure raked its claws up and down my back in a ruthless way.

"Salem . . ." Her name was a guttural sound as my fingers clamped tighter into her hair. She didn't respond, obviously, but she did use one of her hands to wrap around the base of my straining erection to squeeze and rub in time with the bobbing motion of her head. It all felt like a wet fire and the best place my dick had ever been.

She was twirling her quick little tongue around and around all the metal that lived in the head of my dick. She was sucking and tracing the throbbing veins that ran underneath the shaft. She was twisting her hand at the base in way that was making my eyes roll back in my head and there was no way I was going to hold out much longer under her talented and intent manipulation.

I tugged on her hair, the red pieces somehow managed to tangle all around my fingers, and I told her in a voice that sounded like it was coated in whiskey and cigarette smoke, "If you want me to be any use to you anytime in the next twenty minutes, you better let up."

She just laughed and I felt it everywhere. My dick twitched hard in her hands and in her mouth as I leaned more of my weight on the back of the couch because I wasn't entirely certain my legs were going to be able to hold me up any longer. I said her name again—this time in warning, but instead of pulling back or letting up, she snuck a hand between my braced thighs and gave my already overstimulated balls a little squeeze. It was too much.

My fingers clamped down on the sides of her head, I let out a surprised shout and let the pleasure and sensation she had whipped up inside of me go. I was panting and most definitely weak kneed when she finally pulled back. She leaned forward and placed a soft kiss right on the center of the sea beast that covered my abs in angry ink. I couldn't tell if she was trying to soothe more than one monster with the sweet gesture, but one way or the other she succeeded.

I let my hands fall limply to the curve of her shoulders as she rose to her feet in one elegant move. One of her eyebrows danced up and she tapped me on the chin with her index finger as I just stared at her with passion-drunk eyes.

"Grown-up Rowdy has so many fun things to play with."

That made me snort out a laugh as I pushed off the couch to test the steadiness of my legs. They would work well enough to get her to the bedroom. I snatched her hand and started towing her down the hallway behind me. Really my room was the only room in the apartment that I used, so it was the only room that looked lived in.

"You never asked teenage Rowdy to play, so how would you know?"

I turned her around and pressed her against the bedroom door so I could start getting her clothes off. The tank top came easily and so did the black bra that was underneath it. The skirt was so short and tight I was thinking it might just be easier to push it out of my way as my hands moved eagerly across her chest, stopping to play with her metal like she had done with mine.

"You were too young and I was too focused on escaping." She gasped out a high-pitched squeak when I tweaked one nipple just a little harder than the other. I bent down and soothed the puckered tip with my tongue.

"I wouldn't have known what to do with you back then. Hell, I barely know what to do with you now." I got one hand under the hem of her skirt and started to push it up and out of my way. Tonight she was actually wearing something underneath. Lace panties were separating me from the damp arousal I could feel pressing into my middle. That was enough to have my cock twitching in renewed interest.

She groaned as I moved the fabric out of my way and used my thumb to trace her slick folds. Everything about Salem was nuclear hot. I just wanted to jump into the fire and melt into her.

"Oh, I think you know exactly what you're doing." Her head lolled from side to side and I pressed inside of her heat and zeroed in on that place that had her eyes drifting closed and her teeth sinking hard into her lip.

I used my thumb on her clit, pressed hard, and stroked it up and down. I added a couple more digits and scissored them inside of her until she was squirming hard between me and the solid surface I had her trapped against.

"Watching you leave with that deadbeat killed me, Salem." She somehow always had me wanting to pour honesty and the raw emotion that it churned up out at her feet. It was like lancing old wounds so they could finally heal.

She sighed just a little and ran the backs of her fingers across my cheek. "I'm sorry. I never meant to hurt you like that." Even though I could see she meant it, I don't think she knew how deep that hurt had run or how long it had stuck with me.

I felt my brow furrow. "No one that loves me ever does." I needed to change the subject before all that sensual arousal faded out of her eyes and was replaced with doubt and regret.

Her naked chest was rising rapidly and every time her pointed nipples brushed against my own bare chest my dick twitched a little more. She was close, I could feel her body tightening, feel the flood of desire and release coating my fingers. I put a hand under her bottom and hefted her up so that she could wrap her legs around my waist. I was so tempted to just slide inside her welcoming body, but that was a dangerous thought considering neither one of us had had the protection talk. I stumbled over to the massive bed in the center of the room and worked on getting the rest of her clothes off and out of the way.

When she was naked and laid out before me like some kind of offering to the gods, I reached into the drawer of the nightstand and dug out a condom. After getting everything situated, I wasted no time in sliding into her. I loved the way her body gripped me, held on to me like it never wanted to let me go. It had only been a few days since I had been inside of her, but it felt like forever. I got lost in the infinite darkness of her eyes as we both started to move.

We just fit. For every thrust, every tilt of the hips, every touch of a mouth on a needy body part, the other had the perfect response. She moved with me, held on to me, and used her body to make it more than sex. I felt her inside of me somewhere making a place for herself. I kissed her and licked at the jewel over her lip. She pulled on my hair and dug her heels into my ass. I bit her just a little bit on her neck and she left fingernail impressions all across the breadth of my shoulders. When she came she said my name like a prayer. When I came I said her name like a curse. I didn't know what we were going to do with each other in the long run, but I did know that no one had ever looked so at home in bed or under me ever before and that was a first that might just matter more than a first love ever could.

CHAPTER 10

Salem

I GROWLED AT MY PHONE in frustration at threw it on the coffee table, where my feet were propped up. Rowdy looked at me out of the corner of his eye and reached out to mute the loud action movie he was watching.

It had been three weeks since our date at the park. Three weeks in which I no longer went to bed alone or had to chase him or run away from him. After the night at his apartment we just sort of fell into a place where we decided without words being spoken that we would rather hang out together, spend time with one another than be alone. We alternated apartments on a pretty regular basis, which meant Jimbo had two sets of stuff and my fridge now looked like a college frat boy had stocked it.

"What's wrong?" He titled his head at me when I sighed and puffed out a breath to send some of the dark hair that had fallen into my face out of my eyes.

As close as we had gotten and as at ease as he seemed around me now, there was one thing that still set him off

and still made me get buried under doubt and hesitation—
Poppy. We both pretended to ignore the fact that she was
still there, a specter hovering in the middle of this thing we
were building around us, but I was in over my head now and
I couldn't keep tiptoeing around her or the past she shared
with either of us.

"Poppy. She's married to this awful guy and she never
answers any of my calls or texts me back. I'm worried about
her because this dude is a total control freak and she doesn't
have anyone in Loveless to look out for her best interests. I
don't think it's a very happy situation for her."

He stiffened next to me and made a noncommittal noise
in his throat. I saw his jaw go tight and reached up to rub a
finger along the tic that started to work in his cheek.

"It's that bad, Rowdy? I can't even bring up her name?"

Those baby blues shifted away from my probing gaze
and I saw him struggle with himself to get his emotions
under control.

"Nothing changes the past, Salem."

"No, but holding on to something that happened so
long ago so tightly that it's keeping you anchored to the bad
moments and keeping you from moving forward into new,
good moments isn't okay either."

He curled his arm around my shoulders and pulled me
to him so that he could kiss me on the temple.

"I think I'm moving forward just fine."

I sighed and put a hand on his tight stomach muscles.
"Not if I can't talk to you about my sister you aren't. She's my
family, the only member of my family I really have. I love her,

and if I can't even bring up her name without you turning to stone, then you are still very much back there in that place. I know she hurt you, we both did, but if you can forgive me you have to work your way to that place with her as well."

He twisted some of the long strands of my hair around his fingers and took a long minute before responding.

"I had a crush on Poppy from the first second I saw her. She was so sweet. She just seemed like everything I had never experienced before. She loved her family. She was settled deep into the church and school. Even when I was that young I knew her roots ran deep." His tone dropped a little lower and the light from the TV cast weird shadows on his face, making him look almost sinister as the memories swallowed him up.

"She never understood me, never grasped why she was so important to me, and when you left she was my only tie to family, to love and acceptance. I knew I only made things worse by clinging to her, by deciding that all of my happiness was forever going to be tied up in her. It was too much to ask of anyone, let alone a young girl that had never been out of her hometown and out from under her father's rule."

He dropped his chin down so that it was sitting on the top of my head. I moved my arm around his middle so that I was hugging him and rested my cheek on his heart.

"Her terrible taste in men, her endless desire to please your father—I take the blame for some of that. I was smothering her and I think she was doing whatever she could to get away from me without flat-out telling me to get lost. Poppy ended things in a really final way but I think I drove her to it.

So along with the heartache I have carried around for a long time, I also lug around some pretty heavy guilt. I don't like to think about it. I like to pretend none of it ever happened."

"You fell in love with Poppy because you knew she was never going to leave?" It sounded incredible but in my heart I knew it made a lot of sense. Rowdy's mom had died when he was so young and he was used to being unwanted and bounced around, so it totally followed that my sister's simply being part of the fabric of Loveless would be appealing. She was a safe bet and not a threat to his fragile heart.

"Partly. She was also pretty and made me feel like I had a purpose—taking care of her." He chuckled but it didn't have any humor in it. "She never looked at me as more than a friend or a brother, not once. Most of the time she was encouraging me to do what everyone expected. She wanted me to play football, to be prom king, to date a cheerleader, and she wanted me to keep my mouth shut and let the other men in her life treat her like crap. Something your dad and her boyfriends never failed to do."

I turned and rubbed the end of my nose into his chest. This wasn't exactly a pleasant conversation to be having but I think it was long past time that we did.

"What about me? You loved her on first sight because she was stable and planted in the Texas dust, but what about me, Rowdy?"

He chuckled again and this time there was amusement in it.

"To a ten-year-old boy you were the prettiest thing I had ever seen. You were wild, loud, and didn't seem to be scared of anything. I knew you hated to be home, hated all the rules your parents put on you, but you never let it stop you from having fun and being full of joy. I just wanted to be around you all the time because it was like having the warm rays of the sun touch everything that was so cold inside of me. You were the only person that ever made me feel like it was okay to be a lost kid that was really mad about his mom getting killed. You never once made me feel like I should be groveling in gratitude for the bare minimum the universe saw fit to lay at my feet. You were everything to me and then you were gone and I was lost all over again."

That made my throat close up and I cuddled even farther into him. I hooked a leg across his thighs and looked up at him from under my eyelashes.

"I should have tried to keep in touch. I meant to but I was just overwhelmed and lost in my own way. You need to know that leaving you was hard. That leaving Poppy behind sucked, but I really did have to do it."

I should tell him that he was wrong. I was absolutely scared of things back then. I was scared of never getting out of my house. I was scared that my life was always going to be full of endless rules and regulations. I was scared my sister was going to turn into my mother. And I had been scared for him. Scared he was going to get trapped into doing something he didn't love, scared he was going to chase my clueless sister around forever, and scared he was going to let other people decide for him how he should live his life and what his passions should be. I was glad only a select few of those fears had been realized.

"I guess we all *had* to do things that we didn't really want to do in order to make it to where we were supposed to be." His voice was wistful and sort of smoky-sounding. I could hear a hundred different shadows filled with memories coloring it.

Since I was looking up at him, he leaned down and placed a sweet kiss on my lips. That was all it took to turn the moment from something dark and weighted with ghosts and regrets into something hotter, something crackling with desire and need. I wanted to tell him that was what moving forward into the good moments looked and felt like but I needed for him to figure that out on his own.

GIRLS' NIGHT OUT ON THURSDAYS had changed a little over the last month. Cora couldn't drink because she was breast-feeding, Shaw couldn't drink because she was pregnant, and no one wanted to get too out of control and misbehave because Saint usually showed up with Royal, and even when Royal was off of patrol she was still a cop and that meant everyone tried their best to act right. I loved that all these sweet, strong women had invited me into the fold even before Rowdy and I had started hanging out and hooking up. They were an amazing group of women and the fact they believed I belonged among their ranks made me feel really accomplished and pretty proud of myself.

Instead of posting up at Rome's bar or the dive that was next to the shop, Cora had made the executive decision for everyone to gather at a really nice restaurant that was a few blocks over from the new shop, and instead of doing shots until we all threw up, we ordered a bunch of appetizers and sipped on fancy martinis.

Cora was rolling her eyes at Shaw and telling her that she was going to murder Rome. It seemed that now that Rule was going to be a dad, a husband, and a homeowner, Rome was all over her to pack up the house they rented and move into a place they would buy. She swore up one side and down the other that there wasn't anything wrong with the rental, Rome just couldn't handle his little brother being more domesticated and settled than he was. She rolled her multicolored eyes and insisted that if he proposed out of pure competition she was going to shove the ring down his throat.

That bold statement had Ayden laughing and telling Cora that she knew for a fact Cora would snatch the ring up so fast Rome wouldn't even get a chance to put it on her finger. That had the tiny blonde laughing and she didn't deny it.

I looked at Saint and lifted an eyebrow at her. She and Nash were still pretty new in terms of being in a committed relationship, but they were obviously very much in love and meant to be together.

She just shook her head adamantly, the red and gold strands of her ponytail hitting her in her face. She blushed hotly. I knew she was shy and didn't like being the center of attention, but she couldn't help but smile when she talked about her sexy man. Nash was an interesting mix of sweetheart and badass. He was a good match for the lovely and quiet nurse.

"I just barely got my head wrapped around the fact that I have a boyfriend. Marriage, kids . . . none of that stuff is even on the radar yet. I'm probably going to go back to school and Nash is busy with the business expanding. We struggle to make time for each other as it is."

Royal nudged her with a shoulder and wiggled her eyebrows up and down. "You won't have to work as hard at making time if you move in with him like he's been hounding you to do."

Saint blushed even harder and glared at her friend.

"I'm going to."

"What's holding you back?" As always, it was Cora that had to be all up in everyone's business.

Saint looked away and then sighed and looked back at the group. "I don't want him to get sick of me."

Dead silence met the statement and then Ayden started laughing so hard other diners in the restaurant turned to see what was going on. Once Ayden started, Shaw followed, and soon the entire table was chuckling, much to Saint's chagrin.

Saint chomped down on her lower lip and fiddled with her hair. "It's not that funny."

Royal patted her friend on the shoulder. "I told you that you were being ridiculous. That boy is sprung on you. He would keep you in his pocket if he could."

I nodded in agreement. "He would. He talks about how great you are, about how the new shop wouldn't have gotten off the ground if it wasn't for you. Just go for it. You don't want to look back and realize you wasted time with someone that matters to you."

That of course had all eyes on me, so I picked up the hot-pink drink in front of me and met Cora's questioning gaze head-on.

"Are you speaking from experience, Salem?" There was laughter in her tone but something deeper as well. I knew she was really close to Rowdy, looked at him almost like a little brother, so I wasn't going to play coy with her.

"Rowdy and I have a lot of lost time between us. I don't know that I would do anything differently necessarily, but I do know that when I look at him now I see a lot of things I wish I had been around to experience."

"What exactly is going on between the two of you?" That came from Ayden and she didn't have any humor in her tone. Rowdy was her man's BFF and she wouldn't tolerate me playing around with him. It was clear in her amber eyes and the firm set of her mouth.

I shrugged a shoulder. "He calls it getting reacquainted."

One of her dark eyebrows shot up until it almost touched her superstraight bangs. "What do you call it?"

I was going to answer when Shaw suddenly interjected and I realized she was the peacekeeper of the group.

"Leave her alone, Ayd. None of us have any room to talk when it comes to figuring out what is happening with these guys. It was like walking across a shaky bridge with no handrails hanging over the steepest canyon trying to get from where we were to where we wanted to be with all of them, so lay off of Salem. Rowdy is happy, he's not out sleeping with half of Denver anymore, so why doesn't everyone just leave it at that?"

I didn't love having the fact that Rowdy's salacious ways were well known and thrown into the mix but I couldn't pretend he had been saving himself for me. I sighed and ran my finger around the rim of the glass.

"There's a lot of history we have to wade through, so for now I'm just taking it day by day. I came to Denver mostly because he was here, but once I got here I found out some stuff about him and my sister I didn't know, and that's been challenging to work through."

Cora tsked and reached for her plate of food. "He's always been hooked on this idea that there is one true love. We've all tried to tell him that's silly and that there are a million wonderful women in the world that would be happy to have him, but he's been adamant—at least he was until you showed up. His tune changed real quick then."

I sighed again. "He asked my sister to marry him when he was eighteen and she turned him down."

A collective gasp went up from all the other girls that again had the other restaurant patrons looking in our direction.

I shook my head ruefully and forced a lopsided grin. "I knew he had a thing for her, a crush, I thought. I had no idea he was thinking forever and ever with her. I worry that he might have lingering feelings that he can't separate from this thing we have going on now."

Cora snorted and poked the end of her fork at me. "We all do dumb things when we're eighteen. You don't even wanna know about the guy I was with when I was eighteen. It was just a mistake born out of loneliness and insecurity. We all made them back then."

ROWDY   177

Ayden nodded vigorously. "I made really bad choices way before I turned eighteen and my idiot brother had already been locked up more than once by the time he was that age. It isn't fair to hold the past against him."

Saint even chimed in. "Nash broke my heart into a million pieces right around the time he was eighteen. It almost kept me from giving him a fair chance when he came back into my life last year. That would have been the worst mistake I ever made."

I sighed again and picked up my drink to finish the last little bit of it. I needed another and maybe another when I started thinking about Rowdy and his feelings for my sister.

"It's my sister." That was a complication I don't think any of them could really grasp, because as much as I cared about Rowdy, there was no way I was ever going to not have the same blood in my veins as, and undying loyalty to, Poppy.

"What does he say about it all now?" Man, I really did love Shaw. She was always so levelheaded and her entire demeanor was just so loving and open. She was going to make a spectacular mother even if the kid turned out as wild and unpredictable as its dad.

"He says it's not all his story to tell. I've tried to get Poppy to fill in the blanks for years but she always changes the subject or assures me that whatever happened between the two of them was in the past. Something bigger than what I always thought is working underneath everything I'm trying to build on and I don't like it."

"So what if it doesn't work out with you and Rowdy?" Ayden's drawl sounded deceptively languid. "Are you just going to pack up and roll on to the next tattoo shop—the next guy?"

I should've told the sultry southern bell to mind her own damn business but I couldn't fault her for being protective over her friend.

"That's what I normally do." The truth wasn't pretty but it was what it was. "I don't like it when things get messy and complicated."

Her whiskey-tinted eyes narrowed just a fraction. "Sounds like you're right in the middle of messy and complicated to me."

"Yeah, and for once my inclination isn't to cut and run but to stay and fight. Rowdy always mattered a lot to me. Now it's in a different way, but I'm not about to let him go without a very good reason."

Royal suddenly jumped in the conversation in her typically brash way.

"Okay, I'm not part of the inner circle, so I'm going to ask what I know we all have to be thinking." Her eyes were almost as black as my own and they were sparkling with mischief. "Did he sleep with her—your sister, I mean? Because if he did that's kind of weird and I think that along with the proposal might have you wanting to rethink the whole situation."

I recoiled and made a face. There was no way I would've ever let him put his hands on me if I was following in my sister's sexual footprints. "No. I asked her about it all the time when they left for the same college. She never even let him steal a kiss."

Royal threw her fall of auburn hair over her shoulder and leaned forward intently. "So whatever reason he had for popping the question had to have been pretty major and wasn't driven out of true love. I've met Rowdy, I've seen him around other women. That is not a guy that is going to tie himself to a woman he hasn't gone to bed with. No way in hell."

"He says he loved her and she broke him." I hated the pain I heard in my own voice when I forced the words out.

"Maybe he did but there are different kinds of love. Maybe he loved her like a sister or a best friend and he just didn't know the difference. Maybe he was just trying to protect her. I'm not a detective yet but I can tell those things don't add up. Especially not with the way he hustled you into bed the second you gave him a green light. If your sister was *the one,* he never really would've been able to get past the guilt taking you to bed would have caused. Rowdy's a good man, all your guys are. Just because he's telling you that your sister was one thing doesn't mean she really was. Look at his actions not his words."

Her words stung and not just because they were no-nonsense and matter-of-fact but because I knew that if I did what she said I would be the one that ended up crippled by guilt. His actions back then had been clear. He needed me, relied heavily on me, and even knowing that, I still had left. My own wants and needs had outweighed everything else at the time, and now, looking back on it, I realized that while I'd had to leave, there was maybe a better way for me to have gone about it. I let my dad force my hand, had given in to the pressure to run away from all the bad things instead of leaving on my own terms and taking a stand for the shards of good that were buried deep in the Texas soil. Rowdy and I had shared everything—given each other the support we needed to make it in a place neither one of us wanted to be. I should have talked to him, included him in my choice to leave. It still would have sucked, still would've stunned him, but he wouldn't have felt like I just abandoned him. My actions were the ones that spoke volumes and in retrospect I hated it.

However, Royal was also right about the love he had for my sister possibly being something other than true love. He had never treated Poppy the same way he treated me. With her he had always been reserved and quiet—with me there were no boundaries and no shame. I just wasn't sure what that meant now that I was asking him for so much more than his friendship.

Luckily I didn't have to dwell on it for too long because Royal was on a roll and her attention switched to Ayden.

"What is your brother's story?" Her interest seemed far more than casual or professional curiosity.

Ayden snorted.

"Asa's story is one that takes place deep in a small Kentucky town, detours into juvie, drugs, girls, and general criminal pursuits and mayhem." Ayden gulped and her hands curled into tight fists on the tabletop. "It almost ended with a brutal beatdown a little while ago because he decided to rip off a motorcycle club and they retaliated with baseball bats. He was in a coma and almost died. He's never met a rule that applied to him or a law he didn't want to break and it finally caught up with him."

Shaw reached out and squeezed Ayden's shoulder. When it was apparent the brunette was too full of emotion to go on, Cora picked up the rest of the tale.

"Ayden and Jet brought Asa back to Denver so that he could heal and get back on his feet. Much to everyone's surprise Rome took an instant liking to him and put him to work in the bar. I think the Big Guy is keeping an eye on him because he's worried Asa will fall back into his old ways but they have a really solid working relationship and Rome knows all about trying to rebuild a life from the ground up."

It was clear she was proud of her gruff ex-solider for reaching out to Ayden's troubled sibling.

Royal let out a dreamy sigh. "I could just stare at Asa all day."

I had to agree. The Cross siblings were unbelievable to look at. I lifted an eyebrow at her and picked up my drink. "The cop and the criminal?"

She wrinkled her nose. "That sounds like a terrible title for a romance novel."

Cora laughed. "Or a bad porno."

"It doesn't hurt to look, is all I'm saying." Royal settled back in her chair and her dark eyes danced with merriment.

Ayden told her, "He won't go anywhere near anyone with a badge. No matter how pretty you might be. He's not exactly reformed. I'm not sure he ever will be."

"He's still breaking the law?" Now Royal's attention was anything but cheeky and cute.

"No." Ayden sighed heavily. "No, at least not that I know of, but Asa has impulse control issues and that never ends well. He's happy here. He loves the Bar and he has gotten really tight with Rome and even Rowdy, but sometimes when opportunity comes knocking Asa has a hard time leaving the door closed no matter what's waiting for him on the other side of it. That's why I'm worried about what's going to happen to him when Jet and I leave. I feel like part of the reason he's been on the straight and narrow is because he knows I'm here watching."

Her words were a somber reminder that these nights where all of the girls could get together in one place and discuss life and all its challenges and rewards were numbered. Shaw actually teared up a little but blamed it on pregnancy hormones. When Ayden and Jet moved away there was definitely going to be a void left in the group and I realized just how close they all were. They really had formed their own family and blood relations had nothing to do with it.

"I'll be back when that baby is born, you can count on it."

Cora gave Shaw an evil grin. "What if it's twins? I thought I got off easy only having to spawn one giant Archer offspring. What if you end up with two?"

Shaw groaned and put a hand on her still-flat midsection. "Rule is rolling pretty well with the whole surprise pregnancy thing. Two babies instead of one might just be enough to send him over the edge." She smiled and her bright green gaze got a little wistful. "Married, a baby on the way . . . If you asked me a couple years ago if any of that would have applied to Rule Archer, I would've hurt myself laughing." She looked directly at me. "It's amazing the way things can change."

There was no arguing with her about that. All these women had experienced some major life changes and none of them seemed the worse off for any of it. In fact they all seemed stronger and better for enduring those changes and coming out on the other side of things. I always hightailed it before whatever result was waiting for me, even if the result was something that would make my life better.

"Well, all I know is that I'm looking forward to seeing what comes next. So far where Rowdy is concerned I have yet to be disappointed and I'm feeling really fortunate he found such a great group of people to call his own. You guys have taken better care of him than anyone else ever did."

"We love him." Ayden's words were matter-of-fact as Cora and Shaw nodded in agreement.

"He's easy to love." He always had been.

Cora leaned forward and rested her elbows on the table and then propped her chin in her hand. She really did look like a punk-rock pixie.

"I think you probably are as well, Salem. Phil knew good people when he saw them. He never in a million years would have put you on the path back to Rowdy if he didn't think that was what was best for one of his boys. He had to believe *you* are what's going to be best for Rowdy in the long run."

I had never felt like I was easy to love. Too many years spent hearing about how awful I was, about how I would never amount to anything unless I changed my ways, made me believe I was difficult and not worth the work. I think that was why I never stuck around in one place for too long. It cut down on the risk that I would eventually be told I was too much or that I wasn't enough. Neither of those things was acceptable to me, so I just left and I was never anything to anyone.

In the back of my mind I heard Rowdy whispering to me over and over again that at one point in time I was everything to him. I silently wondered if too much time had gone by for me to get back to that place with him. I wanted to matter that much again. Right now it was the only thing on earth I wanted.

CHAPTER 11

Rowdy

I WAS THE LAST one left in the LoDo shop on a quiet Saturday night. My appointment ran late because the burly rugby player that had assured me he had a "high pain tolerance" had actually been a giant baby and the design which should've taken no more than two hours somehow managed to stretch out into four and a half. I was glad to be done and had sent Salem on her way after assuring her I would lock up and put the final payment where it was supposed to go when I was done. She would more than likely have stuck around just to keep me company while I struggled through the appointment, but I think having a pretty girl that kept looking over in sympathy was making the guy act out even more. I was sick of the drama, so I told her I would stop by her place when I was done.

It was becoming more and more common, me going to her place after work, especially when I was at the Marked, since she lived right down the street, and her waiting for me until I was done when I did my shift downtown so we could go get something to eat or grab a drink together. Somehow without noticing it I had slipped into a relationship with a girl I was terrified would leave me again. Asa's words about there being a million different girls for the millions of firsts kept a steady rhythm in my head when it came to Salem.

She was the first girl I kept around for more than one night. She was the first girl I ever actually dated and not just slept with. She was the first girl I could ever remember that made me both hot and bothered and cold and frozen in the same breath. Every time I took her to bed, or put my mouth on her, or held her close, the nagging thought that I better enjoy all of it while she was still around slapped me across the back of the head and reminded me I better be careful because if it had ripped me apart when she left before, I felt like it would hollow me out and leave me empty when she left me now.

I had gone from all the "remember whens" to appreciating all the things she brought with her to the here and now. We were no longer catching up and reminiscing but learning about each other as the adult versions of ourselves, and I had to say I liked all the things that came with grown-up Salem Cruz a whole lot.

My favorite thing was how she seamlessly fit into my life and in with my friends. It was like she had always been part of the Marked family and like she had always been in D-town. She was funny. She was still brutally honest but in a more subtle way than Cora was. She called me out when I got uncomfortable and put on the charm and flirt to distract her from whatever topic I was trying to avoid, usually something having to do with the past and her sister. She had

lived an interesting life in the time since she had left Loveless behind, and her travels and experiences made for a lot
of valuable life experience and a truly independent woman.
I loved that if I was tired or wanted to go hang out with Jet
when he was in town, she didn't care. She was perfectly fine
on her own and I found that remarkably sexy. And while
she was okay letting me just do my thing while she did hers,
when we were in bed together it really felt like there was no
physical way to get close enough.

Sex was nothing new to me. I thought I had seen and
done it all. I mean there were only so many ways two people
could come together. But every single time I was with her
I felt like I was experiencing something brand new. Every
touch, every kiss, every breathless sigh or guttural groan,
every shimmery orgasm, the kind that made my spine feel
like it would snap in half from pleasure . . . all felt new and
overwhelming. I was having a hard time processing what
that meant and I worried if what was happening between us
felt the same to her. It was just another bunch of firsts I could
attribute to the raven-haired beauty.

I was walking out the front door and double-checking
that it was locked behind me since the shop was closed Sunday
and Monday when a soft female voice interrupted me.

"Working late?"

I looked over my shoulder after pocketing the keys and
gave half of a grin to Sayer as I recognized her in all of her el-
egantly cool glory—even at almost nine on a Saturday night
she seemed regal and refined. She looked like she had just
left high tea or court.

"Yep. You, too?"

I had no problem being friendly even if once again I felt like she was standing on the sidewalk in front of the shop specifically for me. Salem had mentioned running into the pretty lawyer once or twice while getting coffee and she seemed to think the woman was harmless. I wasn't so sure I agreed.

She shook her head in the negative. "No. I was actually headed this way and noticed you were still working and I finally worked up the courage to approach you for the real reason I've been lurking around. I was waiting for you to finish your appointment and come out. I was hoping you had a free minute to talk with me. Maybe we could grab a coffee or a drink?"

I blinked at her in shock. First, I had serious doubts I was even slightly her type if her reaction to being in the shop the first time was anything to go by. Second, she knew Salem, so she had to know we had something going on between the two of us, and if she was ignoring that, then all the class she exuded had to be for show. Third, I didn't think I wanted to have anything to do with her *real* reason for semistalking me.

"Uh—no. I'm sort of seeing someone. I'm not interested." I generally had more tact than that but I was still slightly dumbfounded by her and the moment.

She smiled at me sadly and shook her head again. "Not a date, Rowdy. Not even close." She heaved a deep sigh and I saw something working in her very blue eyes. Her hands clenched into fists at her sides and she nervously shifted her weight from foot to foot. She blurted out like the words had been trapped inside of her for a long time, "I'm your sister . . . well, half sister, but still we're related."

All I could do was stare at her while she stared back at me. I was sure she had to be joking. Finally, after what felt like five solid minutes of silence, I threw my head back and laughed. I laughed so hard tears collected in my eyes and my ab muscles started to hurt. It took me another minute to catch my breath and I told her, "That's a fucked-up joke, lady. I don't know what kind of game you think you're playing at but it isn't funny, and I am beyond not interested."

I went to walk around her when she stuck out a manicured hand and latched on to my elbow.

"I'm serious, Rowdy. My dad—our dad—passed away last year from a massive heart attack. I was finalizing his will with the estate lawyer when I was stunned to realize he wanted me to split everything in half with someone I had never heard of before . . . his son." Her eyes were pleading with me. "You."

I shook her off and took a step away from her. She had to be out of her ever-loving mind, but as I narrowed my eyes at her I couldn't help but notice her eyes looked awfully similar to the ones that stared back at me in the mirror every morning.

"You've got to be kidding me right now." I had spent my entire life alone. I had been thrown into an overcrowded system because there was no family to claim me, and now this woman was trying to tell me there had been someone out there all along with my blood in their veins. I couldn't believe it—or her.

"He was married to my mom when you were born." She bit her lip so hard a bead of blood pooled up under the pressure. "He was a very hard man with a lot of secrets. It took months to track you down. Texas has far too many children in the system. When I finally did locate you I couldn't figure out a way to tell you. I actually pictured it going exactly like this. When my company offered me a transfer to Denver, I thought moving here and settling in would give me some time to work up to breaking the news, figure out a way to approach you and get to know you. I just kept chickening out."

I shoved my hands through my hair, messing up the slicked-back style and causing the blond strands to stick up all over the place.

"This is crazy. You're crazy. I don't need to listen to this."

I turned my back on her and started to walk away, when her sad voice stopped me.

"I grew up in a sterile household that never saw an ounce of joy or love. My mom took her own life when I was a teenager because she had had enough of my dad and his cruel and thoughtless ways. I can't tell you how many hours, how many times in my bleak and endless days, I wished for a little brother or sister. I used to dream about you, Rowdy."

She sounded really sad but she also sounded really insane. I didn't want anything to do with someone that had known I was out there on my own and had left me to fend for myself, even if that person was dead and his daughter was here in his stead.

"I don't want anything from a man like that. I don't want

anything from you. Go back to wherever you came from and rest assured I don't want half of anything."

I thought I saw her eyes get glassy with tears but it was dark and I had a million and one things racing through my head, so it might have just been a trick of the lights.

"Rowdy . . ."

"No. Just no. I've been alone my whole life and it sucked. You don't get to show up after all of this time and think we're automatically going to fall into some sort of long-lost brother-sister bond. You're a stranger and I don't want any part of what you're bringing to the table."

"I wouldn't be a stranger if you gave me a shot. I moved here to try and get to know you."

"Fuck that. Fuck all of this." I didn't give her a chance to say anything else. I just hurried around the corner to the paid lot where my SUV was parked and hauled ass up to Capitol Hill to where Salem was waiting for me.

My heart was pounding so loudly in my ears I couldn't hear the traffic around me. My hands were so tense on the steering wheel that I was surprised I didn't break the damn thing in half. A sister. A father. It was all too surreal. It had just been me and Mom and then it had just been me. The idea of having a sibling and a parent that clearly didn't want anything to do with me was beyond overwhelming, and I couldn't get my wheels to stop spinning around and around.

Salem buzzed me in and was waiting for me soon as I pounded on the door. I probably looked like a wild man. My hair was standing on end, I knew my eyes were too big in my face, and I could hear the sound of my breath whooshing in and out in rapid bellows. My hands were shaking when I grabbed her and spun her around to press her back against the front door.

I think she asked me what was wrong. I think she asked me if I was okay. I think she told me to take a breath and talk to her, but I couldn't answer her or do anything to calm down. I was too keyed up. I felt like pure electricity had replaced the blood in my veins and I was alive with it. I was acting on adrenaline and the instinct to grab on to something—someone that had always been so solid and real to me.

Salem was always Salem. Ten years hadn't changed that. Having ridiculously awesome sex hadn't changed that. The fact that my young heart had suffered at the hands of both Cruz sisters hadn't changed that. There was no way Sayer the lawyer and her atomic bomb of a revelation was going to change that, and that's what I needed so desperately at the moment. I needed her just like I always had. Even with all the uncertainty that still crowded in on this amazing thing that was happening between us, she was still my safe place just like she always had been.

Salem was still wearing the long, hot-pink pencil skirt she had worn to work that day. She had on a black T-shirt that had the sacred heart Rule had drawn up for his design on it and the shop name across her chest. Her long hair was set in a bunch of complicated-looking curls that I was probably going to have to apologize for messing up. Her lush mouth was still painted blood red, so when I pressed her hard against the door and devoured her lips I knew I was going to end up with more of her lipstick on me then was on her.

I put my hands on the back her thighs and worked the stiff material of her skirt up her legs. I knew she was confused, could feel it in the hesitancy of her hands as she grabbed my cheeks and tried to get me to slow down. I wasn't having any of it. I just needed her. Needed more than a friendly ear and soft advice. I needed her hot body to burn up all the things that were churning inside of me. I need to hear her scream my name in a voice hot with pleasure so that it melted some of the icicles that were hanging in the vast and empty cavern inside of my chest where my heart was supposed to be.

She had on a pair of lacy panties that were just in my way. I ripped them with a violent tug that had her gasping at me, but I didn't pay attention to any of it. Once I had her skirt up around her waist and her bare underneath it, I hoisted her up and trapped her between me and the door by pressing my chest into hers. I held her upright with one hand under her bottom and used the other to jerk my belt open and to get the straining denim at the front of my pants out of my way. I was trying to disappear inside her. I was trying to get somewhere that felt normal and safe, and she was it. She was nervous, I could feel it. Her arms were tentative as they wrapped around my shoulders and her voice was questioning when she said my name. I wanted to tell her everything was all right, that it would be okay, but I couldn't get a thought past everything inside me clawing with need to get at her.

Once I had my pants down around my ass, I lifted my free hand up to her face and pushed some of her hair out of her eyes. They were so wide and dark I just wanted to fall into them and never look at the light of day again.

"I need you." I sounded like an old man as it wheezed out of me. It was so far from smooth or romantic and I'm sure when I looked back on how callous and uncouth it all was I was going to feel like shit.

She dipped her chin in a little nod and her mouth now robbed of all its bright color turned up on the corners just a little bit. I always needed her, just now it was in a far more adult and intimate way.

"Okay, Rowdy. It's okay."

Her fingers scraped across the short hair on the back of my head as I pushed into her. She hissed a breath between her teeth and I forced myself to stop. She wasn't anywhere ready for me or for all the things I needed to unleash on her. Her body resisted the glide and I let my head fall forward into her neck. Everything inside of me was demanding that I pound into her, ride out all the emotion I was feeling on the wave of a blinding orgasm, but I couldn't hurt her or just take what I wanted and give nothing in return, no matter how out of control I was feeling.

"I'm so sorry." I breathed it into her soft skin and kissed her pulse all the way up to her ear. I felt the tight vise of her body start to loosen just a fraction at the motion. I used my teeth on her earlobe and heard her sigh in pleasure.

She wiggled her hips just a little, and as I traced the out-side shell of her ear with my tongue, the snug fit suddenly let go and I slid in to the hilt, so we were pelvis to pelvis. I rubbed my cheek against her much softer one and she told me, "You just have to give me a second to catch up."

I laughed into her hair and the sound quickly turned into

a groan as her inner muscles started to squeeze and move along my throbbing cock in a way that made my eyes roll back in my head.

"Fair enough." I cupped her around the back of the neck and sealed my mouth over hers as I stared to move now that I had the freedom to do so.

I kissed her so she could feel all the things I was working with. I kissed her so she could feel me. I kissed her so that I could tell her without words how badly I was hurting and how disoriented I suddenly felt. She kissed me back and I felt like it was where my home had always been.

Now that her libido was on board with my own, I dug my fingers into the giving flesh of her backside and really started to thrust into her. She crossed her legs around my waist and I felt her heels dig into my ass. I had to break the kiss to suck in a much-needed breath, and when I did she switched her attention to my jaw and dropped sweet little kisses all along the clenched line. Even while I was powering into her, rutting like an animal into her soft heat, she was still trying to soothe me and make it all better, even though she had no idea what was wrong.

I clamped my teeth on the curve of her neck and sucked hard enough that I knew a mark would be left behind on her dusky skin.

I felt the response deep inside her and that made my dick very happy. Actually my dick was way happier than it normally was when it was buried inside of her and it wasn't until I felt my balls draw up and the orgasm blindside me with a tidal wave of pleasure that I understood why. I inhaled her scent, kissed the red mark I had left on her throat as she shivered and quaked around me as she reached her own pinnacle of release. I told her quietly as she came down and peeled her eyes open to look at me, "I didn't use anything, Salem."

She was quiet for a minute and I almost panicked. We still hadn't had the been-there-and-done-that-with-every-girl-on-the-block talk and I wasn't exactly eager to know who she had been spending her time with in the last decade, so I just used a rubber every time we were together and called it good enough.

She lifted a black eyebrow and put her hands on either side of my face. "We're fine. As long as you don't have any scary things hiding in your sexual closet, I'm on the pill and have been for a long time."

I lifted an eyebrow to match her own wry expression. "Clean as a whistle."

"Me, too."

Well, that was a much easier conversation to have than I had anticipated and I had to admit it gave me an odd kind of thrill to think about having sex without anything between me and her. I had been sexually active for a long time and I couldn't remember ever being with a girl and not having latex be part of the program. Yet another first this woman was for me.

I kissed her again. This time with the care she deserved and with all the gratitude I could put into it. We both made a strangled noise of pleasure and regret as I pulled out of her and bent to lean my forehead against hers. I still had her caught up against the door and I liked the position she was in because we were eye to eye and even if I wanted to it was really hard to look away from her pitch-black gaze.

She rubbed her hands over the sides of my head where my hair was short and reached up to smooth down some of the strands that were still sticking up all wild and out of control on the top of my head.

"Not that I'm ever going to complain about being thoroughly ravished by a blond sex god, but maybe you can explain to me what brought that all on so I can be more prepared for it next time."

I rubbed my forehead against hers as I shook my head and made her laugh when I pulled her off the door and stumbled to the couch still holding her in my arms. My pants were still undone and half off of my ass, so when her damp core hit my lower belly my traitorous dick twitched in awareness. I wondered if I was ever going to get enough of her.

She braced her hands on my shoulders and asked me in a very serious tone, "Rowdy, what happened?"

I thought maybe I could get through spilling my guts easier if I had something else to focus on, so I stripped her cool T-shirt off of her and reached behind her to pop open the clasp on her bra. She rolled her eyes at me and told me I had a one-track mind. I didn't argue and instead pulled my own shirt off over my head and pulled her to my chest so that our hearts were pressed together and beating in time. There was nothing sexier than the slide of metal across my skin as her nipples brushed my tattooed skin. She was the hottest thing in the world.

"You know the lawyer?"

She tucked her head under my chin as she trailed her fingers up and down my ribs.

"Sayer? The one that works down by the LoDo shop?"

"She's the one." I could hear bitterness creeping into my tone as the unbelievability of her claims made my body go tense even though Salem was petting me and rubbing me down like I was a rabid wolf. After the way I had gone after her without any warning it was no wonder she was treading lightly with me.

"What about her? Did she finally work up the nerve to get a tattoo?"

I barked out a choked laugh and decided I needed her all the way naked before I could go on. I urged her up so that she was standing in front of me and pulled her now-wrinkled skirt off of her and settled her back across my lap so that she was straddling me. Everything below my waist took immediate notice of all my favorite parts of her hovering naked and close by.

"No, but she finally worked up the nerve to tell me that she's here in Denver because of me."

"What!"

Maybe that wasn't the best thing to say to the naked woman on my lap but my brain was tired and my cock was getting hard again.

"Not like that. She claims she's my half sister. She said my dad"—I made air quotes in air around the word "dad"—"died last year, and when she went through his estate she was stunned to find out he had left half of everything to a long-lost son . . . me. What in hell am I supposed to do with that?"

"Wow." It was just a puff of sound. "That's insane and intense."

"That's what I said. I told her to leave me alone and that I have zero interest in any part of it."

"Oh, Rowdy." She curled her hand around my neck and kissed me right in the center of my chest. "You can't mean that. I don't know Sayer at all but she seems nice and if she uprooted her entire life to come here and get to know you that means something." She lifted her head to look at me. "Believe me I know, because I did the exact same thing."

I stared at her hard. "I was left alone."

She huffed out a disgruntled noise. "So why would you deny someone that is reaching out to you and trying to get to know you? Wouldn't having a sister mean you would never, ever have to worry about being alone again?"

Her words and her take on the whole thing were making me really uncomfortable. I would have much preferred her saying something like, "Don't you know that now you have me you won't ever have to be alone again," but instead she was looking at me like I had somehow disappointed her.

"I don't need a family, Salem. I went out and found my own and they will never leave me or abandon me." It was an unnecessary dig at her and she didn't miss it. Her dark eyes narrowed and she went to move off of me but I wouldn't let her. I grasped her around her waist and grumbled, "I'm sorry. I'm in a nasty mood."

She cocked her head to the side. "Are you scared of having another blood relative?"

I recoiled and threw my head back on the couch cushions. "Why would you ask me that?"

She shrugged a smooth, caramel-colored shoulder and leaned forward to kiss me on the end of my nose.

"The only family you knew died in a horrible way and started you on a very rocky journey to find the family you have now. It might be terrifying to let someone else in after suffering that kind of loss. Sayer seems like a good person, Rowdy. She helps kids, and even though she obviously comes from a different walk of life than you and I, she never seems judgmental or stuck-up about it. Just consider that letting her in, just a little, might not be a terrible thing. That's a wonderful surprise to have offered up to you."

"If you suddenly had some dude knock on your door and tell you he was your brother, you would just welcome him in with open arms?"

She looked like she was considering it and then she shrugged again. "Maybe not open arms, but I sure wouldn't slam the door closed in his face and then throw the locks." She suddenly giggled a little and rubbed her palms over my chest. "I kept thinking she looked really familiar for some reason. You have the same eyes and the same hair color. She's beautiful and totally looks like your sister."

I swore and it made her laugh. "She said her dad was married when my mom got pregnant."

Salem made a sound of sympathy and leaned forward to kiss me again. "There is a story there. Don't you want to know what it is?"

"I guess . . . maybe."

"No one is going to make you do anything you don't want to, so that means it's up to you to make the right choice."

I lifted both my eyebrows up and grinned at her. I decided I was done talking about Sayer and what the right or the wrong thing to do about her might be.

"So it matters that you came here to get to know me?"

She curled her arms around my neck and scooted closer to me so that she was right over my waist. The very tip of my pierced cock dragged through her folds and it made my eyes twitch in response.

"Of course it matters. You have always mattered, you big moron."

I would have answered but she set herself over my erection and any blood that was left floating around for rational thought shot right to my groin.

"You matter, too, Salem."

I had to say it just in case she didn't know.

"Be quiet, Rowdy . . . my turn to ravish you."

Any time of any day in any place she could think of. I groaned as she started to move over me and just let my eyes drift closed as she instantly made everything seem better just by being.

CHAPTER 12

Salem

WE SPENT ALL DAY in bed on Sunday. I could tell Rowdy was still struggling with learning about Sayer and the fact he had a father that had left him out in the cold . He was not particularly talkative, which went so far against his affable nature that I simply let him sulk and tried to support him in the best way I knew how. I made sure he understood I was there to talk it out with, but I also didn't mind his strong, silent act as long as the results were so delicious and made my body burn. I knew he was going to have to face Sayer and the past sooner or later but I wasn't going to push him into it.

On Monday he wanted me to go hiking with him. Over the last few months I was realizing the way he kept his impressive physique without stepping foot inside a gym— ever—was by doing really strenuous outdoor activity every chance he got. He liked to pick up a football game at the park. He liked to put Jimbo on his leash and go running. He liked to go tromp around in the mountains. He liked to kayak on all the different lakes and rivers that were scattered over the mountains. I, on the other hand, didn't want to do any of that even if it meant I got to watch him get all sweaty and run around shirtless. I was happy being a little round and enjoyed being curved rather than straight up and down.

I told him to ask one of the guys to go with him and rolled my eyes when he grumbled about it. I think he wanted the opportunity to watch me sweat and get all grimy and hot along with him for once, but I was a lady—well, sort of a lady—and that wasn't a look that was good on me. Besides I already had something I really wanted to do before going back to work on Tuesday and it would work a whole lot better for me if he was out of the way and off in the mountains somewhere while I did it.

He rallied Nash and Rome for the venture and was out the door with my dog without even asking if it was okay that he took Jimbo with him while I was still getting dressed and moving a little more slowly than normal thanks to his relentless and amorous attention the day before. Who would've ever thought the sweet little boy from next door would turn into a demon in the sack? He had moves I had never seen before and the addition of that metal cross on the tip of his impressive package kicked things up to a mind-melting level. Even more so without a layer of latex between it and me. Just thinking about it was enough to have me blushing and fanning a hand in front of my face.

I put my hair in a simple braid and opted for a getup that was pretty plain for me. A tight, black skirt and a ruffled top that looked like something an old-time Spanish saloon girl would wear that perfectly matched the red streak in my hair.

I put on some fierce red pumps because there was no way you could go into battle with another woman and not have on footwear that wasn't as impressive as your adversary's and still feel confident. I gave myself one last look over in the mirror and headed down to LoDo.

LoDo was pretty quiet on Mondays, which was one of the reasons the shop was closed on that day. It took me a second to find the law building where Sayer worked because she had never actually given me the exact location, and when I found it I was a little stunned and admittedly intimidated to go inside the elegant brass-and-wood doors.

This was no tiny law practice. This was a giant operation with multiple partners, and everything screamed wealth and opulence as soon as I hit the lobby. There was a security guard at the desk that gave me a curious look when I asked if I could see Sayer.

"Do you have an appointment?"

Did I look like I had an appointment? I bit back a sarcastic comment and smiled, making sure all of my teeth showed.

"No. But if you tell her Salem is here to see her, I bet she'll have you send me to her office."

He shook his head and turned back to the monitor in front of him. "No one goes up without an appointment."

I wanted to growl at him and I was considering just going to the coffee shop and stalking her until she showed up like she seemed in the habit of doing, when I heard my name called from somewhere behind the guard and his massive desk.

I took a few steps back and noticed Sayer coming out of

the elevator with a young woman that was in tears. Sayer
was telling her everything would be fine, that she just had
to trust her, but her soft words seemed to have little effect.
The woman had mascara running all over her face and was
oblivious to the scene she was causing, but she repeatedly
told Sayer "thank you" and accepted her hug on the way out
the lavish front doors.

Sayer made her way over to where I was standing and I
noticed she twisted her hands together. Good. I was glad I
made her nervous.

"Do you have a minute?" I made sure that my tone in-
dicated even if she didn't, she better find one for me real
quick like.

She nodded. "My next client isn't until one but I have
a conference call with opposing counsel for a divorce I'm
working on that I have to make before then."

"I won't take up too much of your time." I would take
as much time as I needed to tell her what I had come to say
to her.

She nodded again and walked over to the desk and
smiled kindly at the security guard. "Marvin, can you sign
in Salem Cruz for me and give her a visitor's pass?"

The guard obviously had a soft spot for her because he
didn't grill her about who I was or why I was there, he just
did what she asked and soon I was following her to the elevator. We took an uncomfortable ride up to the top floor and I
realized belatedly that Sayer wasn't just a lawyer, she was a
partner in this well-established firm and her very classy and
plush office reflected that.

"You're kind of a big deal? Aren't you?"

I settled myself in one of the leather wingback chairs across from her mahogany desk and declined her offer to grab me a cup of coffee or some water.

"My dad was one of the founding partners. I was grand-fathered in. They do a lot of pro bono work and tend to be really active in the different communities the firm sets up offices in."

"How influential were you in getting them to branch out to Denver?"

She flushed a little and leaned back in her chair. "When the proposal to open a new office came up I might have sug-gested Denver as a location, but there is a board that has to vote, so they could have picked Santa Fe or Phoenix, which were the other two options on the table."

"You know you could have explained who you were and avoided the trouble of coming into the shop."

She closed her eyes for a second. "After my dad passed away it took a while to track Rowdy down. The entire time I kept thinking it was one last 'screw you' from a man that had never loved me. I thought it had to be a joke or some scheme to keep me from inheriting his estate. Once I knew Rowdy was a real person—really my brother—I couldn't stop think-ing about getting to know him. Once I got to Denver and settled in, it took me over a month to work up the courage to even look up where the shop was at. It took me another two to walk in the doors. When I saw him—when I saw how much we looked alike . . ." She exhaled loudly and opened her eyes back up. "I knew it was real. I played out every scenario there was on how to tell him. I had nightmares about what his reaction would be. It went about as well as I expected."

"Can you blame him? He had no warning, no way to prepare himself for that kind of news. He's always been on his own, never had a family until he got here and Phil wrapped him up in the Marked family. All of a sudden he has a sister and a dad that didn't want him. What would you do in his shoes?"

She just stared at me for a minute before finally looking away. "I don't know. I never meant to hurt him, but I couldn't keep it from him any longer either. I have to settle the estate. I only had one more week until my dad's attorney was going to move to contact him if I didn't reach out myself."

I sighed and scooted a little closer to the edge of my fancy leather seat. "You need to understand something about Rowdy St. James. He has a huge heart. He's a good man but he has suffered so much loss in his life it's really hard for him to let anybody get too close. You being family—actual blood family—has him scared out of his ever-loving mind."

Her blue eyes were identical to the ones I had been gazing into all weekend.

"I came across the information on his mother's murder when I tried to track him down initially."

"That's just the tip of the iceberg. His mom, and then me. We were really, really close growing up and I left him without a backward glance because I was selfish and young, and then there was my sister." I bit down on my lower lip and powered through. "Rowdy adored her, claimed to be in love with her, and even went as far as to ask her to marry him." My voice cracked a little and I had to clear my throat. "And then there is Phil Donovan. He's the man that started the tattoo shop. He saved Rowdy. He brought him to Denver and gave him a dream job, fostered his art, and let him be the man he was always supposed to be. He gave Rowdy the one thing he always wanted, a home, and he passed away from cancer not too long ago. Everyone Rowdy loves has let him down or left him in some way. That's why he froze you out, why he wouldn't hear anything you had to say to him."

She sucked in an audible breath and put her palms flat on her desk. "That is a lot of loss."

"It is. He's been kicked around a lot by the people that were supposed to take care of him and he's just trying to keep himself safe."

She tilted her head to the side just a fraction and those sky-blue eyes narrowed at me. "What about you? You left and he let you back in."

I let out a dry laugh. "I have a toe in the door but I'm nowhere near back in. Every time I grab my purse, every time I tell him I have to run out for something, he looks at me like I'm never coming back. He knows me better than anyone in my entire life ever has even after ten years apart, but he doesn't trust me to stay with him at all."

"But aren't you involved with one another?" She laughed and wrinkled her nose up a little. "He thought I was trying to ask him out on a date last night and told me in no uncertain terms he was seeing someone."

"We're involved, but I think that level of involvement might differ depending on which one of us you're talking to."

Her pale eyebrows shot up. "You love him?"

I snorted in an entirely unladylike way and tapped my fingers on my knee to dispel some of the tension that built up inside of me at that question.

"I've loved him in many different ways since he was ten years old." She cringed because even I could hear the wistfulness in my voice. "I told you I was here for him."

"How did you know he would welcome you back into his life? Ten years is a long time."

"I didn't. But it was a chance I had to take because in all the time that passed he is the only one that stuck with me. He was worth the risk . . . he still is, even though I know stuff now I didn't know then."

"What are you trying to tell me, Salem? I can see it in all of this but I don't know you, or Rowdy, well enough to put it all together."

I got to my feet and smoothed a hand over the fabric of my skirt. "I'm telling you he's worth it and that eventually he'll get out of his own head and want you to be there. Be patient with him. When he's done being terrified that you're just another person that can leave him or let him down, he's going to come looking for you." I made sure she could see how important what I was telling her was in my steady gaze. "If you're gone or no longer interested when he starts moving toward you, it's going to break him and he doesn't deserve that. So before you make any decisions on really being his sister—on being in his life—think about how committed you are to staying put until he finds his way to you."

She got to her feet also and I had this weird thought that

Rowdy really couldn't have two more different women on every single level there was trying to find a place in his life at the exact same time. One thing was obvious that Sayer and I did have in common was that we were both strong and both determined to force our way in no matter how bad our boy wanted to keep us out.

"I'm not going anywhere, Salem, and if I do, I promise I will do everything humanly possible to make sure he can find me. I will not just disappear. He can find me when he's ready." She crossed her arms over her chest and gave me a lopsided grin. "The funny thing is, I understand all about loss. My mom took her own life when I was pretty young and my dad was a cold, distant man that spent a lot of time working and a lot of time pretending I didn't exist. I mean I physically had a parent in my life, but emotionally"—she shrugged one of her shoulders—"I was just as alone and unwanted as he was and really, he had you. I had no one."

I smoothed some of my hair down and turned to walk toward the door. "Don't hurt my boy and you can have me as well, Sayer. I like you. I think you have class and coolness for miles. That's why I came in peace and wanted to offer you some advice. If I thought you were out for anything other than a real, tangible connection to Rowdy, I would have stormed in with claws out and one of us would have been bloody by the time I was done. Like I said, just give it some time."

I was at the door and pulling it open when she called my name softly. I looked at her over my shoulder and saw that there was a fierce gleam in her ocean-colored eyes.

"I know I don't have the same claim on him as you do but don't let him down again, okay? If you think I could break him, just imagine what it would do to him if you left now that he has you again. He loves you. I can see it, so you have to be able to see it."

"Oh, I see it all right. I just have to make sure he's not looking through the fog left over from the past before I fully believe it. If you wanna talk you know where to find me."

I closed the door behind me and took the elevator back down to the lobby. I winked at the security guard as he cocked a questioning eyebrow at me, clearly wondering what a tatted-up rockabilly chick wanted with one of the partners, but he was too polite to ask.

I was tired. After being up all night with Rowdy and the emotional toll he took on me as well as the showdown with Sayer, I was ready to spend my afternoon off taking a nap. I didn't know how long a hike in the mountains was going to take but I figured I had enough time to grab a burrito at Illegal Pete's and catch a few z's before Rowdy showed back up with the puppy and both of them wanted to play. I got distracted window shopping and saw a really cute minidress that had my mind spinning with ideas of how to turn it into something I could use at the store, and before I knew it I had squandered away an hour and was hustling back to my apartment just in case I missed Rowdy coming in shirtless and sweaty . . . yum.

I was juggling my keys and trying to text him to see where he was at as well as trying not to drop the last part of my burrito that I was still holding on to, so I wasn't paying attention to where I was going or what I was doing. I almost tripped over the long legs stretched out in front of my doorway and succeeded in using every swearword I knew as my very tasty lunch flew out of my hands. My purse and my keys followed my burrito to the hallway floor of my building as I took in my sister's black-and-blue face.

Both of her light brown eyes were ringed in ugly black bruises. Her bottom lip was split open, as was the ridge of one of her high cheekbones. She had an Ace bandage around her wrist that she was cradling against her chest and she was looking up at me from her position on the floor like I was going to kick her with the toe of my high heel. Shiny tears glittered in her gaze and her busted lip trembled as she told me, "Your neighbor let me in. She offered to let me wait in her apartment until you got home but . . ." She trailed off and one fat tear slid across her inky lashes and fell along her battered cheek.

"Poppy." I said her name quietly and crouched down so I could put a hand on her knee. I swore silently as she flinched away from me. I scooped up my keys and offered her a hand.

It made my heart squeeze so hard that it hurt when she hesitated a full minute before grasping it so I could help her up with her uninjured arm. I didn't miss that she didn't put any of her weight on her left foot. I reached out and pushed some of her honey-colored hair off of her shoulder and hissed out a furious breath at the sight of very clear yellow and green fingerprints left around the side of her throat.

She was crying in earnest now and all I could think was I had to get her inside and take care of her. I had the keys in the door and was pushing it open when I heard a familiar bark and suddenly had big puppy paws on the back of my knees.

I looked over my shoulder and had I not been holding on to my battered and abused little sister, there was a good chance I would've orgasmed on the spot. Rowdy had on low-hanging jeans worn white in all the best places. His T-shirt was tucked into the back of his pants like he liked to do and he was indeed sweaty and dirty. None of that was what did it, though. Even though all the moisture-dampened ink covering his torso made me want to drool, what had me ready to howl at the moon like some kind of unleashed sexual werewolf was the fact that he had an old straw cowboy hat on his head and was peering out from under the rim with a sexy grin. It was a look that worked well for him, beyond well, and he knew it. I felt my back teeth clench together as his grin slid away when he saw I wasn't alone.

Recognition crested like waves in a storm as his eyes shifted from happy blue to blustery navy in between blinks.

"Poppy?" His tone was anything but welcoming, and sharp with emotions I couldn't identify. He didn't seem happy to see her and his gaze got even darker when he took in her battered appearance.

"Rowdy?" She breathed the noise out and he pushed the hat up a little farther on his forehead.

Jimbo had no idea what was going on, so he was running around in circles between the two of us, obviously concerned why his humans were just standing around like statues.

"What happened to you?" His voice was hard, and even

though there was a lot of anger in it I didn't think any of it was directed at my now-shivering sister.

I blew out a breath and it sent some of my dark hair dancing on my forehead. "We haven't exactly gotten that far yet. She just showed up and I just got home."

His thunderous gaze shifted from me back to her and stayed on her as she gaped at him in a mix of shock and something else that looked an awful lot like shame. It didn't exactly make me want to jump for joy that he was practically ignoring me during their tense standoff.

Sick of the awkwardness and alive with rage that anyone had dared to put their hands on my little sister in such a violent way, I reached out and shoved the door open. Jimbo darted inside and I snapped at Rowdy, "Are you going to come in?"

He finally looked at me and his mouth pulled down hard in a frown. "No. Call me later."

He pulled his shirt out of the back of his jeans and yanked the hat off his head in a bunch of stiff and jerky movements. He pulled the fabric on over his broad chest and looked at my sister with blustery eyes. "I can't believe you're back in this same place again, Poppy."

He turned on his heel and disappeared down the hallway without a backward glance at me or at Poppy. I locked my teeth together and gently guided my sister into the apartment and then took a minute to clean up the mess I had left in front of my doorway. I wanted to jump Poppy's shit for just showing up out of the blue. I wanted to tear her a new one for not letting me know what had been going on and I wanted to cuddle her up and kiss her forehead because she just looked so beat down and mistreated. My first instinct was to call Saint and have her come look my sister over to make sure she was okay, but Poppy looked like she was about to break apart, so that was going to have to wait.

Poppy drifted over to the couch and just sort of folded in on herself as she sat down. I went to the freezer and dug out a few ice cubes that I wrapped in a dish towel. I gave her the makeshift ice pack and took a seat on the coffee table across from her.

Poppy's coloring all around was lighter than mine and the way the bruises darkened her complexion and shadowed her eyes made me taste murder on the tip of my tongue.

"How did you get here?" I figured I would start out easy with her since she seemed so spooked.

"I drove. Oliver wouldn't let me go to the hospital and I knew my wrist was really messed up. This time he went too far."

I sucked in a breath so fast it whistled through my teeth. "This time?" They had been married for a couple of years now. I didn't even want to guess how long this had been going on. I felt like I should have known better when Poppy started to pull away from me.

She just shrugged. "I called Dad and told him how bad I was hurt and that I needed help. He told me I must have done something to bring Oliver's treatment upon myself." She started shaking and crying again and the hand that wasn't holding the ice to her face curled into a fist on her leg. "After all, Oliver is a deacon in the church and he's a good, God-fearing man, so the fault must lie with me."

"Dad knows this guy has been hitting you and is blaming you for it?" My voice was unsteady with rage.

She just nodded and groaned, as the motion obviously hurt her. "I waited until Oliver left for work, packed a bag, and left. I drove and drove. I had no idea where I was going. I just knew I hurt and felt sick and that the last place I wanted to be was Loveless. It wasn't until I stopped to get gas at the border that I realized I was headed to you."

I reached out and took her hand. "Why didn't you ask me for help? I would've come and rescued you."

She just shook her head and kept on crying. "I'm not a little kid anymore. I knew what was happening was wrong. He has been hitting me in places that no one could see for years. It wasn't until recently he started losing control and I ended up looking like this. It's just gotten worse and worse."

"Poppy . . ."

She barked out a laugh that was so broken and sharp I literally felt it scratch across my skin and leave marks.

"We were discussing having kids. I didn't want to, not with someone like him. Not with a life like this." She tore her hand free and waved it in front of her battered face. "This was the result of me saying no."

"Jesus."

She laughed again. "Jesus has nothing to do with this."

I tucked some of my hair behind my ears and just stared

at her in shock for a minute. "I can't believe I had no idea any of this was going on."

She lifted a shoulder and let it fall. "It's not exactly something I'm proud of. I should be able to do what you did and walk away. I've known since the first time Oliver raised his hand to me that I was in a bad situation. I've been there before and I just didn't learn my lesson."

"Is that what Rowdy was talking about when he saw you?"

"I can't believe he didn't tell you all the gory details, considering you two are obviously way closer now than you were back when we were kids."

"He told me that it was your story to tell."

A tiny smile that actually had some life in it flirted with her broken mouth. "He always did have more integrity than any other man I ever met."

"He told me he asked you to marry him and you turned him down." I sounded like the words had to fight their way out because they bothered me so much to say them.

"No, Salem, he didn't ask me—he offered. That is very different. I was pregnant with the quarterback's baby and the guy told me to get rid of it so that I wouldn't ruin his shot at going pro or ruin his reputation as a squeaky-clean All-American. When I refused to end the pregnancy the guy smacked me around. Rowdy was the only person I felt I could tell about it, and he couldn't miss the black eyes. There was no way I could take him up on the offer—he didn't really love me or want to marry me—so I told him no, that I loved him like a brother, and then he went and almost murdered the baby's dad and took off. He was trying to save me from myself. A week after he was gone I had a miscarriage and the quarterback never even so much as looked at me again."

Who *was* this girl? I felt like I was looking at a stranger in my sister's body.

"Dad was devastated by the breakup with the football star. He loved the idea of me hitching my wagon to a famous athlete." She made a face. "He always said it would help repair the stain that you left on the family name. I was an idiot. I never even liked the guy. I was just doing what I always did and going through the motions because that was what was expected of me. That's how I ended up back in a situation with a man that thinks it's okay to hurt a woman he supposedly loves. I can't do it anymore. I had to break the chains. It was long past time."

"You broke Rowdy's heart, Poppy." I couldn't help but sound a little accusatory.

"Oh, come on, Salem. Don't be ridiculous. Rowdy never loved me. He deluded himself into thinking I was his perfect girl because I was never going to be you. There was no grand adventure waiting for me. There was no risk. No unpredictability. He couldn't have loved me because he was in love with *you*. Still is from the looks of things."

"What?" I was dumbfounded to hear her say it like it was so obvious.

"He never acted like himself with me. He was always the 'church' version of Rowdy around me. With you he was carefree, he was open, and he let himself have a moment where he wasn't always worrying about what was going to happen next. And then you left."

I let my head hang down for a second.

"And then I left." And left a disaster in my wake for the two people I loved the most.

"But you came back."

"I'm not sure how much that matters. The leaving seems to be the thing that sticks." I sighed and got to my feet. "For what it's worth, I'm glad you're here and I will help you shed the chains and anything else you need in order to get away from your life in Loveless, Poppy. No one deserves this." She let me bend over and hug her without flinching, so I thought it was time to press my luck. "I have a friend that's a nurse. You should let me call her and have a look at you." I was going to ask her about filing criminal charges once I was sure she was strong enough to have that conversation. She sighed and pushed some of her hair out of her face without giving me an answer. I don't think she wanted anyone else to see her like this. The shame she was feeling was practically palpable.

"I'm glad I'm here, too, and I think it's awesome that you found your way back to Rowdy even if it took a really long time."

It was funny she used the word "found," because all of a sudden I felt more lost than I ever had been. I didn't know how I had missed my sister being abused and my dad being a tyrant to the point he could ignore the fact that his child was being hurt. I don't know how I had missed that whatever was percolating between me and Rowdy when we were younger

was something more important and went so far beyond kinship and camaraderie than I ever thought. And maybe most
importantly I didn't know exactly how I felt about the fact
that the ghost that was always hovering between Rowdy
and me was here in the flesh and going to be impossible to
ignore, for both of us.

CHAPTER 13

Rowdy

I NEEDED TO GO home and take a shower and wash the sweat and sunshine off of my skin, but I wasn't in the mood to be alone, and the one person I wanted to be with was currently accompanied by the one person I never thought I would see again. That being the case, I headed to the one place where I knew there would be someone I could commiserate with and would feed me booze even on a mellow Monday afternoon.

The Bar was actually pretty busy considering it was still an hour or so before happy hour and Mondays weren't generally big crowd days. The regulars were all lined up in their usual spots at the bar but there was also a group of younger guys gathered around the pool tables in the back that were being loud and ridiculously boisterous. Asa was watching them with careful eyes as I made a place for myself among the grizzled war vets that sat sentinel at the scarred bar top.

"They seem fun." The sarcasm was heavy in my voice as Asa set a beer in front of me and narrowed his eyes even further as a chorus of hoots and hollers went up as Dixie dropped off a trayful of drinks.

"I don't know where they wandered in from but I wish they would find their way back there."

"You need a bouncer to keep the peace."

"Rome used to handle most of the rowdies." He snorted as I lifted my eyebrow at the twist on my name. "But with the baby and Cora, he isn't here as much as he was before. I don't have any problem cracking a head here or there, but I have a record, so I have to watch myself."

"Hire someone to do it if Rome isn't able to."

He moved down the bar to make a round of drinks that Dixie called for and came back wiping his hands on the back of his jeans.

"Rome mentioned some guy he was in the army with. I guess the guy is getting discharged soon and talking about heading here. I think he's holding the spot for him. You know Rome won't pass up a chance to help a fellow soldier out if he can."

I nodded and picked at the label on my beer with a fingernail. "He brought the baby hiking today when we rolled up into the mountains. You shoulda seen him. This giant, burly soldier that looks like he could move the entire mountain range with his bare hands toting around this little pink bundle all wrapped up in bows and sweetness. She's so small in his hands and he holds her like she's glass. They're a good team and it's obvious RJ has her daddy wrapped around her finger."

"Rome's a lucky man. He deserves every bit of good that comes his way after everything he sacrificed in his life."

I pushed the edge of my hat up and looked at him because I really wanted to know his answer to the question I was about to ask.

"Is that what it takes to be rewarded by fate, to find real happiness in life? Sacrifice?"

Asa's gold eyes shined speculatively. "I don't know. Maybe. I know I've never lived a life where I ever put anyone or anything before myself. I can't see a way that I deserve to have the kind of life Rome has or even the kind of real thing Ayden has with Jet. And you know what . . . ?" He leaned on the back of the bar across from me and crossed his arms over his chest. "I'm good with that. I've never done anything to deserve what they have."

"What about turning it around? Being here now and helping Rome out, cleaning up your act so that Ayden doesn't have to live her life wondering what's going to happen to you or what kind of trouble you're going to drop on her doorstep? That doesn't equal repentance and a chance at real happiness and goodness for you?"

I hated to think the past was going to forever define the future for anyone. For Asa especially, because under all his easy charm and reckless demeanor I thought he was a really good dude.

"I've said it before, just because I can act right and be an upstanding guy doesn't mean that's what my default setting is. It's work every day to remind myself what I have to lose if I fall back into old habits, but it's always there—the temptation to take the easy way—the desire to think only of myself. That isn't the kind of man that deserves anything good and real in his life. Pretty sure that if I ever got my hands on something that looked like it was meant to be, I would probably destroy it. Just ask Ayden. I always manage to destroy the good in my life."

I sighed and took another slug of beer. "Well, shit. I stopped by hoping you were going to put me in a better mood."

He pushed off the bar as glass broke in the back and he scowled as Dixie moved over in the direction to help clean it up only to be subjected to a series of derogatory catcalls.

"You did look a little riled up when you walked in. What's up?"

And that was why Asa was so freaking good behind a bar. He could talk about anything. He was brutally honest about who he was and what he had done, which often made the guys that frequented this place feel way better about the things they were battling themselves, and he always seemed like he had an answer for whatever burden was laid on the bar in front of him. Even if most of the advice he doled out was bullshit, it still sounded good when it came with a cocksure smile and was laced with a southern twang.

"Salem's sister showed up unannounced." It was like being shot back in time seeing Poppy all black and blue like that. "I wasn't ready for it. I'll never be ready for it."

I took the straw hat off and plowed my fingers through my sweat-matted hair.

"You had to know that was inevitable. You're sleeping with one sister, at some point the other was bound to make an appearance."

I laughed drily. "Honestly I thought Salem would've

gotten bored by now and moved on like she does. I never thought it was going to get this serious."

"You're kidding yourself, Rowdy. It's been serious since the first minute she hit the Mile High."

"You're telling me."

"So the sister?"

"Poppy. She's a sweet girl. The type that is steady, kind of old-fashioned, and real family oriented. She's married now. I always thought she would be the perfect girl for me but now I'm seeing I might have been trying to protect myself from the fact I knew—even then—that Salem was going to leave me." There was more hollering from the back and another shattering sound as more glass hit the ground. I saw Asa's jaw flex and he started to move toward the end of the bar where it was open to get to the other side.

"What brought the sister here if she has a man back home?"

Dixie came scurrying by as I turned around on my stool and leaned my elbows on the bar as Asa stopped by my side. Her eyes were big and she sounded rattled.

"Those guys are out of control. They had one pitcher of beer and they're acting like it was twenty. They threw two of their pint glasses on the floor and one of them tried to grab me when I told them I wasn't bringing them any more. I'm not serving them anything else."

Asa reached out and patted her on her arm. "You don't have to. They aren't going to be here for much longer."

Asa had always come across as mellow and sort of un-hurried, so it was slightly alarming to see a tic working in his jaw and his normally calm gaze glinting with molten sparks of anger.

"Do you need me to do anything?"

I wasn't just going to sit there while he tried to tangle with an out-of-control group of drunken kids that outnumbered him.

"No. I got this." He laughed a little and copied my pose. "I used to be them."

I made a face. "That bad?"

"Way worse, actually."

"I don't think I would've liked you very much before those bikers beat your ass, Asa."

He looked at me out of the corner of his eye. "Not too many people did. Anyway, finish telling me about the sister?"

"She always had a knack for finding the worst kind of guy to spend time with. From the looks of her, this one took it too far. There is no way her father could've missed it and I think she might've finally had enough. What's the use in being loyal to a family that's going to stand by and watch you be hurt and not do anything about it?"

"That's too bad."

"Yeah, and the fact I may or may not have acted like I was smacked in the face with a bag of bricks when I saw her sure as shit didn't sit well with Salem."

"Gotta be hard for Salem. She has you now but she thinks your sister still has a piece of you from back then. That's a pretty twisted tapestry of history, present and future, she's looking at."

"Poppy doesn't have any piece of me other than sympathy and maybe a big chunk of regret. Seeing her today made that really clear. I was shocked to see her and worried that she was all black and blue, but that was it. The way Salem works me up, the way she just understands me . . . I never had any of that with Poppy. Salem was always the one that I gravitated to, I was just too young and too scared to understand what it meant back then."

Asa made a noise of understanding and then pushed off the bar as one of the guys in the group picked up a pool stick and swung it at the head of one of his friends. The other guy drunkenly ducked and lunged at the attacker's legs. In a split second they were rolling around on the floor in a tangle of arms and legs as fake fighting turned into real fighting really fast.

Asa moved in the direction of the brawl with a determined gait and I quickly followed. The boys were rolling around on the floor, fists were flying, and blood was pouring out of mouths as swearwords and garbled threats punctuated heavy punches. Asa got ahold of the kid that had started the entire mess and tried to pull him off his buddy. One of the other kids in the group moved toward Asa and I just shook my head and told him, "You don't want to do that, friend."

The kid looked at me like he was considering his chances of taking me on, when I got distracted by Asa dropping a long string of swearwords. The kid he had pulled off the obvious loser of the boozy tussle had turned his rage onto Asa and was giving my friend a hard time. Asa had the kid by the back of the neck and one of his arms cranked up between his shoulder blades, but whatever the kid had been drinking had

numbed the pain and he was giving it his all to get loose. He
threw his head back and tried to head-butt Asa and threw
his legs back trying to kick the much taller and much more
sober man.

"Knock it off, you little shit." Asa gave the kid a shake
and looked at me as I bent down to see how the other one
was faring. Not too great if his snoring and bloody face was
any indication. "All of you are done here. Everyone move
toward the front door."

The kid he was wrestling with broke free by throwing
his body forward and surprising Asa enough that he let him
go and the young punk fell face-first on the floor. The guy
rolled over on his back and looked up at us with baleful eyes.

"Fuck you. I can buy and sell this bar a hundred times
over."

Asa looked at me and then looked back at the mouthy
kid who had worked his way up to his knees.

"Well, until your name is on the deed, you and your
friends can get your happy asses outta my bar."

A couple of his cohorts walked up behind the kid and
helped haul him to his feet.

"You gonna make me, Opie? You put your hands on me
and I'll sue you, I'll sue him." The kid pointed at me as I lifted
an eyebrow at him. "I'll sue every single motherfucker in this
place and I'll have you arrested for assault. I know my rights."

I grunted as Asa took a step forward. "Watch yourself." I
wasn't sure the warning was to the kid or to Asa, either way
I could see this situation going even more into the toilet any
second.

"I've been to jail, you little shit. More than once. So what else do you got?"

By now a couple of the other guys in the group started to see some reason and a couple of the regulars had made their way over to see what the ruckus was about. The odds were a little more even now, but the kid in the center of it all was glaring at Asa like he was his own personal archnemesis.

"I got this." The kid grabbed his crotch and Asa took a threatening step forward, so I held out an arm to keep him back.

"You want me to call the cops?" I thought it was a fair question to ask considering the circumstances, but both Asa and the kid glared daggers at me. I held up my hands in a gesture of surrender and took a step back.

"Get. The. Fuck. Out." Plain and simple; there was no mistaking that it was the last warning the blond southerner was going to give the group.

The guy's friends were urging him to just let it go and telling him there was a bunch of different bars they could go to but the guy was in a deadlock with Asa and neither one of them wanted to give in. Finally the kid shook his friends off and pointed a finger at my friend.

"This isn't over, asshole." He looked at his crew and barked, "Let's roll," like it had been his idea to vacate the property all along. He made sure he spit a mouthful of blood on the floor and knocked over a table on his way out.

Asa was practically vibrating with rage and his normally easygoing demeanor was lit up like an inferno. His eyes were glowing in his face and his hands were curled into iron fists. He looked like he was going to put his hand through a wall.

One of the regulars muttered, "I woulda punched him in the mouth," as he meandered back to the bar and Asa let out a heavy sigh.

"Remember when I said doing the right thing is fucking hard? Prime example." He reached up a hand and rubbed it across his face. "A while back I woulda just kicked the shit out of him, taken whatever he had in his wallet and probably his girl, and gone about my way. Or even more likely I woulda found someone to do the dirty work for me and had two sets of assholes out for my blood when it was all over. Now I gotta think that if I do that kind of stuff Rome might get sued, I might go to jail or end up in a body bag, and that sucks."

I agreed with him, so I didn't say anything and just followed him back to the bar so I could pay for my beer and finally head home to take a shower.

"Well, sometimes the right thing is the wrong thing because if anyone deserves a punch in the face, it's that guy." And whoever it was that had used Poppy as a punching bag. I tossed a few bills down on the bar and slapped my hat back on my head. "I'll catch you later, man."

"Yeah and, Rowdy . . ." I stopped and looked back at him. "Your girl just needs to know that now she's the one. Maybe you were confused when you were younger, maybe you were scared and locked on to the safe bet, but now you're taking the chance and she just needs to know it's on her. Nothing wrong with her being the one after as long as she's the last one."

"Damn. You're good at this bartender advice thing."

He laughed. "When all you make are mistakes you learn

how to help other people avoid them. Thanks for having my back. I'm not used that."

"Maybe you deserve more than you think, Opie." He glowered at me and I laughed as I made my way outside and to my SUV.

The sun had gone down but it was still a gorgeous summer night that had just enough of a chill to it to speak to the fact fall was right around the corner. Time had been moving so fast ever since Salem hit town I didn't even realize the balmy summer days were almost gone.

When I got home I stripped down and scrubbed off. My mind was a million miles away, jumping from the past to the present and buzzing around among everything that had happened in the last few months.

I was winding down for bed, watching TV, and working on a few sketches for work the next day when there was a knock on my door. I was surprised at the sound but not at all surprised to see the raven-haired beauty on the other side when I pulled the door open. I propped a shoulder on the doorjamb and lifted an eyebrow at her as Jimbo shot past me and headed right for his favorite spot on the couch.

"Thought you were gonna call." I had told her to call me later.

She tilted her head back to look at me and slowly blinked those midnight eyes. "I didn't really know what to say."

"Why are you here, then?" Eventually we were going to have to have it out—down and dirty over this whole Poppy situation—but I knew it was still too raw and still too fresh to do it tonight. Salem had been just as surprised to see her sister as I was and I was sure she was worried out of her mind at the condition Poppy had shown up in.

She flipped some of her hair back like she liked to do and blinked up at me. It went right to my gut when she batted those long, feathery lashes at me. She told me in a quiet tone, "I don't want to go to bed without you."

Talk about a first that really held some water. She was the first and only girl I didn't want to go to bed without as well.

She brushed past me and trailed her hand along my chest as she went. "I do have a request, though."

I shut the door and watched her walk toward my bedroom like she had been doing it forever and it was the only place she wanted to be.

"What's that?"

She looked at me over her shoulder and her smile was sex, surprise, and everything I ever wanted without knowing it. It also sent bolts of desire shooting hot and fast through my bloodstream.

"Put the cowboy hat back on."

Well, hot damn. Time to saddle up.

WHEN I WOKE UP Salem was gone and so was the dog. I figured she had run back to her own place to get ready for work and to check in on Poppy. There were a lot of awesome things that went along with being a tattoo artist. One of my favorites was that I didn't have to be to work until noon if I didn't want to be. I took my time getting ready for the day by meandering around the apartment and making myself some coffee. I had just finished getting dressed and was pulling on my boots when there was a knock on the door. I assumed that it was Salem like it had been last night and almost fell over when I pulled it open and saw the other Cruz sister standing there.

"Poppy?"

She looked up at me with her black-and-blue eyes and I wanted to throttle whoever it was that had hurt her.

"I was wondering if I could come in and talk to you really fast?"

That sounded like a terrible idea but I couldn't think of a reason to say no to her, so I stepped aside and she entered my apartment, her eyes darting around like someone might jump out and attack her at any minute.

"I assume Salem knows you're here since you know where I live."

I closed the door and leaned back against it with my arms crossed over my chest. She nodded and twisted her hands together as she paced back and forth in front of me.

"I told her I had to talk to you one-on-one. I don't think she was happy about it but she gave me your address and told me how to get here. She's really crazy about you, you know?"

"I would rather not talk about my love life with you, Poppy. Why are you here?" I wasn't sure if I meant here in Denver or here in my house, but she was welcome to answer for either one.

She moved her hair behind her ears in a way that was so similar to her sister but came across as timid and nervous and not sexy and confident like when Salem did it.

"I owe you an apology, Rowdy . . . and so much more."
She let her hands drop to her sides and she faced me steadily.
"You were so nice to me and always tried so hard to save me
from my own good intentions."

"I thought I loved you." It was the first time I had admitted out loud that there was a rock-solid chance I was wrong
about that from the get-go.

"I know you did but you were the only one."

I snorted and pushed off the door. "How did you know I
was fooling myself?"

She tilted her head and a sad smile pulled at her mouth.
"I lived in the same house as Salem and I have eyes. I saw the
way you were with her. She brought you to life and I was
there when she left and you latched on to me like a lifeline.
I understood that you thought I was safe, that I was boring
and never going to change, but come on, Rowdy, what girl
wants to be a guy's safe bet? You never tried to hold my hand
or kiss me, not even when you started sleeping with every
single girlfriend I had. The signs were pretty clear."

I pushed my hands through my hair because I hadn't
gotten around to putting any goop in it yet.

"I followed you to college, Poppy. That had to mean
something." I didn't know if I said it to convince her or
myself of that fact.

She sighed and moved toward me a couple steps. "I was
your security blanket and you were mine. You didn't have
anyone else to hold on to and I was scared to try and be
someone else after trying so long to be the perfect daughter.
Looking back, I should've fought you, should have told you

to cut loose and go to art school like I'm sure Salem would have done, but I was selfish and I was scared." She gripped my hand and gave it a squeeze. "I don't know what I would have done if you hadn't been there when I got pregnant, Rowdy. You were the only person that didn't make me feel like I had committed an unforgivable sin." I saw tears well up in her eyes. "Thank you for trying to protect me."

I swore and pulled her to me so I could hug her. She needed someone to protect her still.

"Why did you go back home, Poppy? Why didn't you go live life and find some kind of happiness for yourself? Why land right back where you started from?"

She was crying now, I could feel moisture seeping into my Meteors T-shirt. "I didn't know how to do anything different. I didn't know how to do *anything*. I was always just this little puppet, this perfect daughter honed in my father's brimstone and fire. I went back to what felt doable and comfortable, and look what it got me."

"Salem would have helped you out of it. Fuck, so would I if you had called me." I squeezed her tighter as she started shaking with the force of her sobbing.

"I thought I deserved all of it. I thought it was my punishment for not doing the right things, for not being a good girl. I had sex before getting married and my baby didn't make it. I thought everything was happening to show me I needed to be better and follow Dad's orders even more strictly. I thought God hated me and this was the result. The first time Oliver smacked me I really, really thought I must not have atoned enough for my sins. I really, truly believed he was the kind of man I was supposed to be with—that is, what my life was supposed to look like."

"Jesus, Poppy." All I could do was shake my head. "We're all sinners in some way or another. No one should have to bear that kind of burden."

"My dad saw my face, he could see the bruises. I know that he knew what was happening and he never did anything to stop it or tried to intervene on my behalf. He's a man of God and he stood by and let his child get beat at the hands of a man that was supposed to love her. I thought for a long time he must believe it was what I deserved as well."

It was just more reason to hate the man that had forced Salem to run. "What turned it around for you?"

She pulled back and looked up at me all bruised and tearstained and I realized I did in fact love her with all of my heart, but it was in a very caring and very platonic way. She loved me like a brother, so it was only fitting that I loved her as a sister in return.

"A bunch of different things. But the fact that Salem found her way back to you and sounded happy, really truly happy in a way that has been missing since she left, was a big part of it. I realized that time could pass and that life could just keep moving forward for everyone no matter what might have happened in between. I've done my penance for any bad choices I might have made and it is my time to be free. I'm never going to be perfect and I'm not going to be punished for them ever again."

I hugged her tighter and repeated one of Rome's favorite phrases: "Atta girl."

I was going to ask her how she knew for a fact that Salem had always wanted me when I heard a dog bark and the door behind me opened up.

"I was worried about you two, so I thought I would poke my head in and see how it was going."

Jimbo ran in excited circles around my living room as I saw Salem's eyes go from black to something even darker when she saw that I holding on to her sister. I let my arms drop and took a step back, knowing it probably didn't look all that great as Poppy hiccuped a little and rubbed her tearstained cheeks.

"It's better now." Poppy's voice was surprisingly clear but Salem looked like she had just tasted something foul and was refusing to meet my gaze.

"Yeah, there was grime knocked off the past and it looks a lot clearer to me now." I was hoping she would pick up on the subtle undercurrent of my words but she just sucked her bottom lip in between her teeth and twisted the ends of her hair around her finger like she did when she was agitated.

"All right. I need to take Jimbo back home and head downtown."

Poppy stepped around me after she reached for my hand and gave it one last squeeze. "I'll take him. I'm still exhausted and I feel like every weight I ever had on my chest is now gone." She smiled at me lopsided and whistled for the hyper puppy. "It was really good to see you again, Rowdy. I missed you."

Well, shit. That was the worst thing to say when Salem already looked like she wanted to skin me alive or pack a suitcase and hit the nearest airport. I could see her ready to bolt out the door and possibly my life, so I caught her arm and pulled her to me before she could do anything rash or permanent.

"She was crying and I felt bad for her. I just gave her a hug . . . that's all."

"Good. She probably needs as many hugs as she can get." Her words said one thing but her stiff body language and the way she wouldn't look at me said another.

"Salem . . ." I put a finger under her chin and forced her to look up at me. "She isn't you. No one is you and no one has ever been you, so don't get any crazy ideas, okay?"

She didn't answer and shook off the hold I had on her arm. "I need to go and so do you. Don't be late for work, Rowdy."

"Salem," She looked at me over her shoulder because she was already out the door. "Don't leave me again."

She didn't say anything and I didn't call her back as she made her way down the hallway and disappeared.

Like I always said, if it wasn't for bad luck . . . Of course she would've had to show up just when I had my arms around Poppy even if it was totally innocent. I was just going to have to take Asa's advice and make sure she *knew*, beyond a shadow of a doubt, that it was only *her*. She might not be my first love but she would always be my last love and I understood what that meant now.

CHAPTER 14

Salem

I WASN'T GOING TO leave him—at least not physically—but my mind was a million miles away, and I hated the places it was visiting.

I wasn't so insecure that I didn't realize my sister needed all the kindness and love she could get, but that didn't change the fact that walking in and seeing Rowdy holding her like she was something precious and rare unhinged something inside my heart. I was confident, I was sure that coming after him had been the right choice, but there was fear, gaping and wide in the center of me that there was still a part of him that was going to see Poppy as the safer choice. Plus there were undoubtedly the protective instincts that had to fire up in him at seeing my sister all broken and battered, and I wasn't absolutely sure that those wouldn't guide him back to the feelings he may have had in the past. I wanted to be more secure in the relationship we had been developing, wanted the doubt to seem foolish and misplaced, but I just couldn't get a handle on all of it, and as a result I took the coward's way out and avoided Rowdy because I just didn't know what to say to him.

Luckily no one questioned me when I called in sick on Wednesday when we were supposed to be at the new shop together. I knew he was mad because he left me a voice mail telling me so. I made sure I had plans to go out with the girls after work on Thursday so I could avoid him showing up at my place to talk to me, which I was sure he was going to do because he sent me a text threatening to. I even called Sayer to see if she wanted to grab dinner on Friday after work to avoid him even further. I just didn't know what to say that didn't make me sound jealous and petty. I also couldn't even begin to fathom what I would do if those fears were realized and he admitted he still loved my sister and what we had was just a fling.

Cora and the girls knew something was majorly off, but I couldn't seem to get the words out to explain everything that was racing around inside my head and clattering around in my heart. I just told them that my sister had shown up unexpectedly and that her husband had been hurting her, so I was stressed out about the situation. They were all smart women and I'm sure they could read between the lines, but they were all kind enough to just let me have a night out and not force me into spilling my guts over a situation that was eating me alive.

I needed a minute to think, some time to figure out what I was doing and how I was going to handle being in love with someone that might very well never be able to love me back, but it was hard because I missed him. I didn't like not talking to him. I hated going to bed alone and I felt like a real asshole because my poor dog kept looking at the door wondering where his playmate was. No one had ever said relationships were easy, but somehow I didn't think they would be this hard or this heartbreaking either.

On top of it all, Poppy was giving me a hard time. I think she knew I was pulling back, pushing space between Rowdy and myself because of her and because of my own hesitation, and she didn't like it one bit. She told me no less than ten times she would not be the reason I sabotaged my own happiness. She reiterated over and over again that things had never and would never be like that between her and Rowdy. She told me to open my eyes and look at what he had done. He had been brave enough, wanted me enough, to take the risk on starting something with me even though he knew there was a chance I wouldn't stay in Denver for very long. Poppy insisted that for him to do that was a true sign of how much he cared for me, and I couldn't argue with her but I also didn't know if it was enough.

On Friday, Sayer and I sat down in a really posh restaurant located really close to the shop and she fed my own words back to me as I begrudgingly told her the details of the entire situation.

"He's worth it."

He always had been but that didn't mean I was as brave as he was and ready to put it all on the line just to end up his second choice. I had never loved anyone after I loved him when he was my only source of joy in my youth and I doubted I would ever be able to love anyone beyond him. He had become my source of everything as an adult.

Unable to think about any of it anymore, I switched the subject and asked Sayer to tell me more about growing up with the man that had left his son in no-man's-land rather than claim him as his own. As she gave me a glimpse into her history I started to think Rowdy may have gotten off lucky and his idea that everything happened for a reason might be valid. There had to be a greater reason for him ending up next door with the Ortegas than just because. He never would've been able to withstand the chilly upbringing and frozen parenting Sayer had been subjected to. It sounded hauntingly familiar and even worse than my own home had been.

I told her about my own father and how his rules and ironfisted control over my family had driven me out of the house in desperation and explained to her why that had left such a lasting impact on Rowdy over the years.

"He was so little when his mom died. He doesn't really remember much about her, but from what he does, I think she was wonderful to him. All he says is that he remembers her being really happy and always smiling. He said her smile could light up a whole room. When she was ripped away from him and he ended up in the system, I don't think anyone knew what to do with a wild kid that was being eaten alive by grief. He just felt so alone." I sighed and noticed that Sayer was blinking really hard to keep her emotion in check. "I remember one day after school I found him sitting on the porch of our house. He was only eleven or twelve at the time and he was really upset. I asked him what was wrong and he told me they were doing a family history project in one of his classes and that the other kids were teasing him because he only had one branch—him. I could see he wanted to yell about it, to cry at the unfairness of it all, but it was just like he had accepted that everyone he loved was gone and he would be on his own forever."

I shook my head and picked up the glass of wine I had been working on with dinner. "I told him the tree just wasn't done growing yet. He would add to it as he got older. He would fall in love, have kids, have in-laws, and make his own St. James orchard. I think it helped at the time but then I turned around and blew out of town and my sister turned him down when he offered to marry her, so neither of us exactly helped ease his long-held fears about being left by the ones he loved the most."

She grinned at me and picked up her own glass of wine. "I would be happy to be a branch on that tree. We could help each other in never being alone again."

I nodded. "He'll figure that out eventually. Poppy keeps trying to tell me he has always loved her like a sister, that he just didn't know it at the time because he was so worried about everyone leaving him. If that's the case, there is no way he won't eventually come around and want to love his actual sister in the same way."

"I sure hope so." She lifted an eyebrow at me and pointed the rim of her wineglass in my direction. "And I hope you realize that you are doing the exact same thing he did. Letting fear decide who you're going to be with. You already spent a decade working your way back to where you wanted to be. It's absolutely foolish to waste that because of something that might or might not be. From everything you've told me and everything I've seen, Rowdy isn't the type to beat around the bush. If he had feelings for your sister at all, he wouldn't be furious at you and hounding you for avoiding him this last week. He's trying to get you to see him looking for you, Salem, the same way you came looking for him after all this time."

I made a face that had her laughing and I couldn't resist ordering dessert when our server came by and asked if we wanted anything else. I was bummed out and missed my man, so ice cream and brownies were absolutely called for.

"I didn't have a choice. I think I've been trying to find my way back to him since the second I left."

"That must have been hard for both of you."

"Yeah. As soon as I left I knew things weren't going to be easy for him but I hoped for the best. The foster family he stayed with through high school were really nice people and I think they took care of his basic needs, but there was no one there to help him figure out his future or to teach him how to follow his heart. Did you know he played football? He could have gone pro if he wanted." I couldn't help the pride that snuck into my tone. "He was amazing but he never loved it. It was just a way to fit in. He loved art and he wanted to draw. He was amazing at that as well and that was his true passion, his real calling."

I moved my hair off of my neck and shoulders and

showed her the field of flowers and birds flying across my back. "He drew this for me when he was twelve. The birds were free and he knew that's the only thing I ever wanted. It was how he tried to give me some kind of liberty from my father's rule."

Sayer leaned closer to look at the design, and when she pulled back she put her hands on the table and looked at me with serious eyes.

"Salem, I don't know Rowdy that well but I can look at that and see someone handing you their heart. I can't believe you have any kind of question about how he feels about you. What other man since then has tried to offer you what you wanted most? He was just a kid at the time and he was trying to make your dreams come true."

Well, shit. Put like that, it made my heart lodge in my throat and my insecurity feel pitiful and petty.

"He's always been a very special guy."

"Well then, I'm sure he figured out he deserves a very special girl. I'm sure your sister is a lovely person, Salem, but she let him chase after her, let him follow her, let him sacrifice his education and possible future for her without a thought. You left, but you also came back. You left your job, your life, and everything you were building in Vegas once you knew he was here. I don't think it's where you go that matters, I think it's where you end up."

I finished my wine with a hefty chug. "You did the same thing."

"I did and I can only hope that eventually he'll realize that matters. I think he already figured it out with you."

I still wasn't one hundred percent sure about that, but when I got home and got berated by my sister yet again for being a no-show when Rowdy came around looking for me, I was starting to believe it more. He texted me twice before I went to bed and I couldn't justify ignoring him anymore, so I responded that I would see him at work tomorrow and we could talk at some point over the weekend. I didn't want the entire shift at the shop to be awkward and uncomfortable between us tomorrow when we worked together. I also told him good night and stopped just short of texting him that sleeping alone sucked. Jimbo gave me sad eyes as he climbed up onto Rowdy's side of the bed and laid his head on my arm.

I patted his rapidly growing head and scrunched-up nose as he licked at my fingers. "I'll get it together, Jimbo. I promise." The dog whined and I sighed. "I know. I miss him, too."

WHEN ROWDY WALKED INTO the shop the next afternoon I expected him to jump all over me and demand answers for my admittedly terrible behavior as of late, but he didn't. He smiled at me in his normally charming way and went to his station to set up since he had back-to-back appointments scheduled throughout the day. He didn't look at me, or try and talk to me beyond what was necessary for business for the entire shift. It stressed me out and made me feel even worse than I already did, and of course since I hadn't seen him for a few days, all I wanted to do was stare at him and remember what he looked like wearing nothing but the battered cowboy hat. It made for a very unpleasant and tense afternoon.

I was going to ask him if he wanted to have lunch with me and by "lunch" meant let me grope him somewhere privately while I tried my best to apologize and explain all the crazy and frantic thoughts that had been hounding me since seeing him with his arms around my sister. He vanished before I could. That put me in a very sour and grumpy mood for the rest of the day. I knew it wasn't logical since I had been the one playing hide-and-seek all week, but I couldn't help it. Luckily the first shipment of stuff for the store came in late in the afternoon and I got to go upstairs and paw through T-shirts, tank tops, jackets, thermals, and old-fashioned button-ups to see how everything turned out.

The guys had come through in spades with the designs. Along with Rowdy's gypsy and Rule's sacred heart, Nash had given me a brightly designed koi fish and, for Phil, an angel that was done in pinup style with tattooed and pierced wings. The older Donovan would have been tickled pink by his son's tribute to him. The designs were fantastic and unique. I just knew people were going to eat them up and this was just the start. I fully intended on making these boys have their own brand that could go on so much more than T-shirts. They were all so talented and had survived so much to get where they were. They deserved notoriety and recognition for being some of the best in the business.

I was in clothes heaven and already thinking about the next wave of designs and apparel as well as getting an online retail site up and running when I heard boots on the stairs. I knew it was Rowdy and looked at my phone to see what time it was. I was surprised to see that the rest of the afternoon had passed while I was up here sorting and organizing and it was well past time to do the cash-out for the day and go home.

When he cleared the top of the landing I noticed he had the bank bag in his hand and that there was a determined slant to his normally smiling mouth.

"Everything downstairs is done. This is ready for the safe. Do you have anything else left to do up here?"

I was going to break down some of the boxes the clothes had come in and try and make a path between my piles so Cora could get through, but that wasn't anything that couldn't wait until Monday. I didn't want to squander my chance if Rowdy was finally willing to talk to me after his chilly treatment all day. I hated that I deserved his brush-off.

"No. I'll finish up on Monday. I'll come when the shop is closed so I can take my time with it."

He nodded and stepped around all my piles of goodies delicately to get to Cora's office. He went inside and came back out carrying a small black bag. He locked the door behind him and walked over to where I was waiting. He wrapped his long fingers around my wrist and without saying a word pulled me after him down the stairs, telling me to hit the lights as we went. As usual I had on heels, so being dragged down the stairs was slightly precarious and he wouldn't answer me when I asked him what he thought he was doing. He didn't even let me go to lock the front door of the shop. Instead he told me to dig the keys out of his pocket and do it for him. Not that I minded the task but I still thought he was being weird and evasive.

"What's in the bag, Rowdy? I told you we could talk after work, so why are you acting so surly?"

"Surly isn't even the tip of the iceberg, sugar."

I knew he had to be really mad if he was using one of his throwaway terms of endearment on me. He further perpetuated that belief when he hauled me to his SUV despite the fact I was peppering him with questions and complaining about my car being in the lot across the street.

He literally lifted me up into the passenger seat and buckled the seat belt around me like I was a little kid. He opened the back door and tossed the black bag on the seat next to another one that I noticed was already there. He made his way around the vehicle, and once he was settled into the driver's seat, he finally turned to look at me.

"Poppy came and got your car when she brought me that bag for you at lunch. Since you've been avoiding me all week I'm taking you somewhere where there is absolutely no place for you to run and we're going to figure this shit out. If you want to ignore me for two more days that's fine, but you're going to be bored out of your mind."

He turned to look out the windshield and I noticed a tic thumping in his strong jawline.

"I told you I was ready to talk." I crossed my arms over my chest because I didn't like being ambushed and I hated feeling chastised.

"You also told me you weren't going to bail on me again and that's exactly what you did this week."

It was true and I couldn't deny it.

"I just needed a minute, Rowdy. I didn't go anywhere. I was here the entire time."

He swore and cut me a hard sidelong look out of the corner of his eye. "You were here but you couldn't have been farther away if you tried."

The SUV pulled onto the interstate and headed north. I watched the city fade into the background and asked him again where we were going.

I could tell he was debating if he wanted to tell me or not just to spite me but eventually his innate kindness won out.

"Phil owned a cabin out in the woods on a private lake in Boulder that he passed on to Nash. Nash keeps it because he can't bear to sell it, and I think he wants to convince Saint to take time off this winter and hide out with him for a week or two since they are both so busy working all the time. He told me I could borrow it for a few days until we get our shit straight. There's no electricity and no modern amenities, so all there is to do is fish, fuck, and talk." He lifted an eyebrow at me with a leer. "I didn't bring any fishing poles."

I looked out the window at the rapidly darkening sky and muttered, "I can't believe my own sister helped you kidnap me."

"Something has to give, Salem. Either we're doing this or we're not, but I have to know one way or the other. Poppy just wants you to be happy. Hell, she just wants *me* to be happy after all this time and the road to that place for both of us runs right through you."

I wasn't sure what to say to that but I did know one thing

that was stunningly, perfectly, absolutely crystal clear to be after the last few days without him. "We are definitely doing this, we just might not be doing it right all of the time, and that road might have a speed bump or two."

At least the tic in his jaw died down after I said that and his hands loosened some on the steering wheel. It must have appeased him some because he turned the radio on and the HorrorPops filled the silence instead of us snapping and griping at each other.

Boulder wasn't really far outside of the city limits, but once we started to head into the mountains and the roads gave way to things that looked like barely there trails, I realized it was going to be well into the night before we got wherever it was we were going. It was still warm enough out that I could roll the window down and listen to the sounds of the forest and smell the things that made Colorado such a beautiful place to be. The pine, the hint of fall in air, the way everything felt so untouched and natural, even the dust the tires kicked up made it feel like someplace I had never been before and was lucky to be now. The night crickets and the call of the animals in the surrounding woods were lulling and almost enough to put me to sleep, but I didn't want to miss any of it. I wasn't a nature girl but the peacefulness and serenity of this place was really welcome after a week spent on the edge of doubt and confusion.

When Rowdy finally stopped over an hour and a half later, I decided calling this place a cabin was being generous. It looked more like a wooden shack in the center of the woods and I would bet my best pair of heels that no woman had ever been inside the ramshackle building. All I could think was that if it looked this bad at night, I really didn't want to see it in the daylight.

Rowdy climbed out of the SUV and took our bags to the stairs and dropped them in front of the door. He moved around to the back of the vehicle as I climbed down out of it and I watched as he muscled out a big cooler and went to deposit it by the rest of the stuff. He looked at me questioningly, so I sighed and delicately made my way to where he was waiting, careful not to break an ankle on the uneven ground in my tall heels.

"I'm not exactly dressed for this, Rowland."

He smirked at me and got the door open and ushered me inside the tiny space. I almost turned around and ran back out the door. There was nothing there. Four walls, a wood-burning stove, no lights shining, which led to everything being cast in creepy shadows. A beat-up chair that looked like it had dropped from the back of a garbage truck and an old-style army cot were the only furnishings. I balked and turned to tell him flatly, "I'm not sleeping on the floor and there better not be bats."

He laughed out loud and hauled all of our stuff inside. He disappeared to the back of the SUV again and brought in a giant Rubbermaid container that he set down by me with a thud. He popped it open and pulled out a couple of lanterns that he lit up right away and an air mattress that had an adapter to blow it up off the cigarette lighter in the car. He also produced several blankets and offered to let me dig through the supplies he brought to find something to eat.

There was plenty of beer, some bottles of water, and stuff for sandwiches and breakfast. I had to give it to him, he was superprepared for this venture.

Once he muscled the inflated air mattress back inside and made up the makeshift bed, he kicked off his cowboy boots and flopped on his back to stare at the ceiling. He put his hands behind his head and just lay there in silence, so I took my own shoes off, grabbed a couple of beers, and went over to join him. I set the cans on the floor and sat next to his hip on the squishy bed.

"How are you going to survive not having junk to put in your hair for a couple of days?" I playfully poked at the slicked-up blond strands.

He caught my arm in his hand and brought it down to put a kiss on my fluttering pulse on the underside of my wrist. He lifted an eyebrow and tilted his chin down so he could look at me.

"I brought my cowboy hat."

Oh, sweet baby Jesus, we needed to make up real quick, then. I reached out so I could trace the line of one of his golden eyebrows.

"I'm sorry you felt like you had to go to such an extreme just to talk about our relationship. That isn't right and it isn't fair to you. I was just freaking out and I know I didn't handle it correctly."

His chest rose and fell as he exhaled loudly. He caught my hand and used it to pull me over him so that I was lying across his broad chest.

"It's not the freak-out or the way you handled it that worries me. It's the fact that you felt like you *had* to freak out in the first place. I know the whole Poppy thing is tricky and uncomfortable, but I think I have it figured out now. But even if I didn't, it has been you for months now, Salem. I just don't get how you can't know that."

He brushed his fingers through my hair and it felt so good I wanted to purr like a cat and rub up against him.

"I don't know. I guess it's the same as me telling you I'm here because you're here and that means I'm not leaving and yet you still look at me all the time like I'm going to vanish into thin air. We can *know* one thing, Rowdy, but our heart holds on to something else."

"I don't want it to hold on to that anymore. I just want it to hold on to you."

I squeezed my eyes shut and had to swallow around how happy and terrified his words made me.

"Yeah?"

He nodded and his chin rubbed against the top of my head. "Yeah."

"We just need to let everything go. We have to trust each other if we're going to be together. I missed you this week and so did Jimbo."

He yawned so loud I heard his jaw crack and he squeezed me closer. "I'm older now and a lot bigger than you. Getting away isn't going to be as easy as it once was, Salem. I'm not going to let you run anymore."

He sounded so sure, and for the first time since this all started between us I just believed. I believed in him. I believed in me and I believed in this thing between us having enough legs to be real and forever because that was what fate, and maybe something bigger than fate, wanted for both of us.

"I'm not looking to get away, Rowdy."

I was expecting some kind of clever comeback, one of his off-the-cuff quips, but all I got was a steady rise and fall of that strong chest and his breath moving my hair as he breathed in and out above my head. The big jerk had fallen asleep on me.

I sighed and wiggled off of him so that I could wrestle his legs up on the air mattress so that he would be more comfortable. I couldn't blame him. It was a challenging drive after a full day of work and I'm sure his week hadn't been any better than mine. I was bummed out that his crashing out early shot all my visions of playing sexy cowgirl on top of him with no one around to hear me scream in pleasure all to hell.

Slightly put out, I dug around in the bag my sister packed until I found a pair of yoga pants and a tank to sleep in. I made a PB&J for dinner and tried to send Poppy a text to make sure she took Jimbo out before bed but was further disgruntled to find that this far out in the woods there was no service. I killed an hour and then decided all there was to do was curl up next to Rowdy and try to sleep, so I shut down the lanterns and curled up next to him as close as I could. His massive frame took up most of the available space.

I listened to the lulling sounds of the forest and the

night. I listened to Rowdy's rhythmic breathing and sighed when he wrapped his arm around me in his sleep and hauled me tightly to his side.

I realized it really was all about where I had ended up and not where I had been, because as long as he was there, wherever that happened to be was going to be where I was supposed to be at as well.

Even if that place was some forgotten cabin in the Colorado mountains.

CHAPTER 15

Rowdy

IT WAS THE FIRST full night of sleep that I had gotten since she walked away from me earlier in the week. I don't know what woke me up before dawn, maybe the fact the air mattress was sagging in the middle or the call of the birds in the pine trees, but something had my eyes popping open before it was even light out. I automatically reached for the body that was supposed to be curled up alongside mine and jerked up into a sitting position when I came up empty.

The cabin was tiny, so it was easy to see I was alone and I couldn't for the life of me figure out where my city girl would've gotten off to before the sun was even in the sky. I mean there was no bathroom, the place was beyond rustic, but I didn't think Salem was the type to go tromping through the woods without letting me know where she was going or waking me up to hold the flashlight for her. So I pushed my messy hair off my face, pulled my boots on, and went to find her.

It didn't take long. The cabin was in a clearing that sat

on a crystal-clear lake that was fed from runoff from the mountains. The area was a national forest and the land that wasn't part of it was privately owned by guys like Phil that just wanted a quiet escape from the city. This wasn't a lake that allowed anything with a motor on the water, but there was still a weather-beaten dock for rowboats and kayaks jutting out from the rough shoreline. Salem was sitting on the end with her legs dangling over the side, a blanket wrapped around her shoulders while she watched the first rays of dawn break across the sky. When I got closer I noticed she had an open beer in her hand and a soft smile on her beautiful face. If I had had paper and something to draw with, I would have captured the moment for posterity.

I sat down behind her and trapped her between my longer legs and wrapped an arm across her chest to pull her back so that she was resting against my chest.

"Breakfast of champions." I took the beer from her and took a swig, making a face as I did. It was too early for Coors Light, but whatever.

"I couldn't figure out how to turn the little stove thing on."

I'd brought a camp stove up so we could have breakfast and coffee but I hadn't bothered to hook the propane up to it. Good thing. She probably would have blown us up messing with it. Beer was a poor substitute for coffee this early in the morning, though.

"You're up early." I linked our fingers together on one hand and rested my chin on the top of her head. There was nothing like sunrise and sunset in the mountains. The entire sky turned orange and red and looked like flames racing across the jagged peaks.

"It was quiet and it's never quiet. I wanted to enjoy it for a minute. I don't think I've ever seen anything so pretty."

"Me either." Granted, I was talking about her and she knew it, because she laughed and it made her soft hair brush against my chin.

"Rowdy . . ."

"Salem . . ."

It was such a nice moment, one that had taken us so long to get to. I couldn't think of any place on earth that was better than this. And I knew for a fact that there wasn't any better girl.

"You make me very happy, you always did." It was all there in her voice. The way that the past and the future were all tangled around each other but still had us standing strong and together right in the middle of it.

I blew out a deep breath and took the can of beer from her and set it down so I could turn her around in my arms so that we were facing each other. She wrapped her legs around my waist and curled her arms around my neck as we stared at each other. The blanket fell away and she shivered as the cool morning air brushed across her shoulders. I collected her ebony hair in one hand and used it to tug her head back so that she was looking up at me with sleepy and sexy eyes.

"I always thought it was the firsts that matter, but now I know that it's the lasts that stay with you."

Her mouth puckered into a little frown of confusion and I bent down to kiss that ruby above her lip. She shivered again and this time I knew it didn't have anything to do with the chill in the air.

"I believed for a long time that I was never going to get past the first girl that made me feel like I was in love. I used it as an excuse to keep other women at an arm's length because I was terrified of being hurt again. I was afraid, I still am, but I realize that the fact I want to be with you, that I care so much about you, means so much more than the fear."

She sighed and moved one of her hands to rest in on my cheek. "I don't want you to be afraid of me, Rowdy."

"You were and have been the source of a lot of firsts for me, Salem. The first girl I kissed. The first girl I ever cried in front of. The first girl I ever gave a present to. The first I never forgot. You're the first girl that has ever kept me up at night and the first girl that makes me hurt badly with the way I want you. Looking back, I think when you drove away that day you took a piece of me with you that I didn't get back until I saw you at the shop. All of those firsts are important and made me see things more clearly without the filter of time and resentment in the way, but what really matters is the lasts."

I bent down so I could kiss her. I just pressed my lips lightly against her parted mouth and whispered to her, "You are the last person I want to kiss. The last woman I want in my bed. I want you to be the last girl that touches any and all parts of me, Salem, and that means so much more than a first. Who cares if Poppy was there first or if there were nameless people in between? All that matters is that at the end of it all there is just you, only you, and no one else."

She didn't say anything for a long time. Her dark eyes were so deep and fathomless it made it hard to read what was going on inside her head. She rubbed her thumb up and down along one of my sideburns and then leaned forward to return the same kind of soft and sweet kiss I had just given her.

"It took me a long time to get here, Rowdy. It's where I was always supposed to be. This is my final destination, so at the end there is just you and only you as well. The journey in the middle shaped both of us, there is no denying it, but I like being your last . . . just as long as I can keep surprising you with some firsts along the way."

I laughed because that was typical Salem. Nothing could ever be just good enough. We could be together, would love each other, end up together, but she was always going to want it to be new, challenging, and surprising. That was one of the main reasons I had never been able to get past her and never would.

"I've been around the block. Not too many firsts left." It was the truth but she had managed to pull one or two out in the months we had been together.

One of her jet-black eyebrows shot up and she smiled impishly at me. "Is that a challenge?"

I laughed again because I was happy. Really, truly happy for the first time since she left when I was fifteen. "It can be."

I almost melted when her dark gaze switched to something sizzling and hot. The arm she had wrapped around my neck tightened, pulling me closer to her, and she traced her fingertip across the outside edge of my mouth.

"Have you ever had sex outside by a lake while the sun is coming up after drinking Coors Light for breakfast?"

I nudged my hands under the edge of her tank top so I could hold on to her waist as I leaned over and flattened her beneath me on the discarded blanket she had brought outside with her. She parted her legs for me and I trapped her face between my palms so I could kiss her with everything that had been missing from my life for the week we had been apart. I wasn't ever doing that again, being apart, and she needed to be able to feel that.

"Nope. The only one of those things I have ever done before is have Coors Light for breakfast."

She laughed and it pushed her chest into mine. I felt her nipples bead up against the thin fabric of her top. I wanted it out of my way.

"I've seen your fridge, so that doesn't surprise me. Let me be your first and last, Rowdy . . . and you can be mine."

I let her kiss me again and helped her yank my shirt off over my head. Goose bumps raced across my skin as the mountain air hit naked flesh.

"First and last, Salem." I practically groaned the words at her because she was wiggling out of her tank top without separating where we were pressed together, so each little strip of bare skin she revealed rubbed and pressed enticingly against my own.

She smiled at me and it made my dick twitch painfully behind the fly of my jeans. "If you think I'm coming to the middle of nowhere in the woods and getting busy with anyone else, then you're insane. You are the only person in the entire universe I would ever want to get naked with in a place like this." She got her hands on the button of my jeans and told me matter-of-factly, "I pretty much want to get naked with you whenever and wherever."

I sucked in a breath as the backs of her fingers rubbed against the aroused length of my cock. "Good to know."

She muttered something I couldn't hear through the river of blood rushing between my ears and the hammering of my heart as she used the pad of her thumb to rub all across the head of my erection between the multiple piercings that decorated the sensitive surface. "The feeling is absolutely mutual, just so you know." I sounded gruff and slightly strangled.

She chuckled low in her throat and gave the heavy shaft a tight squeeze. "You don't say?"

Enough of the playful banter. She had left me alone for almost a solid week and I had been twisting myself up over her and this thing we had. It was well past time that she just *knew* it was her for me and no other would ever do.

While she was busy sliding her fist up and down and then back again, I reared up enough to slide her legs out of her stretchy pants so that she was all creamy, bronze skin and wild dark hair and eyes. I loved the pops of color that decorated her skin, loved the way she wore her life like badges captured in art on her body. I loved that when I touched her, when I put my hands on her tattoos, it looked like our colors just bled into one another. We became one giant painting of swirling colors and heated skin. She was a perfect work of art in more ways than one.

I sucked one of her pierced nipples into my mouth and used my teeth on the hard, metal ring. It made her arch her back up off the dock and she reflexively squeezed my dick at the pleasure-pain of the action. It made me groan against her now-damp flesh and had me tightening my fist in her hair where I was using it to brace myself above her on the rickety wood.

She was working my jeans down around the curve of my ass and still working my cock up and down. I thought the top of my head might blow off with every flick of her wrist. I moved over to the other breast to lick and suck until she was writhing under me and had curled her legs up around my hips. She finally let go of my dick and shoved both her hands into my hair so she could jerk my mouth up to her own. She arched up against me and her wet center brushed erotically across the eager tip of my erection. Her arousal dotted the metal studs that were rubbing against her outer lips in sexy, slippery moisture and it made both of us gasp through the kiss.

Her tongue skated along the ridge of my lower lip and she told me with desire-laced humor, "You have so much gunk in your hair I'm never getting my hands back."

She wiggled her digits in the messy strands and I laughed. It did take a lot of hair crap to rock a pompadour.

"Good. We can stay like this forever."

I thrust my hips forward just a fraction so that the tip of my arousal just barely parted her folds. She wiggled impatiently against me and her eyes got heavy lidded. She bit her bottom lip and arched her back just enough to draw me another inch inside her hot and welcoming body. She dug her fingernails into my scalp and I followed her silent urges and just let my body meld into hers. She made mewling sounds and her eyes drifted closed as I seated myself inside of her as far as I could go. We really did just fit together like we were a matching set, and every time I was with her like this I felt like it was where I was supposed to be.

Her thighs tensed around my hips and her hands tugged at my hair. She threw her head back and lifted her hips up into mine. I guess the week apart hadn't been easy on her either. She was demanding with her body all the things I wanted to give her anyway. I kissed her again and braced my weight on my forearms that I left caged around her head and rose up on my knees just a little. Thank goodness I still had my jeans halfway on or else I would be picking splinters out of my skin for days. She angled her hips up to match the new position and I felt like I went even deeper inside of her. She was swallowing me up and I never wanted to get free.

Her inner walls started to move, to quiver and flex as I thrust in and out and her hands got more grabby and insistent in my hair. I resisted the urge to just drive into her, to just lose myself in the feel of her body and the peacefulness of the setting. I was trying to imprint on her how important this was to me, how important she was to me, and I couldn't do that if I just dove off the cliff into a sea of pleasure without appreciating the climb to get there.

I freed one of my hands from her tangle of hair and hooked the edge of my thumb under the hoop in the center of her nipple. I tugged on it at the same time I dropped down to nip at her bottom lip with my teeth. It made her move up—hard—against me and I could feel the liquid response where we were joined. She murmured my name and lifted her hips against me so that our pelvises were grinding hard together and I almost lost the steady and smooth rhythm I had been working on. I pulled on the piercing again and her dark eyes snapped open at the same time she gave my hair a rough pull.

"More."

I kissed her along her jaw and sucked her earlobe in between my teeth. "More what?"

She groaned and dug her heels hard into my ass. "More everything."

I was going to tease her, tell her that good things came to those who waited, but she short-circuited my brain and made my dick jump when she freed one of her hands from my hair and the goop in it and managed to get it between us so she could touch herself.

"Shit."

"Ohhhhh . . ." Her eyes drifted back shut and I felt the way her body changed at the added stimulation. She got so tight, burned so hot, I thought the metal cross was going to weld us together in the best way possible.

As much as she was touching herself, her questing fingers kept brushing along the top of my erection as I moved in and out of her. My control split and all I wanted to do was pound into her until we both saw stars and couldn't catch our breath. I let go of her breast and wrapped a hand around her backside so I could hold her up. I thrust into her, let my forehead fall forward so that it was resting against hers, and just let it all go. It was only me and only her. We were connected in ways that spanned time and all the other nonsense that just didn't matter.

She gasped my name and I felt her rush of pleasure coat both of us. It made me swear again, and as her body went slack in my hold and her inner muscles started to loosen around me, I had the freedom to really move. I pushed into her, closed my eyes, and just let go of everything that had been before there was her. I felt her kiss me on the corner of my mouth, felt her hand switch from teasing herself to teasing me by making a circle with her thumb and forefinger and wrapping it around the very base of my cock and squeezing—hard. That was all there was to it. Pleasure snapped and popped along my spine and it was my turn to douse us both in pleasure and wetness. Nothing would ever feel as right as me and her together in this moment.

I collapsed on top of her, all sweaty and spent, and she laughed huskily in my ear. "I'll be your first and last for whatever you want as long as it feels like that."

I turned my head so I could nuzzle her ear and told her, "And I'll make you happy as long as I possibly can if this is what it feels like."

It had taken us a long time to get here but really all of it was worth it in the end if this is what the destination looked like. Thank God I'd had Phil there to put both of us on the right track. I owed him more than my life and the way he had fostered the art in my soul. I owed him my future and everything that was tied up in this woman that I felt like I needed in order to keep living. Phil had taken care of me in the most significant ways possible just like Nash told me he was doing. Phil Donovan wanted his family safe and loved, and putting Salem squarely in my path was his last gift to me before he had passed on. Clever bastard.

WE SPENT THE REST of the day just hanging out together. I got the camp stove together and made real breakfast and instant coffee. We put all the things still lingering between us to rest. I told her that I would stop obsessing about her packing a bag and running off on me if she would stop trying to put me back in a place where she thought I was in love with her sister. I think we were both realistic enough to understand that nothing was perfect and we were bound to run into roadblocks in the future but being together was worth the work it was going to take.

She spent well over an hour after seeing me walk around for most of the day wearing nothing but jeans, boots, and that lucky cowboy hat trying to tell me that I should be on a calendar for the shop. She told me if I could get Nash and Rule to agree, as well as the other guys, Jet, Rome, and Asa, the thing would fly off the shelves. She told me she would call it *The Marked Men* and it would make so much money we could retire if we wanted. I just rolled my eyes at her and tried to change the subject but I could see the wheels turning in her head and Salem was nothing if not persistent.

Poppy had packed her a pair of flip-flops, so we walked around the lake and then took a nap early in the afternoon.

I woke up with her mouth around my dick and her tongue doing delicious things. We learned the hard way that the air mattress wasn't intended for that kind of extracurricular activity. After a pretty rough round of sex on the cabin floor, we made the executive decision that we had done enough damage to nature and it was time to head back to the city early. She had a bunch of stuff she wanted to take care of now that some stock had arrived for the store, so I packed up and agreed it would be nice to spend the night back in a comfortable bed. Plus I missed the dog and I think she really wanted to check in on her sister.

We were just getting into the city limits of Boulder when both of our phones suddenly got service again. Salem's dinged with a few missed messages but mine blew the fuck up. Jet had called no less than twenty times and I had ten missed text messages from him. I frowned and called him back even though I didn't like to be on the phone while I was on the interstate.

When he answered he sounded like he was in the middle of a crowd.

"Where the fuck have you been all day?"

I scowled and looked at Salem, who had obviously heard Jet's raised voice.

"I was at Phil's cabin with Salem. We had some stuff we needed to work out and needed some space to do it. What the hell is going on?"

"I'm trying to get on a plane out of Boston to get back to Denver, but there's fog and nothing is getting off the fucking ground." He growled something I couldn't make out and told me, "I need you to take care of my girl for me. Asa got arrested last night and I know she's about to lose it."

"What!" I was so shocked the car swerved a little and Salem shouted my name. I apologized to her and pulled over onto the shoulder so I could focus on what Jet was telling me. "What happened?"

"I don't know for sure. Ayden didn't even find out from him. Royal called her." He sighed and I could just picture him pacing and shoving his hands through his messy, black hair. "She's the one that took him in."

"You've got to be kidding me."

"I wish I was. All I know is my wife is there and I'm here and it's a bunch of bullshit. I need you to make sure she's okay."

"Of course. We'll be back in the city in just a few. She'll be my first stop."

"Thank you."

"Of course. For what it's worth, I think Asa is a good dude. I really think he's turned it around."

Jet swore again. "I thought so, too, but I'm not surprised by anything that guy does anymore. I gotta go. I gotta figure out a way home. Thanks, man."

I hung up and just stared at my phone for a second. I looked at Salem and shook my head. "Royal arrested Asa last night."

She bit her lip. "For what?"

"Jet didn't know. He's worried Ayden is freaking out over it."

She nodded. "I bet. Hold on a sec. I'm gonna text Saint.

She and Royal are attached at the hip. She probably has the insider info."

I lifted an eyebrow at her. "You don't think Ayden would have tried that already."

She shrugged. "Maybe."

I pulled back into traffic after sending Ayden a text saying I was headed her way. It was a solid ten minutes before Salem's phone pinged and then pinged again.

"Assault. Some kids came into the police station and lodged a complaint against him. She says one was pretty busted up and claimed that he went back to the bar to apologize for some ruckus he and his buddies caused and Asa jumped him in the parking lot." She frowned and looked up at me. "Aren't there cameras at the Bar?"

"Not outside. Shit. I bet I know exactly who those kids are."

"You do?"

"Yeah. There was this group of punks in the bar the other day while I was there and they were giving Asa a really hard time. He let it go but kicked them out and the one kid told him he would regret it. It wouldn't be hard to find out Asa has a record and claiming something like assault means the cops would have to pick him up." I tightened my hands on the steering wheel. "Son of a bitch."

"You need to tell Royal."

"We need to get him a lawyer." I looked at her out of the corner of my eye. "His history is pretty nasty. It won't look good in front of any judge."

"Well, you were a witness and if there are cameras inside the bar you can prove this kid has some kind of vendetta and . . ." She paused and reached out to put her hand on my thigh. "If you need to get him a lawyer, I know someone we can ask to help with that."

She was talking about Sayer. Good God, could the rest of this day get any more out of hand.

"She does family law. We need a criminal lawyer."

"She's smart and she cares about you. If you ask her for help I have no doubt she will find you the best criminal attorney in the state. You have to give her a chance, Rowdy. Just like you did for me. We both came here for you, you're the one that has to open the door to let us in."

I didn't want to because once that door was open I would never be able to slam it closed again and the sexy brunette in the passenger seat was living proof of that. The more people that I let in, the more people I had to risk losing later on down the road, but for Ayden and for Jet I would just have to suck it up.

"Call her." I gritted the words out between my teeth and raced toward D-town to try and pull Asa's ass out of the fire.

CHAPTER 16

Salem

IT WAS HARD TO tell who was more anxious as we sat in Sayer's office as brother and sister stared at each other across her fancy desk. Rowdy couldn't sit still and Sayer kept clearing her throat and twisting her fingers together nervously.

"He didn't do it. That punk kid set him up." Rowdy was adamant and his tone was hard.

Sayer was trying to be impartial in a very lawyerly way, but I could see she wanted to fight this battle for him. "That may be, but Asa has an extensive record with some pretty nasty stuff on it, and with a corroborating witness the charges against him will be hard to refute."

Rowdy raked his hands through his hair and cast pleading eyes in her direction.

"What about the surveillance tapes inside of the bar?" I asked the question hoping it would help calm him down.

"The owner, Rome, pulled them and is sending them over. I really think the best bet is to post Asa's bond and hire him an attorney. The police report from the patrol unit that took him down to the station stated that it looked like he had indeed been in a fight. His hands were busted up and he had blood and scratches on his face."

"Those little shits probably jumped him and set him up. I'm telling you I was there. This kid was a nightmare and just looking to start something. He was pissed right the hell off that Asa kicked him out of the bar."

I reached out and grabbed Rowdy's wildly flailing hand and pulled him over to my side. He was practically vibrating with the intensity of being this close to Sayer and the stress of the situation with Asa. Ayden was already at the precinct trying to bail her brother out and Jet had finally managed to get on a plane, but he was still four hours away from home. Rowdy had offered to go to the police station with Ayden, but she was more worried about getting him represented than she was about getting him out of lockup. She said getting him out eventually was the easy part, getting someone to represent him, someone that could prove he was innocent, was the tricky part, so she had tasked Rowdy with that chore. Personally I thought she wanted her brother to know that she was the one specifically bailing him. There was bad blood there and Ayden needed Asa to know she was standing by him even if she hadn't always done that.

"I get that, and the fact you can attest to that, as well as the rest of the patrons in the bar during the event, is very helpful to Asa's case, but it's still an uphill battle. Asa's record and the fact he didn't defend himself, just went quietly with the police and never argued against the arrest makes him look bad—really bad. Innocent people don't generally surrender to the police that easily. On top of that, the kid that lodged the complaint and pressed the charges is as squeaky-clean as they come. He doesn't even have a speeding ticket."

Rowdy growled and sat on the edge of his chair. Sayer's blue eyes were sympathetic, and deep down I think Rowdy appreciated she wasn't just throwing sunshine at him because it was what he wanted to hear.

"So what do we do now?"

She cocked her head to the side and considered the two of us thoughtfully. "There is this guy, Quaid Jackson, and I know firsthand that he's a barracuda. I've never had to work with him directly since he's a criminal attorney, but his reputation is vicious. No one wants to go up against him in court." She smiled a little bit and reached for her phone. "One of the other partners represented him in his divorce a few months ago. The wife was a real piece of work. The firm saved Quaid from having to pay over three grand a month in maintenance payments to her. Let me give him a call and see if he can help your friend out."

Rowdy let out a breath he must have been holding for a while and reached out his hand to wrap it around the back of my neck. I leaned into his touch and patted his thigh reassuringly. I was the one that had called Sayer to set up this meeting, but now that we were here I could see some of the reservations and coldness Rowdy had walked in with thawing around him. Sayer hadn't judged, hadn't assumed the worst based on what Asa looked like on paper. All she cared about was trying to help her brother's friend out because he was in some serious trouble and she was in a position to try and fix it.

Her conversation with the other attorney was brief and cut right to the chase. She laid out what the other guy would be facing and then frowned at whatever his response was. They went back and forth for a few more minutes and then Sayer stated flatly, "The cost isn't an issue, Quaid. Keeping an innocent man out of jail is." I felt Rowdy's fingers flex involuntarily around my neck and I looked up at him in concern. He looked back down at me and I was surprised to see a little grin pulling around his mouth.

"She's tough."

"And pretty. Just like you." He rolled his eyes at me but bent so he could brush his lips across the crown of my head.

Sayer hung up the phone and grinned at us in a way that could only be described as victorious. "He's in. I knew he couldn't resist the challenge."

Rowdy cleared his throat. "He sounds expensive."

I knew everyone would pitch in and help out to cover the cost if need be but Sayer just shook her head. "He's going to do it as a favor to the firm. All the client will have to cover is the typical retainer he charges, which is five grand."

Five grand was still a lot of money but it was totally doable.

"Thank you so much, Sayer." I wanted to hug her.

The blonde nodded at me and her attention shifted to Rowdy. She took a deep breath and let it out slowly. "I know it's not the reason you're here but I feel like it would be remiss of me not to mention that you have a substantial inheritance at your fingertips if you need it."

I felt Rowdy jerk a little next to me and the leg I was holding on to went rock hard under my fingers.

"I . . ." He trailed off and I saw his head sort of drop. "I can't think about that right now. I appreciate you helping us out and riding to the rescue, but trying to get my head around the money and you . . ." He shrugged. "I don't know that I'm ready for that just yet."

Sayer smiled a little sadly. "I understand. I guess as long as there is an option for you to get your head around it at some point, I can wait—and I will."

He cleared his throat again and got to his feet. He walked over to the desk and stuck his hand out to her so that she could shake it. Seeing the two of them next to each other like that . . . there was no denying they were related. They looked so strikingly similar, except for the classic elegance that Sayer possessed and the delicate femininity of her features, there was no missing the fact they were brother and sister.

"I'm sorry I acted like such an asshole when you told me who you were. I don't do so great with surprises."

I saw her squeeze his hand. "Don't worry about it. I took a swing at my dad's lawyer and called him a liar when he broke the news to me. I understand it's a lot to take in."

He nodded and took a step back toward me. "You seem like a really nice person, Sayer. Half sister or not, you didn't deserve to have that bomb dropped on you like that any more than I did. It was a shitty thing to do to both of us."

Sayer snorted and got to her feet behind the fancy desk and took a few steps around the side. "Dad was a pretty shitty guy." She lifted her chin a little and changed the sub-ject as she told us, "They never moved Asa out of the lockup at the city precinct. He's probably still there until his sister posts his bond. You can probably catch up with them if you head that way now."

Rowdy nodded and thanked her again. I scooted around him and wrapped my arms around her. "Thank you."

She hugged me back. "Of course." She looked over my head where I was sure Rowdy was watching our exchange.

"I told you he would get there."

"I think your friend with the shady past might've sped the process up."

I laughed a little and let her go. "Well, they do say every-thing happens for a reason."

"I guess so. Good luck. Call me if you need any more help. Quaid is the best in the business but I'm always avail-able if you need me."

"You're amazing." Rowdy's voice was soft and there was a wealth of emotion coloring it. He took my hand as we left the law building and made our way back up toward Capitol Hill, where the downtown police station was lo-cated. It actually wasn't too far away from the Marked, and the closer we got, the tenser and more agitated Rowdy seemed to get.

Spotting Ayden as soon as we entered the doors was easy as could be. She was pacing back and forth in a frantic matter, the heels of her red cowboy boots clicking on the li-noleum floor. She jerked her head up when Rowdy called her name and then flew into his arms with enough force that it rocked him back a few steps. The poor girl looked exhausted and harried, but over all of that she looked furious.

"Asa didn't do this." Her golden eyes gleamed with such certainty that if I had had any questions about Asa's innocence before, Ayden's zealous faith in her brother was enough to squash them.

"I know, Ayd. I was there the night the kid started shit with him. I think he set Asa up."

Ayden pushed her hands through her dark hair and pulled at it in frustration. "Asa has gotten into all kinds of trouble since he could walk, but he isn't stupid. He wouldn't put the bar or Rome at risk like that." She gulped. "When I accused him of being involved in that robbery a while back and he shut down, pulled away from me, I knew . . . he wants to be here and he's changed. I can't believe this is happening all over again."

Rowdy ran his hand up and down her back soothingly. "We'll get it figured out, Ayd. We got him a lawyer that doesn't mess around and there were plenty of witnesses there that can give statements to the fact that it was the kid that started harassing Asa not the other way around."

Ayden barked out a bitter-sounding laugh and started pacing again. "All I can keep thinking is what would've happened if I was in Austin when this happened? Who would be here to get him out? Who would be here to believe that he was innocent? It's making my heart hurt and stomach turn over and over."

I could see she was spinning herself out of control and Rowdy was at a loss as to how to get her back on track. I stepped around him and grabbed her wrists to pull her hands out of her hair.

"Ayden, breathe for a second." Her whiskey-colored eyes flashed at me and for a split second I thought she was going to take a swing at me, but she did what I said and took a series of deep breaths and I noticed her hands unclenched. "We're here. We know he didn't do this and we are ready to help him fight to prove it. He won't be alone."

"I've been here for over three hours waiting for them to bring him out. It gave me too much time to remember what this is like. Seeing your brother or anyone you love in handcuffs sucks."

"I know, honey, but this time trouble found him, he didn't go looking for it. That might happen from time to time and it wouldn't matter if you are here, in Austin, or on the moon. Your brother just has that way about him."

I wasn't lying to her. It was there in Asa's wicked grin and effortless charm. Boys that pretty and that smooth were bound to end up in hot water from time to time even if they were actively trying to avoid it.

I think she was going to say something back, but just then Rowdy called her name as Royal and a man also in a dark blue police uniform guided Ayden's brother to where we were waiting. Royal wouldn't meet Ayden's gaze, so she settled on looking at me. I could see in her dark eyes a hundred different levels of turmoil as she said, "Sorry it took so long. Getting the paperwork together took longer than it should have." She sighed. "You're lucky they let you bail him out without having to go in front of a judge first."

Ayden gasped and Rowdy swore when Asa stepped around the police officers and the damage to his face became clear. One of his eyes was swollen entirely shut, his lips were puffy and swollen, and there was a gash across his chin that looked gory and nasty. It looked like it probably could have used a stitch or two to hold it shut.

"Oh my God, Asa! Are you okay?"

He caught Ayden before she could plow into him the way she had done to Rowdy and then winced when she hugged him too tightly.

"I've been better."

"You need to go to a doctor, or let Saint look at you." She sounded like she was going to cry.

"Naw, it's nothing that won't wash off." His eyes flicked over to Rowdy and they exchanged some kind of guy look that clearly communicated he was in way more pain than he was letting on. "Thanks for getting me out, Ayd."

That was what sent her over the edge. Big fat tears started rolling off her inky lashes, and even though it obviously pained him to do so, Asa pulled her closer to hug.

"It's fine."

"Why didn't you tell them you didn't do it?" Rowdy asked the question to Asa, but he was looking at Royal and I saw her wince. Her partner scowled at the lot of us and crossed his arms over his beefy chest.

Asa didn't answer but he looked over his sister's head right at Royal. The two of them had a weird stare-off until her partner obviously got sick of it and instructed all of us, "He has a court date in a few days. Try and keep him out of trouble until then." He made a face. "Next time I doubt so many people will be willing to pull strings to spring him loose so quickly."

He nudged Royal as he turned to walk away. She bit down on her lower lip and looked at me somewhat pleadingly. How I became the ally I wasn't sure, but I didn't hold anything against her. She was normally so full of fire and sass it was odd seeing her sort of reserved and almost apologetic.

"I was just doing my job." It was a job she loved and was good at. I knew that even though I had only spent a handful of hours in her company.

"We all know that, Royal." I was trying to reassure her but her gaze had locked on to Asa and I don't think she was talking to the rest of us at all.

Ayden pulled away from her brother and looked at the redhead balefully. "I can't believe you tossed him in a jail cell with his face looking like that and kept him overnight."

I saw a pink flush race up Royal's throat and she opened her mouth to defend herself, but Asa cut it all short.

"Stop. If I was someone else, someone better to begin with, none of us would even be here. I used to know better than to underestimate a slick kid with a lot of hate and entitlement. Leave the pretty cop alone, Ayd. She even apologized when she put the cuffs on me last night." He winked at Royal out of his good eye. "Let's get out of here. I don't need to spend any more time in a police station than necessary." He smirked, at least I think that's what it was supposed to be, but considering the current mangled state of his handsome face, it was hard to tell. "Even if they are like a second home by now."

Ayden gritted her teeth and told him, "You're not funny," as she hurried to apologize to Royal for biting her head off.

We were all ready to be anywhere but here, so I gladly followed Rowdy as he headed toward the front doors of the station. Ayden was right on my heels and I didn't miss hearing Asa tell Royal before he followed us, "It's a shame, Red, you, me, and handcuffs could be a whole lot of fun in a different context." Only Asa would be throwing out lines while he looked like crap and still smelled like jail and dried blood.

I thought I saw Royal blush again and I know for sure I saw her jaw drop open just a little bit, and immediately thought they were both asking for trouble. Asa was a careless flirt and obviously not going to be interested in a girl that had arrested him. If he was, it was all about the game and revenge for a guy like him. Royal was lively and full of spirit, but I had seen the hint of vulnerability in her when she walked the sexy southerner out to us, and a guy like Asa would devour that, and her, if he got the opportunity. I thought it was probably for the best her badge and gun were enough to keep him from seeing how gorgeous and wonderful she was underneath them.

It was well into the night by the time everything was all said and done. Ayden was arguing with Asa about going to the ER or at least letting her to ask Saint to give him a once-over, and Rowdy took a call from Jet letting him know he had just landed at DIA. It had been a long, exhausting day and hadn't ended at all the way I expected after my super-sexy morning on the dock with Rowdy.

We were back in his SUV headed toward my apartment when he reached over and grabbed my hand and pulled the back of it up to his lips. He kissed it lightly and then put it down on his thigh.

"Thanks for sticking with me today. That was rough."

I curled my fingers into the denim. "Of course. It was rough, but it could have been way worse. You have good people on your side and so does Asa."

His teeth flashed white in the dark shadows of the car. "I have you on my side. I forgot how much that made me feel like I could do whatever I needed to do, whatever I wanted to do."

That made warmth rush all the way through me. "Oh stop it. You have an amazing group of friends and family here. It's really touching the way you all just rally around each other and take care of one another." I sighed a little as emotion welled up inside of me. "You found your family tree, Rowdy, and the branches are stronger and sturdier than most people with blood relatives have."

"Yeah." His tone dropped to a lower timbre. "It's the one time in my life I can actually say I feel like luck was on my side. I was lucky to end up here." He looked at me in the darkness and I could see the blue of his eyes burning hot. "I also feel pretty lucky you found me after all this time."

I shifted in my seat as emotion welled up in my throat. "I didn't even know I was looking for you, but as soon as I saw your picture on the website when Nash called to offer me the job, I felt like that was exactly what I had been doing for ten years . . . looking for you."

It was a somber conversation, and on the tail of such an emotionally draining day, it left us both spent. When we got to my apartment Rowdy walked me to the door, spent ten minutes wrestling around on the ground with Jimbo, and chitchatted briefly with Poppy while I chewed her out for being on his team instead of mine. As much as I wanted him to spend the night so I cuddle up into that big body and just unwind, I think we both knew it wasn't in the cards for tonight.

He kissed me before he left and it was almost enough to make me tackle him and drag him into my bedroom, and it wasn't until he was gone and I shut and locked the door that I realized I had made out with him in front of my sister and hadn't even worried about it a little bit.

I flopped down on the couch next to her and grunted as the rapidly growing ball of fur that was Jimbo plopped his heavy body across my legs.

"I'm in love with him. Like real and forever." The words rushed out and I wasn't even sure that was what I had intended to say to her, definitely not before saying it to him. Poppy nudged me with her shoulder.

"Duh. You think I would have helped him abduct you if I didn't know that? You were miserable this entire week and for no reason. I want you to be happy and in love, and the only person you've ever felt that way with was Rowdy."

I threw my head back against the cushions and scratched Jimbo hard between his floppy ears.

"For something that sounds so easy, why does it seem to be so hard? Like why can I just blurt it out to you but the idea of telling him makes me want to hurl?"

She rested her head next to mine. "I don't have the answer to that, but I wish I did. Love is complicated and can hurt so much."

"You aren't going back to Loveless, are you, Poppy?" She couldn't. I don't think I would let her even if she was an adult and in charge of her own life.

"Eventually."

I gasped and turned to glare at her. "No way!"

"Calm down, Salem. I just meant I have to go back and get my stuff. I'm not sure how to do that and not have an ugly showdown with Oliver, but yeah, I need to go back to show him and Dad I'm not afraid and that what they did is wrong."

"Well, I'm going to go with you, then. You aren't going to face either of those assholes alone."

"It was a fight I should have fought a long time ago. Just like you did." She was quiet for a long minute and then told me in a soft and broken-sounding voice, "I love you, Salem."

"Back atcha, Poppy."

I had spent the day surrounded by love, spent it watching family of all different kinds of relations fight for each other and help one another. It made me realize how alone and solitary my life on the move had really been all these years. I was just starting to build a family tree of my own and it wasn't surprising at all that the roots of it rested at

Rowdy's booted feet. He had always been the one single constant in my life even when miles and memories separated us.

I could stomach the idea of returning to a place I had sworn I would never set foot in again only because I knew he was where I would be going back to. He would always be my lighthouse, guiding me home through any kind of storm, just like that sprawling tattoo on his chest said.

CHAPTER 17

Rowdy

I WAS NERVOUS WALKING into the Bar. I think I had asked her to meet me here instead of one of the classier, more upscale places in LoDo to try and put us on more equal footing and I was never one to squander the home-field advantage.

I was early by a good twenty minutes, but the longer I sat around thinking about sitting down with her one-on-one, the closer I was to talking myself out of doing it. So when I entered the dark interior of the Bar on that Friday night two weeks after Asa's run-in with the law, I was relieved and surprised to see Rule sitting at the bar talking to Rome. The Archer brothers were bound to keep my mind off my own little reunion that I had on the schedule for the night. I should have manned up and approached Sayer and had this powwow a month ago, but I just now was able to think about talking to her without wanting to bolt in the opposite direction.

I took a seat next to Rule and clapped him on the shoulder as Rome lifted his scarred eyebrow at me.

"Where's your lady?"

My lady . . . I would never get sick of hearing Salem referred to as mine. "She's with Saint and Royal helping Saint pack."

It seemed like it had taken forever to get Nash's girl to agree to move in with him, and now that she had he was wasting no time in getting her and her belongings under his roof for good.

"I'm actually meeting someone else for a drink."

Both the brothers turned to me, and if it was possible to burst into flames or be frozen on the spot from the disapproval in both pairs of blue eyes, I would have been a dead man. I held up my hands in surrender from all the disapproval and shook my head.

"No. Not like that. Jeez, have you met Salem? She would cut my balls off and feed them to me if I was screwing around on her." I lifted up my own eyebrow and curled my hands on the edge of the bar. "I found out a few weeks ago that the guy that contributed the other half of my DNA was out there all along and knew about me. His daughter—my half sister—found out about me after he died and left me half of her inheritance. She tracked me down and has been trying to get to know me for a couple months. She's actually the one that found the lawyer for Asa."

Rome let out a low whistle and turned to get me a beer. "That's some straight-up soap-opera shit right there."

Rule and I both laughed. "Tell me about it." I shoved Rule on the shoulder hard enough that he almost toppled off the bar stool. "Why aren't you home with your pregnant wife?" I never thought the original wild child of the Marked family was going to settle down, but Rule had taken to being domesticated like a champ and I had to say it looked damn good on him.

He righted himself in the seat and snatched the beer out of my hand so he could take a long swallow out of it. He gave it back after making sure to slobber all over the top of it and I could only fake-glower at him while I laughed at his antics.

"We went for the ultrasound today and I think we both needed a minute to get our heads around it. I guess it kind of made it all real. I'm gonna be a dad. I'm having a kid with the last person on earth I ever thought I was going to fall in love with, and now I don't have any kind of life without her in it. I heard the heartbeat and almost fucking cried." His pale eyes got huge in his face. "What am I supposed to do if he turns out just like me?"

Rome chuckled and I asked, "You're having a boy?"

He rubbed his hand across the back of his neck. "Yeah. I think a girl would maybe be easier. She would be sweet and soft like Shaw. God help us all if this kid takes after his old man."

Rome snorted. "I have a baby girl, and while she is sweet and soft she is also ornery and demanding."

I smirked at him. "Just like her mama."

"No kidding, but I wouldn't have it any other way." He told Rule, "You'll be fine. If he is like you then you know what you need to do to keep him in line and remind him that it's okay to be difficult and to make your own way in this world, but that he also has to let the people that love him in."

The brothers shared an intense look that spoke to battles won and lost and I had to agree with Rome's assessment. In order to lighten up the mood a little, I told Rule, "And at least it isn't twins. I don't think Denver would remain standing if there were two more of you unleashed on the Mile High."

The quip had the desired effect and some of the tension unleashed from Rule's shoulders. "True. Cora pouted for a full hour when Rome told her it was just one baby and not twins."

"I bet she did."

Rome looked up and nodded over my head as someone came in the door. I turned to see who it was and looked past Asa as he walked in to the young woman that followed him in the front door. She was short, about Cora's height, but curved more like Salem, she had hot-pink hair and a snarl on her pretty mouth. She looked mad at the world and not happy to be at the Bar at all. The little thing practically breathed out bad attitude and discontentment. She walked past all of us without acknowledging our existence in any way, shape, or form. She literally emanated anger and displeasure like a thick, black cloud in her wake.

Rome grunted at her thunderous arrival and quipped, "Speaking of Cora, that little lady right there can give her a run for her money in the attitude department." The older Archer sounded disgruntled about that fact.

"Who is she?" This came from Rule as he pointed in the direction the pink-haired sprite had gone.

"Brite's daughter, Avett. He asked me and Asa to find a way to keep her out of trouble for a few months. She got kicked out of college and fell in with a pretty bad crowd. She's shit with the customers, so we tossed her in the kitchen to help Darcy out, but considering they're mother and daughter, it isn't going well. One of them is bound to walk out in the middle of a rush sooner or later." He chuckled drily. "I think Brite is hoping Asa might be a good influence on her, as crazy as that sounds."

Brite Walker was the guy that had sold the Rome the Bar for a song. He was also the ex-soldier's mentor and really the all-around voice of reason when it came to burly, stubborn men making dumb choices. I knew there was nothing Rome or Asa wouldn't do for Brite, including giving his unpleasant offspring a job and looking out for her.

I lifted up my eyebrow. "She seems like a real delight."

Rome just grunted a nonanswer and told us, "I have plans with Cora tonight, so I need to work on getting out of here. Joe is babysitting and I'm taking her out." Joe was Cora's dad and so in love with his new baby granddaughter that he had packed up his entire life in Brooklyn and moved to Denver to be closer to his girls. He was a huge part of Rome and Cora's life.

"What's the occasion?" Rule's question was simple, but the way Rome stiffened and the way his eyes blazed neon blue made me think there was something more to his plans than just a date night.

"No occasion. I have a gorgeous woman that gave me a beautiful daughter and she always deserves to know that she is the most important thing in the world to me." Oh yeah, Rome wasn't a major talker and that kind of sentiment was far more flowery than he usually expressed. Rule and I shared a knowing look. Something was definitely up.

"Gonna go get Asa ready for the night shift and then bounce." He lifted his chin at Rule and told him, "You're going to be a great dad, Rule. Just like you're a great husband, a great brother, a great friend, and a rock-solid business partner. You and Shaw were meant to do this."

Rule nodded his head and I saw him swallow hard. "Thanks."

I turned around so I could see the door. I didn't want to miss Sayer when she showed up and I admittedly didn't want to miss her reaction when she saw the Bar. Sure, Rome had cleaned the place up, every surface was restored or new, but it was still a dive bar and there was no way to mask that.

"What do you think is up with him and Cora?" I went to take a drink from the beer and then remembered Rule sticking his tongue all over it and just handed it to him with a scowl.

"I dunno. He's been bugging her to move. He wants to buy a house, but who knows. Those two fight fire with gasoline and I think they both get off on watching it burn."

"Never boring, I guess."

"No way. Could you ever imagine anything with Cora being boring?"

I laughed and stiffened up when I saw the tall blond woman come in through the front door. Rule took note of my sudden change in posture and followed my gaze to where Sayer was looking around the dimly lit interior for me. She caught my eye and started in my direction. She moved like she was part of a royal wedding procession.

"She looks an awful lot like you, Rowdy."

"Yeah, I know."

Sayer stopped in front of me and shifted a little uneasily. "Hello."

"Hey. Sayer Cole, this is Rule Archer. He's a coworker and a longtime friend."

She stuck out her hand for Rule to shake and I was impressed her gaze didn't linger at all over the colorful cobra had that decorated the entire backside of Rule's hand.

"Nice to meet you." Her voice was firm and she didn't seem uncomfortable at all, but her gaze kept meeting mine and then dating away. I wondered if she was just as nervous about spending time together as I was.

"You, too. Thank you for helping Asa out."

The case had fallen apart in a most spectacular way when the guy Sayer had put us in touch with to represent Asa had come on board. Quaid Jackson was indeed a barracuda and he left no stone unturned when it came to defending Asa, even with Asa's history being less than stellar. Really the nails in the coffin of the case had come down to arrogance and foolishness on the kid's part. The ringleader, the little punk that had started shit with Asa in the bar, had been brash enough to post cell-phone video on YouTube of him and his friends surrounding Asa in the parking lot after the bar closed. The assault that was shown was violent, unprovoked, vicious, and completely unfair. Of course Asa had fought back and the kid did indeed get his ass handed to him, but that was nothing compared to the beating Asa took out, numbered five to one. Really he was lucky his face had just gotten banged up. It really looked like things could have been far worse for him.

Quaid found the video, not that it had been hard to find once it found its way to Facebook and Twitter, and took it to the powers that be in the justice system in order to get the case dropped. The ringleader of the entire circus was now looking at false reporting charges and some serious assault charges of his own. Quaid had been nice enough to only charge Asa a grand considering he never actually had to go before a judge. It was pretty much a win for Team Asa even if he still wouldn't explain why he hadn't protested his arrest or defended himself to the police when they hooked him up and put him in the patrol car.

"He seems to have a knack for landing in hot water." Sayer said it lightly and without censure.

Rule got up off the stool and threw some money down on the bar. "It happens to all of us now and then."

He told me good-bye and hollered the same to Asa as he appeared behind the bar. I introduced the bartender to Sayer as well and he thanked her in much the same way Rule had, only with far more charm and a grin that was designed to make her want to go to bed with him. I hoped it didn't work. I was just getting used to the idea of having a sister. I couldn't even begin to try and work my way through how the idea of her sleeping with a lothario like Asa made me feel. He told us drinks were on the house for the night and gave me a smirk like he knew exactly what part of the gutter my mind had nose-dived into. I flipped him off as I followed Sayer to one of the tables that was up near the stage Rome had built during his remodel of the Bar. It was going to get busy later but for now it was quiet enough we could talk and not have to shout at each other over bar noise.

I was surprised when she took a bottle of Coors Light instead of ordering a mixed drink or a glass of wine, though I wasn't even really sure they served wine here that wasn't the equivalent of the stuff that came out of a box.

"I'm glad you asked to meet with me." She talked in a way that was very cultured and even but her constantly moving hands gave away how nervous she was.

"Sometimes it takes me a minute to work my way around to where I'm supposed to be. Like I told you in your office you didn't deserve that kind of treatment. I'm usually a pretty decent guy."

"Maybe not, but I get that this is all kind of hard to process."

I picked up my beer and looked at her over the top of it. "You had to process it as well."

She nodded a little and picked at the sticker on her beer bottle. "My dad was always finding new and perfectly horrific ways to mess with my life. I'm used to trying to process through it all." Her eyes that were an identical match to mine darkened like a cloudy day. "When I started trying to track you down I was mad at him. I was alone, you were alone, and he knew it all along. We could have had each other and helped each other and he purposely kept us apart until he was gone. I'm pretty sure he counted on you being a greedy, selfish bastard that would just snap the money up without a thought. He was trying to hurt me, but really he gave me the one thing I always wanted." The corners of her mouth tilted up just a little bit. "Someone else to call family, someone else to care about and share things with. The fact that you are a good man, and that you turned out so amazing all on your own, really is an epic 'screw you' to the old man. I could love you unconditionally for that alone, Rowdy."

I paused with the beer halfway to my lips and just looked at her. That was probably one of the nicest things anyone had ever had to say about me.

"I'm really not interested in taking half of your inheritance, Sayer. I don't make lawyer money but I do all right and I can support myself just fine." I finally took a slug of the beer and put it back down on the table. "It sounds like you earned every single cent in the hardest way possible."

She moved some of her hair over her shoulder and leaned a little closer to me so that she could prop her elbow on the table and rest her chin on her hand.

"I'm going to be really presumptuous and overstep my bounds for a second, so don't get mad at me."

I lifted an eyebrow at her but grinned because she really looked concerned about what my reaction might be. I couldn't blame her. I hadn't exactly rolled out the welcome mat for her thus far.

"I've spent some time with Salem. I adore her and think she's about as perfect for you as any girl could ever be. I know you guys have some history lingering between you but from the outside the two of you act like you're a team. Before you dismiss saying yes to money that is rightfully yours, you might want to think about the fact you are not operating independently anymore. That money could pay for a wedding. It could pay for a down payment on a house. You could use it for a new business, or for college if you have kids down the line. It's no small sum, and honestly, Rowdy, you earned it just as much as I did."

Fuck me. I hadn't even started to think about what an unexpected windfall might mean if my relationship kept moving forward with Salem the way it was. There was no doubt she had ahold of my heart and had always owned my soul. Sure I was probably going to put a ring on her finger down the line and the way this group was popping out kids left and right that would probably be on the agenda at some point as well. I just hadn't really thought about it in terms of being right around the corner.

"We *are* a matched set." I liked Salem's way of looking at how we fit together. Sure there had been others along the way but no one fit in the empty places the way she did, no matter how hard I might have tried to force them. "You're right. I need to talk to her before just turning the money down cold."

"She's a very dynamic young woman."

I laughed because that was one way to put it. "She's a force of nature."

"The tattoo she has on her back, the one you drew for her when she was a teenager, I've never seen anything so beautiful. I think your drawing is amazing and the fact she carries her favorite gift she ever received with her every day is pretty special."

I had never really looked at it that way before, but Sayer was right. It was special. Really special, just like the relationship I had with Salem was. "I always thought I had bad luck, ya know?" I leaned a little closer to her as well. "My mom died because some dirty bastard tried to carjack her." I sighed and felt the weight of that loss settle on me like it always did. "I'm sure you know that because you dug into my life trying to find me, but what you don't know is that she was out that night because I was sick. I had a fever and was throwing up, so she was just running to the store real quick to grab some 7 Up and kid's Tylenol for me. We didn't live in a good part of town, so she never would've been out unless it was for me."

Emotion crawled up my throat and made it hard to talk. I had to look down at the table because the sympathy in Sayer's gaze was too much for me to handle.

"Then there was the Cruz sisters. I needed Salem and she left. I thought I loved Poppy and she didn't want me. More bad luck." I gave a broken laugh that sounded like it was coated in rust. "Then there was football. I was good at it, really good, but I didn't love it and what I did love I couldn't see a future in."

I cleared my throat and then looked back up at her. "After the last month or so I've started to change my mind about that luck. Salem came back and set my world right even though I didn't know it was upside down. Poppy will always be important to me in a different way that still really matters. Phil found me and taught me how to make a living off of art. My mom might be gone but everywhere I turn now I run into someone that loves me and considers me family . . . including you. That's more good fortune then most men get in a lifetime."

Her eyes got really shiny and she told me, "You're going to make me cry."

I grunted a little and decided to change the subject. "What about you? No one was pissed about you picking up and traipsing off to find your long-lost little brother?"

She made a face and it was her turn to be unable to meet my gaze. "I was engaged before I left, but it just wasn't a good fit. I broke it off before I moved and the fact I was more concerned about you and what you would think than him and how I might have hurt him was a huge indicator that splitting up was the right choice."

"That's a bummer. Were you together for a long time?"

"Five years, engaged for two. He was a nice guy, just not the right guy for me."

"That's still rough."

She lifted her chin up and gave me a grin. It so surreal how much of myself I could see in her when she looked back at me.

"I think I'd like to hold out for something like you seem to have with Salem. I want someone that looks at me like I'm the beginning and end of everything. That's the way you look at her."

"My first and last."

She cocked her head to the side and looked at me in confusion. I picked up my beer because she might be my sister but she was still a virtual stranger and getting all personal and gooey and emotional wasn't really what I had planned for this meet-up.

"Salem was the girl that was a lot of firsts for me even if I didn't recognize it at the time. Now that she's back in my life I'm trying to focus on the lasts that she'll be to me."

Sayer nodded and picked up her own beer. "Like the last girl you're going to love?"

"Exactly."

"That's what I want." I was going to tell her to hold out for it and to ignore Asa as he walked over with two more beers and put all of his southern charm and hospitably on display, but I didn't get the chance because Zeb walked in looking like he had been rolling around in sawdust and Spackle for hours. He had wood particles stuck in his beard and grime streaked across his forehead.

I was used to his burly and unkempt appearance but I thought it might intimidate Sayer when he pulled out a chair without asking and ordered, telling Asa to bring him a beer. Asa walked away laughing and sent Dixie back over with a drink for Zeb.

"Who is this?" His voice sounded like it was hewn from the mountains and rattled with thunder. I wasn't sure but beneath the beard and dust I think he was leering at Sayer.

"My sister. Sayer, this is my buddy Zeb Fuller. He actually designed and built the new tattoo shop in LoDo." I was surprised how effortless calling her my sister was and how much I liked the way it sounded.

Zeb's leafy-green eyes glinted in humor. "You have a sister? A hot, classy sister?"

I saw Sayer blush and look at me with big eyes. Zeb kind of resembled a grizzly bear and there was nothing about him that came across as welcoming and cuddly, but I think he was actively trying to flirt with my sister.

"It sure looks that way." I narrowed my eyes at him and tried to kick him under the table. It was like jamming my boot into a tree trunk.

"Full of surprises, aren't you, Rowdy? First the cutie from back home and now a gorgeous sibling you've been keeping all to yourself. Who else is gonna come crawling out of the woodwork after you?"

I didn't want to give him the satisfaction of telling him Poppy was also in town, so I just glowered at him while he continued to grin at me through his beard. I was expecting an awkward silence to descend, but like she kept doing, Sayer surprised me by being able to talk shop with Zeb like a pro. As it turned out, she had purchased an old Victorian in Governors Park and the thing was in absolute disrepair. Two beers later I think they had plans in place for him to come check her property out and look over the work she thought her current contractor was ripping her off on. She also didn't bat an eyelash when Zeb disclosed his criminal past. She in return informed him that because she was a lawyer she knew all too well that sometimes the legal system got things wrong. By the fourth beer I think she was actively flirting back with my giant friend and I was distinctly uncomfortable and feeling like a third wheel.

I texted Salem to see if she was home yet, and when she responded with a selfie of herself in bed, curled up with her glasses on and from what I could see nothing else, I bid a hasty good-bye and headed to my girl. Poppy let me in the door and just laughed at me as I brushed past her with hardly any kind of greeting or acknowledgment on my way to Salem's room.

She was awake and waiting for me and she really did only have on those trendy black frames she only wore when she was at home. Her black-and-red hair was a wild mess all over the pillows and it took me about three seconds to strip down and join her. At some point when I was making her moan and holler my name, it occurred to me that we weren't exactly alone in the apartment and I should have some consideration for Poppy, but then her hands started rubbing over the piercings in my dick and I couldn't think about anything but how amazing she was and how I never wanted anyone to put their hands on me again besides her.

We fell asleep wrapped around one another, spent and satiated. Her hair was stuck to my chest and her taste was all in my mouth and it was perfect. Her soft weight on top of me was kind of like the anchor that I had tattooed on my neck. It held me in place, kept me grounded, reminded me she was my home port when we had both been adrift for so long.

I JERKED AWAKE AND SWORE in aggravation when Salem's elbow landed in my gut as she scrambled up and out of bed. At first I couldn't figure out what she was doing, but then I heard Poppy frantically knocking on the bedroom door and the dog barking his fool head off. I groaned and reached for the jeans I had left on the side of the bed the night before. Salem had commandeered my shirt, so I was only half dressed as I made my way out into the living room to see what all the commotion was about.

I told Jimbo to hush and fetched him a tennis ball to distract him as Poppy shrieked incoherently at Salem. I was about to whistle and tell everyone to chill the fuck out when the buzzer from the security door at the front of the building went off on the wall unit. It buzzed and buzzed like someone was leaning on it. It was only four o'clock in the morning and this obviously wasn't a locked-out neighbor.

"What in the hell is going on?" I scrubbed my hands over my hair and made my way over to the girls.

Salem looked at me over her shoulder, her dark eyes worried and fathomless. Even with her tawny complexion I could tell she was pale.

"Poppy thinks it's Oliver, her husband."

I frowned and crossed my arms over my chest. The buzzer went off again and I looked at it balefully. "How on earth would he even know how to find you?"

Poppy was shaking her head back and forth and crying big fat tears. "I don't know. Oh my God, he's going to kill me."

I felt my eyebrows dip low over my nose as I made my way to the intercom. "It's probably just some drunk that can't get in and keeps leaning on the same button." I hit the response key and barked, "Move it, dude. Not one is letting you in. It's four in the morning, don't make me call the cops."

There was no response, but as soon as I let up off the call button it started buzzing again. Salem was watching me like I should know what to do, so I just shrugged and said, "Fine, I'm gonna go out there and help them get their damn finger off the buzzer. Whoever it is." Poppy started crying harder and Salem frowned at me.

"You saw her when she got here. This guy is unpredictable and unhinged. I don't want you to get hurt. Maybe we should just call the police."

The buzzer started trilling once again and Jimbo growled at it low in his throat. I reached down to scratch him between his ears.

"Let me handle it first. This guy doesn't get to harass my girls and maybe he needs to pick on someone his own size."

Poppy hiccuped. "He's insane, Rowdy. He nearly beat me to death because I wouldn't agree to have kids with him. What if he has a knife or a gun? I don't want you getting hurt because of me."

I gave both of them a lopsided smile and pulled the door open. "Don't worry about me. I'm good at taking care of you, remember?"

They both called my name as Jimbo darted past me and bolted to the end of the hallway where the security door was located. I grabbed his collar just in case and pulled the first door open and made my way to the second where the intercom was located. There was a man standing in front of the console pressing the button with Salem's apartment number on it and not letting up on it.

He was pretty unremarkable-looking. He was shorter

than me by quite a bit, and he was wearing nondescript khakis and an untucked polo shirt. His hair looked like it had been raked through with aggravated hands, and when his dark eyes landed on me I could see fury blazing out of them.

"Hey, man. Knock it off. I don't know who you are but you have the wrong apartment." Jimbo growled low in his throat and tugged at my hold on his collar. He was a good dog and never aggressive, so it made me frown at the guy. "Move along, buddy."

The guy stepped away from the console and looked me up and down. Granted I looked like I has just been loved hard and woken up grumpy, which I had, but I still towered over him and there was no missing the apprehension that crossed his puckered face. His gaze landed somewhere on the pirate ship inked on my chest and he asked me with a sneer, "Who in the hell are you?"

I was so taken aback all I could do was blink. The dog barked a loud, high-pitched yelp and the guy gave him a dirty look.

"The guy on the outside of the security door doesn't get to ask the questions. Like I said, get lost or I'm calling the cops."

His chest puffed up and red rage flooded into his face. "My wife is in there and I'm not going anywhere until I talk to her."

Poppy was right. This guy was missing a few screws.

"No. You aren't getting anywhere near her. I saw your handiwork last time you 'talked' to her and that isn't happening again."

"She belongs to me!"

I took a step forward the dog lunged at the guy's crotch. "People are not property. Poppy is a sweet girl who deserves better than an asshole that uses her as a punching bag and a dad that looks the other way while it's happening. Go back to Texas and forget about her."

He took a step closer to me and almost lost a finger when he poked me in the bare chest with it.

"I know about you. The orphan with no family, no roots. You have no one and nothing. Poppy didn't want you then and there is no way she wants you now. I'm going to talk to her even if I have to go through you to do it."

I probably would've let it go, probably would have managed to maintain my cool, but before I could form words to tell the guy to fuck off, he lifted his foot and kicked Jimbo square in the side. The dog howled in pain and jerked out of my grip. I didn't have to worry about swinging first because the little bastard tried to get in a sucker punch when I turned to see if the dog was okay. I caught his fist in my hand and jerked his arm behind his back. When he was off balance I clocked him once hard in the mouth, which split his bottom lip open and had blood dripping down his chin. I was just so much taller than him that really he couldn't get any leverage as he wiggled against me and I turned him around and clamped him in an unmovable choke hold.

He threw his head back and tried to head-butt me, so I grabbed him by the back of the neck and bent him forward so that he was wrenched over at a totally awkward and painful angle. I marched him out of the breezeway and down the sidewalk to the street. I shoved him away from me with enough force that he stumbled and fell forward on his hands and knees.

"Don't come back, dude. I'm taking Poppy to get a restraining order today, and believe me, if you think I'm bad you don't even wanna see what her sister has in store for you if you come around again. Only piece-of-shit men hit women and you're lucky I don't do to you what you did to her."

He turned over to look back at me and I swore he was plotting my death as he glowered at me. I really should smash his nose in to teach him a lesson or at least kick him in the ribs to pay him back for the dog.

"Poppy is mine." It came out garbled and I just lifted an eyebrow at him.

"She feels differently about that. Someone along the way shoulda taught you how to respect women."

I whistled for Jimbo and laughed out loud as he limped over to where the fallen intruder was still lying and lifted his leg. Poppy's husband tried to scramble away to avoid the golden shower but he wasn't fast enough and Jimbo was obviously proud of himself as he bounded back over to me. We watched as the guy got to his feet, swearing at us and calling us names the entire way as he stormed off to his car.

I patted the dog on the head and told him "good boy" as we went back inside to the girls.

Salem was pacing back and forth and Poppy was curled up into a tight ball on the couch when we went back inside. Salem launched herself at me as soon as I cleared the front door, so I wrapped her in my arms and kissed her on the top of her head.

"I called Royal. I had to."

I kissed her on her trembling mouth when she looked up at me and tugged on the ends of her hair. "Probably a good idea to have your sister talk to her. She's right. That guy has some serious issues. I think he really might be a major threat to not only her, but you as well. She needs an emergency order of protection and you should see if Royal can arrest him for animal cruelty." I nodded toward the dog, who had made himself comfortable on the couch next to Poppy. "He kicked Jimbo in the side."

Salem gasped and then called the guy every bad name that was in the book. "I'm so glad you were here."

Poppy poked her head over the back of the couch and said, "Me, too."

I kissed Salem again and told her, "I'm always going to be here."

She wrapped her arms around my waist and rested her cheek over my heart, which I swear was beating just for her.

"So am I, Rowdy." I actually believed her when she told me that now, and nothing made me happier.

CHAPTER 18

Salem

IT WAS IMPOSSIBLE TO go back to sleep after all of that, so by the time Rowdy and I had to go to work we were both dragging. Him even more so since he had to go in earlier than normal to make up for the appointment he had missed the day he was late and hungover. Poppy didn't want to be at the apartment alone and I couldn't blame her. So I decided to take her to the shop with me and put her to work up in the store. Everything was finally tagged, organized, and inventoried. We were only about a week out from having a fully operational store above the tattoo shop and there were already inquires in my in-box about online orders for merchandise. The shops were both so busy, the guys and the new artists all booked out over a month in advance, so I knew that Nash and Rule were going to have to hire someone specifically to manage the retail aspects of the business. It was a good problem to have, I just hoped the guys saw it the same way.

Cora was excited to have extra hands around for the

busy day. She actually had scheduled a couple of piercings for the afternoon, so she put Poppy to work in the office updating portfolios and working on some kind of spreadsheet that had something to do with office supplies and stuff the guys ordered for their stations. She was in a tizzy about paper towels or something like that, which made Poppy laugh. Cora seemed even more hyper and more boisterous than usual, enough so that Rowdy asked her about it. She just brushed him off and the subject was dropped, at least until she walked up to the counter with her client, a girl that had wanted dermals put in behind her ears and I noticed a big, fat, sparkly ring on that all-important finger as Cora handed me the checkout paperwork.

I felt my jaw drop as I reached out to snatch up her much smaller hand in my own. "Did you get engaged?"

The shop was busy and there was plenty of chatter going on in the background, but when I asked the question the place was suddenly quiet enough to hear a pin drop. Cora yanked her hand back and a hot-pink flush colored her face. Her turquoise eye flashed at me in humor and the brown one got all melty and soft.

"Maybe." I laughed at her and reached back for her hand to look at the ring on her left hand.

This was Cora after all, no boring diamond or traditional gold setting would do. Instead it was a ring that twisted around her finger and had two gems sitting offset next to each other, one a creamy golden topaz and the other a pristine blue sapphire. It wasn't an exact match to her two-tone eye color but the idea was there and obvious. I never would have pictured a big, gruff guy like Rome Archer getting something like an engagement ring so perfectly right.

I felt Rowdy over my shoulder as he reached out and took Cora's hand from mine.

"I knew he was up to something last night. Secretive bastard." He let Cora's hand fall and reached out to squeeze me on the back of the neck. I wasn't sure if it was a warning not to get any ideas or a warning that something like that beautiful ring was in my near future. "Congratulations, but why didn't you say anything, Tink?"

I thought it was really cute the guys all called her Tink. It was short for Tinker Bell because she was so small and blond. Even if her personality was more shark than woodland sprite, the nickname fit.

Cora lifted a shoulder and let it fall. "I dunno. I'm still kind of in shock."

Rowdy laughed. "Oh, come on. We all know Rome's an old-fashioned guy at heart. Of course he was gonna make an honest woman out of you and ask you to marry him."

She held her hand out in front of her and turned it so that the light from outside shimmered and glinted of the jewels. She really did look like a hip and trendy version of a Disney character.

"He didn't ask me." Both of her eyebrows shot up and a sardonic grin pulled at her mouth. "He told me."

That made Rowdy laugh and I just gaped at her. "You've got to be kidding me!"

"Nope. He took me out to dinner, which was really nice since we haven't really had a ton of alone time together since

Remy was born. We went back home and I thought my dad
and the baby were still going to be there but Rome asked Dad
to take her for the night." She blinked rapidly and wrinkled
her nose. I think she was about to cry before she reined it
in. "He also asked my dad for permission, which is so crazy.
Rome never asks anyone for anything, ever." She put a hand
to her chest and sighed. "He got down on one knee and told
me he didn't care if we lived in the rental forever or if we
lived in a tent in the woods as long as we were together forever. Then he told me I was going to marry him, that I didn't
have a choice." She flashed the ring at me. "Then he put this
on me and told me I'm never allowed to take it off."

I didn't think that sounded very romantic but apparently
it had been because it was the only time I could remember
ever seeing Cora look so dreamy eyed.

"Well, congratulations." I was really happy for her. She
was a very cool chick and had a beautiful family. It was a nice
change of pace to the early-morning horror that had been
just outside my door.

"I was engaged a million years ago and it was a shit
show. It all feels different when it's the right person. Like it
just settles into your bones and you just know it's the way it's
supposed to be."

Rowdy's fingers tightened on the back of my neck and I
looked up at him by tilting my head back a little. His sky-blue
eyes were glowing in his face.

"Well, tell the big guy we're all happy for the two of you
and you do realize this means Rule is going to be in charge
of Rome's bachelor party when the time comes, right?"

She opened her mouth and then snapped it shut with her
teeth clicking together. She narrowed her eyes at Rowdy.
"Over my dead body."

She turned on her combat-booted heel and headed back
up the stairs. Rowdy let go of his hold on me and propped his
hip on the edge of the desk. He changed the subject to the
one I was trying to actively avoid thinking about.

"I think you should pack up Poppy and come stay at my
apartment for a few days while the cops try and find that
Oliver guy to serve him with the restraining order."

Since my sister's estranged husband wasn't from the area
and we couldn't figure out how he had located Poppy, finding him was a much more difficult task than it should have
been. And really a restraining order wasn't any kind of guaranteed protection. Royal had been brutally clear with Poppy
when she explained that all it did was enable the police to
arrest Oliver for violating the order, but he could very well
walk right through it if he was as intent on getting to her as
he seemed to be.

I propped an elbow on the edge of the desk and looked
up at him through my lashes. "Yeah. That would probably
make her feel a little better about things." I sighed. "It would
probably make me feel better about things as well."

He reached out and tugged lightly on the ends of my
hair. "They'll find him."

"How do you think he even knew where to look for her,
where I lived?"

"I dunno. Maybe he searched for you on the Internet. All
he would have to do is search Google and you pop up as the

manager of the shops here. I'm not sure how he narrowed it down to what apartment complex you live in, though. Do you think Poppy might have told someone she was staying with you?"

There was subtext there I didn't want to hear even though it was loud and clear. I sighed and moved to rest my forehead against the hard muscle of his thigh.

"You think she talked to one of my parents, don't you?"

He put his hand on the back of my head and massaged my scalp. "Walking away for you was different. You never cared what they thought, never wanted to fit into the mold that they had crafted for you. Poppy wasn't like that. She valued your dad's opinion. She wanted to please him and have him love her unconditionally. That's a hard habit to break free from."

I lifted my head up and stood so that I was right next to him. If we were anywhere but at work I probably would have jumped him and kissed him all over.

"Can you watch the front for me for just a second? I want to go upstairs and talk to her really quick."

He nodded and crossed his arms over his chest. "Take it easy on her. I know it's been a long time and a lot of miles for you, but try and remember what living under his thumb and under his roof was like."

I couldn't resist the urge to run my fingertips over the way his bicep flexed enticingly as I moved around him and made my way upstairs. The door to Cora's office was open and she was on the phone at her desk. Poppy was standing in front of one of the fun-house mirrors making faces at herself, which made me laugh out loud and had her turning around to glare at me.

"What? Isn't that what you're supposed to do in them? I don't know how anyone is going to use them when they try on clothes. They make your reflection crazy and totally unflattering."

"There are normal mirrors in the dressing rooms. These are just for fun."

She made her way over to me and took a seat on the vintage velour lounger that was now right in the middle of the room. It was covered in purple velvet and just as wacky and gaudy as the rest of the decor of the shop. It was a nice place for boyfriends and husbands to sit down while their ladies shopped.

"This place is so cool, Salem. I see so much of you in it. This really is the perfect place and the perfect job for you."

"It's going to be even better when the guys find time to add art to the collection, and I'm still working on Rowdy to convince the gang to make a sexy calendar."

She laughed at that even though I was dead serious about it. Those boys would have them flying off the shelves if I could just get them to agree to it. I knew it was a long shot but I still really liked the idea.

I reached out and put a hand on her shoulder. "I want to ask you something and I want you to be honest with me, Poppy. Did you tell Mom or Dad you were here in Denver with me? I just want to know how Oliver would've found out exactly where my apartment was. Denver is a pretty big city. It's not just like he stumbled upon it out of luck."

I saw her pale under her caramel-colored complexion. Her honey-colored gaze got wide and I saw her bottom lip start to quiver. I squeezed her shoulder in comfort and pulled her forward into a one-armed hug.

"Poppy, it's fine. I just wanted to know. I want to keep you safe."

"I called Mom to let her know I was okay. It was one thing for Dad to justify Oliver hurting me, but I figured there was no way a mother could condone that happening to her child. I told her I was staying with you and that I would be back soon to get the rest of my stuff and that I was going to file for divorce." She gulped and pulled away from me so that she could shove her hands through her hair. "Mom told me to come home. She said everything can be worked out if I have enough faith and that I should trust God and look into counseling.. She told me she was disappointed in me and that Dad was devastated by my betrayal." She laughed so sharply I was surprised it didn't draw blood when she spit it out. "*My* betrayal. Can you believe that?" Well, of course I could. That was why I had left, but she kept talking, so I didn't get the opportunity to tell her that. "I didn't tell her where you apartment was, though. I would never do that to you. I know if you wanted them to know where you lived, you would've have told them yourself."

"Oh, Poppy."

"I know. I feel like I should have known better. The idea that Oliver might have been watching you, could have followed you home from work or something, makes my skin hurt. I know he's dangerous and I can't believe I would so recklessly put you in harm's way after you took me in without question."

The idea that her husband might have followed me to find out where I lived had never occurred to me but it made my skin crawl. That was definitely unnerving.

"It's hard when you realize the people that love you the most actually care about you the least. Dad has always been way more focused on the church and his image than he was on what was happening under his own roof. He thought control and dominance was a substitute for love and understanding." I rolled my eyes at her. "And Mom just follows his lead. There was never room in that house for us to be anything but their little, perfect dolls. We weren't supposed to individuate, and when we did"—I shrugged—"they just couldn't handle it. You need to tell yourself over and over again that none of this is your fault."

"I feel like it all is, though."

I hugged her again, realizing my sister was going to eventually need some professional help when all of this died down. She had been in the mix of my dad's machinations and in an abusive relationship far too long for my love and support to be enough to get her head around everything.

"Rowdy wants us to come stay at his place until we know for sure Oliver has been served with the protection order. Royal said when they find him the police will try and convince him the best course of action is to just head back to Texas, but until that happens we'll camp out at the bachelor pad."

She grumbled something under her breath and got to

her feet in front of me so that she could pace back and forth in front of me in an agitated matter.

"You and Rowdy should be hanging out and enjoying spending time together. It took you a lifetime to finally get together and here I am right in the middle of it once again."

Not too long ago the idea of her being between him and me would have had me freezing Rowdy out and pushing him away again. The fear that what he used to feel for her would somehow overwhelm what he now felt for me was gone. I could see it when he looked at me now. I felt it in every touch and saw it in every rakish smile he threw my way. When he loved, he loved wholly, completely, and forever. I knew it deep down in my bones, just like Cora had said. What was between us was just right, it had always been. We both needed time to grow up and let it find its way to a solid and healthy place so we could both enjoy it.

"You aren't in the middle of us, you are surrounded by us because we both care a lot about you and don't want you to be hurt anymore. We've both been protecting you from afar for years. Now we are a united front and God help anyone that tries to get through us." I lifted up my eyebrows and gave her a hard look. "Mom and Dad included."

She squeezed her eyes shut and pushed the heel of her hands into them. "I'm just so tired of it all, Salem."

Who could blame her? I looked up as Cora came out of the office. She had a permanent smile on her face and really, with that pretty ring and the even prettier man that had given it to her, she had every reason to be lit up from the inside out with joy.

"I don't mean to pry." Of course she did. It was Cora's lot in life to be smack-dab in the middle of whatever drama was going on in the Marked world, so I just rolled my eyes at her and got to my feet. "But you both look exhausted and my dad still has my kid, so I don't need to be home until later. Why don't you go on and head over to Rowdy's so you can rest for the remainder of the day?" Her pierced eyebrow danced upward, making her look like a mischievous fairy. "I'll watch the front and shut down the shop when the last client leaves."

It was official, I was part of the family. Cora was swooping in to take care of me just like she did the rest of the crew. I could have kissed her for it. I looked at my sister and had zero doubt a nap would do her some good. She had dark circles under her eyes and looked worn down and empty. I could literally see the way her heart and soul were hurting in her shadowed gaze.

"I think that's a good idea. I'll call Royal on the way and see if they have any information on Oliver as well."

Cora told me solemnly, "This isn't the first time a guy that just couldn't take 'no' for an answer has wreaked havoc with one of our girls. I know how stressful and dangerous the situation can be. You need to take care of her."

I walked around the lounger and wrapped Cora in a tight hug, and something really struck me as permanent and definite when I told her thank you and she pulled back and told me point-blank, "We take care of our own."

Poppy climbed to her feet as well and offered Cora a wobbly smile. "I'm so glad my sister found you guys and this place. I really think it was where she was always destined to be."

Cora laughed and followed us down the stairs as we headed back into the shop. "Of course it's where Salem was supposed to be. Rowdy is here and I think it's pretty obvious to anyone that's been paying attention that they were bound to end up together."

We went downstairs and I had to wait a second for Rowdy to look up from what he working on. When he did, those summery eyes chased some of the chill of fear and worry away.

"I'm gonna take Poppy to your place. She's exhausted and hanging on by a thread."

He looked around me at my rapidly wilting sister and nodded his head. "All right. Wanna give me twenty minutes and I'll follow you so that I know you're safe? I can cancel my last two appointments for the day."

I would feel better with him there, but I figured Poppy and I would be okay as long as we stuck together and we weren't going to my place but to his. "I think it'll be fine, but if you want to come home early when you're done, I won't complain. Poppy really needs to rest. Can you stop by my place and grab Jimbo and some stuff for her on your way?"

He told his client to give him a second and set the machine he was using down and snapped off the black latex gloves covering his hands. He got to his feet and dug his keys out of his pocket. He fiddled with the ring until he handed two loose keys over to me. He placed them in my palm then bent low so that his mouth was right next to my ear and whispered, "Another first. No girl has ever had the keys to my place before."

I got hot all over and wanted to kiss his face off, but we were at work and it wasn't the time. I curled my fingers around the metal and smiled at him. "First and last."

He lifted his chin in agreement and turned back to finish the impressive geisha tattoo he was putting on his client.

I went back to Poppy and hooked my arm through hers after thanking Cora again as I guided my sister out of the shop. She sort of shuffled alongside me, and once we got to the car she slumped down in the passenger seat and didn't say anything to me as she gazed out the window. It was depressing and disheartening, to say the least. I just let her be, and once we got to Rowdy's apartment complex, it was by some unspoken agreement that we planned to hustle inside just to be safe. Neither of us wanted to linger out in the open until we knew for sure the authorities had located Poppy's soon-to-be ex-husband..

I had some stuff scattered around Rowdy's place already. I had been making my way into his life, into his space, subconsciously for weeks and weeks. I was making myself at home without even realizing that's what I was doing. I just needed my dog and some provisions for my sister and I could camp out there indefinitely.

I was just about to shut the car door and click the locks closed behind me when another car motor revved and screeching brakes made me pull up short. I looked over the top of the open door I was holding and felt all the blood rush out of my face.

A sedan stopped right next to my car and the driver's-side door swung open violently. Before I could react in any way other than to freeze in surprise and shock, a short man got out of the car and pointed at my sister where she was hovering nervously next to my car on the curb. I knew this wasn't a good situation.

"Get in this car, Poppy." He didn't yell, didn't posture, he just told her what to do in a coolly clam voice that was terrifying.

"No." Poppy didn't say it. I did. But there was no way I was letting her go anywhere with him. He looked unkempt and crazed and there was obvious danger stamped all over him.

He vibrated in rage when I barked the negative at him, and instead of letting the argument escalate or raising his voice and coming after me, he methodically produced a gun from somewhere behind his back and pointed it right at me.

I had lived in a lot of big cities and not always in a good part of town. I had seen guns before and even witnessed gun violence at a club here or there along the way. What I had never had happen to be me before was to be facing down the barrel of one with a man clearly ready to pull the trigger on the other side of it.

"Get. In. The. Car. Poppy." Each word was hollow, deliberate, and laced with evil.

I could hear my sister whimpering and felt the tension between all of us wind up and scream with the need to break. My hands curled around the frame of the door as I stared unblinking at the gun.

"Move! I will shoot your sister. I should do it anyway as a favor to your father."

I swallowed hard but refused to react. I had a feeling if I so much as twitched an eyelash the wrong way he would feel justified in pulling the trigger. Why hadn't I thought this through? Of course, if he had followed me home to see where I lived, the lunatic would have followed me to Rowdy's as well. Hell, the creep very well might have been lurking outside of the shop all day just waiting for his moment. I felt like an idiot, and my sister was the one who was going to suffer.

"Oh my God." Poppy whispered the words and I saw her move out of the corner of my eye.

"Don't!" I couldn't stop the command and jolted when the gun went off in a thunderous BANG. I gasped and watched at the bullet skated across the hood of my car. I jumped involuntarily and couldn't stop shaking in terror. I had always been independent and confident that I could take care of myself, but right now I was lamenting not just waiting twenty minutes for Rowdy to come with us. Not that I wanted him in danger, but something about having him close by gave me the feeling things would be all right no matter what, and that was a feeling I could desperately use right now as the gun was leveled at my face once again.

"I will shoot you. I don't care about you. I just want what's mine."

Poppy had moved so that she was between me and the gun. I wanted to reach out and grab her and pull her back to me, but now I didn't want to risk him pulling the trigger and shooting her.

"Poppy, if you get in that car he's just going to shoot me as soon as you close the door. He's going to hurt us both."

She was shaking so badly that she could hardly stand up. Her honey-colored eyes were gigantic in her face and I couldn't see any way this was going to end without bloodshed.

"No, he won't. Put the gun down, Oliver, and I'll get in the car."

He laughed and it sounded as deranged and crazy as he looked. "You don't get to give orders. I give the orders. Get in the fucking car, Poppy."

"Listen, the police are already looking for you. You just fired a gun in a crowded metro area. How long do you think you have before you're surrounded by cops? If you want me to go with you, put the gun down and I will. I'm not getting out of the way until you do. You'll have to shoot me if you want to hurt Salem."

Shit. This wasn't good. Not at all. I went to tell Poppy to run, to move, to do something—anything besides getting in that car with a man that had already proven he could break her, but I didn't get the chance. Oliver went back the driver's door of his car and tossed the gun in the direction of the backseat. If Poppy did get in the car like she seemed determined to do, there was no way she could get to the weapon before he could.

"Now get in." Apparently his desire to have my sister under his control outweighed his desire to threaten and harm me. "I'm not telling you again. An obedient wife listens to her husband."

"Don't do this, Poppy." I was pleading with her in desperation.

She looked at me over her shoulder. "Get in the car and call the police."

"He's going to hurt you—kill you. You can't go with him."

"I have to. You'll save me. You always do."

She pulled open the passenger door of the sedan and slid inside. Oliver looked at me over the hood of his car and made a finger gun. He pretended to shoot me right in the head just as the faint sounds of sirens could be heard. He slipped inside of the car and raced off with my sister's horrified face looking at me out of the passenger window.

I dove for my cell phone and called 911, Royal, Rowdy, my parents, and Sayer in that order. The police were already on their way, and before I screamed at Rowdy that I needed him and that he had to come hold me together, I was surrounded by detectives and patrol officers. They were all asking me a million questions.

What color was the car?

Did I see the license plate?

What was he wearing?

What was Poppy wearing?

Did I know what kind of gun it was?

Did I think he was going to hurt Poppy—or himself?

Where would he take her?

The questions were endless and I couldn't answer most of them coherently. I felt like I was numb. I felt like I had walked into a bad shoot-'em-up movie and the plot had just twisted in a glaringly obvious way. How did I not know better? I was crying silent tears. I was shaking so hard my muscles hurt. I felt like all the words being spoken to me were just white noise over the roar of my blood and the thundering of my heart. I wanted to curl up in a fetal position on the ground and rock. I wanted to get in my car and go speeding off in a random direction like I would just magically find Oliver and my sister if I did that. I wanted to throttle Oliver, kick my dad, and shake my mom within an inch of her life.

I heard my name hollered through the chaos. I caught sight of Rowdy's tall frame and blond hair as he made his way through the throng of law enforcement, intent on getting to me. As soon as his arms closed around me I shattered into a million pieces. I collapsed and let him hold me up as I cried and cursed and swore vengeance on everyone. I had never had anyone I cared about taken from me before. Sure, I had left, walked away because I felt like I had to, but having someone I loved ripped from me in a brutal and vile way left me torn open and aching. It gave me an entirely new appreciation for those wounds Rowdy had suffered with his entire life. I curled my arms around his waist and swore to God, the universe, and whoever else happened to be listening to me that I would never let him go again.

I felt him kiss the top of my head as he squeezed me back. "I've got you." He did. He absolutely did and I had him.

"I know you do. I've got you, too."

Now we just had to stay strong and hold on to one another while Denver's finest went after the lunatic that had kidnapped my little sister.

CHAPTER 19

Rowdy

I T WAS A MISERABLE NIGHT. The police weren't being very helpful, and if it wasn't for Royal showing up and being the unofficial liaison between Salem and the detectives working the case, I felt like there was a pretty good chance my girl would have ended up in lockup herself.

She was understandably frantic, but more than that, she was furious. She was mad at herself for leaving the shop unescorted even though I kept telling her it wouldn't have mattered. Oliver had a gun and he was determined to haul Poppy off. Regardless if I had been with them or not, a bullet was a bullet and chances are he would have seen me as a threat and shot first just to get me out of the way. I should've kept quiet because that just made her angrier and more distraught. I knew the feeling. The idea of a crazed gunman pointing a weapon at her and firing it off anywhere near her made me want to hurt everyone.

She was angry at Poppy for going with Oliver, but she was absolutely livid that the reason Poppy had tied herself to a man like her husband in the first place was because of their father and his damaged way of parenting. I could see a storm lurking there and figured I would just do my best when it finally crested. For now all I could do was hold her, tell her everything would be all right, and give Royal silent pleading looks over the top of Salem's head as she held on to me and alternately cried and cussed out the world.

I was scared for Poppy as well. I had seen how unhinged her husband was up close and personal. The fact he had pulled a gun on two innocent women in broad daylight showed he didn't care about repercussions or getting caught. He was zealously focused on claiming what he determined was his and that made Poppy less than human in his eyes. She was trapped in a car with an armed assailant that viewed her as nothing more than property. To him she was just a possession and people broke and destroyed their possessions all the time. I couldn't think about it too hard or it made everything on the inside of me want to shut down and I couldn't do that and take care of Salem like she needed me to.

I might not love Poppy the way I loved Salem, but she was still important to me. She still held a place in my history and in my heart and she was undoubtedly part of my ramshackle family. I had lost enough people I cared about in this lifetime. There was no way I was going to lose another.

I was sitting on the couch in Salem's living room. It was early the next morning and she had just fallen asleep after pacing the floor for what seemed like endless hours. Even in her slumber she was whimpering and restless. I was rubbing my thumb absently around her temple in circles and staring sightlessly at the television. Across the bottom the ticker was running with the information to be on the lookout for Oliver and the sedan. It was absolutely surreal to see Poppy's description there. It made it feel like she was a stranger, just one more unknown face that ended up in a bad situation. I hated that and hated that this was happening to her and to those that loved her.

Jimbo was curled up on the other side of me. He was getting too big to be allowed on the furniture but he hadn't left Salem's side since the police had cleared out and I think the poor guy was feeling bad he hadn't been able to help. The dog's big, golden eyes were locked on Salem as she murmured in her sleep and twitched. I reached out with my other hand and petted him on the top of his wide head.

"It's okay, fella. It's hard to keep your lady safe." He blew out noise through his nose like he knew exactly what I was talking about and the tip of his tail flipped back and forth.

I looked down at Salem and saw that her brows were furrowed and that she had deep lines etched between the raven arches. I used my fingertip to smooth them out and sighed.

"It's probably the worst time ever to tell you this, but I . ." She suddenly turned so that she was lying on her back and looking directly up at me. That endlessly black gaze had my past, my future, all my secrets, and every dream I had ever had in them. It was like looking into forever and knowing that she was always going to be there right at the center of it. " . . . love you. I will love you unendingly and forever."

Her long lashes swept down for just a moment and then

lifted back up. Like stars in the night sky I could see her feelings for me twinkling up at me from the midnight depths.

"I love you, too. I couldn't do this without you. You always made me stronger than I ever was alone. I've always needed a reason to stay; with you that has never been the case. With you staying is the only option I have because the only place I want to be is wherever you are at."

That was the only thing I had ever wanted her to say to me. I bent down so I could kiss her softly. "It might have taken me a long-ass time to figure out the difference between first love and real love, but, Salem, there is nothing more real than what I feel for you."

She was going to respond but her cell phone went off and we both went stiff and stared at each other with big, nervous eyes. I reached for the phone and winced a little when I saw that Royal's was the number on the screen. I couldn't believe my hands were actually shaking as I swiped across the screen to answer the call.

"Hello."

"Rowdy?" Her voice was low and I could hear a lot of commotion in the background of wherever she was calling me from.

"Yeah, I'm with Salem. Do you have any news?"

Salem pulled herself up and clutched my free hand with both of her own. She was pale and her dark eyes looked like they were swallowing up her entire face. The fear shining out of them settled like a rock in my gut and made my chest twist with the need to be able to do something for her.

"Maybe I should talk to Salem." Royal's voice stayed

steady and low but her words shook like an earthquake through my entire being.

My heart sank and my fingers curled around Salem's hands reflexively. "I'll just put you on speaker."

"Okay." She waited a second as I moved the phone away from my ear and held it between me and my girl after switching on the speaker.

"Go ahead, Royal."

She sighed over the line and I heard sirens and commotion in the background. "First of all, Poppy is all right. She's in an ambulance on the way to a hospital in Albuquerque."

Salem made a noise and fell forward so that her forehead was resting on my shoulder. "Thank God."

"Yeah. The State Patrol picked up on the alert for the car her husband was driving after he had already crossed the state border. It looks like he was headed back to Texas with her."

"Figures." I was relieved, but there was something about the way Royal was talking, the distant, professionally smooth recounting of events, that was off-putting. I could literally feel the other shoe waiting to drop.

"Umm . . . Poppy was in pretty bad shape when the cops finally got to her. I don't know what the extent of the injuries is but I know it isn't good." I could tell she was glossing it over for Salem's sake. Fat tears were glittering on Salem's black lashes and I could tell she was reading between the lines as well.

"What else, Royal? Just lay it all out so we can work on getting to New Mexico as soon as possible."

She sighed again and finally her cop persona cracked just a little. Her voice quivered just a little bit and there was just enough of a thread of emotion in it to turn her from her professional role into a friend.

"The husband didn't go easily. The cops cornered him at a rest stop after a forty-five-minute car chase. He still had the gun." She paused for a second and I froze as Salem's nails dug into my skin hard enough to break the skin. "There was a standoff."

"Shit." It just slipped out but Salem nodded. It was like listening to our worst fears being played out.

"Yeah. He had the gun to Poppy's head. He threatened to shoot her, threatened to shoot himself. The State Patrol called in a critical response team to negotiate the hostage situation. It'll be all over the news within the next hour, I'm sure."

Salem shook her head numbly back and forth like she could deny any of this had happened to her little sister.

"At the end of the day the SWAT team took preventative measures to mitigate the threat."

Salem let go of her death grip on me and got to her feet. She looked exhausted and fragile, but as always there was that core of strength in her that just wouldn't bend.

"What happened, Royal?"

"Oliver Martinez is dead."

I let out a deep breath and shared a solemn look with Salem. "Good."

"Yeah, well, at the end the hostage was rescued . . . but, Rowdy . . ." Her voice faded out and she had to clear her throat. "That poor girl went through hell. She had to witness someone she was married to die right in front of her. It doesn't matter how much he might've hurt her, or how awful he was . . . that changes a person. She isn't going to be the same after this experience."

I pulled Salem to my chest in a one-armed hug as the tears finally escaped the trap of her feathery lashes. "Of course not, but we'll take care of her and help her heal. It's what this family does."

"I know. She's lucky to be part of the fold."

"Thank you for the update, Royal."

"Sure. If you need anything else let me know. I'll text you the info I have for where they are taking her."

Salem mumbled a thank-you that was lost in the fabric of my shirt as I ended the call and used both arms to squeeze her to me as tightly as I could.

"She'll be okay. Poppy is a Cruz and you girls are fighters."

She wrapped her arms around my waist and laid her cheek on the spot in my chest where my heart was thudding erratically from adrenaline and relief.

"Yeah, but a lifetime of fighting gets old after a while." She pulled back and looked up at me, and I could see it, feel it, and smell it in the air. The storm had hit land and she was ready to level everything in her path. "It's time for a knockout once and for all."

All I could do was shrug my agreement. "Let's go take care of your sister first."

She moved away from me with a nod. "I love you and I

love that you know what I have to do and aren't freaking out about it."

I was already on my phone looking at flights out of DIA to Albuquerque. Luckily it was a short flight and wouldn't take us too long to get to Poppy's side. I looked up from the screen and gave Salem a half grin.

"You'll always have a little bit of gypsy in you, Salem. As long as you return to me, I'm willing to let you go wherever it is you want to go. I'll be right here when you get back."

I saw her bottom lip tremble at my words, and before I could hit send on the ridiculously expensive last-minute flight, she launched herself back at me and I had my arms full of quivering, shaking female. She grabbed my face in both of her hands and kissed me in a way that had forever laced all the way through it.

"Gypsies can see the future in their crystal ball, Rowdy. Do you wanna guess what I see in mine?"

"Us?"

She laughed just a little and kissed me again. "Definitely us. I'm gonna grab some stuff to take to Poppy and we need to figure out what to do with Jimbo since we're both going and have no idea how long we're going to be gone for."

I had a plethora of people that I knew for a fact would ride to the rescue to help me out with the dog, but for some reason the first person I put a call in to was Sayer and it didn't have anything to do with the fact she had a giant backyard.

Sayer, of course, told me she was dropping everything and headed over to get the dog. She was also genuinely over-joyed that Poppy was all right, but took a minute to quietly tell me that she had the names of several victims' counselors that she could refer Poppy to when the time was right. Sayer was good people and remarkably understanding. The more I talked to her, the more that I let her in, the more I realized how proud I was to have the same blood as her running through my veins. I was happy that she wanted me to be part of her family and I was looking forward to introducing her to the rest of mine.

It only took half an hour for Sayer to show up and collect Jimbo. The girls hugged and more tears were shed as I hustled Salem out the door and we rushed to the airport. Both of us were jittery and anxious as we trudged through security and waited impatiently to board. Since neither of us had slept the night before, nodding off as soon as the plane hit cruising altitude was bound to happen, and when the wheels touched down and we both jerked awake, it was with the knowledge that someone we both loved was hurt, alone, and more than likely fundamentally changed by the recent tragedy she had just survived. It made the vibe between us heavy and thick, but we held on to one another and didn't let go.

At the hospital it was a little bit of work to get in to see Poppy. There were still a bunch of law enforcement officials running around and the media was lurking like vultures. The nursing staff knew who Salem was right away and started to usher her back, but she didn't want to go without me. Since I wasn't immediate family they weren't going to let me in to see Poppy. I thought it was more important that Poppy see a familiar face than it was to fight the rules, but Salem was having none of it. And in her typical way she charmed and maneuvered everyone that she needed to in order to get me clearance to go into the room with her.

I almost wished I had stayed in the hall. Poppy looked dreadful. Her face was practically deformed from the beating she had endured. Her hair was a tangled and matted mess that had dried blood caked in the strands, and even though both of her eyes were black and blue and swollen to the point that I had no idea how she could see out of them, I could see the weird, hollow cast in the typically glowing depths. She just looked beyond broken, and while I wanted to turn around and pretend like none of it had happened, Salem marched right in and scooped her sister up in a gentle hug as they rocked together around the tubes and monitors that were plugged into Poppy.

There was no regret. There were no useless words of condolence. All Salem could do was hold Poppy as she cried and cried. There was nothing that was going to make the situation, or her sister, any better and Salem knew that, so she just offered up her strength, which was really the only thing that Poppy needed at the moment. I wasn't really sure what to do with myself, so I just hovered by the doorway and watched the heartbreaking scene unfold. As a man that cared about these two women, who had loved both of them in different ways for a lifetime, it filled me with impotent rage that they were both suffering so deeply and there was nothing I could do about it. If Oliver hadn't already been dead I felt like I would start a manhunt so I could take him out myself.

Poppy must have felt the heat that my anger and unease

were putting off because she tapped the hospital bed next to her hip and motioned me over.

I sat down as delicately as I could and picked up her hand. Her fingernails were all broken off and tattered and there were black finger marks from her wrist to her elbow. Whatever Oliver had inflicted on her, she had fought back like a champ. It was never easy to see anyone like this, let alone someone that was important to you.

"I'm so glad you guys had each other while this was going on." Her voice was scratchy and sounded like it took a whole lot of effort to make it work. She squinted at me out of her puffy eyes and I could see her sincerity and her heart shining back at me. "I know this had to be pretty hard for both of you."

I never wanted to lose anyone I loved ever again, but this incident, this act of senseless violence and maliciousness, made it very clear that no matter what choices I made, fate very well might have other plans and loss was just a part of life. It was a far better idea to enjoy the time I had with those that matter than it was to obsess and worry over what would happen when that time ran out.

"All that matters is that you're okay and that we get to take you home."

She turned her head to look at Salem and then let her battered eyes drift shut. "I don't even know where home is anymore. That's what Oliver kept saying to me: 'You belong at home with me.' What kind of home looks like this?" I saw her tremble and saw Salem's spine go stiff.

"Home is where there are people that love you and need

you. Home is where you belong no matter what your faults are or what your life looks like to others. Home is where you can leave but always know it's there to go back to. Poppy, home is where I am. Home is where Rowdy is. You're coming back to Denver with us so we can take care of you and get you some help."

That was the final fight. Salem wasn't going to let it all rest until she had it out with her father for the final time. She was going to cut the ties, break the strings that kept her and Poppy tied to the past, break them for good. She was going to go back to Loveless.

Everything inside of me wanted to demand that she let me go with her. I wanted to be her dragon slayer, her offensive line, but I knew I had to let her go alone. I had to let her go so she could come back. I had to let her do it alone because it wasn't my fight. I would take care of Poppy and make sure she was okay while Salem did her best to set them both free.

Poppy didn't have the energy to argue or talk much more. I knew Salem was going to want to stay at her side, so I left the two of them alone and went to update everyone back home about what was going on. The troops did what they always did and rallied. Rule and Nash told me not to worry about work. Cora asked me if I needed her to pack up the baby and drive down to New Mexico. Ayden told me she would go get the dog and was stunned when I told her my sister already had him. That was going to have to go on the top of the to-do list when I got back to D-town. Everyone was going to have to meet Sayer, since she was obviously going to be a big part of my life moving forward.

It took two more days until Poppy was released and the police were done with her. By that time we were all ready to be back home. Poppy was sick of being poked and prodded and the constant reminders of what had happened to her. She was also arguing vehemently with Salem about her plan to return to Loveless and confront their father. Poppy just wanted her to let it go, but Salem was adamant that she was going to get Poppy's things and have some final words with their dad. I was trying to stay out of it because I saw both sides of the argument and I knew there was no stopping Salem once she had her mind made up about something. In fact I was going to fly home with Poppy and get her situated while Salem was renting an SUV and driving to Loveless from New Mexico. It was a situation that had both sisters uneasy for different reasons.

On the day Poppy was finally discharged we were standing in front of the hospital waiting for the taxi to take us to the airport and I could tell Salem had something on her mind. She was fidgety, playing with her hair, and wouldn't look me directly in the eye. After five minutes I had had enough and hauled her to me by her upper arms so that we were eye to eye. I kissed her on the tip of the nose while she dangled there and told her softly,

"Stop it."

She scowled at me and swatted my bicep as I put her back down on her feet. "Stop what?"

"Whatever you're thinking. Just stop. I'm trusting you to come back. You gotta trust me that I'm just taking care of my family. Your crystal ball shows us, remember?"

She made a face at me and sighed. "I know. She's just so broken and you're just so sweet and want to make everything better. I just had a brief flash of doubt is all. I know you're the best person to help her heal right now. You're the only person I trust with her."

I bent so I could kiss her on her sassy mouth. She always tasted like the best of everything. I loved the way she just melted into me and the way her tongue twisted and curled along mine. I pulled back and rested my forehead against hers.

"You know how you said you wanted to still be the first at some things so you could surprise me?"

She laughed a little and nodded, bumping our heads together. "There is a really important first I want you to do for me while you're in Texas."

She pulled back so we were staring at each other and I think she had to have seen in my gaze how important my request was because she agreed without me even telling her what it was.

"I'll do whatever you want me to, Rowdy."

I gave her a lopsided grin and explained to her what I needed for her to do for me. By the time I was done, we both had tears in our eyes and needed to hold on to one another for just a second.

The doors behind us whooshed open and Poppy was wheeled out looking like a shattered doll. I would help her heal and so would everyone else in my errant family. We were made up of the fragmented and damaged and it was only together that we learned the value of ourselves and what unconditional love and acceptance looked like. It was

342   *Jay Crownover*

the perfect place for Poppy to forget about the past and find her peace and her future.

I helped load one Cruz sister into the taxi and kissed the other one good-bye with everything I had in me. It was oddly reminiscent of ten years ago. Once again I was taking care of Poppy and watching Salem go off to do her own thing. Only I knew this time it had a different ending, and instead of cursing fate and bad luck, I was thanking both of those things for bringing these women into my life for better or worse.

Whatever happened from here on out, I would always be grateful for every single moment I had with everyone I loved.

CHAPTER 20

Salem

I HADN'T STEPPED FOOT inside of a church since I left Love-less a lifetime ago. I didn't have anything against religion. I believed that faith and the trust in something bigger than yourself was an important part of people making peace with how hard and trying life could be at times, but leaving my old life behind also meant leaving behind hours spent in a pew listening to my father piously lead his congregation.

It was an odd feeling to be back as an adult. It felt different knowing I could get up and leave at any point in the sermon that I wanted to. Now that I was out from under his control, lived a full life beyond him and this town, his words seemed so hollow. Where I always thought my father was full of religious conviction and driven by faith, as I watched him at the pulpit now I wondered if it was all just an act.

Sure he was just as passionate as he always had seemed. His words echoed from the wooden rafters and the people surrounding me were obviously moved, but there was something there, something I could see clearly now that time had passed, and he no longer seemed so intimidating or all-powerful like he had to my young eyes. His smile was just a little too bright. His eyes were just a little bit too wide and the cadence of his voice was just a little too practiced and theatrical to ring true. All his words about love and respect, about doing God's work and living a life of sacrifice, hit a chord in me as I realized he was very much preaching "do as I say and not as I do." It was hypocritical and I wished instead of being wrapped up in my own misery at home when I was younger I could have seen him and his dictates for what they were. I felt like it probably could have saved me from making a lot of mistakes along the way.

My mom had caught sight of me when I entered at the beginning of the service and took a seat in the back. She kept shooting nervous looks over her shoulder at me like she was worried I was going to jump to my feet at any given moment and lay all my family's sins bare for all of the loyal parishioners to judge. I just kept smiling at her with a lot of teeth. I didn't see any reason to put her mind at ease, not after the way she had sold Poppy out to a murderous creep under the guise of trying to do what was best for her. Every time she caught my eye, she gulped and nervously looked back at my father.

I figured he knew I was there as well. His entire sermon centered on forgiveness and sin. The sins of the body. The sins of the mind. The sins of the well-meaning and the sins of parents and children. He talked a good game about nothing in this world being unforgivable by God and then turned my stomach when he offered a prayer for Oliver Martinez and reminded everyone sitting inside the picture-perfect, small-town church that it was only up to God to forgive and judge Oliver for his misdeeds. Not one word about Poppy or the horror she had suffered and he most definitely didn't mention that he was the primary reason Oliver had found my sister in the first place.

I wanted to get up and march up the aisle to the front of the church and knock him off the altar. I wanted to stand on the pew and scream that all these innocent people were listening to a fraud and that my father really thought his opinion and his beliefs were just as important as the deity he claimed was the only one that could sit in judgment. I didn't do anything. I sat there with my arms crossed over my chest and watched him through narrowed eyes.

I knew he was trying to get a rise out of me in front of all of these people he considered his sheep, his blind followers. He had long since declared me an embarrassment, a loss, a wayward soul that was godless and not worthy of his guidance and tutelage, so I wasn't about to prove him right in any way, shape, or form.

My phone vibrated from where I had it stashed and I pulled it out to glance at the text.

Love you.

It was simple. It was sweet. It was a reminder that after this was all said and done, I had somewhere to go. I had someone that would always want me. I had never returned to anything or anyone in my entire life, so it sent warm and gooey threads of love and happiness shooting all through me so that I absolutely couldn't wait to get back home. I wanted to get back to Rowdy. The days I had to spend apart from him felt years longer than the decade we had previously spent separated.

I missed him. I was worried about my sister. I wanted to cuddle with my dog. I wanted to get back to work, and as much as it surprised me, I really missed the crystal-clear Colorado sky. I had found my place and it would take a real act of God to remove me from it now. I sent him back the return sentiment and stood up as the service ended with a final prayer and everyone started to file out.

Exiting church took forever. Everyone had to say hello. Everyone had to stop and shake my father's hand and tell him how much they appreciated his kind words and giving nature. I had to literally bite my tongue when more than one person muttered under their breath about the shock that they had felt about what had happened with Oliver and my sister. The sympathy the churchgoers so readily offered my father and mother as they told them to stay strong during this trying time made me see red. The fact that the lunatic that had held my sister hostage, put a gun to her head, and beat her senseless more than once had been so skilled at hiding all of his evilness while my sister suffered alone and in silence made my insides boil with rage. The injustice of it all left a vile taste in my mouth and had fury coiling tight along my spine.

Rowdy had gotten Poppy home without incident, but once they were in Denver, my sister had started to break down. She was a mess and Rowdy was at a loss as to how to help her. Poppy didn't want to be at my apartment, she didn't

want to be alone with him at his place, so out of desperation Rowdy had called Sayer and asked her to take both of
them in until I got home. Luckily Sayer had plenty of room
at her Victorian and she was well versed in how to handle
my sister in her fragile state. Sayer Cole was turning out to
be a lifesaver, and the fact that she had dropped everything
to pursue the same man I had pursued was undeniably for-
tuitous, and I was so grateful she had found her way into
our lives. Rowdy's endless prophesizing that all things happened for a reason really did seem to be true. There was a
lot of really nasty stuff and a lot of really ugly bumps in the
road we had all had to overcome, but in the end it really felt
like all of us had ended up exactly where we were supposed
to be. For me, I knew without a doubt that was wherever
Rowdy was at, but I felt like it rang true for Poppy and Sayer
as well.

I was the last one to leave. I felt like I was saying good-
bye to this life and this place the right way this time. I wasn't
running in a blind panic. I wasn't sacrificing all the good that
was in my life just to escape the bad. I was leaving on my
own terms and taking a stand to prevent any of the evil that
lived here from reaching out and getting its tentacles into
me and my sister ever again.

I smoothed my hair down. Tugged at the hem of my shirt
and took a deep breath. I wasn't nervous so much as I was
anxious and ready for it to all be over with. I had to squint
into the sun when I exited the church doors. My mother and
father were standing on the top step waving to the last of
the parishioners as they exited the parking lot for the rest

of their Sunday afternoon. I flinched away when my mom reached out a hand to touch me. After ten years . . . it had been so long, they looked older and far less impressive than I remembered. I saw my dad's eyes skate over all the tattooed skin that was exposed by my white, ruffled top and immediately saw the censure and disgust rise up in his gaze.

"It wasn't bad enough that you desecrated our home with your lack of morals and lack of respect, you had to go and violate your body in an unholy way as well?" He shook his dark head at me like I really had shamed him in some unforgivable way. "Why am I not surprised?"

At another point in time that dig would've stung. It would have made me feel guilty for the choice to wear art on my body and for claiming my skin as my own, but now I saw it for what it was, a desperate attempt to belittle me, a way to exert his control and put me back under his disapproving thumb. I lifted an eyebrow at him and looked back and forth between him and my mom.

"I didn't think you would want to do this here on the steps of the church, where any of your followers might happen by, but that's fine by me. I don't have anything to hide. Can you say the same thing, Dad?"

I saw my mom start out of the corner of my eye and saw my dad's shoulder tense just a fraction. My mom reached out again and this time I let her fingers land on my forearm.

"It's been ten years, Salem. This is not a proper homecoming."

I laughed, an actual laugh, and shook her off. "No, and that's because this has never been any kind of home." I tucked some of my hair behind my ears and glared hard at both of them.

"You ran me out of town on purpose when I was too young to know any better. You made it impossible for me to stay, and as a result you destroyed Poppy and you forced me to leave the only boy I ever loved behind." I poked my dad squarely in the center of his chest and saw the way his eyes flared with veritable hatred for me. "I see it now. You knew I wasn't going to break, wasn't going to come to heel, so you made it so that I couldn't stay and would never come back. Well, I'll hand it to you, you won that round, Dad."

He scoffed at me and wrapped his arm around my mother's shoulders. I thought I saw her flinch but I wasn't about to break eye contact with him, so I couldn't be sure.

"You were willful and godless. You were wrapped up in a boy that was too young and had no family. There was no good in you, Salem. It was the best thing for this family for you to go out on your own. Your sister would have fallen victim to your heathen ways."

I rolled my eyes. "My heathen ways led me to a wonderful career, a life full of great friends, and put me back on the path to the guy you forced me away from. My heathen ways led me to exactly where I was always supposed to be. You turned your daughter, your own flesh and blood, into a victim, into a shell of herself, because she was so scared of disappointing you. You nearly got her killed. How do you think your parishioners would feel about that, Dad?"

He tilted his chin defiantly and looked down his nose at me. He would never give in, never admit what he had done was wrong. Not when it came to me or to Poppy, but there was fear there. I saw it in the way his mouth tightened and the way he paled just a fraction. I could pull the mask off and everyone would see who he really was. I had the upper hand but he still knew how to dig his way under my skin.

"Poppy made many mistakes. She had a penance to pay." The blame would always fall on someone else.

The rage that was riding me so hard burst bright and hot between my eyes. I wanted to smack him across his smug face. Instead I curled my fingers into my palms and dug in so hard that I drew blood.

"She had sex, Dad. Most girls in college do, and that is not an unforgivable sin that she needs to pay penance for the rest of her life."

He was going to disagree and this was going to be an endless battle of words and wills, so I cut it short.

"Look, I don't care what you think. I don't care if you spend every single night trying to will me to my own special corner of hell. What I do care about is Poppy and making sure she is happy and safe moving forward. You are not to contact her. You are not to reach out to her. You are not to try and make her feel bad or vilify her for being involved in the death of a terrible man. I want you to leave her alone. Do you understand me?"

My mom made a noise in her throat and my dad grunted at me. "You don't speak for your sister, Salem. There is still hope for Poppy to find her way back to the flock."

I growled and took a step forward. "If she contacts you, all you are going to do is tell her you are happy she is okay

and that you support the choices she is making. You do not
want to push the issue with me, Dad. I'm not a kid anymore
and I will fight you tooth and nail for her."

"You can't threaten me, Salem."

"Oh, really? If you think you're embarrassed by the way
I was when I lived under your roof, just wait until I drag out
all the dirt that's under my nails from the things I did to
survive when you ran me off. Did you know I was a strip-
per? How do you think you would like some of those videos
and pictures uploaded to the Web with your name and the
church attached?"

I lifted a challenging eyebrow and watched him weigh if
I was serious or not.

"How about the years I spent as a burlesque dancer or
the time I worked for a freak show on a boardwalk, or the
time I hosted a drag show in a gay bar? What about a sex
tape? You have no idea the kind of skeletons I can drag out
of the closet, and once something ends up on the Internet,
it never dies. I can drag you and this entire parish into the
mud. Don't push the issue with me, Dad. I will do whatever
I have to do to keep Poppy safe. Oh, and that kid next door
that had no family and wasn't good enough for us is actually all grown up, wildly successful, and willing to fight right
by my side. Did I mention his sister is a lawyer? I'm sure he
would love to tell the world all about how you pushed Poppy
to date that quarterback and then turned on her when he
got her pregnant and left her alone. What kind of man of
God are you? The kind that gives his daughter's location to
an abuser and covers up the fact that he's been protecting a

wife beater. The farce you have going on will disappear in a puff of smoke. I won't just pull the mask off, Dad, I'll shatter it into a million pieces."

I crossed my arms over my chest as we faced off. I could see he wanted to fight, wanted to believe that he was beloved enough, had people enthralled enough, that all my dirty deeds wouldn't tarnish his glow, but my mom suddenly moved out from under his arm and looked up at him pleadingly.

"She's right. This has to stop." My dad opened his mouth to argue and she held up a hand to silence him. "Enough. We lost one daughter already and Salem is right: we nearly got another one killed. I won't be part of this anymore. This isn't a righteous life." She pointed a finger at my dad's stunned face and told him flatly, "If you think your reputation can survive what Salem is threatening, then know this. It absolutely won't survive your wife leaving you on top of it. You are going to do as she says and that is all there is to it."

My father looked dumbfounded and furious. My mom looked shaky and kind of sick. She turned back to me and gave me a sad smile.

"I thought Oliver was good for your sister. She was never the same when she came back from college. I didn't realize he was hurting her until it was far too late, and I allowed your father to convince me that Oliver had changed and was remorseful for the way he treated your sister. He told me that Oliver was healing through prayer and counseling. I was wrong to blindly believe and trust. I have been very wrong for the last decade. You take care of your sister and give her whatever she needs. We won't get in the way." She looked over her shoulder at my father and firmed her mouth. "I'll make sure of it."

I wasn't going to say thank you. She didn't get gratitude for finally doing something she should have been doing my entire life. It was her job to stand between her children and this man. I nodded and turned to walk away from both of them for the last time.

"Salem." I looked over my shoulder as my mom called my name. "I need you to know it broke my heart when you left all those years ago."

It broke mine, too, but not because I was leaving her. It broke my heart because I had left Poppy and Rowdy with waves of sorrow in my wake.

"Then you should've done something so I didn't have to go, Mom."

I saw tears in her eyes and genuine regret but it was too little too late.

"I'm glad you found your way back to that boy. You were always so sweet together. He was wonderful with both of you girls."

"He still is." And I knew he always would be. Where he was is where I needed to be, not here on these church steps . . . only I had a stop to make on my way out of town first.

I didn't bother with good-byes. I didn't bother with a final look or a wave. I just left it as it was. The door was finally closed. I wasn't being run out of town, I was leaving with a clear and important destination in mind. I wasn't running from my past. I was heading purposefully toward my future, and it made me full and complete in a way all my bouncing around from place to place never had.

Before I got to where I was going, I pulled over to the side of a dusty road and jumped out of the rented SUV that was packed full with my sister's personal effects so that I could gather a fistful of Texas bluebells in my hands. They matched the field of flowers on my back so perfectly that it made me smile and had my heart swelling. I gently laid them on the empty seat next to me and drove the rest of the way to the cemetery that was about thirty minutes outside of Loveless's city limits.

It seemed like a really forgotten and lonely place. There was no bright green grass and rows of elegant headstones decorated with every kind of flower under the sun. Instead the ground was covered in brownish-green remnants of grass and the headstones looked sunbaked and worn. There were no other mourners milling about or paying respects, so all I had was a six-year-old's memory of where to find the grave site I was looking for. It took longer to find her than it should have, and by the time I did, the bluebells looked a little sad. It was fitting. The whole atmosphere was somber and I was a little surprised that tears sprang to my eyes as soon as I saw the inscription on the plain headstone.

Gloria St. James
1975–1996
A Loving Mother with a Beautiful Smile

I wondered who had added the last part if it was only her and Rowdy, but I was glad it was there for him to see whenever he managed to make his way back here to see it. I crouched down and rested the flowers next to the cold stone and sort of just fell to my knees as I stared at the grave. I had so many things I wanted to say, felt like I had to catch her up on her son's entire life, but nothing could make it around the lump in my throat.

I took a second, let a few tears fall, and then cleared my throat.

"Hello, Gloria, it's nice to meet you. My name is Salem Cruz and I'm hopelessly in love with your son."

I had to clear my throat again and my vision got hazy as moisture collected in the corners of my eyes. This was a lot harder than I had thought it was going to be when Rowdy had asked me to do it outside the hospital.

"I've known him most of my life and he has always been a good soul. You brought a wonderful man into this world and I just know you would be so proud of him and the life he has made for himself. He carries you very close to his heart."

I reached out and traced her name where it was etched in stone. It matched the tattoo on Rowdy's side almost perfectly.

"It took us a long time to figure things out, but now that we have, he really wanted me to be the first and last woman in his life that meets his mom." I was crying in earnest now because of how important this moment was. It really solidified the resolution that Rowdy wanted me as his forever. "I'm going to do everything in my power to take care of him for you for the rest of my life. I just want you to know that."

I let my head fall forward and I squeezed my eyes shut. Emotion and a lifetime of what could have been swirled all around me. I felt a hot breeze move some of my hair off of where it was sticking to my neck and the sweet scent of the flowers floated up into my nose. I put my hands on my thighs and lifted my head back up as I gazed thoughtfully at the headstone.

"I'm not going to waste moments ever again. I'll bring him back here so you can see how amazing he is and so that you don't ever have to wonder if he found someone to love him after you. He has me, he has an entire family he found for himself, and he has all the wonderful memories of you."

The wind moved again, sending the petals of the flowers I had laid down dancing. I felt like it was time to go. I kissed my fingers and touched her name. I climbed to my feet and headed back to the SUV. Walking away from my own parents felt final and hollow. Saying good-bye to Rowdy's mom felt peaceful and right. I felt like she had somehow given me her blessing to keep her son's heart safe for her. It was a task I was going to dedicate myself to until the end of time.

I texted Rowdy to let him know I would be back home sometime the following evening and freaked out just a little when he replied that he was back at his own apartment because Poppy was having a really hard time being around any guy at the moment. I hadn't been brave enough to ask her if Oliver had sexually assaulted her as well as beaten her and she hadn't volunteered the information, but the evidence seemed to be pointing in that direction.

I called to check on her, and after an awkward conversation with a bunch of single-syllable answers, I hung up after

making her promise over and over again that she was okay.
She told me she was just jumpy and that Rowdy was too big.
Accidently running into him in the hallway, or bumping
into him coming out the bathroom, was just too much for
her nerves right now, so she had asked him to go home. He
hadn't wanted to, was still hovering over her, trying to help
her feel safe, but that was just exacerbating the problem. I
told her I would be home soon and she laughed and told me I
needed to just get to my guy. Apparently, after the run-in by
the bathroom, she was well aware of what I was missing out
on and was all for me getting back between the sheets with
Rowdy and every fun thing he was working with. I didn't
disagree, so I hung up with every intention of Rowdy's place
being my first stop as soon as I hit the Mile High.

WHEN I PUT THE key he had given me in the door to his
apartment it felt like the end of a long journey. Really it was
only a little over twelve hours and I had stopped to nap once
along the way, but it still felt like too long since I had seen his
face or been able to touch all that toned and tattooed skin.
Jimbo greeted me at the door when I pushed it open. His
tongue lolled out of his mouth and he jumped up and put his
paws on my legs. He was going to be huge when he finally
grew into his fuzzy body and I was overwhelmed at how
happy I was to see him. I dropped to my knees and rubbed
my face in his neck as he licked me all over my face. I was
obviously missed and I had to say it was just one more reason
I knew I was finally where I was supposed to be.

    It was late, so the apartment was dark. I checked the

dog's food and water, trying to be quiet in case Rowdy was already asleep. I was winding my way toward his bedroom when a haphazardly discarded sketch pad lying on the couch caught my eye in the dim light. I paused for a minute to pick it up and felt my heart stop and then start to race as I flipped through the first few pages.

There were a couple of drawings that were obviously for clients, tattoos that hadn't made it from paper to skin yet, but most of the pristine white pages were covered with images wearing my face. There was mermaid me, and naughty-sailor-girl me. There was sassy Indian girl me with long Pocahontas braids and there was sexy devil me standing next to angelic me. There were dozens of them all in different shapes and sizes, but every single image was undoubtedly modeled after my distinct look. I wasn't sure if he had drawn them all over this last week while I had been gone or over the months we had been chasing each other in circles. Either way it made my heart swell and the full certainty that I was it for him settle deep inside my bones.

I set the pad down and tiptoed through the hall. Jimbo took one look at where I was going and huffed out a disgusted-sounding snort. The poor guy had learned early on that he wanted no part of what happened between his humans when they were together in the bedroom.

The light was off and Rowdy was sprawled on his stomach across the covers. His blond hair was sticking up everywhere and he hand one arm bent up under his head. The only thing that could have made the sight better would have been if he hadn't bothered with the black boxers before crashing out. Even with them obscuring the view, I couldn't complain. I let out a breathless sigh and crept closer so that I could lean over and touch my lips to that anchor on the side of his neck. I felt his pulse leap and tasted the salt on his skin as he murmured sleepily and rolled over onto his back.

Those infinitely blue eyes glowed at me in the dark as a grin pulled up the corner of his mouth.

"Hey."

I was leaning over him, so I bent down to kiss him quickly and rub the end of my nose against his.

"Hey."

He reached up a hand and tangled it in my hair where it slid over my shoulder and landed on his chest.

"How did it go?"

I sighed and lifted a hand to trace my fingers along that scrolling tattoo along his rib cage. The ink and name that rested there seemed so much more important to me now than it had before. "I met your mom and said good-bye. It broke my heart just a little bit, but I'm so happy you asked me to go and see her. And I may have threatened my father with a sex tape." The last was muttered under my breath as his eyebrows shot up and he used his grip on my hair to pull me over him so that we were both sprawled across the bed.

"Do you have a sex tape?"

"Hell no, but he doesn't know that and he wouldn't put it past me. Surprisingly my mom stepped up to the plate and agreed to leave Poppy be. She admitted that she fucked up pretty majorly. I wish it mattered."

His chest moved as he sighed. "It's too late for any of it to matter now."

"That's kind of how I looked at it. How's Poppy doing?"

He swore a little bit and shifted under me. There was evidence of how much he missed me the last week poking me in the hip. It made me smile and had me wiggling enticingly on top of his hard body.

"Not good. She's withdrawn, jumpy. She doesn't want anyone to touch her and she wakes up screaming almost every single night. Sayer is really good with her, but I'm worried."

I nodded and brushed my mouth over the flat nipple that was closest to my mouth. I heard him suck in a breath and it made me smile against his skin.

"Me, too. I think we're just going to have to stand strong for her and wait until Poppy's ready for us to help. My sister is stronger than any of us ever thought." My voice got husky on its own accord.

"She is." I felt his hands tighten in my hair as he pulled my head up so that he could devour my mouth with his own. "I missed you." I could taste his missing me in the way he kissed me and held me. He also sounded just as rough and needy as I did.

"I missed you, too." And I was past ready to show him just how much.

I moved my mouth down to the other side of his chest so I could run my tongue around the other flat disk and worked my hands down his sides so that I could get them under the waistband of his boxers. I gave the rock-hard globes of his ass a squeeze for good measure and worked the dark fabric out of my way. He helped set his straining erection free and the taut skin burned in my hand and I wrapped it around the turgid shaft. I loved the way his body throbbed and pulsed at my touch. It was a heady thing to know this was the way he always responded to me.

I used my thumb to caress the hot metal that rested on the top of the head of his cock and looked up to see blue blazing down at me.

"Thank you for coming back to me." His voice sounded like a love song.

I used the hand that wasn't around his dick to draw a heart on his chest with my finger. "Always. I love you. Thank you for always being there for me to come back to." I moved my thumb to play with the bottom of the piercing and he groaned.

"I don't think I've ever not been in love with you, Salem."

I kissed the place on his chest where I could feel his heart thundering in time to every sweep of my thumb and every twist of my wrist. I let go and started to slide my hand up and down as he went stiff underneath me.

"I know the feeling, Rowdy." I also knew the feeling of wanting to have him, to feel him, to be all over him and under him as pleasure covered both of us like a blanket. I was done talking and moved so that I had something in my mouth to prevent further conversation.

He barked out my name as I took him between my lips and circled that creatively pierced head around and around with my tongue. I adored the tang of metal and man as I licked him like he was my favorite dessert treat. I felt his stomach muscles tense and his thighs go tight as I worked him with my hands and mouth. There was something insanely satisfying about making that strong, tattooed body quiver and quake under my command. It was a feeling that would never get old. Neither would the way he said my name like a curse and pulled on my hair. I loved the way his palms cupped my head and the way I could feel how close to the edge he was as I rolled those metal balls back and forth across my tongue.

He arched his hips up off the bed, which totally threw off my rhythm and had me pulling up to tell him to cool it, but as soon as I was vertical he started pulling at my clothes, ripping my shirt off over my head, and practically wrestling my tight, black pants off of my legs. My underwear disappeared under impatient hands that were sexy and rough as he pulled me over him and placed me over his cock, which was all shiny and slick-looking thanks to my mouth.

He cupped the heavy weight of my breasts in each of his hands and mimicked the way I had been playing with his piercings on my own. It made me suck in a sharp sound of pleasure. I sat myself down on his erection and let each inch by delectable inch slide inside my welcoming heat. I braced my hands on his chest and leaned forward so that we were cocooned in the dark fall of my hair. Everything about us just felt so good and so right. As we started to move I groaned and whispered.

"You are my perfect match."

His eyes got heavy-lidded and his breath started to whoosh in and out as I really started to rock on top of him.

"And you're mine."

There wasn't any space to talk after that. There were only the sounds of kissing, of bodies moving together, of flesh on flesh and pleasure as it filled the room. There were hands on faces, there were hands between legs, there were kisses and bites, and there was more than one orgasm as we moved together and against one another. There were soft sighs and dirty swearwords, and at one point when he had his mouth between my legs and knees up around my ears, I was pretty sure I saw the God I had always heard so much about.

Hours later, when morning was just starting to creep in, I laid my head on his chest after he dragged me into the shower and settled into the only place I was ever supposed to be.

The journey to get here had been long, often filled with wrong turns and missteps, but at the end of it, all that really mattered was the destination no matter how long it took to get there.

EPILOGUE

I WAS TRYING REALLY hard not to smile at the disgruntled expression on Salem's face as she glared at me in the reflection of the bathroom mirror. It would have been easier to believe she was actually upset if her lipstick wasn't smudged across her pouting mouth and the hem of her dress wasn't up around her waist as I drove into her balls deep, from behind. I had one hand on top of hers where she was braced against the mirror and the other on the edge of the sink so I had the optimum amount of leverage.

"We're going to be late." I could tell she wanted to sound annoyed but it faded away on a sigh when I moved a hand around to her front and tickled her inner thigh as I searched for her hot center.

I had to laugh. We were late a lot. That's what happened when your girl looked like her and had a preference for skirts and dresses and not wearing anything underneath them. Her head dropped forward and I felt her body get tight around me. I bent a little so I could kiss her on the back of her neck where her hair was pulled up in a complicated twist that looked like something from a *Good Housekeeping* ad from the 1950s.

"No one cares if we're late." They all knew the reason why by now, and as long as I was happy, as long as Salem and I showed up smiling, no one gave a shit if we rolled in a half an hour or so behind schedule.

She swore at me but her dark eyes glittered where they were locked on mine in the mirror and I could tell she was close. That was a good thing because I wasn't going to last much longer. I tapped her clit with my thumb, sank my teeth into her neck, and that was all it took. I felt her shudder under my hands and against my chest, I felt her come apart for me, and I quickly followed.

When I pulled back all I had to do was get resituated and zip my pants up. She had to redo half of her makeup and make sure she didn't look thoroughly debauched and rumpled. I grinned at her because even as she slicked red lipstick back on, there was no hiding the languid and satisfied gleam in her dark gaze.

"You're a sex fiend." She was laughing about it now because even though she might not like showing up late, she never told me no when I turned all my amorous attention onto her, which I did a lot since I had moved her into my place almost as soon as she had unpacked from her trip to Texas.

For a while we had thought Poppy would want to move into Salem's old apartment, but as of now the younger Cruz sister was still bunking with Sayer and it seemed like she was in no hurry to leave. It had been months, and while Poppy was making tiny steps of progress, she was still skittish and jumpy, still a shadow of the young girl I had known so long ago. The only person she really seemed comfortable around was my sister, and as long as Sayer was willing to be her guiding light, neither Salem nor I saw a reason to push the issue.

"You love it." I made sure I didn't have her lipstick all over my face and walked out of the bathroom.

She followed me, rolling her eyes. "I love you—*it* is just one of the side benefits."

I chuckled and helped her into her long coat. It was the middle of December and all the ups and downs of summer and fall had changed just as fast as the Colorado weather. The new shop was a raging success. The store was generating steady income and the online market was so busy that Salem was trying to convince Nash to hire someone specifically to manage that branch of the business. The grand opening of the store has been a major party, and every last Saturday of the month Salem arranged different art installations that turned the store into an eclectic gallery showcase. It was opening doors to new customers, to a new breed of clientele, and showcased tattooing and art in the same kind of light. She was brilliant and she was making all of us a whole lot of money. So much money in fact that Rule and Nash were throwing around the idea of opening a third store in either Boulder or Colorado Springs the following year. Salem had turned the Marked into its own little tattoo empire.

Tonight we were headed to the Bar for a combined baby

shower–farewell party. Shaw was due at the end of January
and Jet and Ayden were moving after the first of the year. It
was a bittersweet celebration and there were bound to be
tears of sorrow and happiness. Life just kept moving forward
and everyone had to find the path they were meant to be on.
As bummed as I was to see my best friend go, I knew it was
what was best for him and his wife. Jet deserved to be happy
and the only way for him to do that was to be with Ayden as
much as he possibly could. Besides, with a baby on the way
and a wedding lurking on the horizon, it wasn't like Ayden
and Jet were going to be strangers. They would be back
often and they would always be welcomed with open arms.

The Bar was packed when we got there. Rome had closed
the business to the public for the night but that didn't mean
the place wasn't filled to the brim with family and friends
wanting to say good-bye and welcome the newest addition
to our crazy family. Salem looked at me with wide eyes as
we walked through the door because we were obviously the
last to show. There was no missing the way Asa winked at
me in approval from behind the bar or the way Nash gave
me a high five. I just shrugged at her and gave her an incor-
rigible grin. She wacked me on the stomach with the back of
her hand and glided away on those sky-high heels that were
part of the temptation that made us late to start with.

Jet walked over and handed me a beer that I clicked
against the top of the one he held in his hand.

"Gonna miss you, dude."

He nodded as we watched both of our ladies hug. That
was a lot of dark-haired beauty to take in.

"I know. You'll come to Austin." It wasn't a question and it didn't need to be. I would go to Austin to visit.

"You know it."

"I would have been worried about you if Salem hadn't shown up to stake her claim. I'm glad you have her."

She threw her head back and laughed at something Saint said to her and reached out to put her hand on Poppy's arm where she was hovering uncertainly off to the side of the group where the girls had gathered.

I was going to say something dirty about *having* her up against the sink not even twenty minutes before but I caught sight of Zeb moving toward my sister where she was leaning against the bar and talking with Asa. He had been working on her house for the last month and every time we talked he dropped none-too-subtle hints that he would like to nail more than her rotting floorboards. I wasn't sure how I felt about that yet or if I was even allowed to have an opinion, so I just watched him pursue her with a scowl.

"She makes everything in my life better. She always did. I love you guys and was really lucky when Phil brought me here and I finally found a place where I fit in and belonged." I pointed at Salem with the top of my beer and lifted and eyebrow at her when she caught me staring at her. She grinned back at me and slicked her tongue across her bottom lip. It made me chuckle and want to pull her dress up over her ass again. I looked back at my friend. "But she is my home. I didn't know I was wandering until she found me."

Jet muttered his agreement and we both had to grin as Shaw waddled with her big belly to where Ayden was so they could hold on to each other. They were both crying and blubbering all over each other and as girlie and emotional as it seemed, it was really beautiful. Those girls really loved one another and both of their lives were about to change in major ways.

Rule was sitting with Rome and the brothers had their heads bent close together. They were talking in quiet tones as Cora sat next to them with a wiggling Remy on her lap. The baby was a handful, full of energy, babbling away between words and not quite words, and looked like she was ready to get up and go at just ten months. She was starting to walk just a little bit, so Rome kept telling Cora to let her down, but mama bear was adamant that the baby was not going to crawl around in whatever might be on the bar floor. Rome acted insulted, like the bar was spotless, but when he took little RJ from her mom he didn't put her down either. He just bounced the little bundle up and down on his leg until she squealed in delight.

Rule shook his head, probably because it was his future playing right out in front of him, and got up to go collect his pregnant wife. She was still crying when he got to her, so he pulled her into a tight hug and rested his cheek on the top of her fair head. Jet didn't say anything but silently left my side so he could collect his own crying lady and offer whatever comfort he could. Like I thought, tears of happiness and sorrow.

I put my beer back up to my lips and was going to make my way over to my own girl when I saw Saint suddenly pull away from the group with her phone to her ear. She had to leave early on more than one occasion because of work, so I hoped the hospital wasn't calling to ruin her evening. She was talking rapidly and I saw her gaze shoot up to Nash where he was talking with Cora's dad. He immediately stopped midsentence and found his way over to the pretty redhead's side.

I frowned in concern as they both shared a frowning look as Saint continued to talk animatedly into the phone. I was going to go ask if everything was all right when a light hand touched my elbow. I looked down and smiled softly at Poppy. It had taken months to get her comfortable enough to even be alone in a room with me again, so the fact she was okay with person-on-person contact was a giant leap in the right direction.

"How's it going?"

She nodded a little bit and forced a tight grin. "Every day gets a little bit better. It's hard not to appreciate making it out alive in such a beautiful place filled with so many wonderful people." She cleared her throat and reached out to squeeze my hand. "I never did tell you thank you. Thank you for bringing me home. Thank you for trying to take care of me. Thank you for welcoming us into your family. Thank you for loving my sister . . . just thank you for being great."

I thought she would probably get uncomfortable if I tried to hug her, so I just brought her hand where it was resting on the top of mine up to my lips and gave it a light kiss.

"Anytime, Poppy. None that stuff makes me great, it just makes me a man trying to do right by someone he cares about."

That heartbreaking smile was back on her face as she

pulled away from me. "I think you are the only man in my entire life that has ever tried to do right by me."

I was going to reply that she should only let people in her life that did right by her from here on out but got interrupted when Nash and Saint went rushing by shoving arms into coats and looking wild-eyed and slightly frantic.

"Whoa . . . you two okay?"

Saint didn't stop. She was pulling her long hair out of the collar of her jacket and practically jogging to the front door of the bar.

Nash paused for a second and looked after his girl with darkening purple eyes.

"That was Saint's boss at the ER. They just rolled in multiple injuries from a police shootout in Five Points. She knows that Saint and Royal are friends, so she called her to give her a heads-up that Royal and her partner were two of the officers they were bringing in. She couldn't give her any more information, but Saint being Saint she isn't going to wait around and find out how bad the situation is, she's going to dive headfirst into it. We're headed to the hospital now. Can you tell everyone why we're bouncing early?"

I nodded solemnly and watched as he turned to race after his lady. Suddenly the beer in my hand didn't seem as appetizing and the festive mood didn't fit right. Royal had been lying low ever since she had put cuffs on Asa. I think she was worried about the reception she would receive from everyone for locking up one of ours.

I walked over to the bar so I could set the beer down and shrugged when Asa looked at it and then up at me.

"Not in the mood to drink all of a sudden."

His amber eyes flashed in question. "What's up?"

"Nash just said that a bunch of cops got hurt. He and Saint left to find out if Royal was one of them."

His gaze narrowed just a fraction and he put his hands on the bar in front of him. "That's a pretty girl with a shitty job. I hope she's okay." His drawl sounded a little more pronounced, a little thicker than it normally did, and I wondered if he was saying something I wasn't entirely hearing.

"Me, too."

I sighed as Salem suddenly appeared at my side. She settled her hip next to mine and wrapped her arm around my waist. Her head rested on my shoulder and her hair tickled my chin. She was so much more than my lady—she was my best friend, my muse, my lover, my future. Without her the road stretched dark and endless in front of me; with her the path I wanted to travel was crystal clear.

"You all right? I felt your mood crash from across the room."

I tilted my head so I could rub my cheek against the crown of her head.

"Nash and Saint just left for the hospital because Royal may or may not be hurt."

She was silent for a second and then pulled back so she was looking up at me. She put a hand on my chest and tapped her fingers against my heart.

"Let's go."

I lifted my eyebrows at her. "Really?"

She nodded at me and said, "Royal went out of her way to help us with the situation with Poppy, and Saint is going to need a friend if things are bad. Besides, Nash spent so time in a hospital with Phil I'm sure he could use a distraction from the bad memories if they are going to be there for awhile. That's what we do, take care of one another."

"I more than love you, Salem. Every day it feels like so much more than the day before."

I agreed that we should go and asked Asa to let everyone know what was going on if they asked. I didn't want to make an announcement because I knew if I did the entire bar would pack it in and head on over to the ER and today wasn't a day for that. There was too many good-byes to say and too many firsts to enjoy.

I got Salem's coat and told Jet what was going on. He gave me a tight one-arm hug that had more back pounding to it than actual embracing and told me my cowboy boots needed Texas dust back on them. I really was going to miss the tight-pants-wearing son of a bitch.

Once we were in the car Salem reached out and put her hand on my knee as we drove the dark Denver streets.

"No matter how the road winds and turns, as long as you are there at the end of it I'll be happy, Rowdy."

I felt her words spread and expand in my chest so there was no room for it to be empty, no room there to be afraid of what might or might not happen in the future. Any bad luck I might have had paled in comparison to the supreme good fortune that had given me this woman as my own. I looked at her out of the corner of my eye and told her the only thing I could:

"I'm a lucky man."

Asa and Royal's story to be continued . . .

I just wanna say quickly that I know it's a lot more complicated to get someone out of jail than I made it seem with Asa. I try really hard to write as true to life as I can, but sometimes a scene, and in this case not just the scene, but an entire future book, sort of hinge on me bending the rules of reality just a little bit.

I also know it is nearly impossible to get in touch with a lawyer on the weekend!

Just play along with these little inconsistencies for me ☺. The threads that tie Asa and Royal together are interesting and complicated, so I had to take a little creative license in order to start weaving them together.

Rowdy and Salem's Playlist

(It's a doozy! I could listen to it all day long.)

Nikki Lane—"Gone, Gone, Gone," "Coming Home to You"
Patterson Hood—"Belvedere," "Back of a Bible"
Ryan Bingham—"Guess Who's Knocking"
American Aquarium—"Casualties"
Devil Doll—"The Things You Make Me Do"
American Aquarium—"I'm Not Going to the Bar"
Hank Williams Jr.—"Family Tradition"
David Allan Coe—"Mama Tried"
John Paul Keith—"She'll Dance to Anything"
Carl Perkins—"Honey, Don't"
Scott H. Biram—"Lost Case of Being Found"
The Cramps—"The Way I Walk"
The Reverend Horton Heat—"Jimbo Song"
Justin Townes Earle—"Baby's Got a Bad Idea"
Old Crow Medicine Show—"Wagon Wheel," "Hard to Love"
Dirty River Boys—"My Son"

JD McPherson—"Wolf Teeth"

Empress of Fur—"Mad Mad Bad Bad Mama"

Dwight Yoakam—"Little Sister"

The Meteors—"Psycho for Your Love"

Hayes Carll—"Love Don't Let Me Down"

HorrorPops—"Dotted with Hearts"

Buddy Holly—"Because I Love You"

Chris Isaak—"Baby Did a Bad Bad Thing"

Jason Isbell—"The Devil Is My Running Mate"

Lindi Ortega—"When All the Stars Align"

Three Bad Jacks—"Scars"

Kasey Anderson and the Honkies—"My Blues, My Love"

ACKNOWLEDGMENTS

I have the greatest job ever. A bad day doing this is still a hundred times more rewarding and fulfilling than a good day doing something else I didn't have my heart in. I have the BEST readers in all of book land. You're funny and sweet, supportive and endearing, and full of heart and fire. Not a day goes by that my life isn't enriched by interacting with you in some way. It makes my heart happy that you love this little slice of book world I've created as much as I do. Anytime you choose to spend your hard-earned money on something I created just makes a little piece of my writer soul fill with both pride and gratitude. I just need each and every single one of you to know how much I value you and how much I appreciate all the wonderful things you have brought into my life. If we ever get a chance to meet out there in the big, bad world, know that I am the one excited and thrilled to meet YOU!!! It's an honor to hug you and tell you thank you for buying my books and giving me a fresh start when I so desperately needed one. I hope you know that with every book, every story, I go into it knowing that I owe all of you everything. Thank you for letting me be me and not being too freaked out by all my spazziness and boisterousness. Thank you for embracing my crazy and the fun that can go along with it!

Like I always say, I love to hear from you, so feel free to chat at me and know if I could I would buy each and every single one of you a beer on release day.

Holler at me: jaycrownover@gmail.com

Along with having the best job I have been blessed with the best people to help me do it. Amanda Bergeron is the coolest editor a gal could ask for. She is tiny and mighty and she really does make sure every book that ends up in your hands is the best it can be. She makes me better even when it makes me want to murder all the things.

The entire team at HarperCollins is amazing. Jessie Edwards and Alaina Waagner take supergood care of me and they work really, really hard to make sure all the readers in book land know what's going on with me and they try really hard to keep the business end of putting a book into readers' hands fun. I hate to fly but don't mind traveling to New York as much when I get to hang with these awesome ladies once I get there. The entire HarperCollins/William Morrow crew is just kick-ass in general and they all really just love books and romance and want readers to have the best experience possible. I feel like I landed in the right place and ended up in the right hands . . . kinda like Rowdy and Salem ☺.

My agent, Stacey, is a superwoman. No one works harder

or takes better care of me in the book world. I have endless amounts of love and respect for her . . . again even when what she tells me makes me want to murder all the things! She's just good people and I feel superlucky she believes in me and I still get a thrill and rush of pride when she reads one of my books and tells me how much she likes it.

http://www.donaghyliterary.com

I appreciate all the work the ladies at http://literatiauthorservices.com/ do to keep my book life running smoothly. Karen, Michelle, and Rosette are aces when it comes to organizing cover reveals and blog tours. They handle all the little details and prevent me from throwing my computer out the window.

I just added the amazing and wonderful K. P. Simmon of Inkslinger PR to my team and there are no words to describe how lucky I am to have her as not only a friend but also a major part of my Book world!

Melissa Shank is a doll. Honestly I didn't know they still crafted women like her in modern times. I just adore everything about her and love her soul and her passion for books and readers. I never thought I needed a street team or fan page or that anyone would be interested in something like that. I was wrong, and Mel is amazing for taking a tiny little corner of Facebook and turning it into something fun and interactive. She's just wonderful and I want to smother her in love. I also need to shout out to Katie Marcum for helping keep the Crowd rolling like a well-oiled machine. You both have my undying thanks. If you wanna join and come hang out, it's pretty fun and Mel gives stuff away on the regular!

https://www.facebook.com/groups/crownoverscrowd/

I have another Mel that makes my life a treat. She reads all these books before the masses and before I send them off to Amanda. Her input helps me tell the best story I can and I appreciate having someone there to catch all my crazy ideas and help me wrangle them into an exciting, romantic journey. The Marked Men wouldn't be what they are without her . . . none of my boys would.

There are not enough words in the world to explain all the ways I need to thank my folks, so I'm settling for "thanks for everything, Mom and Dad." They can fill in the blanks because there are a zillion different things I should thank them for every single day. They're just the best.

I love my bestie. I love all the things about her and really I just need to thank her for being her. She's amazing. That is all.

Thanks to all my book friends, new and old, for making signings and being out there in the book world a real treat. It's always superfun to meet fellow authors and bloggers and I love getting to know all about the gears inside the industry that make this business tick. Book people are simply the best all-around, so thanks for proving that to be true time and time again.

Blogger nation . . . oh, how you are the oil in the machine and I am so endlessly grateful for all you have done for me and the boys. Thank you for all that you do so selflessly. Thank you for getting my covers out there, for joining my blog tours, for wanting to interview me, and for asking me to do blog tours even though I have to say no because I have NO

TIME!!!! Thank you for sharing your love of books. Thank you for writing reviews that are often better crafted than the book I wrote. Thank you for keeping book land united and connected. Thank you for spreading the word and sharing the things you love . . . and the things you don't love as much. I love how punk-rock blogging feels. How grassroots and DIY it tends to be. I love how a passion for books and reading built an entire platform for people to stand on and shout about their passion to all that will listen. It's supercool. As always, thanks to all of you bloggers that have morphed from reviewer to friend and confidant. I appreciate the early feedback and the reviews that hit my ears before they hit the Internet. Thank you for making me want to do what I do even better.

I always end with a shout-out to my pack. I just love their furry little faces so damn much. I wish there was a way for them to know how much they mean to me!!! Smooches Charley, Pistol, and Duce . . . And to Mike Maley (who will never even see this) because I wouldn't be able to leave and come meet all you wonderful readers if he didn't take such good care of my furry family for me when I'm gone.

Our favorite Southern charmer, ASA,

is up next.

But first . . .

have you taken a trip to Jay Crownover's

The Point?

Turn the page for a sneak peek at

Better When He's Bold,

the explosive second installment

in the suspenseful, sexy new series . . .

CHAPTER 1

Brysen

SOME MEN ARE IMPOSSIBLE to ignore. It's like everyone else around them is moving in slow motion, like everyone else is painted in black and white and he's the only spot of color; the only thing moving in the room. Race Hartman was that kind of man. Even though an entire room full of loud, drunk, and excited party people separated us, even though I doubted he knew I was at the same house party as he was, all I could see was him. Tall and blond with a face and body designed to make the fairer sex stupid with lust, he was undeniably beautiful and delicious, like everything that was bad for you tended to be. I didn't want to keep staring, but I couldn't stop myself. He was just that dynamic—just that bold—and in my world where things were gray and lifeless, he was a sensory feast and I was happy to gorge.

I missed the days when I just went to school, partied, had a good time and acted like I didn't have a care in the world. Those days were long gone so I needed to stop gaping at Race like an idiot and get on with trying to enjoy the one night I had off from work and wasn't needed at home. My little sister was at a sleepover, and my dad had agreed to stay home with my mom. It was a rare occurrence when I got to behave like a normal twenty-one-year-old, and I was squandering it by lusting after my best friend's older brother, and probably the worst, most inappropriate guy in the entire world to have a crush on.

"Do you know him?"

My friend Adria was the one who had convinced me to come out tonight. I remembered parties like this being more fun. I took a sip of lukewarm beer out of a red plastic cup and fought the way my eyes wanted to magnetically drift to Race.

"He's Dovie's older brother."

"Really?"

Her disbelief was justified. Where Race looked regal, like some kind of golden god sent down to rule over us mere mortals, Dovie Pryce was a rumpled redhead covered in freckles and about as unobvious as one person could be. She was cute at best, not impressive and heart-stopping like her brother was. She was also the nicest person in the world. I was pretty sure Race didn't have a nice bone anywhere in his impressive body.

My fingers curled around the cup tighter when his head turned and those mossy green eyes met mine.

"Really." My voice was huskier than normal even to my own ears.

"How can that be?"

I liked Adria. We had Business Finance together and she

was one of the few people who hadn't ditched me when I was forced to move back home after everything with my mom went down. I didn't have much fun anymore, which meant I didn't have many friends anymore either. Trying to explain to her the complicated dynamics in the Hartman family, though, was not something I planned on spending the evening doing. Race and Dovie's lineage wasn't a story that was particularly good times, and that's what I was after tonight—a good time.

I gulped because Race was making his way through the crowd of dancing and grinding college students toward where we were standing. People just instinctively moved out of his way. It was like there was a force-field of badass that surrounded him that only those who liked to live dangerously dared to test. I wasn't one of those people. At least that's what I told myself every time I was around him.

Sure, I was dangerously attracted, had been ever since the first time I saw him when he dropped Dovie off at work, but he would never know. Race wasn't a good guy and my life was hard enough without adding in the kind of complication he was bound to be.

To keep Race and those traitorous feelings at bay, I was awful to him . . . I mean really, really awful. I was cold. I was disinterested. I was rude, and sometimes I was flat-out mean. I acted like he was annoying, treated him like he was a vile, nasty human being, and when that didn't work, I ignored him and acted like he wasn't worth my time. It was getting harder and harder to do, and the more disdain I tossed in his direction, the more charm and liquid sex appeal he leveled at me. We were involved in a tantalizing back and forth game that I was terrified I would eventually lose. Race wanted me, and he didn't make that a secret. I didn't know how much longer my wayward lust was going to be held at bay under the assault of those evergreen colored eyes and that gorgeous head of spun gold hair.

He flashed a million-watt smile at me and stopped so he was looming over me. Even in five-inch heels he towered over me.

"Well, hello, Brysen."

I rolled my eyes and raised the cup to hide my involuntary gulp as his gruff voice slid over my skin.

"Race."

Adria nudged me in the side with the sharp edge of her elbow. I cleared my throat and inclined my head in her direction.

"This is my friend, Adria."

He stuck out a big hand and clasped her much smaller one. I practically saw her panties melt and her vagina throw out a welcome mat.

"What are you doing here?"

I should be asking him that. This was a college party, filled with drunk coeds and undergrads. I actually attended the university around the corner, but Race had long since given up the academic life for one that involved crime and lots and lots of illegal activity. He was the one who shouldn't be here.

"Just out having some fun." I tried to keep my tone flat and uninterested, but if he could hear the way my heart pounded, the jig would be up for certain.

He lifted a blond eyebrow at me and flashed a half grin.

Gah . . . he even had a killer dimple in his left cheek. I wanted to lick it so bad. I dug the tips of my fingernails into my palms and took a deep breath.

"I'm surprised you know how to do that, Bry, have fun."

He was right, so all I could do was narrow my eyes at him and put on the ice-queen mask I perpetually wore in his presence.

"What are you doing here, Race? Shaking down poor college kids for their student loan checks?"

His other eyebrow shot up to join the first one, and when he unleashed a full smile on us, it practically knocked both Adria and me over. Something darker flashed in his green eyes and I wanted to take a step back. Race was dangerous in more ways than one, and I needed to remember that.

"Most college kids have zero sense and like a challenge. That's a breeding ground for a guy like me. Plus football season starts next weekend and I just needed to check in on a few early clients." His eyes slid over the top of my sleek bob to the toes of my pointed black heels. "I stayed longer for the scenery."

Adria cleared her throat and looked back and forth between the two of us.

"Clients? At a house party? What exactly do you do?" If she only knew the kinds of illicit things Race did.

He cocked his head to the side and the blinding smile he wielded like a weapon fell off of his face. There were a lot of facets to Race Hartman, and this darker, harder side of him had only made an appearance when he decided he was going to take over the reins of a major crime syndicate after he had had a major role in bringing the kingpin Novak down. Race wasn't just a bad guy, a criminal, he was *the* bad guy. He was running numbers, loan-sharking, operating illegal gambling houses, helping his best friend chop and move stolen cars, and making sure every man, woman, and child in the Point knew he was the guy calling the shots on the streets now. He was too pretty to be that awful, but because of Dovie I knew exactly how filthy Race's hands had become since taking over Novak's empire. Not to mention his new business partner was a pimp, a money launder, and absolutely ruthless and cold. Nassir had to be shady and enigmatic considering he ran every underground operation that existed in the inner city and it seemed some of that had rubbed off on Race.

"I make money, sweetheart."

And he did. I shifted uneasily on my too tall shoes and tried not to let him see how my pulse fluttered under his unwavering gaze. There was something about being desired by a man that you knew could destroy anyone in the room. It shouldn't feel good, shouldn't make my thighs clench and my insides pulse, but it did, he did.

I smirked at him and tossed the longer part of my razor straight bob over my shoulder.

"Race is an entrepreneur of sorts." The kind you would only find in a place that was as dark and as broken as the Point.

Adria obviously wanted to ask more questions. I saw her open her mouth, but before she could get a word out, a loud BANG rang out and the typical college party I had been using to try and escape the aching reality of my everyday turned into a chaotic riot.

There was no mistaking the smell of gunpowder as pandemonium erupted and more shots rang out. I went to grab Adria, but because we were so close to the door, a flood of panicked bodies separated us in a split second. I felt hard hands grab me and pull me out of the way of the stampede. My face was pressed into a rock hard chest and a big hand held my head down as I was roughly moved through the press of running and flailing bodies.

My heart was in my throat and I heard the gun go off one more time, followed by the shriek of a female voice. Race let out a litany of swear words from somewhere above my head, and he let me go for just a second. I heard glass breaking, felt him shift, pull me along behind him, and then the cool night air was around us. He set me away from him a little bit, but grabbed my hand and proceeded to pull out me along behind him. Our feet crunched over the broken glass of the back door he had obviously shattered in order for us to escape.

I was panting and running in stilettos and skinny jeans after a guy with legs twice as long as mine, which was practically impossible, but I did it. He didn't stop until we had rounded the yard on the other side of the house and made our way across the street. Most of the other partygoers had dispersed, and the wail of sirens could already be heard in the distance. I put my hands on his chest and pleaded with him,

"We have to find Adria."

His eyes were practically black, full of emotions I was scared to name.

"I can't be here when the cops show up, Brysen. I have to go."

I gasped at him and balled my hands into fists so I could thump him on the chest—hard.

"Help me find her, Race!"

He just shook that perfect blond head and gazed down at me.

"You're the only one I was worried about."

My heart tripped, but the sirens were getting closer and he was moving away from me. I grabbed onto his wrist and realized I was shaking so hard I could barely hold onto him.

"Don't leave me." My voice sounded scared and lost. I didn't know what to do in a situation that involved guns and violence. It unnerved me how nonchalant he was with it all.

The shadows in his eyes moved and his mouth turned down at the corners. Before I could react, his hands slid around the back of my neck, under the edge of my hair, and he yanked me up onto the tip of my toes. I clasped both hands around his wrists, tried not to freak out when my chest flattened against his and pretty much just dangled there while he proceeded to kiss the shit out of me.

It was dark, people were stumbling about drunk and bewildered, I was worried about my friend, and I was angry at him . . . always angry, but for the first time since I had laid my eyes on him, all that want, all that tangling, greedy lust was let loose, and I kissed him back.

It wasn't romantic, it wasn't sweet and filled with tangible longing or loving care. It was brutal, violent, hard and hot, and nothing in my entire life had ever felt better. His tongue invaded. His teeth scraped. His hands bruised, and I could feel his erection through the front of his jeans where we were pushed together. I should've protested, said something to make him stop, but all I could do was moan and rub against him like some kind of wanton cat in heat.

And just when I was contemplating curling around him, coiling into that big body and making myself at home, he dropped me, stepped back, left me blinking up at him like an idiot, shook that golden head, and disappeared into the darkness without another word. I stared at the spot where he had been, wrapped my arms around my chest, and tried to keep from falling apart on the spot.

"Brysen!"

I jerked my head up as Adria came barreling into me. She almost took both of us to the ground.

"Oh, my god I was freaking out! Where did you go?"

I hugged her back, mostly to see if that would stop the shaking. It didn't.

"Race took me out the back for some reason."

Her eyes were huge in her face.

"Why would he do that? No one knew where the gunman was."

I just shook my head. "I don't know, I just followed him." He didn't really give me a choice.

"Some guy caught his girlfriend with another guy. Can you believe that? All that for something so stupid."

I didn't get to ask her how she knew what the ruckus was

all about because the police were finally on the scene and they were giving those of us left lingering about the third degree.

The university and the house where the party was at were both located on the Hill. Things like random gunfire, jealous boyfriends, and cheating girlfriends belonged in the Point; at least that's what most people from the Hill tried to fool themselves into believing. By the time it was all said and done I was exhausted, and could still taste Race on my lips. My night out in order to forget had turned into one that I would remember forever, even if I knew how bad an idea it was to hold onto this memory. Maybe gray wasn't such a bad shade to be surrounded in after all. It was boring and bland, but it was safe.

I drove Adria back to her apartment, fielding questions about Race the entire way. She was fascinated by him, could feel that magnetic pull he just naturally had. I tried to tell her that he was bad news, that the world he operated in was so far away from her almost MBA as she could imagine, but of course that only added to his mystique and appeal. What nice girl from the Hill didn't lust for a naughty boy from the Point? It couldn't have been any more clichéd if it tried. By the time I was headed home, I had a headache and my stomach was in knots.

When I parked in front of the cookie-cutter tri-level my parents had built before everything fell apart, I had to really think about whether or not I wanted to keep the engine running and just keep driving until I was somewhere else, until I hit a different life. Two years ago, everything in my world had been cheery and full of color and light. I was living in an apartment with girlfriends, attending college, fending off boys with only one thing on their mind. I was silly. I was carefree, and I never thought about any of it going away.

Now I was living back at home, taking care of one parent suffering from a crippling bout of depression and had a tendency to self-medicate, and another who was a workaholic and obviously burying himself in his job to avoid the troubling things going on at home. Mostly I came back to keep my little sister, Karsen, from being affected by the sadness and the darkness of it all. She was sixteen, a straight-A student, and bound for college in just a couple more years. I could tough it out until then. After all, my parents had always worked hard to keep our family on the fine line between the Hill and the Point, and I felt like it was the least I could do to repay them. We had never been obnoxiously wealthy, but we had never been forced to try and survive on the battleground that was life on the streets of the Point either. I really felt like I owed them for that at the very least.

Sighing, I made my way inside. There were no lights on because Karsen wasn't home and my mom was undoubtedly passed out in bed. I swung by the kitchen to grab a beer that was actually cold and puttered by my dad's office on the way up to the floor where my room was. He was seated behind the computer, like always. His balding head bent down and his eyes locked on whatever was on the screen. I frowned a little and twisted the cap off the neck of the bottle.

"Hey."

I saw him start and his gaze jerked away from the monitor. "Brysen Carter, you scared the piss out of me."

"How was she?"

He cleared his throat and returned his attention back to the computer. "Fine. Everything was fine."

That was highly unlikely.

"Did you even check on her tonight, dad?"

"Brysen, this is very important. Can this wait?"

Not really, but everything came second to his job. I didn't say anything, just pulled off my shoes and wandered around the corner to where the master bedroom was located. The door was cracked and the TV was on. I pushed the door open with the flat of my hand and hissed out a swear word.

My mom was sprawled sideways across the bed. Her head was hanging over the edge and the same whitish-blond hair that I had on my head was in a tangled mess, touching the floor. An empty bottle of vodka was resting on the pillow and light snores were coming from her. I put the bottle of beer down on the dresser and went in to set her to rights. Clearly dad hadn't bothered to pull himself away long enough to make sure she was all right. He had just left her to her own devices, and this was always the end result.

She peeled one watery eye open to look at me and mumbled my name as I wrestled her under the covers. I snatched up the empty bottle and resisted the urge to smash it on the floor. Just barely. She hadn't always been this way. She was always a little off, wrestled with emotional ups and downs, but then a car accident, a horrible back injury and endless amounts of pain, plus the inability for her to go back to work, and my mother had become this drunken, sad shell of a woman. It always made my heart twist and my guts tug because it didn't have to be this way. She could get help, my dad could support her, and maybe my life could go back to some kind of normal, but that wasn't happening and for now I just had to make do until Karsen was old enough to get out on her own.

I flipped off the TV and shut the door behind me with a thud. It would take a tornado to rouse her from that kind of drunken slumber anyway. I finally found my way to my room.

Living back at home as an adult was so weird. It wasn't like I had a curfew, or the same rules and regulations to follow as I had when I was a teenager, but everything about this childhood room felt wrong. I felt like left some part of myself outside the door every time I resigned myself to another night, another day spent here.

I pulled my phone out of my back pocket and pulled up the last message I had sent to Dovie asking her to go to the party with me tonight. Now that she had a fulltime job working at a group home for all the kids lost in the system, I hardly saw her anymore. Add in the fact that she was living with and involved with the only guy in the Point I considered scarier than Race, meant I rarely went by her house or saw her outside of school anymore. Tonight she had declined the invite because she had homework to do, but I secretly wondered if Bax had told her not to go.

He hated everything that had to do with The Hill. He was from the streets, an ex-con, a thief, and there was no doubt he was up to his eyeballs in Race's criminal enterprise. Shane Baxter had a reputation in these parts that was as legendary as the man who sired him. The man he and Race had taken down. They were not the kind of guys you wanted to mess with, but I really liked Dovie so I braved the shark-filled waters she swam in to keep her in my life and call her my bestie.

I twisted my phone around and sent her a message:

Saw Race at the party tonight.

It took a few minutes for her to answer back.

What was he doing there?
He said working.
I bet.

I rolled my eyes a little at what constituted as "work" for him and typed out:

*Someone had a gun and fired off shots inside. Race got
me out but took off because of the police.*

I was still pretty steamed about it, and still heated from the inside out by that kiss. Why did he have to taste so good, feel so right, yet be so wrong?

She answered back in a matter-of-fact way only someone firmly immersed in the Point could do:

*He can't risk messing around with the police. No one
from here really can. I'm not surprised he took off. Is
everyone okay?*
Fine. Everyone was fine.

I wasn't fine. Having an idea that someone was a criminal, that they might not be on the up and up was something
entirely different than having the proof right in front of your
face. I didn't understand that world, didn't want to understand, it therefore, no matter how hot he was, how much he
pulled me out of the monotony of my day to day life, Race
Hartman would never be the guy for me, and that made
things deep inside me burn.

We chit-chatted some more. Me about nothing in partic-
ular, and her about the guys. Bax scared me so I was nervous
and anxious around him, and I think she tried to make him
more human, more likable in my eyes, to offset that. And
Race, well, he spun me around and it took every effort I had
to pretend disinterest instead of rabid curiosity every time
she mentioned something about him. It was getting harder
and harder to do.

I told her goodnight and sent a message to my sister to
tell her goodnight as well. Karsen was a good egg, a kid who
deserved to make it out of this house unscathed and un-
scarred from the state the Carters were currently in. She was
a small little thing, with the same pale hair I had, but our
mom's brown eyes instead of dad's blue like I had. She was
as sweet as could be, and when she shot back a smiley face, I
finally settled into my routine for the night.

It was while I washed my face and climbed into the shower that I could finally admit that I was lonely, that I was sad, that I was overwhelmed with all the things I was feeling and the battle of always keeping the things churning inside me in check. In the shower I could cry and no one could tell. This wasn't the life I wanted. This wasn't where I thought I would be at twenty-one, but I had to adapt, had to change in order to do what was best for everyone, and that was just the way it was going to be. I didn't have any choice in the matter.

I toweled off, ran a brush through my hair, and climbed into a pair of yoga pants and a tank to sleep in. The adrenaline from everything started to leach out of my system and I finally got to fall onto the mattress face first. I was letting my eyes drift shut, trying really hard not to relive every flick of Race's tongue, every scrape of teeth, when my phone lit up with a new message. It was late, and the only person I thought it could be was Karsen, so I bolted upright and swiped a finger over the screen.

It wasn't from Karsen. It wasn't from a number I recognized at all. It was five words, no big deal, but the rock that settled in my stomach when I read them told me something was off.

You looked so pretty tonight.

I just stared for a second before answering back.

Who is this?
So sorry I missed you.

What in the hell was that supposed to mean? I asked who it was again, and when I didn't get a response back, I just switched my phone off and tossed it back on the nightstand. I sat there in the dark for a long moment with my pulse thrumming hard and a creepy sense of unease making the hair on the back of my neck stand on end. I shivered before laying back down on the bed and pulling the covers all the way up over the top of my head.

Talking about missing someone when gunshots had been going off wasn't funny, and I was raw enough not to like it one little bit. I closed my eyes and my brain started to question why exactly Race had pulled me out the back of the house when everyone else had been stampeding toward the front door.

This is why I didn't have time for a guy like Race. If he had been anyone else, his motivations would have never even been in question. And what had he meant by 'you're the only one I'm worried about'? It was just because he wanted me, like to played games with me because I was a challenge. But that was it . . . right?

Ugh. I didn't have the time or the space for any of it. And yet when I finally drifted off it was his pretty face and his perfect mouth that followed me into dreamland and not the anxiety and apprehension that was gnawing on me after that weird text.

A MARKED MEN NOVEL

Asa

BY JAY CROWNOVER

Starting over in Denver with a whole new circle of friends and family, Asa Cross struggles with being the man he knows everyone wants him to be and the man he knows he really is. A leopard doesn't it change its spots and Asa has always been a predator. He doesn't want to hurt those who love and rely on him, especially one luscious arresting cop who suddenly seems to be interested in him for far more than his penchant for breaking the law. But letting go of old habits is hard, and it's easy to hit bottom when it's the place you know best.

Royal Hastings is quickly learning what the bottom looks like after a tragic situation at work threatens not only her career but her partner's life. As a woman who has only ever had a few real friends she's trying to muddle through her confusion and devastation all alone. Except she can't stop thinking about the sexy southern bartender she locked up. Crushing on Asa is the last thing she needs but his allure is too strong to resist. His long criminal record can only hurt her already shaky career and chasing after a guy who has no respect for the law or himself can only end in heartbreak.

A longtime criminal and a cop together just seems so wrong . . . but for Asa and Royal, being wrong together is the only right choice to make.